BURNED

GREAT SOCIETY TRILOGY: BOOK TWO

G.K. LAMB

MONOLITH

CONTENTS

"Monsters exist, but they are too few in number to be truly dangerous. More dangerous are the common men, the functionaries ready to believe and to act without asking questions."
— Primo Levi

CHAPTER ONE

THERE IS NO REST IN THIS DARKNESS. I float in shadow somewhere between consciousness and restless sleep. I can feel every twist and bump on the ambulance's path, but I cannot make sense of the journey. It could be hours or mere moments since we burned rubber from the streets of Einsam. I've never been out of the city, and I wish I were awake to see it. Somewhere away from the twisted, soaring monoliths freer and less suffocating. Open fields with air so clear you can see the horizon. Endless stretches of tall pines swaying to the rhythm of cool mountain breezes. Quaint houses standing proudly over fields of vibrant green crops in row upon row.

The darkness swirls abruptly. A sharp turn. We're picking up speed. Nausea takes the place of stillness. The silence is interrupted by a high-pitched ringing steadily building in my ears. There are no picturesque farms, no stands of tall trees, no life. This is the Great Society, leaving Einsam doesn't change that. Imagining it, even in this dream world, doesn't make it any more real. The weight of that turns in the darkness like a vortex.

Everything is broken. The world is on fire. And she's never coming back.

My stomach lurches as if I were being thrown from the thirty-first floor. In a rush from darkness into light, I snap out of my trance and return to the back of the ambulance.

Everything is a smear of red until my eyes compensate for the glowing white lights above. My body is in revolt. Every muscle is trembling, and I feel as if I need to expel everything I've ever consumed.

I try to fight it, but the waves of nausea are too intense.

"Quick Gette, get the bag!"

Without a moment's hesitation, Georgette leans in from across the van and holds the bag open for me. Just in time.

I retch into the outstretched barf bag. My throat, nose, and eyes sting like a swarm of angry ants are burrowing their way out of my stomach. Dizzy and exhausted I collapse back onto the narrow, padded bench.

"I'm so sorry," I say. My voice is thin, almost ethereal.

"Don't fret. Just lay back and rest. I think you got exposed to some of the chemical agent. Thank God you were wearing your mask, but I think it got on your skin." Cornelia's words are matter of fact, but I can tell she's fighting back panic. Probably not for my sake, but for Georgette's.

"It must have soaked into the ash. I had to dive into it to

avoid the bullets," I say.

"You did nothing wrong, Evelyn. If you weren't out there to see the ambulance, we'd probably be buried alive in the sewers."

I turn my head and catch Cornelia's gaze.

"She's right Evelyn," says Charles twisted around in the passenger seat. "What you did was very brave. You saved us. I'm glad you're okay, and… I'm sorry."

"There's no need to discuss that now Charles," Cornelia says, her words scolding him into silence. He twists back around to stare into the sliver of tarmac illuminated by the headlights.

"You really are brave, Evelyn." Georgette's words are genuine and sweet.

I try to smile, but the effort is too great. I rest my head back against the thin foam on the bench and close my eyes.

The bouncing road and relentless speed are almost too much to bear. Every inch of my skin crawls and writhes from stinging invisible fire. I try to drift into sleep, but what I find there is more unbearable than the pain. Mother's eyes stare, cold and unmoving, back at me from the darkness. I try to look away or blink and banish her ghostly gaze, but nothing dislodges her. With Mother branded into my mind's eye, I focus on the creeping pain on my skin. The profound ache of bruises. The heaving of my chest, the unreachable itch of hairline cracks in my ribs. Tears well in my eyes and fall in big splashes against the cold bench. I can't deny it any longer: I loved her. She loved me, and yet we never truly told each other. I never let her know I cared, that I'd miss her when she was gone. I took her for granted, and I threw her love away. I pitted her against Father—I even took his side—when all along she was the one that actually cared. A mistake I can never rectify. Her eyes burn a hole in my heart that no time and no new love will heal—a chasm invisible and unending.

And what now? I can't just give up, I can't stop and cry. I'm angry, but I can't wallow here. I have to be strong. I have to keep going. She gave her life so that I could keep mine. I have to make her sacrifice matter, make it count for something, and I almost threw it away. I put my mask on by instinct, an instinct she gave me, and it was the only thing that kept the poison from getting into my lungs. I'd be dead, buried in the ash. Victor, Charles, Cornelia, Georgette, and Mr. Herrington would have been entombed. But how do I hold both of those truths at the same time? The masks are a weapon against the people, a tool of oppression—*cell block me*—but the silver trucks are real. The poison in their bellies blisters, chokes, and kills. *Wear Your Mask.* Always when I think I'm getting somewhere, when I think I'm free, the concrete walls close in again. Tearing down this dark highway, in the middle of the night, with no clear destination, what am I supposed to do?

A warm hand rests on my shoulder. I roll over and look up at Cornelia.

"It's been a rough road darling, and I think you deserve to rest. I'm going to hook you up to an IV and then give you something to help you sleep. Don't worry about us, Victor and Charles will keep us safe until you're feeling better."

"Yeah don't worry Evelyn, we've got your back!" Georgette's words are so sincere that it's hard to fight against them.

I want to stay awake, alert for the dangers surely lurking just beyond the narrow swath cut by the headlights. But I can hardly keep my eyes open—my mind aches from pains physical and phantom. Maybe she's right, I can't fix anything now. I should rest.

Contracting my abs, I sit up. The effort feels like bending an iron girder. Cornelia smiles, then turns away. Rooting through the metal cabinets, she pulls out orange pill bottles and studies their labels. After discarding a half-dozen bottles, she finds one that fits the bill.

"This is strong, but it should let you rest." She plops two white pills into my hand and offers me a bottle of water. The tablets are chalky and the water warm, but placebo or not, real relief rushes over me like a cleansing rain. I feel her tug my arm toward her.

"This will sting, don't look."

The IV needle punches through the crook of my elbow. Pain flashes and then recedes into the mellow waves of relief washing over me. Painkillers cover me in a blanket shielding me from the eyes in the darkness.

"Now lay back. It's going to be a long journey, and we need you healthy."

I let the tension in my muscles go, and gravity quickly pulls me back to the bench. The aching is gone. I'm weightless—my body has melted away. With my eyes fighting to stay open, I catch a glimpse of Victor in the driver's seat. His face stern and alert—eyes fixed on the road ahead. *He can handle this.*

I blink my eyes open. An odor, pungent like six-month-old asparagus rotting in the back of the fridge, sears through my nostrils pulling me out of sleep.

I sit up to search for the source of the smell—the world wobbles nearly as much as my stomach. I get my first real look at the ambulance—austere, metal, and glass. Dawn is pouring through the two small windows in its rear doors. Golden light refracts through the glass in a thousand brilliant beams. Beautiful.

Georgette is curled up asleep on the opposite bench. The spot Cornelia was in last night is empty. A quick scan reveals that she and Charles are both missing. Victor is passed out. The exhaustion from driving all night is enacting its revenge—his eyes twitch, and he's practically panting.

I turn back to the shafts of light. The sky behind them is a hazy brown, but it's clear enough to reveal a bright and angular ball of light. For the first time in my life, I have to avert my eyes from the sun—only now realizing the real power it radiates.

I follow the beams through the glass and find the source of the smell. The largest beam illuminates Mr. Herrington. When the sewer water dried, it left the sheet stiffened around the contours of his face. Golden light pools in his gaunt cheeks and sunken eyes—a mockery of the brightness he radiated in life.

With the ambulance turned off, the air scrubbers are dormant, and the smell won't go away until they are on again. Although it won't really go away, it'll just be—like everything else in this world—masked.

I can't bring up tears—sorrow pours into the chasm and the pit grows deeper to swallow it. Soon I fear only a truly great torrent of loss will coax tears to fall. *What has this world made of me?*

I look up at my IV bag. It's empty, and for the first time in a long time, I feel like myself in my *own* skin. I pull the needle out and wince. I wasn't expecting to have sensation back so quickly—I guess the pills have worn off. A small trickle of blood races to the edge of my elbow. A single droplet falls before I can clamp the puncture shut.

I don't want to wake Georgette, and with Mr. Herrington covering the floor, exit through the double doors will be difficult. The gap between the front seats is narrow, but I make it through with little effort and plop into the passenger's seat. Through the front window, I can see a sparse forest of brown-gray trees. Most are barren, but here and there small patches of dry brown needles cling to spindly branches.

Victor is slumped over the steering wheel. He must have collapsed onto the dash not even a moment after he put the ambulance in park and turned off the engine. I don't remember what time we left, but we must have driven for several hours, and there is no telling when the last time he slept was. When he wakes up, I'll have to thank him for getting us out of the city in one piece.

I turn to the door and clasp the cold metal handle and begin to twist when the small yellow warning plastered above it forces me to pause. *Wear Your Mask. Ensure your mask is properly sealed before exiting the vehicle.* Months ago, I would have obeyed without question. Days ago, I would have scoffed. And now? Now I'm not sure. I chart the many possible truths of the mask: it isolates us, *it keeps us safe*, it controls us, *it keeps us safe.* My thoughts spiral. Always, the Caretaker's words shout themselves in defiance of my protests. *Wear Your Mask.* I want to fight it, deny their power over me, over everyone, but then the sores on my skin start to itch. I look down at the back of my hand. The skin is red and raw. Small blisters are pushing their way out. The poison is real. The danger is real.

I reach back and grab my mask. It's been scrubbed clean. That's one more thing to thank Cornelia for. I flip it around and stare through the eye ports. I close my eyes and give in to the routine. Press. Exhale. Empty. Tighten. Breathe.

Open again, I see the world filtered through rubber and glass. The door clicks open, and I step out onto the pine-needle-littered dirt. My feet crunch on the unfamiliar terrain nearly drowning out the faint rustling of the needles still clinging to the trees. The cool breeze cuts through my soiled jumpsuit. I rub my shivering arms and press on.

A few dozen meters ahead, there is a small clearing. Cornelia and Charles are there. Charles has his head down to his chest. His face is hidden behind a mask, but his body is limp—his arms lay motionless at his side. He shifts his weight from one foot to the other like a boat listing at anchor. Cornelia stands rigid. Her hands gesticulate at her waist in the body language equivalent of an enraged whisper. As I approach, my footfalls alert them. Their conversation dies, and they both turn toward me. Splitting the distance, we meet at the edge of the clearing.

"You look like you're feeling much better," says Cornelia. The hints of frustration and argument have yet to drop entirely from her lips.

"I am. Thank you. Thank you for taking care of me—and getting us out of there."

"No thanks are necessary. We owe you and Victor a great deal," says Charles.

The conversation fizzles. They plainly wanted, or needed, to continue what they were doing, and there is no way they are going to with me around. But there isn't time or space for personal squabbles anymore—no matter how justified. I step past them and into the clearing. From my new vantage point, I can see the ground slope down to a large flat plane below. The road cuts the expanse in half like a black scar. On the near side of the road stands a squat fueling station with another building that looks like a diner. I take the scene in. Quivering blades of yellow grass cling to life in ash soaked soil. Swirling ash-devils twirl peacefully. A dozen chrome cars are parked in a row along the side of the diner. Their engines idling, belching smoke, to keep the wipers running in an endless battle against the ever-falling soot. Apart from the people eating in the diner, there doesn't appear to be anyone around. The road in both directions is empty as far as the haze will let me see. We didn't stop for the view, so why did we? Thick black rubber hoses swaying in the breeze at the pump grab my attention.

I turn back to Charles and Cornelia. They are looking anywhere but at each other, yet they're standing shoulder to shoulder in a failed effort to make it look like nothing's wrong. I shake it away. This used to bother me, consume me. But the world is full of so many bigger problems. These petty grievances mean little in the grand scheme of things. Or maybe I have it wrong; perhaps they mean everything, and that's why nothing changes? I speak to break that train of thought.

"How do we get the gas?"

Charles's glazed eyes snap to life. He steps toward me. Cornelia shadows him. Focused on the gas pumps coming into his view, he doesn't seem to notice her.

"I have a can. I pulled it from the ambulance. I should be able to pump a few gallons before anyone notices."

"But what happens when they do?" I say. I don't want to think about what will happen if a Peace Officer happens to be sitting there on the other side of the glass, sipping on a coffee. But without gas, we're sitting ducks in this wasteland.

"That's why Gette and I will go inside and get some food," Cornelia clenches her fists. "We'll draw their attention away from the gas pumps."

"Absolutely not! How many times do I have to tell you no? I can't risk that. No, no way."

"This isn't all about you, Charles. Gette and I are in this just as much as you are. Victor is passed out, Evelyn is still dehydrated and suffering from a concussion—and God knows what's in that poison gas. Yes, it is the only way. If we can get the gas, everything will work out. Then we can get to Glen Fois without any more stops."

"What if they detain you? What if they start asking questions? What if there are Peace Officers in there? No. I mean it, no! It's too dangerous. We can make it farther on the gas we've got. If we use the back roads, we can make it to Bergholz—it'll be easier to get gas there." Charles is beginning to heave. The extra effort of arguing in his mask is taking its toll on him.

"That will push things back a day or two. A day or two we don't have. He's dead Charles, it's all lost. The network is gone, the safe houses are compromised. Einsam is dead to us. It's just us, and Glen Fois is the only place we know we can find a little peace in this storm. We have to take risks, Charles. Bernard took risks, his whole life was a risk. And he wouldn't have it any other way."

"Don't bring him into this! You think I don't know what's going on? He was like a father to me, I loved him, and it's all gone now. It's all gone because of some damned kid with a badge and a gun."

As the words leave his mouth, Charles crumbles. Falling to his knees, he sobs. Cornelia's stiffness melts away. She rushes to his side, holding him in her embrace—nestling her head on his neck—she starts to whisper.

"You can't lose us, Charles. We're yours for now and always. We'll always be with you. Bernard is still alive in you."

"I can't lose you. I can't."

As though the skies opened and a great torrent of rain burst from the heavens, I feel the chasm fill to bursting. Mother's eyes, tired, bloodshot, and full of tears, stare back at me. *Run!*

Tears blur my vision. Rage fuels my muscles. I don't remember grabbing the gas can. One moment my hand was empty, and the next it was clenched around the metal handle threatening to break it. One muffled shout told me to stop. But I can't stop, I can never stop. She told me to run.

Barreling down the hill, the perspective of the world closes in, and the once open plains now feel like the jaws of a hungry beast inching toward my neck.

Belches of black smoke plume from the cars idling in the parking lot obscuring the windows of the diner beyond. *How many eyes are staring back on the other side of the darkness?* I look away from the building and lock my focus on the pump.

I skid to a stop; I'd gained more speed than I thought. My lungs heave—the taste of copper floods my mouth. But a pulsing, boiling energy courses through my veins, keeping fatigue in check. My hands fumble with the metal cap—they jitter and fidget in rhythm with my pulsing heartbeat and the surging adrenaline carried in my veins. In my haste, the cap flings off into the soot. I drop the can and dive after it. Snatching it up, I get back up and try to decipher the instructions on the pump. *Pull handle, insert nozzle, raise lever.* How hard can that be?

I pull the handle on the lever. It's heavier than I thought it would be, and the rubber hose fights me. It twists and bends as I try to position it in the can. Getting the nozzle into the opening, I flip up the lever. Gas shoots from the nozzle in a torrent. A small glass façade hides white plastic wheels spinning wildly to count the cost. I have no way of telling how full the container is. I think it must be ten liters, so I fix my eyes on the numbers. 2.3. 2.6. 3. It's filling up quick, but I can feel eyes piercing into my back. I chance a glance over at the diner. The only movement is the stirring clouds of black smoke. I turn back to the wheels. 8.9. 9.3. 9.8.

"Hey! You've got to pay for that!" A voice—static and distorted—roars out over loudspeakers.

Fear darts through my spine. I rip the nozzle from the can. Gas sprays everywhere soaking instantly into the thirsty soil. I twist the metal cap on. It seats with a satisfying *click*.

The weight of the full tank slows my launch. Heaving it up

into my arms, I secure a better grip and begin my dash back up the hill. I can't look back. The adrenaline is still pumping, but its power to fight the building rebellion in my heart and lungs is fading. I wish I could rip this mask off and let more air in, but even now the fear of the gas keeps it firmly on my face.

Eyes fixed on the tree line at the top of the hill, I concentrate on nothing but the chase. Left, right, breath in breath out, left, right. Like fresh mountain air, the trees appear unmoving, a mirage, ever out of reach.

Run!

The weight of her final word coalesces with the strain, and together they sink their teeth into me. My right leg buckles and my knee slams to the ground. A deep resonating pain shoots out from the point of impact and rattles through my bones. I recover fast, but the pain lingers and slows every step. I grit my teeth. My mind is running wild trying to put down the myriad rebellions and conflicting messages erupting all over my body and keep me focused on the goal.

I force my momentum forward, fighting the pain, doubt, and fear that reverberates with every step. I summit the hill and break through the tree line. Charles, standing in the clearing, breaks free from Cornelia's arms and races toward me. His massive frame moves with a feline grace and hurricane speed.

"Get Victor to start it up!" Charles says, spinning his hand in a circle over his head.

"On it!" replies Cornelia already sprinting back to the ambulance.

Charles reaches me. He takes up the canister gasping under its weight. At least it's heavy for him too.

"Just hop in. We'll fill up somewhere safer."

"Right!"

I turn my focus toward the ambulance. With the canister gone, I'm rejuvenated. My knee still aches, and my lungs still scream, but with respite so close at hand, the rest of me muffles their cries and doubles their efforts to get me there.

Cornelia pulls open the passenger door and jumps in with one liquid motion. Through the windshield, I see her grab Victor's shoulders and shake. He jerks awake and instinctively throttles the car to life. Georgette, mask-less, pleads to know what's going on. Though her words are too distant to make out clearly, I don't need to hear any of them. I'm asking the same things.

I rush around to the back and throw open the double doors. Pulling myself in, I'm face-to-face with Mr. Herrington. *This isn't a dream. You're here. Run!* I shake my head to rid it of the shouting.

Charles emerges from around the corner, not a heartbeat later. I retake my place on the bench and turn to help him pull in the gas can. It takes every ounce of strength I have left to keep it from falling. I pull it next to me on the bench and secure it with a thick canvas strap hanging from the wall.

Charles jumps onto the opposite bench and slams the double doors shut. Ripping off his mask, he turns to Victor.

"Drive!"

The ambulance lurches to life. Victor weaves us deftly through the trees, down the hill, and away from the pumps and the café.

Leaning back, I pull my mask off. The overhead filtration system is working overtime to recycle the air in the cabin and is blowing a gale of cold air from the vents in the ceiling. The fresh air feels good against my hot, sweat-drenched skin. The smell is mostly gone, but now that I know that it's there, I can't shake it from my nose.

Charles leans back against the wall and closes his eyes. His chest rises and falls in rapid succession. Then without warning, it stops, his eyes open, and he focuses on me.

"That was reckless! You can't just run off and do whatever you want—you can't play hero all the time! You have to think of all of us."

His words pierce and sting like needles. Was I acting? Playing a role? Am I selfish? All good questions answerable some other time.

"Not now," I say. My tone is far more humble than my words.

"Why I—" before he can finish, Georgette places her hand on his leg. She looks into his eyes and the fire in them dwindles. Crossing his arms, he leans back against the wall and pretends to sleep.

The cabin grows quiet. Only the sound of dirt crunching beneath our tires and the squeal of struts bounding over rocks in the field dares challenge the silence.

I squeeze my eyes shut, hoping to get some reprieve. Mother stares back at me in the darkness. I can't lose you, Evelyn.

I can't throw my eyes open fast enough. With nowhere to look that won't make me deal with the past or confront the tension of the present, I turn up to the ceiling and the air vents desperately fighting their never-ending battle against the stench of death and the noxious smog.

Victor breaks the tension.

"Where are we headed?" his voice both confused and distressed.

"Glen Fois. And then we can all rest," says Cornelia through a laden breath.

I keep my eyes focused on the vents and let my body sway with the bumps and curves in the road. It's going to be a long ride to Glen Fois.

CHAPTER TWO

TENSION IN THE AMBULANCE is as thick as tar. We all need to vent, to come to terms with what is going on. But there is no time, no space to crawl into a corner and scream until your lungs are hoarse. We could snap. Go after each other, break apart what little community we have left. But that delicate flame, that shining hope in the darkness—that perhaps we can all get through this together—forces us to bottle up our frustrations, fears, doubts, grief, and pain into a knot in our chests. Even Georgette seems to fully appreciate the mood and the severity of the events around her. I'm not sure I would have been able to handle this when I was her age. I sat in front of the television and pictured myself up there alongside the cartoon characters and adults dressed as animals. I lost myself in the television's twinkling fantasies. It took me years to figure out that the only way to get the better world I wanted was to go out and make it. But I think Georgette and I have lived very different lives. My parents sheltered me from everything, yet she seems aware of so much. I guess that's the difference between living in the basement versus the penthouse.

Hitting an unusually large pothole, the ambulance lurches. My head bobbles around, breaking my staring contest with the vent above. *I guess I lose.*

"Everything alright, Victor? Do you need me to take a turn driving?" says Cornelia.

"No. I'm okay. It was hit that one or the canyon on either side of it. I chose the path of least resistance."

Without thought, laughter floods from my mouth—my eyes and cheeks hot from the sudden burst.

Charles looks up from his morose trance.

"What could possibly be so funny?"

"Victor taking the path of least resistance? Yeah, right!" I say, although just barely over the sound of my own laughter.

Charles's face remains stoic, then in a flash, his eyes grow wide, and a broad smile reveals his shining teeth. A great belly laugh bursts from his stout chest buckling him over. His eyes are closed tight—each giggle pushes a small tear out of the corner of his eyes. The tension in the ambulance shatters, and we all erupt into uncontrollable fits of laughter. Victor jerks the wheel sharply to the left, then corrects himself. We pause for a moment and look around at each other then break into another fit of laughter.

"That's rich kid! Least resistance! Ha!" Charles forces his words out through wheezing breaths.

"You're one to talk, Charles! You even make your sandwiches the hard way." Cornelia attempts to give Charles a grave look, but as soon as their eyes meet, she melts back into laughter.

Catharsis. Each laugh frees a snake from the Gordian knot of emotions strangling my heart. It lifts and elevates us. It pulls us from the present and into somewhere else, some other time when we didn't have to worry about bombs and bullets, poison and subversives, suffering and death. But reality, like gravity, will not be denied. You can push against it, fight it, but in the end, it always wins. There is no other way.

"Papa, Bernard would have liked this."

Georgette's innocence cut us like a knife. It was lost on no one that Mr. Herrington lay dead in the narrow floor between us. How could we avoid it? His death swells inside the cabin threatening to force all the air out of the cramped space. My hand grasps at the invisible constrictor collapsing my lungs. All of us, in our own way, set events in motion that put him in that van and put those bullets in his heart. I can't handle it. I slam my eyes shut.

Run! Bang! Arrest her! Bang! Is he breathing? Long live the Great Society! Cinnamon! I don't know kid.

Tears run down my cheeks—red and chapped—in lines like rivers. At this rate, they will hollow out grooves. Charles sinks his head into his hands, attempting to flee from the crumbling world around him. Victor stares straight ahead at the road, his sniffles fighting the unending tide of grief trying to pull him back into the depths. Cornelia reaches for Georgette.

She did the right thing. She pulled us back to the present—to escaping, surviving. I want to be upset, but I can't blame her. I wish I knew Mr. Herrington better. How can I judge her words from our few hours together? Every time I feel myself connecting with someone, the world conspires to rip them from me. It's as if my punishment for the truth is to remain—to linger on after everyone else has gone.

I close my eyes and witness a never-ending slideshow of my mistakes and disappointments. As horrible as these visions are, they're better than anything I can look at in this ambulance.

The drive feels like an eternity. Hours down the road the gas finally gives out to fumes. Victor pulls into a thick grove of trees growing around a leaking, above-ground water main. The soot tries to stifle life, to cover everything in its gray embrace. But where there is even a crumb of nourishment, life has taken root to stand tall, vibrant, and defiant against the dying world.

We putter to a stop. Charles pulls on his mask and jumps out the double doors. I unhook the gas can from the strap and pass it to him. The weight is immense—the effort is magnified by my growling hunger. He takes it from me, our eyes avoid each other. He closes the double doors and disappears. With the engine off, the silence crinkles like midnight static. It shouts and pulls at us to fill the void. Yet no words will fall from our lips. We'd rather suffer the raging silence than speak and crack it open.

A sudden burst of noise from the doors opening saves us from saying anything. Charles passes me the now empty can. Anticipating its full weight, I nearly lose control and bang the container into the wall. A flash of red-hot embarrassment shoots across my face. I look away from him and focus on the fuel can. Feed the strap through the handle, insert the buckle, *click*.

"That should get us the rest of the way there. How far now, Victor?" Charles' voice sounds alien and distant like speech imitating itself.

Victor lets out a profound sigh. Pointing to the glove box, he turns to Cornelia.

"The map is in there. I have a pretty good idea of where we are, but we should check."

Cornelia nods and opens the glove box. The map was hastily shoved in there before and is now hopelessly crumbled. Cornelia takes a moment to unfold it, inspect its creases, then refold it to its proper shape. She hands it over to Victor, who takes it from her with a slow and deliberate motion. He lays it out over the steering wheel. His finger stabs at Einsam on the map and begins to trace our path.

"We followed this road west, then here, this is where we got the gas. I followed this ridgeline until here, and then I've followed the road north. We should be here."

His finger stops just south of a small hamlet named Bergholz.

"It's a little farm just north of here, right along Wolf Run Creek."

Before any of us can jump in with a suggestion, Victor takes charge.

"If I take this road around to the east, we can circle back and around to avoid Bergholz altogether. It'll take longer—we probably won't get there until nightfall—but it should help us avoid any more," he pauses to find the least inflammatory word, "complications."

I know I've messed things up, but what do they want from me? How are you expected to act when everything is blowing up around you? I want to scream—burst from this damned ambulance and tear across the hills until I run out of earth then press on until I fall off the edge into oblivion. Strapping my frustration back down, I take a deep breath.

"That's probably for the best. I vote the longer route."

"Agreed. We're holding on by a string as it is. The long way, Victor." Cornelia's words resonate with Charles and Georgette, who nod their agreement in concert.

Victor capitalizes on the silence. Passing the map back to Cornelia, he twists the keys and brings the engine grumbling to life.

We return to the roadway and pick up speed. The little patch of green fades into the distance, and the landscape once again returns to a uniform yellow-gray.

Away from the city, the night is too dark. Expanses of nothingness fill me with anxiety. Trapped my whole life in the tight confines of the mask, the city, the penthouse, the schoolroom—this openness feels unnatural, like an illusion ready to crumble around me at any moment.

To avoid being seen, we're driving without lights which has slowed our pace to a crawl. We are near a creek now, and the dusty yellow fields have yielded to thick clumps of dark green. The hedges have encroached upon the road, and the clean-cut lines from saw blades show where they are beaten back in an endless struggle between civilization and the unstoppable march of nature.

Down dark and narrow driveways, dim yellow lights illuminate small rundown farmhouses. We continue to slowly curve and twist through this alien landscape. Each new bend revealing whole worlds I could never have imagined in the choking confines of Einsam. Abandoned, unidentifiable hulks of metal reflect a rusty red in the scant moonlight. Their corpses litter the byways as the world's last reminders of some ancient robot war.

Seeing the puzzlement on my face, Charles breaks our long silence. "This whole area used to be farms. But about twenty years back, a little before you were born I think, the drought got *real* bad. The dust came in, and well," he drifts off staring into the moonlit world framed in the front windshield, "the wrecks speak for themselves."

"I'm surprised to see so many lights on at the farmhouses," Cornelia says. "The way Bernard spoke it was as if everyone fled to the city."

"That was the impression I had too. We may not be as safe as I thought we'd be. Last time I was here with him I was helping him gather up some family heirlooms before boarding up the place."

"I guess people will do anything to survive, to regain what they've lost," I say. The observation has been rattling around in my mind for days now, and it only just found a reason to come out.

"That's what we're doing, so I can't really blame these people for doing it too," says Cornelia.

"Let's just hope Glen Fois is still the refuge we need it to be."

"Well, we'll find out soon enough. I think it's down here at the end of this driveway," says Victor pointing off toward the vacuous darkness between two thick groves of vines.

"At least there are no lights down there. That's a good sign. Should I go ahead and scout it out?" Charles says.

Cornelia pulls herself around in the seat to look directly at Charles.

"You can't preach to me about losing people and then offer to cavalierly walk into the unknown," she says.

"Well someone has to go, and well, I'm the most familiar with the place."

"At this point, Charles, if one of us gets caught then we all get caught. Plus, am I supposed to just sit here in the road idling while you go scope things out? That seems like an excellent way to draw attention to us."

"You're right. I just," he lets out a deep sigh then inhales sharply. "I just want you to be safe."

"We're safest together," I say.

"I'm staying with Evelyn." Georgette nods her head forward to add emphasis to her declaration.

Cornelia smiles then twists back into her seat, "Well, you heard the lady, Victor."

Creeping forward, the ambulance quickly eats up the remaining few meters of road. The transition to gravel is loud and abrupt. Whereas the roads are semi-maintained, it's clear no one has graded this road in ages. Deep ruts and grooves jerk the cabin left and right while giant rocks send us all flying in our seats. With only the rays of moonlight peeking through the clouds to guide us, Victor is having a terrible time avoiding the hazards.

The road grows darker. The distant lights of farmhouses appear as tiny dots like stars. Soon even they grow dim, and only the moon lights our path.

The deep ruts start to even-out, and patches of grass begin to replace gravel. The claustrophobic driveway slicing through the vines finally ends, revealing a large clearing. Moonlight highlights the edges of a small two-story house. A porch wraps all the way around the exterior, and a small round window on the second-floor shines like a beacon with reflected silver. Next to the house is a barn that looks just like all the others I've seen in films and textbooks. The roof is caved in at the corner, and even in the dark it looks unstable. At the far end of the field, there is a tall windmill gently spinning in the wind. Next to it stands a series of dull, round containers barely visible in the darkness. But most breathtaking is the towering oak tree. It stands at least as tall as the windmill. Its branches spread wide and cover the side of the house in inky shadow. Its full leafage shimmers in the breeze—twinkling in the moonlight. It's glorious. Transfixed as we approach, my eyes are unable to wander from the dancing leaves. The sight of it brings a tear of disbelief to my eye.

When Victor stops in front of the barn, the sudden jolt forces me to gasp. I hadn't even realized I was holding my breath.

"It was quite the place back in the day. Bernard's mother, Florence, she kept the place spotless. The house was always painted a soft shade of blue and trimmed out in white. It looked sharp."

We all pause and soak in Charles's words. The sight of Glen Fois, and the isolation and vastness around it, fills me with comfort and warmth. I wonder if this place will ever be back to the way it was? Or has too much time passed, and the dust and decay have found a permanent home here? It seems hopeless to believe in a bright future, but then the glistening leaves grab my attention. Even in such a barren and abandoned place, this mighty oak has stood the test of time and continues to thrive in spite of what the world throws at it. Even in the short time I knew him, Bernard seems to have a lot in common with this oak tree. Who's copying who?

With the engine off, the sounds of night creep into the ambulance. Hisses and croaks bounce around in my ears. I've never heard real crickets or the droning dirge of the cicadas. Miles away from the city but a world apart.

"The house doesn't have any air filters, and I doubt we need them here, but bring your mask along just in case. They could be releasing gas, and we should be ready."

I grab my mask and squeeze it tight. It's so strange to need it again.

"I'll lead the way. I think I still remember where the bed-rooms are. We should all try and get some rest, and then we can figure out our next move and give Bernard a proper burial in the morning."

"Right then, lead the way, Charles. Gette, hold Evelyn's hand and keep close."

I reach my hand out to Georgette and smile. She smiles back and together we press open the double doors and hop out of the cabin.

My legs are stiff from the hours of sitting. It takes a moment for the blood and sensation to get back to normal. Georgette's grip is solid, and she seems steady. The air is crisp. A gentle breeze blows—goose pimples crawl across my flesh. Charles jumps out after us and turns on his flashlight. The beam cuts through the darkness. I shoot my free hand up to shield myself from its brilliance. He aims it at the porch. The light reveals fading and chipped paint. The light cutting though the porch banisters casts the door in spider-like shadows.

"I'll lead the way. Evelyn, Gette, stay close."

In unison, Georgette and I nod to Charles and follow behind him. His bulk blocks most of the light, so we follow his silhouette into the abandoned house with careful footsteps. The wooden steps up the porch are warped and creaking. No matter how carefully we choose our footfalls, they shout a shrill cry into the darkness. Most likely there isn't anyone inside, or even in earshot, but every moment, breath, and step tolls like a bell ringing in the silence. Charles's outline freezes in front of the door; his large hand engulfing the small brass knob. The wind blows cold, and the sound of my heartbeat crescendos into thunder. *Kertoosh. Kertoosh. Kertoosh.*

The door creaks open. A swirl of dust billows enshrouding Charles in a beautiful aura of dancing sprites. He enters the house, and I press forward, propelled by the thunder in my ears. Georgette keeps pace—her grip tightening as we pass the threshold.

"Anyone home?" Charles speaks into the dark and empty house.

We wait. The sound of settling dust and groaning joists unsettles the peace. Charles waves the light back and forth as if trying to hold back the endless tide of darkness and is as successful as holding back the waves. A long minute passes then Charles relaxes the frantic sweeping of his light and moves toward the kitchen. With Victor and Cornelia crammed into the foyer with us, I tug gently on Georgette's hand and push us a little farther into the room. The sound of drawers rattling and cupboard doors creaking fills the house.

"What are you looking for Charles?" says Cornelia.

"Candles. Grandma Herrington never trusted the electricity here very much, so she used to keep the place stocked with candles and matches."

"I wonder if that's where Mr. Herrington got his aversion to computers from?" Victor asks. His voice is tired, strained.

"I doubt it, she loved television. No, it's just these rural power lines 'progress you can see!' they said when they put it in. Never did it right, though, or got around to fixing it up much."

"Sounds about right," I say. Brevity feels both comforting and wrong. It fights inside me like twisting, scratching wolves.

"Ah-ha! Here's one."

The match bursts to life and blossoms on the candle's wick. The fire shares its dance and soon both candle and match rage against the darkness. Transfixed, Charles lets the fire burn a little too long—orange fire licks out at his pinched fingers.

"Ouch!"

Shaking the match out of his hand, Charles bites his tongue to keep from letting loose a string of obscenities.

"Here, Charles, let me get the candles lit. There is some burn ointment in the ambulance. And Victor, why don't you bring in anything we can use. Bottled water, food?"

"On it," says Victor.

Charles nods to Cornelia, disappearing into the night with his flashlight.

Cornelia lights the candles, and soon the whole kitchen is ablaze.

"Can you both draw the curtains, or block the windows somehow? It's probably best not to advertise that there is some-one in the old Herrington place."

"On it," I say, echoing Victor. I move toward the front win-dows. The yellow and red flower-patterned drapes are just barely visible in the candlelight. Only a step away, something tugs at my arm. Georgette's hand constricts around mine. I turn to look at her. Fire writhing in her big eyes.

"It's alright, Georgette. You can come with me." I flash her a smile. "Come on. It'll be fun. I bet I can cover more windows than you!"

"Nu-uh, I can!" Her hand drops from mine, and she takes off toward the windows at the back of the house. I turn around and dash toward the windows as fast as I can. The drapes are thick and covered with an equally thick layer of dust. Pulling them closed, I unleash a plume of neglect. Covered, I dash to the living room windows. A curved bay window—flanked by two thin rectangular ones—shimmers in the tendrils of moonlight passing through. A long, wall-length curtain rod makes the task simple. With a single *zhhwhip*, I pull the curtain closed and cut off the shards of silver light. I turn back toward the kitchen. Behind Cornelia is a single square window over the sink. My hackles rise—alerting me to the other set of eyes staring down the kitchen window. In the entry to the hallway, Georgette stands poised to dash into the kitchen. As soon as my eyes meet hers, she takes off. I try to keep pace and follow, but my muscles ache, and my joints protest. If I really wanted to, I'm sure I could force myself to win. But letting her earn this victory, as small and trivial as it is, will help us both keep our spirits alive in this mess.

"I did it! I won. Told you I could get more than you!" Georgette's words fight their way out through short breaths.

"Good job, Gette! You're so quick! Now you and Evelyn take these candles and do the same upstairs. Dad and I will see what we can scrounge up for dinner."

"I'll see what kind of sleeping arrangements there are while we're up there."

"Good idea, Evelyn." She extends two candles to Georgette. She grabs them, one in each hand, and then walks toward me with a slow and deliberate pace.

Taking one of the candles from her, I retake her hand and head up the stairs to the second floor.

Our rummage through the upstairs is quick. The curtains were already drawn on most of the windows. We find three single beds in two rooms. There is a small staircase that leads up to an attic, but it hardly seems worth exploring in the darkness. We return downstairs just as Victor and Charles return from the ambulance.

"Find anything useful?"

"Just some bottled water. No food, not even a morsel," says Victor. The bottles of water glimmering in his hands.

Cornelia sighs, "Same here. Cupboards are bare save for a few cans of well-expired beans. I'm hungry, but I'll take a growling stomach over food poisoning."

"At least we'll be able to sleep in relative comfort. There are three beds upstairs. You and Georgette can take the room with two beds and Charles, you the other. Victor can have the couch, and I'll take the chair."

"No, Evelyn, you and Victor should get a bed each. You've both had a rough time of it, you need to really rest up," Charles says.

"Don't you want to sleep in our room, Evelyn? It'll be way more comfortable than that chair." Georgette's eyes dart to the faded burgundy wing-backed chair in the living room. Even with little light, it's clear to see its most comfortable days are behind it.

"I think the arrangement I laid out will be best. That way you can stay close to Georgette, and everyone else can get some sleep."

"Let me at least take the chair, you'll sleep better in the bed."

"No, I think—"

"Please, Evelyn, you deserve the sleep. I may not have done the things you did, but we'd be trapped, stranded, or dead if you hadn't of acted the way you did earlier. I'm not sure I like it, but I have to respect it. Please," he gestures toward the staircase. I can feel my cheeks turn red. I hadn't done any of those things for praise, and his words make it sound like I'm a selfless hero. I just did what I had to. I try to open my mouth to speak, but the words choke up in my throat. I can feel all their eyes on me. Little Georgette is looking up at me like I'm a superhero.

Charles claps his hands, breaking the awkward tension. "Well then, let's get to sleep. We've got a long day ahead of us tomorrow and a lot of things to figure out. We might not get a chance to rest like this for a while so let's take full advantage of it."

We agree in silence. I feel his words ring ominously true. The future now is cloudier and more obscure than ever. Where will we go? How will we find food? How will we stay safe? Is there a safe place? All questions that burn without answer—that gnaw without nourishment.

Cornelia takes Georgette's hand and leads her up the stairs.

"Goodnight my darlings."

"Goodnight Papa."

Victor's words freeze me as my foot hits the first step.

"Goodnight, Evelyn."

His tone stirs the world inside me. I can hardly process this. Was there longing in his voice? Or was that just concern? More questions and still fewer answers. I shake my head a little.

"Goodnight, Victor."

I ascend the staircase and pause at the landing. Georgette runs from her room and embraces me in a hug. Her tiny arms wrap around me and squeeze tight. I hug her back—my arms wrap around her neck and head.

"Goodnight kiddo."

She pulls back and smiles up at me, then darts back into the room. Cornelia mouths a silent goodnight. Her eyes are kind though exhausted. I return the courtesy and watch as she pulls the door shut.

With only a candle to light my path, I find my way to the second room. The door creaks open. A petite single bed fills most of the space. There is a small dresser with a mirror crusted over in cobwebs—dust fills the rest of it. I navigate the narrow path to the bed. The covers are coated with a layer of dust as fine as powder. I grab at the corner and pull it back slowly to keep as much of it in place as I can. Hot wax drips down the candle and over my fingers. Startled, I wince blowing the candle out. Blackness rushes in. The ghost image of the candle lingers in an orange dancing outline. Moment by moment the darkness seizes more of it until it's gone.

Run!

Alone in the darkness, Mother's words find me again. Eyes open or closed I'm unable to escape her face, her startled eyes, her panicked voice. I feel the tears come. I drop the candle letting it clatter on the floor. I'm suffocating.

I tear off my mask and let it fall. The mustiness of the room accosts me. I breathe in—daring my lungs to burst—and cry. I muffle the sobs with my hands. *I'm so sorry, mom, I love you.* I say these words to myself over and over until they are the only words I can remember.

CHAPTER THREE

HOURS OF SLEEPLESS DARKNESS brings the room into focus. Illuminated by a single splinter of light through the window, the bed and dresser take shape as gray outlines against gray walls. Light commands great power over darkness; the dark may be ever ready to fill the void, but even a single candle, or beam of moonlight, holds it at bay. I move to the window, tracing the beam's path through the room. I lean into it and press my eye to the window.

The yard is bright in the brilliance of the full moon. The great oak tree stands magnificent. Silver dances on the shimmering leaves waving to the rhythms of the wind. *No wonder you believed peace was possible when you lived in a place like this.* For Mr. Herrington, Einsam was the anomaly. A dark sinkhole of oppression and sorrow. He knew that just outside the city's boundaries, tall oak trees fought the acrid air and stood defiant against drought and hardship. With the moon and stars above, hope is almost tangible. If I had been born here, lived here, things would have been so different. But how can I even think that? I am who I am because of where I came from, because of the people who raised me. The people who loved me.

As if a tempest suddenly burst from pure stillness, my body is propelled to action. I cannot lay Mother to rest, but I can make sure Mr. Herrington receives the dignity he deserves.

Affixing my mask, I move like a clumsy ghost through the house. The floors creak and groan at my every step, but it seems exhaustion has everyone firmly asleep. The few remaining candles flicker on their last strand of wick—wax spills down their sides freezing into delicate waterfalls.

The front door opens with a sharp metal screech, and the wind greets me with icy fingers. I step into the cold. Uncontrollable shivers rack my body, but I press forward through the night toward the barn. Under the silver moon, the world is ethereal. It's a beauty I've never seen before. The best of the world illuminated in radiant, gentle light. The wind whispers rustling the leaves. I'm glad Mr. Herrington can be at rest here and not in the bowels of smoldering, choking Einsam.

The barn door is large and rotting. Chained shut, the long years of abandonment have rusted and warped its every surface. I push against the right door which stands ajar. The heavy chain bangs against the wood. *Bang! Run! Arrest her!* That moment burned forever into my mind. Just when I think I've seen it for the last time, it comes again, pulling me back to watch my life go up in flames.

I breathe deeply. I listen to the symphony of the meadow

and refocus on my grim task. I push against the door. Again, the chain bangs against the weathered boards. Braced for the sound, I keep the hot flashes of memory from engulfing me. I slip inside scraping against the splinters on the edge of the doors. Inside the barn is so dark my vision fails me. I'm forced to stand still and wait for it to recover. The wind pours through the gap in the door. Its whispers sound sinister now, and the images taking shape are twisted tall and cruel. My heart quickens, each breath is rapid and shallow. I fight the urge to run. To race back to the illusionary safety of the house. Head pulled under the dusty covers, I could pretend that this darkness doesn't exist, that all is warm and safe in the world. But I know better, and I've plunged depths far deeper.

With patience, my sight returns enough for me to make out the rough outline of a shovel leaned against the near wall. I step toward it deliberately—each footstep slow and cautious. I reach out and grab the handle. It's rough, and pulling it to me, it feels rickety. Unconvinced of its ability to help me complete the task, but unable to see an alternative, I turn back to the meadow bathed in silver.

In contrast to the barn, the field feels as bright as day. The finer details of the land come into focus. The wide twisting branches of the oak. Trees swaying in the distance under the watchful eye of the ever-spinning windmill. Thick hedges stand like ancient walls around the meadow. The amber glow of farmers' lights is the only reminder that beyond this hallowed glen the Great Society is embroiled in conflict.

Standing beneath the tall oak tree, I take a moment to remember the few moments I got to share with Mr. Herrington.

"We will build a better world. I will build a better world. I'm so glad to have known you."

My words meld with the whispers of the night. Two faded and fraying strands of rope dance to the rhythms of the wind. I walk over to them. I run them through my hands—they are rough burlap. Looking down, I see a piece of wood with the bottom half of the ropes tied to its ends. The grass and earth have grown over it, and within a few years, I'm sure it will disappear altogether into the soil.

I plunge the shovel into the ground. Using my foot, I force the scoop deeper. I pull back the first load. The dirt is clumpy and dry—grass clings to it desperate for water. I strike again. With the surface broken up, progress is marginally faster. Scoop after scoop the pile grows. Scoop after scoop my pace quickens.

Sweat beads on my forehead. My hands grow raw—the rough handle blisters my palms. I pant as the exhaustion that has already taken my friends catches up to me. I struggle against it—I keep at the grave.

Faster now, I thrust the shovel into the dirt with all the force my arms can muster. *Tshoop. Tshoop. Tshoop.* Tears fall as they will. My mind swirls with grief and anxious anticipation. *Tshoop. Tshoop. Tshoop.* With every inch added to the mounding pile of dirt, I feel the weight of reality press that much harder on my heart.

The wind's whispers turn into a howl. In my focused frenzy, I hadn't seen the storm approaching. Dark clouds rumble toward the glen. The moon is swallowed by the storm front roiling the sky. The *pitter-patter* of rain crescendos. I keep my head down. *I must finish this.* The wind picks up speed. The bitter cold bites into me, and I cannot hold the shivers at bay. My aching hands begin to tremble. I lose control of the shovel. It falls to the ground—its impact silenced by the rush of coming rain. I crouch low to pick it up. The momentary reprieve afforded to my hands is enough to keep them from taking the shovel up again. Pulling my hands back, my fingers are still curled up and seized together. I force them to retake the shovel, and they protest with angry shouts of white-hot pain. Standing up, my back too begins to cry. My body joins in, adding a dozen more voices to the angry mob. *Stop! Enough! Rest!* Demands their collective cry.

I must finish this. Pulling the shovel back for another blow, the world conspires with my body to make me stop. The rain hits me in a sheet—gorged droplets drench me in an instant. Total darkness smears away the world. I wince away from the stinging droplets.

"I have to finish this!" I scream at the clouds. I brandish the shovel like a sword against a dragon.

A thunderous roar deafens me, and a blinding flash overwhelms my dark-adjusted eyes. A lightning bolt strikes the windmill—a violent shower of sparks explodes in a burst of red and orange leaving their ghostly trails dancing in my eyes long after the rain snuffs them out. An instant later, a massive invisible force whacks into my chest. The energy of it rattles through my bones and echoes in my lungs.

Dazed, I stand quaking. The shovel falls away from my aching hands. I crumble to my knees; the soft, muddy earth easing my fall. I hang my head and add my tears to the downpour.

The ground hastily drinks in the water far past the point of bursting. The hole rapidly turns into a muddy pool.

Rising to my feet, I head back to the house. Each tread is labored and slowed by the deepening mud. A second bolt of lightning strikes nearby straightening my spine and keeping me moving. The solid steps of the porch fill me with relief.

Beyond the point of breaking, I stumble up the stairs and fall into my room.

CHAPTER FOUR

I'M WRECKED. Dawn streams through the window refracting into rainbows along the cracks in the glass. The light has only just hit me but sweat is already percolating on my face—condensation clouds the eyelets of my mask.

I push myself off the floor and move to the window. The act is comforting. It's something I've done a thousand times before, but it's all different now, and the darkness weighing on me stomps out my nostalgia. A different landscape, a different me.

Beyond the window, all is dust and grass. This world is more than foreign, it's completely alien to the one I lost.

I have to keep moving and finish what I started last night. Yet the thought of one more step into the unknown, of stumbling into some new nightmare, pulls on my neck like heavy chains hooked to my bones. This is becoming a far too familiar feeling.

I wish I were a hero. Bold and brave. Confident that there is meaning in sacrifice. But I have no armor. No noble quest fuels my purpose, only the fear of stopping and admitting what

I've become compels me forward. But I suppose that means I always know exactly what I'm going to do next—keep running.

Each step down to the first-floor creaks at the slightest touch. The old house seems to shudder in the presence of people; having been abandoned for so long, it's as if it forgot how to be a house. I can hear voices coming from outside, but in here it's still silent. Apart from the activity in the kitchen last night, it still looks as if no one has lived here in years. Muddy trails disturb the dust and wind paths leading up to the bedrooms and make swirls around the kitchen and living room. Looking closer, more paths emerge. The fantastical whimsy of wind has carved small dunes into the layers of dust. Intricate lines snake around the house. Thousands of tiny little mouse prints paint a desperate trail seeking out the last bits of edible food. Crossing over it all, I stand at the threshold. Prepared to go outside, I check the seals on my mask. I press my hand over filter and vent. I trace my fingers along the rubber edge around my face. I vent again just to be sure.

I haven't felt this way—the utter terror of simply being outside—since I was a child. But slithering past my defenses, fear has returned to its home in my chest. It has a spare key, and I can't retool the locks.

With a twist and push, I step out into the light. The wooden beams groan underfoot. The door's hinges squeal in desperate need of oil. When I was in the city, choked by fumes and the endless skyscrapers blotting out the sky, I had dreamed of pastoral lands—bright days and green fields far in the distance from the city. I dreamed of the crunch of real earth under my feet. Now that I'm here, I feel strange, uneasy. It feels so exposed in every direction. Underneath the skyscrapers—and their tens of thousands of hidden eyes—I felt invisible and yet here, with trees, grass, and gentle wind I feel utterly exposed. As if my every move is being watched by a thousand eyes lingering just beyond the horizon or in the skulls of murderous birds lurking in the trees.

Cornelia and Georgette are holding shovels and punching them into the earth where I was digging last night. The mound of dirt is twice as high as it was before—the earth muddy and yielding from last night's tempest. Charles and Victor are out of sight, but I hear the telltale signs of them working in the barn. It sounds as though they are cutting wood and hammering nails. I suppose they're making a coffin. How do you bring up the subject of death? How do we talk about this? I don't think any of us know, so we just work and let our silence speak for us.

None of us are ready for this. I wasn't at all ready to see him go. I'd only just met him. I had just begun to learn things from him—to see a different world and a different way of being. And now he's gone. Ripped away in an instant. This must be just as difficult for them—no, more so. They lost a man like father and grandfather, and I wouldn't know anything about that—I never had a real father, only the shell of one.

I know nothing about woodworking or making coffins, but I can dig a hole. I cross the grassy field. The soil doesn't crunch as it did last night—it's soft, squishy. But I can tell it will be back to crunching soon—so desperate for water it's drinking deep, saving the precious liquid in secret chasms far beneath the surface. I approach them slowly. Cornelia looks exhausted—her eyes webbed with burst blood vessels. I stop in front of her, and we share our grief without words—neither of us can think of the right ones. *Thank you*, I want to say to her. Thank you for continuing what I started. But it feels wrong to say thanks in a time like this.

Gette continues to dig. Given up on the full-size shovel, her little trowel takes small mounds of dirt and adds them to the growing pile. The wind blows between us. Distant cicadas and rhythmic sounds of saws slicing into wood fill the air.

"Mr. Herrington always loved the rain. 'It's the Earth's way of starting anew' he'd say." Cornelia's eyes are clenched tight holding back tears.

"Rain makes the flowers grow. That's what I remember pappa Herrington saying."

Tears swell and fall, trapped on my cheeks by the seal of my mask. I wish I knew him better. I wish I knew how he could see beauty in the soot. How he could see a future through the darkness. We need someone with his vision and optimism now more than ever.

Cornelia grasps my shoulder. Her hands are rough with blisters, but her touch is soothing.

"He was like a father to Charles and me. He was a good

man. He had his faults, we all do."

"I know I do."

Cornelia reaches out her other arm. Grabbing me by both shoulders, she pulls herself in line with me. Her vibrant, gray-blue eyes sear into me.

"That's not what I meant. I don't blame you for this. From what Charles tells me, Bernard really liked you. I think given more time you two would have grown to be fast friends."

"It doesn't feel that way. It feels like I dragged him—and now all of you—into my mess."

"It's our mess, Evelyn. The bombs would have gone off anyway. Fowler would have unleashed her chaos anyway. Domhnall would be ruthless anyway. Bernard died in pursuit of a better tomorrow. He couldn't have asked for more, and he couldn't have asked for a better champion of that tomorrow."

Her words stab at my heart. What do others see me as? A champion? I am anything but. I'm a wreck, I'm stumbling around breaking everything I grasp. The sobs come back. The pain, the guilt, the anguish.

"I'm no champion." Spittle and tears spray with every pained word.

She pulls me into a hug, swaddling me with her arms. Tangled together, time slinks forward—our shadows shift beneath our feet as the sun creeps toward its zenith.

The soft squeeze of little arms around my leg alerts me to Georgette's presence. She looks up at me. Her face smeared with dirt. Her hair is ragged, and dark circles cloud her young eyes. But through it all, optimism shines through. It's as if she's seeing a different world than the one we're standing in.

"You got us out of the city and got us here safe too. I don't really know what a champion is, but you're my hero."

Uplifting and overwhelming. It's exactly what I need to hear and exactly what I don't. Everything has been a frenzy of action and hasty decisions. It's encouraging to know that not all of them have been wrong. Yet I can't shake that I'm in free fall; reacting to everything but unable to really control or change anything. Maybe none of us can.

Fresh tears swell, but these have the tinge of joy, and I feel a smile crack on my face for the first time in what seems like an eternity. I swoop Georgette up into my arms and squeeze her tight. She nuzzles her head in the crook of my neck. I'm so unaccustomed to this kind of intimate contact that it catches me off guard. Nervous shudders emerge then quickly fade into a comfortable warmth I can't ever recall feeling. I think this is what Mother always wanted to give me but couldn't.

We hold on to each other for a solid minute. The wind passes around us—the soft soil pulls us down.

The sun had finished its climb and was dipping toward the

horizon before the grave was ready. Taking turns, Cornelia, Georgette, and I dug it deep and wide. We took great care to keep the edges straight, to do it properly. Blisters, red and oozing, cover our hands. Our stomachs growl together in a somber choir. Sticking the shovels into the mound of freshly disturbed earth, we lean against the tall oak tree and rest. Getting the weight off my feet feels incredible. I sink into the small nook in the roots and close my eyes. The bark of the tree is warm from the midday sun, and it radiates relief to my aching back. Sleep tugs on heavy eyes and pulls me under. Like plunging into water and bursting again from the surface, my mind fights and embraces sleep until I take a final plunge down and stay beneath.

Half lucid, I wake sore and starving. My face is flush and dripping under the mask, and the deep rumbling in my stomach threatens to shake my teeth loose. The weight of this reality takes hold and sits on my chest. I let out a deep sigh then rise. Standing over the empty grave, I turn to the barn. The sounds of hammering and sawing have ceased. The only sound is the shivering of the green oak leaves in the evening wind now biting and quickly turning cold.

I cross the field to the barn and feel the anxiety of the openness bombard my senses. My ears perk up and pull back startled and alert. The hair on my neck stands on end, and I feel my breaths grow shallow and quick. *We're alone here, we're alone here* I tell myself over and over to take control of my nerves and shake the sickening feeling coursing through my veins.

Placing a hand on the half-open door of the barn, I breathe deep then push my way inside.

Victor and Charles stand over an open wooden box. One-meter-wide by two-meters-long, it's unmistakably a coffin. Crafted from the fallen and abandoned timbers of the barn it looks rough except in the small areas of exposed cuts that appear a few tones lighter than the mottled-gray everywhere else. The pungent smell of mildew seeps into my mask. It's an unfamiliar and not entirely unpleasant smell, but looking down at the coffin, and the linen-wrapped body inside, I know I'll never be able to associate it with anything else.

"We used linens from the house. We couldn't find anything else that seemed fit to bury him in. All his old clothes were moth-eaten and mildewed. These were the best we could find," says Charles. Somber and sounding exhausted, he turns to look at me. We meet eyes then look back down at Mr. Herrington. Wrapped up in the white floral linen he looks peaceful and dignified.

"He deserves better," Victor says without looking away from the coffin.

"I think you've both done him proud. He looks at peace, and he'll be buried at home, surrounded by people who love him. What more can we give him?" I say.

"Some justice, some proof that this isn't all for nothing," Victor says. He's shaking and shifting from foot to foot. He seems ready to burst from his skin. "I don't know," he sighs,

"I don't know. I wish he were here. I wish Damian were here. They'd know what to do."

Charles steps behind Victor clasping him by the shoulders.

"I want that too. I miss them. But we got to keep our heads screwed on tight. We can make it through this. If we lean on each other, we'll get through this."

Victor bobs his head.

Charles turns and points behind me.

"Let's let Bernard rest."

I turn to look where he's pointing. Two hammers lay next to a pile of thin, rusted nails. I pass a hammer to Charles, pick up my own, then take a handful of nails for us both. Victor sets the lid onto the coffin. Methodically, Charles and I hammer the nails into place. I've never swung a hammer before, and the first few nails go in crooked and bent. But halfway down my side I get the hang of it and drive the rest home neatly.

Setting the hammer down, I look at my rust-covered hands. I can't escape being reminded that there is blood on them and that I'm to blame for so much of it. If I hadn't gone back for my parents, he'd still be alive. But then, Georgette and Cornelia could be dead. I hate these choices. Even with hindsight, I feel unable to pick a path that I can live with.

Cornelia and Gette peek through the barn doors, the setting sun silhouetting them in an orange-yellow glow.

"It's time," says Charles.

Using rope from the barn, we lower Mr. Herrington into the ground. We each grab a shovel, and before long, the grave is covered. A large black stain in a sea of yellow-green grass. We stand in silence. Death hangs heavy on us all. With a black paint-pen found in the ambulance and a scrap piece of wood, Cornelia writes a headstone. *Bernard Herrington. Scholar, Activist, Father. He is loved and dearly missed.*

CHAPTER FIVE

"WE CAN'T STAY HERE." Victor's words stir us from our solemn wake. Scanning the table, it's hard to gauge everyone's reaction by the scant candlelight flickering in our eyes. The sun hasn't set, but with the curtains drawn it might as well have. I try to study their faces, but I can't take my eyes off their shadows dancing on the walls behind them to the chaotic rhythm of the flames.

Victor jumps back in satisfying our unspoken desire for direction. "We have to find a way to Lufthaffen. My sister can help us find a place to stay, maybe even get us out of the country."

"It's too risky," Charles says, pulling himself out of his slouch. "How will we get there? That's almost six-hundred miles." He brings his index finger and thumb together along his lower eyelids smudging away the tears lingering in his lashes. His face sobers. "Probably more because it won't be safe to use the highways. We don't have permits—real or fake—to make the trip and POs are going to want to ask for them at every inter-state border and travel control point. Maybe six months ago we could have gotten through with a few slaps on the wrist, but I'm pretty sure we're wanted—they might even be looking for us. All it'll take is one PO running an iris scan, or trusting some twinge in their gut, and it'll all be over."

"It is risky," I say, leaning over the table—candles warming my cheeks. "But what other choice do we have? We can't go back to Einsam, and we need help. We can't do this by ourselves." I lean back and stare up at the shadow theatre on the ceiling. "But you're right, we need papers to travel. And we'll need money, food, provisions. Nothing we have here."

"It's a gamble," Cornelia says emerging from the velvet darkness as she leans in. "But every step from here forward will be. If the Sheffield's still live down the road, they might be willing to help us."

"That's a big maybe—there's no telling if they are still there. And it's been twenty years. How do we know if they're still sympathetic to people like us?"

"People like us…" Gette supports her chin on her fist. "You mean Subversives?"

Charles sighs, "I suppose that's what we are." His attempt at a smile says anything but, 'I know that sounds bad, but it's okay.'

"I don't want to get lumped in with Fowler." I take Gette's hand, "But you've got a point. We're fugitive subversives on the run from," I let go of her to tally our enemies until I run out of fingers. "Everyone."

"I don't want to be a bad guy. We're not bad guys… are we?"

Cornelia reaches across the table and squeezes her daughter's hand. Gette's face is scrunched, her eyes darting around to each of our faces. "We're not the bad guys my darling. But the Caretakers and the Peace Officers don't know that. They think we're bad people."

"Can't we just talk to them? I'm sure once they'd met us, they'd know we're not bad, and we wouldn't have to run anymore."

"Yeah let's walk on up to a checkpoint and explain ourselves," says Victor pumping his arms in a mocking march.

"Hey!" barks Charles. "Where's your head at? We're carrying enough as it is—we don't need your snark."

"I'm sorry," Victor shakes his head, trying to pull himself back together. "And I'm sorry Gette. It's just so frustrating being lumped in with radicals."

"To be fair, Victor, Damian was one of us," I say.

"So now he's a radical? Now we're subversives? Maybe we should just go and throw our lot in with Fowler? You knew him for five minutes and you brand him a radical and lump him in with murderers?"

"He did murder people Victor—he attacked and killed innocent people."

"And what about you? How did you get out of the apartment?

Huh? How did you get out!"

Air catches in my throat.

"Enough!" Cornelia's chair clatters to the floor sending up a small cloud of dust. Gette whimpers. Her lips tremble. My fingernails dig into the edge of the table. I'm seething. "We're all hungry, exhausted, and grieving. But that doesn't excuse us to go after each other. Charles, try and get everyone something to eat, and I'll go talk to the Sheffield's. They'll remember me, and I should be able to get them to help."

"Cora, no—you can't go alone. We should go together."

Cornelia shakes her head. "I hear what you're saying—and I know what I said—but Mrs. Sheffield is a jumpy woman, and I think she's less likely to spook if it's just me. We don't have time to argue, I need to get to her house before sunset if there's any chance she lets me in."

Charles opens his mouth to protest then relinquishes with a nod. What other option do we have?

The creaking of the house melds with Gette's sobs. Our fears manifest in the twisted shadows skittering around the room.

Cornelia turns to leave. I stand—my chair screeches against the hardwood floor.

"I'll go. You have Charles and Gette to look after. If something happens to me, well, that's okay. I'm expendable."

"Absolutely not. You're not, in any way, expendable. I need

you to stay here with Gette, keep her safe."

Gette turns to her mother and then to me.

"You're coming back real quick, right?"

"Always darling."

Gette bursts from the table and leaps into her mother's arms. Cornelia squeezes her tight then sets her down.

"I'll be back soon."

The door slams behind her. We sit motionlessly and listen to her footsteps as they fade into silence.

Charles gets up from the table. "Come on, Victor, I think I know where the emergency provisions are buried. Hopefully, they're still there and still edible."

Victor keeps his eyes on his feet and follows Charles out the door. Alone, Gette turns to me.

"Everything is going to be okay, right?"

Her words are so frail, the stress is getting to her. The light in her eyes is still there, but every moment in this world threatens to snuff it out. I kneel and take her hands in mine.

"It's going to work out. I promise."

Her cheeks lift into a smile.

"So, we've got some waiting to do while your mom gets us help. What do you want to do?"

She looks around the dark house, to the door where her mother disappeared into the twilight, then back into my eyes. Distress melts into anxiety then a spark in her eye catalyzes into gleeful mania. "Mom said there's an attic full of cool old stuff. We should go adventuring!"

The idea of playing feels wrong, but maybe she's right—what we really need is a good distraction. Plus, it might actually be fun. And if the world can use anything, it's more fun.

"Race you up the stairs!" I shout, leaping to the air before Gette even knows the race is afoot.

My feet fly up the stairs and I'm nearly to the landing before I hear Gette's protest.

"No fair!"

I pause at the top. I see the room I slept in¬—the door still ajar, a dried muddied mess stands out against the uniform layers of dust. Similar disturbed trails of muddy feet trace lines into the other bedroom where Cornelia and Gette slept. I follow the unbroken patches of dust to the attic. A tight twisting stair only wide enough for one person at a time. But I'm too slow. In the time it took me to gather in my surroundings, Gette stole the lead.

"Hey!" I shout. Though out of breath, aching, and hungry a real sense of joy washes over me. I haven't played in so long it feels nice to pretend I'm a kid again and the world outside this house doesn't matter.

"Too slow, I win!" Gette stands triumphantly at the top. The single shaft of light coming from the rose window bathes her in glory.

"That was no fair, I didn't really know where we were going," I say, putting my hands on my hip.

"You started before me, so I think maybe it's a tie then. Does that sound okay?"

I step toward her and extend my hand as an olive branch.

"A tie."

A wicked smirk tugs on Gette's cheeks—just visible under her mask.

"Nope, I win!" As quick as her words, she races into the attic.

"Get back here!" Gette giggles and avoids my clumsy swipes at her. Our feet stir up the dust. My giggles mix with hers. She deftly outmaneuvers me for two full laps of the cramped attic—her little feet giving her the edge in the narrow walkways between mounding boxes. But she can't get away. Catching up to her in the corner nearest the window, I finally get my hands on her stomach.

"Winners get tickled!" My fingers dance about wildly. Gette crumbles into a laughing heap on a pile of newspapers. I fall after her and continue my relentless tickle attack.

"Stop, stop. It was a tie. It was a tie!" I stop my fingers and roll over onto a stack of old newspapers. Heaving breaths through my mask, we both giggle and stare at the golden dust dancing in the stream of sunset coming through the rose window.

Having caught our breath, we turn our attention to the space around us. I sit up to take it in. A lifetime, or perhaps longer, of accumulated stuff is strewn about in disorganized heaps. Thick dust covers documents, furniture, pictures, and mysterious objects shrouded in moth-eaten tarps. Gette digs into the pile of documents beneath her. Bank records, pay stubs. Receipts from forty years ago for dry cleaning. Interspersed with it all are decades of old Caretaker pamphlets. Handed out on street corners, they're just one of the many things I took for granted in the city. As commonplace as the soot, they hardly register my attention. But seeing them piled together is like looking through time.

The words I have grown so accustomed to—*Keep Your Opinions to Yourself! Wear Your Mask*—aren't as unchanging as I thought. *United, We Rise! Against Subversion We Are One. Make Our Society Great Again—Do Your Part to Build a Better Tomorrow.* The tone is similar—someone is telling us what to do, what to think—but the fear, the anxiety is missing. I thought that was how it had always been. It feels like it. I think that's what I saw in the machine. But here it is, in muted pastels on yellowing paper, a different past, a different Great Society. How did it change so much, how did we end up here? Every stone overturned obscures more than it reveals.

Gette holds up one of the oldest looking pamphlets to me.

"We're trying to make a better tomorrow, right?"

"I think so. Though, I'm not really sure how we'll do that. That's the goal, I guess."

"We just have to do better today than yesterday?"

"Anything is better than yesterday."

"I don't know, today was pretty bad too. Papa's really gone." The pamphlet trembles in her hand. I can feel the void crushing down. The bubble of laughter and joy we built could only last so long. I have to push back, keep from slipping deeper into that darkness. I dart my eyes around looking for a distraction, a way out of this conversation, this reality, and back into the bubble. Pamphlets, bus tickets, dry cleaning stubs, theater tickets, newspaper articles. I focus in on the closest headline. Only part of it is visible underneath the other papers. *Protests Rage at the Halls of Justice Over…* The rest is obscured. I can hardly push the other documents away fast enough. This is something real, something important, and I have to know what it is. *Radical New Law.*

Holding it in both hands, my eyes race across the page. 'Protesters argue that corruption between Personal Protection Supplies CEO Sexton Domnhall and High Caretaker Pruitt is unlawful… Citizens will be required to purchase, maintain, and wear an approved gas mask at all times… Domnhall argues the threat of subversion is too great to go on as normal… Protesters claim this law is nothing but corporate cronyism and an abuse of the Council of Industry… High Caretaker Pruitt condemns the protesters' actions as subversive and influenced by foreign terrorist groups.'

Transfixed, my obsession diverts Gette's gaze away from her grief.

"Are you okay?" she asks.

This is beyond what I can handle. I don't know what to think, let alone know how to respond.

"Here," I say. The word almost a whisper. Gette takes the paper with some hesitation as if the words will jump off the page and attack her. I watch her eyes drag back and forth, pausing on some places and staring at others. Her brow is furrowed, and she takes an eternity to read the short article. Every instant thumps in my head like a drum. *How does this all fit together?*

"What does it mean?" Gette says.

"I'm not sure. This is new to me. I don't even know what to say."

"Mom and dad will know."

"We'll ask them about it later, but right now let's look for more articles. Maybe if we can find some more, things will start to make sense."

Gette nods and begins to sort through the piles of documents.

"Found another one!"

"Quick give it here, I'll make a pile." I pluck the articles from her hand and place them on a small patch of cleared floor.

We search frantically. Hidden in the boxes of junk are articles from before I was born about the New Laws and the gradual changes to the Great Society. Fifteen years ago is the newest one. A short strip with a single line ripped from the editorial page. *Brutal Crack-Downs Trigger Backlash; Subversion Here to Stay.* After that, nothing. Either people stopped caring, or the papers stopped talking about it. There are so many articles, all saved for a purpose. And it's clear whoever saved them knew they would be dangerous and split them up.

Gette hands me a few more articles, and I add them to the growing pile. Protests, riots, lawsuits—there was so much activism, so much resistance to the world we live in now. The Caretakers have done a good job of wiping it all away. *But is that even possible? Did they take it away or did we choose to forget?* The information was there, I could've known I guess, I could've found these things out. Why didn't I look harder? Why was I so selfish? All that matters now is that I'm trying to do the right thing. I'm doing what I can to learn from my mistakes.

I sort the articles by date. Oldest to newest. Gette hands me more, and I slip them into the system. Twenty, thirty, forty, the stack of articles piles up. Gette hands me yet another. At first glance its headline seems to fit in with all the others—*Protests in Liberty Square*—but something makes me pause. I set down the stack of articles and turn my full attention to this one. My eyes shoot to the upper right scanning the date *December 23, 416.* I was born that summer. I would've been six months old.

Strange to think that I was alive at a time that was so different from what I've always known. It's as if I was born into one world and grew up in another.

I scan down the page to the picture. A palm-sized, black halftone image shows the familiar cobblestones of Liberty Square. People holding banners march in circles around the middle of the square in an area cordoned off by concrete barriers. The quality of the photo is too poor to make out what the banners say, but it's clear they're protesting the Caretakers' decision to implement the New Laws. I pull the paper close and study the image. The longer I look the more it makes the hair on the back my neck stand on edge. Cold dread washes over me as I recognition blooms on the horizon of my memories. I can't say where I've seen this before, but I know that I have. I scrutinize every detail desperate for any sign, anything to let me know where I've seen this before. And then I see it and my heart stops.

On the left edge of the image, blurry, but clear enough, is Mother. There is no way to tell for sure—the quality of the image is terrible, and time has done in its damage to the article—but I know it's her. The way she used to sweep her hair to the left, the ruffled mustard-yellow blouse and woolen skirt she used to wear. The way she held herself when I was little, shoulders back chin up. Seeing her like that is a shock, but it's who she's with that slams a fist in my gut and sends fire surging down from my temples into my throat.

She holds a banner aloft in one hand with a child bundled

to her back—*that's me.* I shake out a tear and look back, hoping to see something different. Seeing me on her back makes sense but what I can't understand is the person standing to her left. Holding her left hand is a girl. She looks like me. But I was only six months old, and I don't have any siblings. At least I don't think I have any siblings.

Her black hair is cut into a bob. She's thin, almost frail, but her hand is raised in defiant protest, and her mouth is open wide screaming a chant. She can't be more than six years old, and already she's such a different girl than I was at that age. The fires surging down my neck meet the ice snaking from gut. The room swirls and I can barely hold on to the paper.

"What is it? Does it say something bad?"

Unable to speak, I hand Gette the article. She looks it over intently looking for something horrific. Unable to spot the monster, she looks up at me perplexed and offers the paper back to me. I take it with trepidation. It can hardly weigh more than a few grams, but it feels like a lead weight.

"I don't know what it means Gette, but I think it changes everything."

"Is it something in the picture?"

"Someone. My mother and my sister."

"I didn't know you had a sister?"

"Neither did I."

Gette is just as confused as I am. We started this game as a distraction from the world, yet it led us straight into it. A single tug on the story I've spun of my life and everything I thought I knew—the person I thought I was—has started to unravel.

Mother, I thought I knew her. I thought she was trapped, scared, and alone. Maybe she was when I can remember her, but there she is in the photograph, defiant and alive. I thought she didn't really love me. I thought she didn't stand for anything and that she was too afraid to even leave the house. This proves that for all the observing I've done, I never thought to turn around from the windows and notice her. I was so sure that she was someone I didn't want to know—didn't need to know—that I tuned her out through the glass just like she and Father blocked me out with the television.

The guilt of letting Mother die, of never knowing her and deliberately shutting her out, stabs at me digging and twisting its steel into my heart. I took her on face value, and I was wrong. But it's not just Mother, I've been doing that with everything. I've taken the Great Society at its word—*wear your mask, keep your opinions to yourself.* I thought I was defying those commands, but I think it's clear now that all I've ever done was obey them.

But what good does knowing any of this do? It's too late. Yearning tugs and squeezes in my gut. She was someone. Someone I want to know. Someone I want to be like. How did I never see it? What happened between this photograph and my memories? How do things change so much? Nausea creeps over me sending shivers down my shoulders and neck. I don't think

I'll ever know—I'm not sure if there's a way to know—but I have to try.

Muffled from the distance, the front door slams shut with a *woof*.

"I wonder if mom is back?"

"I don't know, let's go see," I say, my voice fluttering.

"Should we bring the articles down to show everyone else?" Gette asks oblivious to the anguish roiling inside me. My impulse is to say yes, bundle them in my arms, throw them on the table, and demand answers. What does this mean? How did you not know these things about Mother—about the past? But I'm also afraid. Afraid of those answers and where they might lead.

"Let's…" I look Gette in the eye "… leave them here for now. Once everything settles down maybe, we'll have time to bring your parents up here, and they can tell us all about it."

"Okay," she says, her face beaming. Gette jumps up and runs back toward the stairwell.

I get up slowly to keep the spinning world from crashing. Once I'm sure I have my feet, I look down at the article in my hand. I must keep it safe. I fold it once, then again; I fold in until it's a tiny square and all the strength in the universe couldn't help me fold it any smaller. I unzip my jumpsuit a little and put the article into the inside pocket next to the storage sphere. Compartmentalized, I re-zip the jumpsuit and head downstairs.

Cornelia hasn't returned, but Charles and Victor are standing in the kitchen.

"Oh, there you are," Charles says, stepping forward to run his fingers through Gette's curly auburn hair. "We were just about to start looking for you. Victor and I found the emergency kit hidden in the barn. Some of it was spoiled, but I think we have enough food for tonight."

"Oxtail soup and broth," says Victor. He's not wearing his mask, so the disgust dripping from the corners of his lips is plain to see. Charles reaches into the box Victor is carrying, grabs the crusty tin cans, then sets about brushing the rust off their tops. *Cleaned*, he sets them down on the kitchen counter. Victor makes short work of opening them with an old-style can opener that zips through the lids in a rocking motion like a scythe through grain. Charles dumps the first open yellow-brown can into a bowl. The contents have separated. Sickly orange liquid rests on the top. Dark brown mush sinks to the bottom and a murky brown something fills the middle. Victor audibly gags.

"Now I really don't want to eat it."

"It's still well within its expiration date. See here," Charles stabs a massive finger at the peeling yellow label. "Look, it says right here. 'Contents may separate. Safe until printed date.' I don't like the look of it either Victor, but we have to eat—we have to keep our strength up." He turns his attention away from Victor down to Gette. "Here, darling, let me get you a bowl."

Gette pulls off her mask and walks toward her father. Dark

rings around her eyes stand out on her young face. She's far more fatigued than she's letting on.

"Looks like bathwater papa, I'm not sure I can eat it." Holding the bowl of soup, Charles kneels in front of Gette.

"I know darling. This isn't what I want for you, but you gotta eat something." Gette forces a smile and takes the bowl from Charles. She sets it on the table then pulls out a chair and sits down. Charles pours bowls for the rest of us. Taking them, we follow Gette to the table. Looking around at everyone, I see that I'm the only one still wearing my mask. Watching the others die that way has really stuck with me and I'm now—more than ever—afraid to take my mask off. But I can see that they're alright, they're not dying. I exhale sharply and pull off my mask. The stagnant odor of the house hits me—dust, decay, neglect.

Spoon in hand, I dip into the broth. The dark mush swirls underneath while orange fatty liquids dance around on the surface. Normally I just wouldn't eat this. I'd push it aside, throw it away, but the nagging, chewing, overwhelming hunger in my stomach begs me to eat it. I fill the spoon and raise it to my mouth. My eyes can't seem to get over the fact that it looks like dog food, so I close them and go for it.

It's not that bad—meaty with a hint of mushroom. There is an unpleasant sourness to it, but in my current state of hunger it almost adds something—excitement. I open my eyes and look down at the broth pleased to discover that it no longer looks repulsive. I dig in.

Spoon after spoon, I devour it all. Gette looks at me from across the table and hesitantly sips a tiny bit from her spoon. Her eyes light up and she too digs in. Charles smiles and does the same taking big, heaping spoonfuls. Victor still looks unconvinced but dips his spoon in. He holds his nose and clenches his eyes tight. Smacking his lips, he examines the broth looking for any excuse not to eat it. He opens his eyes and nods his head a little.

"Okay, I guess it's not that bad. But it still looks awful!" We all chuckle.

"I won't disagree with you there," Charles says, smiling.

We share a few minutes together in silence listening to the sounds of metal spoons against clay bowls—slurps and sloshes—enjoying the first meal we've had in days.

Having licked our bowls clean, we sit back and hold our stomachs. Even this little amount of soup seems to be overwhelming. With hunger held—temporarily—at bay, all I can think about is taking a nap.

Charles is way ahead of me. He's leaned back in his chair, arms crossed over his chest, with only the occasional snore rattling his calm. Gette has passed out on the table her head buried in her arms. Her little chest rising and falling rhythmically. It's just Victor and me still awake.

He's studying my face. It's strange. I've only just met Victor, yet I feel so comfortable around him. It must be everything we've been through together, but he feels familiar, like a brother I never had. Though I can't shake that he's looking at me as more than that. Is he looking into my face and seeing more than a sister, more than a friend?

"If you're looking for answers in my face, I'm sorry to say you're not going to find any there," I say, shaking Victor out of his trance. He blinks himself alert.

"Sorry, I didn't mean to stare. There is so much running through my head. You think Cornelia can find us help?"

"I hope so. But I'm not sure what kind of help she can find. This place seems to be abandoned. Everyone's gone to the cities or somewhere else. Somebody still out here, they won't have much."

"We have to try, right? We have to ask?"

"Of course we do—because we're not giving up. We're working on getting out of this mess, some way to make it better."

"But how, how can we make this better?" Victor asks.

"I'm still trying to figure that out."

"Well let's hope we figure it out before things get worse."

I look away from him and sigh. He's right. How do you make things better when you're not entirely sure what made them go bad? How can you have a conversation about the masks when bombs are going off, and gunmen are rampaging in the streets? I just hope Damian's actions don't permanently brand us subversives. How can we try to lobby people for peace if they think we started this? I don't want to think about this right now. We need to think about getting out of here. Finding some stability, food, shelter. We need to find new friends—all the ones we know of are either dead or too far away.

I stand up, push my chair back, then collect the bowls and drop them into the sink. There's no running water, and I have no intention of washing them, but it feels good to do something that makes the world feel orderly, normal. Standing in the kitchen, I look through the window over the sink. The sun is nearly set—an orange-red glow hangs over the hedgerows. It's beautiful. I wonder if Mother ever looked at a sunset like this or if she ever saw the world as beautiful? How could she have had another life? A whole life I never knew about? Do I really have a sister? Or am I connecting dots that aren't there, looking for something, anything, to make this better? Whether it's true or not, only time will tell. But in the meantime, it's a nice distraction to think that perhaps Mother was a better person than I have given her credit for. To think that she *did* fight. That she *did* try to break free from her prison.

I assume so much of people. I assume what I see on the outside is the same on the inside. I know that's not true of me, so why is it so hard for me to see that in others? Maybe if I had an older sister, someone to help me figure it all out, maybe then I'd be a better person. But here I stand at the window looking out on the sunset delving into the what-ifs reminiscing about the past I've just created for myself. I don't even know if it's true. I'm building this whole future, this whole life, this whole reality from one article and a grainy picture.

I always knew something was missing. Spare rooms filled with things to distract from the emptiness they personify. Masks piled high to bury the pain. Maybe I did have a sister. And I think she died.

I look down at the sink, dirty bowls stacked on top of layers of dust.

"Do you really think your sister can help us?" I say, turning back to Victor.

"I kept in pretty good touch with her. She has a stable job and some connections inside the bureaucracy. She can help us once we get to Lufthaffen."

"But how do you make that trip? Isn't it almost 1,000 miles? I don't have any money, ID badge, anything. Plus, if that weren't enough, they're looking for me—I'm wanted."

"How do you know you're wanted? Surely there's enough else going that no one is worried about you."

Victor doesn't know. Nobody knows. His earlier accusations where stress, not condemnation. I haven't told them, and I don't know if I can. I don't know for sure, but it's possible the bombings and the violence have overshadowed my actions. Even if that's true, I'll still know what I did. I shot those Peace Officers. Their higher-ups would've known they were looking for me. I've had run-ins with Fowler, and she just started this mess. There is no telling what they think I am or if they think I'm working with her.

"Things happened in the apartment. Things I'm wanted for."

Victor stares at me intently—his eyes trying to peel back my face and see what I'm hiding.

"Whatever you did, you had to do. You're here now, that's all that matters."

"Did I though?"

I haven't said it directly, but now I think he knows—he knows what I did.

"Everyone runs from Peace Officers that's normal, it's fine. Something wrong with that?" He doesn't know—he hasn't connected the dots. "It's not like you killed them."

His words ring in my head. *Bang. Bang. Bang. Bang.*

"You're not a murderer, Evelyn. You're a good person. Besides, they're probably looking for everyone—everyone is a suspect now."

I feel sick. I don't know what he would do if he found out what I did. Or what any of them would do? Would Charles and Cornelia still trust me with their daughter? Would Victor still look at me like he can't look away? I'm not even sure if they should. Backed into a corner, I lashed out, and now I have to live with the consequences of that forever. I saw something in myself that I didn't want to see. Even now I don't want to acknowledge that it's there. Primordial violence, utter disregard for others. I sometimes think I lack empathy, that I don't really care who people are—*they're all just ants to me.* I know that isn't true—it's not the whole story. I do care. I want things to improve.

"We have to figure out a better mode of transportation. We can't take an ambulance all the way there. How are we going to get past the checkpoints? Say they are looking for me, it doesn't really matter because I don't have ID. No matter which way you look at it that makes me a subversive."

Victor nods—the wheels in his head turning. "True," he says—he says more, but the words trail off into muttering.

"Perhaps there's a way to get fake papers or new papers," I say. "Maybe Cornelia will find someone, and they can help us out of this mess."

"I hope so. I really do."

Feeling the conversation grind to a more-or-less satisfying halt, I move to the living room and slump into the wing-backed chair. I shift myself around trying to find comfort in the lumpy springs. I catch Victor looking at me as I close my eyes.

A porch step cries out and rips me from sleep. I snap up and scan the room. Everyone is right where I saw them last, eyes closed and fast asleep. *Clump, clop.* More footsteps—one person maybe more—they're on the porch now and nearly at the door.

I dart up and sneak as fast as I dare next to the door. I peek through a clean smudge on the window. Ice water pours down my back, skin tightens, muscles clench. Cornelia's there, wearing her mask, but she has a shadow.

Cornelia's inching forward, hands tugging at the seam of her jumpsuit. A shadowy figure looms behind her prodding her toward the door.

Woosh. Woosh. Woosh. I'm lightheaded, and my heart's pounding. To my left is a coffee table, I crouch behind it grabbing the lip for support. The porch creaks—the shadow is at the door.

CHAPTER SIX

TWILIGHT GLINTS OFF THE GUN barrel emerging through the door. It's a stubby, antique weapon. Its barrel discolored and blue from a lifetime of use. The old, gaunt hand wrapped around it is resolute and practiced—their index finger hovers just outside the trigger guard coiled and ready.

Should I rush for the door? Do I run? Fear digs its fingers into my muscles.

Too late.

An elderly woman enters. Kyphotic and gray, she manages to fill half the doorway—just. Her mask is a budget model that hasn't protected her from any real danger in years—the rubber along its edge is crumbling and gray. Her knobby, arthritic fingers look contorted and upset to be gripping the pistol.

Startled, I pop up. My shoulder catches the underside of the coffee table with a bang. The unexpected commotion sends the woman wheeling toward me—the pistol leveled at my chest.

"Don't shoot, don't shoot!" I scream, my hands darting over my head. There is rustling and creaking behind me—Charles, Gette, and Victor must be waking up.

"Girl! I almost shot you. You shouldn't jump out at an old lady with a gun. Now come on over here to the table and sit down."

I obey her command. I move to the table with cautious steps careful to keep my hands raised where she can see them. Charles stands up from the table and broadens his shoulders. Her eyes narrow and she orders him back down with the pistol.

"You too. Get over to the table. Come on—the little girl and the boy too." The three of them obey, raising their arms in surrender. Gette whimpers. Cornelia enters the foyer and places her hand on the woman's shoulder.

"See? It's all as I've said. Now, please put the pistol down."

The woman keeps the pistol aimed at Charles and thinks for a long second. She shifts her weight while she's thinking—the floors squeaking under her. She uncocks the pistol with a loud click and returns it to the oversized pocket on her overcoat. A shudder of relief washes over me, and a collective sigh rushes out of the room.

"Thank you," Cornelia says.

The woman remains in the door primed. Cornelia moves out from behind her and goes to Charles. Cornelia places her hands on Gette's shoulders, and she reaches up and grasps her mother's hands.

"This isn't normally how I introduce myself," the woman looks down at the pistol in her pocket, "but the world's a hornet's nest right now and you can't be too careful. I'm Colleen Sheffield," she tips her head in a rural curtsey. "Cornelia filled me in about your predicament. Can't believe Bernard is gone, he was a good man. I'm not really sure though—what do you people want of me? I don't think I can help you that much."

I clear my throat to speak and shake loose the bundle of nerves threatening to choke me.

"Mrs. Sheffield, we need help getting to Lufthaffen."

Colleen laughs.

"I don't know what you expect me to do," she shrugs her shoulders and flips over her hands revealing empty palms. "I'm trapped here just the same as you. If I could get outta here, I would."

"We'd be grateful for anything. Perhaps you know someone who could help us? You don't have to do anything yourself, just point us in the right direction."

"You're strong-willed. I like that. It will serve you well for what's to come." She chews a wad of something bulging out of her bottom lip. "I can't help you myself, but I might be able to point you in the direction of someone who can."

"That's wonderful, thank you. Who?" I ask, smiling.

Colleen's face remains stone. "Maurice Reinhardt. He runs

the plantation north of town. He's wealthy and he has connections. If anyone can get you out of here and get you on the road to Lufthaffen, it's him."

"Reinhardt? As in Reinhardt Agriculture?" Charles says.

"Yes, those Reinhardt's."

Charles roils in his chair. "I don't trust those people. I saw what they did to the Herrington's and the other farmers. We have to find help somewhere else."

"I told you—I can't help you. I don't trust the Reinhardt's either they're bad people. Always have been, always will be. And Maurice especially so," she leans forward spitting a hearty glob of dark spit onto the floor. The desiccated floorboards pull in the moisture in an instant turning the spit into a little pool of mud. She sniffs loudly, turning her face up in disgust, then drops her eyes down in defeat. "But I don't know where else you can turn. It's just me and the few other families still clinging onto the dirt we still own."

"So, what happened to everyone else," says Charles, "where have all of the farmers gone?"

"They work for Reinhardt now. When the drought hit, and the crops died, we were all going broke. He lent his money on the condition that the farmers go work for him on the plantation. Thousands of them are living there now—in dorms—working to pay off debts they can never repay. The only thing I can think of is doing some legwork for him. Maybe it'll get you papers, or maybe it'll buy you safe passage to Lufthaffen."

"Are you insane? You'd have me put my daughter to work in that prison? To beg for help from that monster? I'd rather take my chances on the road in the ambulance."

"Look here sonny, I don't like that option either—you don't see me working on his plantation—but it's the only one I see, and the only thing I can suggest. I've got nothing but dirt here, he at least has some money and maybe a way out."

"I think she's right Charles," Cornelia says. "What option do we have? We can't keep driving around in the ambulance. There's no way we would make it past 1,000 miles of roadblocks without some help, without some paperwork."

"You're right. I know you're right, but there has to be some other way." Charles turns an accusatory finger to Colleen. "You said it yourself he doesn't make debts people can repay. You work for that man until you die. I for one don't intend to die on some man's plantation." Colleen glares but offers no retort.

"So we just try our luck on the road?" I say.

Charles looks from his wife and daughter to Victor and me then lands on Colleen with a scowl. "Yes. I think we have to take our chances on the road. We'll only drive at night. We'll go slow, be cautious."

"We only just made it here." Cornelia pulls Gette tight into her. "Things aren't going to get better, Charles—things are going to get worse."

"I'll go. I'll go to the plantation," I say. Every eye turns on me. The room drops ten degrees. "I'll figure out a way to get us papers. The rest of you can stay with Mrs. Sheffield while I figure it out."

Colleen raises her hands in protest. "I never agreed to that. I can't feed that many people." She takes a step back straddling the threshold.

"Absolutely not, Evelyn," Cornelia says. "We need to stick together—we can only get through this if we stick together." She offers me her hand. I take it and look into her eyes. I see concern there—desperation. She doesn't like this plan either, but what choice is there?

"We go to the plantation, we get our paperwork, and we get the hell out of here. We stick together—we'll figure it out," Victor says, nodding his head.

I've jumped at the first exit every time. I see an opening and I go for it. Taking the first path available has gotten me this far, but it's been a bumpy road, and I regret more than a few decisions. Maybe we should heed her advice. Reinhardt sounds like a terrible person who exploits his power for his purposes—and his purposes only.

"No way," I say.

Victor looks at me as though I stabbed him, "but you just—"

I cut him off. "If Reinhardt is only half as bad as you've made him out to be," I say aiming my words at Colleen, "then we can't take that option. There is no telling if he would help us or turn us over to Peace Officers. Charles is right. We need to take our chances in the ambulance. If we stick to the side roads, we could make it to Lufthaffen. It's all unknown, but I don't think jumping in with Reinhardt is our best move right now. We'll get boxed in, and I think staying mobile is the best thing we can do right now."

Cornelia squeezes my hand, "I'm not thrilled with it. But maybe you and Charles are onto something. Gette and I are with you." Gette clenches her jaw in resolve and throws me a curt nod. Cornelia runs her fingers through Gette's hair and pats her back. Victor sighs, shaking his head in defeat.

"Can you help us out with the map Mrs. Sheffield?" I say, trying to carry the conversation forward into action. "Point us in the right direction?"

Colleen looks me up and down, spits out a glob of mucus through the front door onto the porch, then pulls out a chair from the table.

"Get your map, and I'll set you straight."

Colleen traces the roads on the map with her finger for the better part of an hour. She mutters intelligible things to herself marking intersections with big looping Xs or dread-inducing question marks. After circling all the highways and byways within a hundred-mile radius of Bergholz, she caps her pen then leans back in her chair.

"That's as much as I know. And like I said, if I were you, I'd assume the question marks are checkpoints by now."

I look over the map. Taking my finger, I imagine a course out of the farmland and into the rural mountain roads. My finger begins to trace a path then runs into an X. I back up a step, this time taking a left rather than a right, or vice versa. Each journey starts and then abruptly stops. Some roads are totally hopeless—no matter which direction you turn, there are a half-dozen checkpoints in the way. With a stolen car and no papers, it's safe to assume that any run-in with Peace Officers will be the end of our escape. Then, something promising. By back-tracking a little, there is a safe path; by using the little-used roads, there is a route through the mountains that could take us all the way to Mansfield. This might just work. We might be able to get there.

However, elation vanishes in a flash. My fingers begin to plot the path from there to Lufthaffen—my eyes see it, and my finger stops dead in its tracks. Mansfield is only a quarter of the way there. Beyond that is the start of the Heartland Delta. A huge swath of land shaded in deep blue on the map. Industrial cities and military bases run together into a nearly impassible labyrinth of inter-connected highways and thoroughfares.

"I don't know how you're going to get through that mess there. You'll need to ditch the ambulance and think of another way," Colleen says adding her own finger to the map. "I'd try and grab a train out of Mansfield. The coal trains get checked for bombs and are heavily guarded. But if you could slip inside of one you'd get dumped right in the heart of Lufthaffen."

My stomach swirls. Maybe this isn't a great idea. There is a dense gridiron of deep blue country in between us and our promised land. The enormity of the challenge is manifesting on my shoulders and it's growing harder to even sit up straight. Is this the right decision?

"That's a good suggestion," Charles says, "the coal trains could help us bypass all the checkpoints and random searches."

"It's a possibility. Just cross your fingers and hope you end up in a car headed for a coal heap and not one that goes straight into the boilers."

Charles looks up from his hunched perch over the map.

"We'll make sure," his words aim for confidence but hit nervousness instead.

"We'll stick together, and we'll get through." Cornelia takes Charles' hand. "We can't look at the whole journey. We know how to get this far," she says, stabbing her finger at the spider's web of a train terminal in the heart of Mansfield. "We'll figure out the rest once we get there."

The house creaks and drones. My heartbeat pounds in my ears.

Colleen leans forward in a hurry—the front legs of her chair slam into the ground with a bang. Startled, we all jump. Victor, being far more intent on the map than I realized, lets out a gasp.

"I'll leave you to it then," Colleen's eyes survey our gaunt faces. "My offer still stands though. If you come to your senses, I'll drive you into town. It ain't the best choice, but Reinhardt could help."

"Thanks for the information, Mrs. Sheffield, but we'll take our chances on the road," Charles says, corralling her to the door. Colleen shrugs and stands to leave. He opens the door keeping his body square with Colleen—his eyes follow her unblinking.

Mrs. Sheffield pauses in the doorway. "If you change your mind, scribble a lightning bolt on the mailbox and I'll come back." She sighs long and for show. "I shouldn't, but the Herrington's were good people."

"We are indebted to your kindness," Cornelia says.

Mrs. Sheffield scoffs. "I wish you good fortune." Tipping her head goodnight, she takes three short steps then disappears into the dark.

The sound of the door closing echoes away into static before anyone speaks.

Leaning on the table with both arms outstretched, Charles addresses us—eyes fixed on the map. "Victor, make sure the van's ready. Evelyn, study that route—I'll need you to navigate." He drops to one knee and wraps his arms around his wife and daughter.

"We'll make it Charles," I say.

He lifts his head from Cornelia's shoulder. His eyes are

growing red and watery. His mouth starts to open then he decides against it choosing to nod instead.

"Well, I guess I'm driving then," Victor says, standing abruptly. His face is severe, his shoulders pulled back, jaw clenched. He doesn't like this plan, not in the slightest. I want to say something, say anything, to assure him that we need to try. But we're beyond words at this point. We've made our choices. All that's left are the consequences.

CHAPTER SEVEN

THE NIGHT STRETCHES before us like an oil-slick ocean. Indiscernible shapes flit along the sides of the road—their pallor ghastly-white from the sliver moonlight peeking through the clouds. Victor is leaned as far forward as he can—his head nearly touching the windshield. His eyes dart left and right like windshield wipers desperately trying to peel back the impenetrable fog before us. His knuckles have long since turned white, and every time we turn I wince at the grating sound of his clenched fists on the leather steering wheel. He's tense like a bound wire ready to snap. He liked this plan least of all, and now it's resting on his shoulders to see it through. I try my best to focus on my task. Keeping my eyes peeled, I study the darkness for the unmarked twists and turns we need to make to get to safety.

A grueling hour passes. We had to cut back the way we came, driving away from Mansfield and toward Einsam to get to the mountain roads that should take us all the way there. Running alongside towering powerlines constructed in a lattice of riveted steel, the roads cut across the landscape like a knife.

I remember Speer talking about these kinds of infrastructure projects in class. The Great Society Works Progress Administration built many of them in a flurry of construction immediately following the Great Societal Revolution. Thousands of workers scoured the landscape clear and left the sinew and muscles of civilization in their wake. Too bad no one thought it'd be a good idea to maintain it. Like so much else, these once glorious byways of the Great Society's power are now unkempt, overgrown, and crumbling.

The ambulance was never built for roads like this, and all of us bounce around clutching desperately onto anything we can grasp to steady ourselves. I'm thankful at least to be in the front where the bucket seats and shoulder belts do much to keep me from sloshing about. If our plight were not so dire and the stakes so impossibly high, this could almost be fun. Like an amusement park ride. One look at Victor and all the amusement drops away.

"How are we doing Evelyn? How long before we're back on pavement?" Victor says—his eyes fixed forward.

I look back at the map and trace our path with my finger. I follow it back down highway 52, across rural route 115, and onto service road 76. I jab at where we should be.

"We're getting close to the 51. It shouldn't be more than a few minutes now. After that, it should all be tarmac. Look, here's the turn!" I say, pointing my finger across Victor's face. He harrumphs then expertly careens the ambulance up onto the pavement. My stomach lurches from the transition.

"All okay back there?" I say, twisting around in my seat.

Cornelia has Gette wrapped up in her arms on one side of the cabin while Charles has his arms extended out to each side bracing himself—the thin strap across his waist doing little to keep the bulk of his torso safe.

"Fine. We're fine. Keep your eyes on the road—"

Like night flipped instantly to day, the world erupts in piercing yellow light. Victor slams on the brakes. I surge forward. The belt holds me fast digging into my collar.

"Hang on!" Victor cries, slamming the gear lever into reverse. The transition grates and squeals then we lurch backward.

"This wasn't on the map!" I shout—panic ringing in my ears.

"Cora, keep her head down!"

The ambulance bellows—the cabin quakes. My arms spread out for stability. One hand on the roof, the other Victor's bicep. No time to process that, red siren lights spark to life in front of us. The bulbous shape of a Peace Officer cruiser barrels toward us. Squat, gray and with angular red slashes for headlamps, the cruiser looks like a demonic panther ready to pounce.

Our engine revs louder, Victor spins the wheel hard to turn us right-way round. Top heavy, the ambulance groans as its tires leave the earth.

We crash down against the passenger side. The shockwave ripples through me as my lungs seize empty and shut. Searing pain like molten needles shoved into my temples forces out a silent scream. I gasp, gulping air that both saves my life and adds vigor to the pain.

Windows shattered, and without my mask, the smell of burning rubber and oil clings to the back of my throat. Looking left, Victor is dangling above me, suspended there by his seat belt. He's limp. My heart sticks in my throat. No—you can't be dead. *Thump. Thump. Thump.*

"I really fucked that up," Victor moans rubbing his head.

Relief washes over me. Before another thought can cross my mind, the cabin doors swing open. In the rearview mirror, I see the black featureless silhouettes of two Peace Officers— the floodlight's beams casting them in a heavenly halo. My hands fly to the buckle release. Quivering, they feel like wet sand. They paw frantically at the clasp. My breaths come in rapid-fire shallow gasps.

Like shadow puppets on the wall, I watch as Charles leaps at the Peace Officers. Taken off guard, the first one doesn't even have time to raise his arms in defense. Charles swings his clenched fists like clubs striking the Peace Officer on the side of the neck. He crumbles out of sight. The other swivels the rifle from his back. Cornelia jumps into the fray, throwing herself onto the weapon. Her weight pulls on the rifle and its strap forcing the Peace Officer down.

My fingers find the clasp. The belt *zhhwhips* back.

Grasping either side of the front seats, I pull myself through the narrow gap. I stumble forward. My arms dart out to catch my fall. They save my face from the sharp geometric shards of glass littering the floor, but in return a half-dozen glass slivers embed themselves into my palm. Nausea swells as I stand—my legs tremble. I unhook the fire extinguisher from the wall—designed for emergencies, its latch is wide and pops open effortlessly. The metal is cold in my stinging hands. I step forward with a crunch and raise the extinguisher ready to strike. Charles is twisted together with the first officer he attacked—his massive bulk evident against their leaner frame. Cornelia is still on the ground. The Peace Officer with the rifle was able to twist free. Rising to their feet, they train their weapon at Cornelia. *Run!*

Mother's final moments explode from the darkness before me. Inches from the barrel, another mother faces an eternal fate—her own daughter struggling to get free of her restraints an arm's length from me now.

Could I have done something to save Mother? Could I have leaped forward and attacked the Peace Officers? If I had, would I be dead now? My body slumped on the cold polished floors of the penthouse? *Damn it Evelyn, don't you know that I love you?*

I lunge like a fury. Sorrow, delusion, and rage erupt from me like Pandora's box unhinged. My weapon strikes the Peace Officer on the temple. *Crack!* The composite shell of their re-breather splinters open sending twinkling black shards falling like rain. I maintain my assault, landing another blow in the same spot. This time the impact resonates with the crunch of blood and bone. I jerk the rifle free from around their shoulders and bring it to my own. The other Peace Officer has gotten the best of Charles; now on top of him, she's landing blow after blow with her baton along the side of his face. Charles' eyes roll wide—his grip on her brown trench coat slackens.

"Enough!" I bellow. Aiming the rifle square in her face, the Peace Officer lowers her baton and stands.

"Stand down Citizen," she says, her voice amplified from the mask and labored from the fight.

"Not a chance! Drop it—"

"Citizen—"

"Drop it!"

She squats low, placing the baton on the ground gently. A crunching from inside the cab draws our attention. Gette has helped Victor free of his restraints and the duo is clambering out of the cabin.

"Get something to tie them up with," I say to Victor.

"You don't have to do this, Citizen. Hand over the weap—" Before she can finish her sentence, Charles brings the baton down on her neck. *Kursgoosh!* Grabbing at her neck, she drops to one knee.

"Give me the rifle!" Charles demands.

I cannot form words. Towering over her, Charles is seething.

Spittle and blood spray from his mouth with every heaving breath. In one hand, the baton twitches to deliver another blow while the other reaches for the gun.

I step back, shaking my head. "Enough… Enough!" I take a moment to inhale and let the tears stream down my face. The floodlights beat down on us casting everything in long, stretched-out shadows. The whirling red lights on the cruiser resonate in my skull like distant drums.

"Give me the rifle!"

I look down at the weapon in my hands. The power to take, to end, but never heal. Turning my hips into the throw, I hurl the rifle into the woods.

"What are you doing?"

"Enough. God damn it, enough! Tie them up, take their radios and then we leave."

"We can't leave them alive—"

"Yes, we can. That's the only way," says Victor a spool of medical tape already in his hands.

Charles flings the baton into the ground grunting. It clatters away, skipping across the asphalt. The Peace Officer offers her hands up to Victor and he promptly winds the tape from her wrists to her elbows. Cornelia pulls the unconscious officer's arms out from under him and crosses them in the small of his back. A small pool of blood shines like the moon under his head. I feel faint.

I shouldn't have hit him the second time. What have I done? Did I kill him?

Victor finishes taping them up. The night swirls in surreal brilliance and vibrant gloom.

We run through the night down the service roads. Bumbling along as fast as we are able, we heave and strain across the broken ground. Each crunch sends fresh waves of terror down our spines. The clouds have vanished revealing the moon in all its splendor both aiding our flight and adding to our angst—what sees can be seen.

With our blood still hot from the brawl, it takes nearly an hour before the night's chill creeps into us. Gette feels it first and I'm not far behind. The howling wind laps up the sweat glimmering on my skin, turning me to ice.

Everything went sideways in a hurry. The plan should have worked—there wasn't supposed to be a checkpoint there. Maybe Colleen did that on purpose? Or maybe she was just wrong, or it was new, or it was a total fluke. Trying to find a justification does nothing to change the fact. Only a few miles from where we started and farther away than ever.

When at last we reached Glen Fois, all our moods have soured. Panicked, and trapped within ourselves, the night looped in a terrible spiral bringing up every word, every action that led us into this mess. Victor is seething the most. Opposed from the onset, he's reacted the way I feared he would. Indignation burns in him like a coal furnace.

Charles carries Gette up the stairs under Cornelia's thorny gaze—her eyes seem to convey a conflicted mix of both resentment and appreciation.

I collapse onto the couch—the thought of even a few more steps up the stairs are out of the question. Victor sinks into the wing-backed chair across from me. His heaving breaths condense in jets of water vapor illuminated by the slivers of light tracing through the windows. Shivering, I curl up into the couch and close my eyes.

"Thank you, Victor."

Exhaustion pulls me into sleep like a weigh stone dragging me to the ocean's depths.

I'm conscious, but I'm not awake. My body floats like a marionette as I glide through the crystalline void. My arms and legs articulate in close approximation to movement—rigid and forced. Twilight shades of purple and black glint and disappear along hidden lines of complex geometry. I'm weightless and burdened both; in control and utterly helpless. I'm trapped in a sickening loop of acceptance and refusal—conscious and unconscious mind tangles in ethereal melee.

The space before me swirls into recognizable shapes. A platform beneath me forms first. My feet connect with it, and a rush of tingling pressure fills my body in an odd simulacrum of gravity. Then before me, three ordinary doors emerge in a row. Three doors that could be any door. So nondescript and devoid of features that what unique character they do have—a swirling knot in the pine or a diagonal striping of the grain—flit between them until each is no different from the others. They are familiar. Not in the way that all doors are familiar but in an intimate way. A flash of memory solidifies their shapes, and the features lock permanently onto each door. The first is the most obvious and should not have vexed me at all—the door to my apartment. 1745 gleams in silver letters centered at eye level. A long subtle tiger-stripe pattern stretches the length of the door. Now that I see it, the other doors fade away—the hidden geometry of the void swallows them back into darkness.

I step forward on tingling feet. My arm extends toward the door, and I catch a glimpse of a twinkling purple glint on a silver strand around my wrist. It stretches off into infinity. *Do I want to open the door, or am I made to open it?*

I press inside and am immediately somewhere else. I glance back over my shoulder hoping to find the void to orient myself, but I find my childhood bedroom instead. The world slides over itself parallaxing in time with waves of nausea. Then just as odd, sudden, and strange, I rush into the moment with a snap.

My room feels smaller. The walls are where they always are, but everything in them has shrunken down. My bed is short and narrow. The bedspread is a tufted duvet the color of muted thistle. Above the white metal headboard, hanging on the wall are posters for the Blue Scarf Girls. *Pride. Duty. Friendship.* Atop the white three-drawer dresser against the far wall is my scarf. The color is a vacuous blue. Carefully folded—its creases perfect.

I turn my gaze back around quite sure of where I am but finding it difficult to pinpoint a 'when.' I bounce into the central living area of the penthouse on the tiny legs of my seven-year-old self. Adult figures dressed all in black loom around me. Their faces twist and wobble in a mist—forgotten.

The mood is dour. I don't remember these details, but this feeling—crushing gloom—I know it well. It pulls on me like grasping tendrils from the floor. With each step toward the wall of windows, all the giddiness within me melts away. There is something in front of the window. Something stripped away. Like a thick stroke of a painter's brush and as colorless as coal. But it does not wobble and protest like a faded memory struggling to condensate. No, it lingers permanently etched away. No angle can reveal itself to me. No straining rebuilds its absence.

I struggle to bring it into view. I stare into its ashen depths and rake my mind for the answer. *Is this really a memory? Or merely a dream? Am I dying, or have I died, and is this what lies beyond?* Questions bloom and burst in a chain reaction each rippling out a thread into the void.

The world around me shudders. The walls crack open, and the hidden geometry of the dreamscape beyond this door gleams through like hot iron. Dust, but not dust—wraithlike tendrils of forgotten memories—flood into the room. Everything except the gaping scar disappears into the swirling miasma.

A violent tremor sends the world shifting over itself; different images overlap passing in and out of each other concealing and revealing tiny corners of the scar. The shifting images accelerate until my world is nothing but an endless stream of questions feeding the torrent of memory like the headwater of a mighty river.

It all becomes clear. For a single instant. A flash before the world crumbles into darkness, I see what was taken away. A platform draped in black silk. A mahogany casket with silver hardware. I have only this instant, but I dare myself to look inside. Pleated white pillows cradle a young woman's head. Her hair is short—molding around her tear-drop face like an ebony halo. Her skin has a deathly paleness, but she is still fierce and beautiful.

The dream takes the moment away, and I'm ripped back through whatever maze I traveled to get here. Silver leashes tugging at my wrists, I'm unable to fight back. I'm frozen. A name forms on my lips and manages to slip from them just as the waking world pulls me to the surface.

"Hannah."

CHAPTER EIGHT

CONSCIOUSNESS BLEEDS IN SLOW assembling a picture that makes no sense. I'm surrounded by long warping blobs, writhing from unseen tides against a crisscrossing geometric solid, framed by a piercing white rectangle. Details swim over each other—their names and purposes escaping me. I blink hard and concentrate. When I open my eyes again the abstract world snaps back into reality—curtains ripple in front of the square window illuminated by the dawn. I sit up and the world wobbles again. I clench my eyes shut and reach out for the arm of the couch to steady myself.

"Are you alright? You look like you're going to be sick."

I crack my eyes open. Victor has sprung from his chair and is now knelt on the rug in front of me. His chestnut eyes are alert, studying me.

"Have you ever woken up, and for a minute, everything is," I pause to find the word, "unreal?" Victor clasps his hand on my knee and tilts his head to the right.

"No, that's not it," I continue, "the world is still the same as always, but you can't remember it, so it's all strange and you don't know who, what, or when you are." He's earnest—his thumb strokes my knee sending a jolt of electricity up my thigh.

"And then all of a sudden—"

Snap. Victor snaps his fingers, "And then it all clicks into place and you can't remember how you didn't know those things."

I take his hands and move them off my knee into the open space between us.

"Exactly. I just had that. But worse than I can ever remember having it before."

"I know what you mean. These last few days have been," he scoffs, "they've been unreal."

I smirk, then let it grow into a smile. A long moment passes in which the rising sun crests the hedgerows, replacing the white glow with squint-inducing shafts of orange light. The house creaks and bellows as if it too is waking from a restless night. Feet slide off beds onto the floor above us. Their crash brings the moment down.

"I'm sorry for last night," I say. "You were right, we never—"

Victor squeezes my hand. "We had to risk it. You did the right thing, you kept your cool," Victor turns his eyes down to the faded swirling floral pattern on the rug at our feet. "I'm upset, but I'll be alright. We're all trying to do the same thing—get us someplace safe. I understand that but—"

"But it's hard to accept," I say. He nods with a hmm.

"They'll be up soon," he says standing. "I'll see if I can scrounge up some breakfast."

Our hands slip out of each other's as he walks away. I let my hands linger, twisting them around in the morning light. Blistered, cut, filthy—every fingernail is packed with the black dirt of Mr. Herrington's grave.

The Standish family limps down the stairs in a somber parade. Each of Cornelia's steps shoots a wince across her face. The kaleidoscope of yellow and purple marbled across Charles' face does little to hide his discomfort. Gette is sheepish, hiding behind her father's choppy gait. I open my mouth to greet them and strike the 'good' from my voice before it crosses my lips. The result is a quivering, "Morning."

Cornelia doesn't miss a beat, "We look that good, huh?" I try to smile but that comes out quivering too.

I meet them at the table and sit myself down. "Did you at least get some rest?" Charles and Cornelia shake their heads in near unison.

"We're not as young as we used to be—it's getting harder and harder to bounce back from things like that," she says speaking to me but looking squarely at Charles.

"Feels like I've lived that night every day of my life," says Charles.

"Come on, it hasn't always been that bad."

"No?" Charles retorts.

Cornelia's face betrays no retreat. Charles hangs his head, "No. No, you're right. There was a time when this kind of thing didn't happen very often."

"Was that when people didn't wear masks?" Gette says. "Evelyn and I saw pictures in the paper of people without their masks—she even saw her mom!"

Cornelia and Charles turn to their daughter bemused, then to me. I shrug.

"When you went to find help, Gette and I explored the attic. I've been meaning to ask about it. I guess now is as good a time as any."

"When were they from?" Cornelia asks.

"Most of it was twenty, thirty years ago. But there were some articles from when I was a little kid. My mother and I think—" I gulp in a breath. "I think my sister was in one of them."

"I didn't know you had a sister," says Charles.

"Neither did I."

They exchange a concerned look. Cornelia looks me over with wide, gracious eyes. "I don't know if we'll have any answers, but we'll tell you what we can. What would you like to know?"

"Well," an avalanche of unformed curiosity clutters up my

mind. "Well, I guess I thought people in the Great Society always wore their masks. At least since Neptus."

Cornelia leans an elbow on the table—her eyebrows perk up. "Charles was telling me you saw something in the Oracle Device." She laughs, "here you are asking me questions and you are the one that got to see one of Neptus's unfiltered memories."

"She's right," Charles says. "We'd been trying to get our hands on one of those for years."

A discomforting brew of guilt turns in my stomach. People have been risking their lives for decades, slowly, carefully building up resistance to the Caretakers, and then I come along. Yes, I saw—no, lived—the memory, but Fowler no doubt has it now. Whatever hidden truth was on it, is lost on me.

"But see, that's what I don't understand. Neptus and Daedalus wanted the old world forgotten, erased. They gave their partners whatever they wanted and brutally crushed their enemies. I didn't see much, but enough to connect the dots. But the New Laws? I don't know how to make that fit."

Charles nods somberly. "Wearing your mask wasn't always the law, it was just a good idea—the air was bad… real bad. When I was a boy, growing up in the Under City, there were days you could cut the air it was so thick."

Gette's eyes are like saucers, "Did people die papa?"

"Yes. Yes, they did darling. Maybe not right away, but they'd die young. Especially if you were sick, newborn, or very old."

Cornelia rests a hand on Gette's back. She looks as though she doesn't want Charles to tell her more but also that she knows it must be said.

"One winter, thirty," Charles starts.

Cornelia's gaze drifts to the ceiling—an invisible abacus working. "No," she interjects. "Thirty-five, years ago now."

Charles nods, "Right, oh right. Thirty-five years ago, the streets got hit with a smog so bad people were dropping dead in the streets. *The Pestilence* is what we called it. There was a run on the stores. Masks and filters were sold out everywhere. People flocked to buildings with filtration systems installed. People in the tenements, in the Under City, they were an afterthought. I was just a boy then—tens of thousands of people died on the streets of Einsam."

"What did the Caretakers do?" I ask.

"Nothing. Not a damn thing," Charles replies. The anger not vented in his words is adding a bloom of crimson to the malted yellows on his cheeks.

Cornelia jumps back in mouthing 'language' to Charles, "The nation was in an uproar. When the smog lifted, people took to the streets and demanded change."

"They didn't budge at first, the Caretakers," says Charles, "but then it seemed they might do something to clean up the air. Then Domnhall got his fingers into High Caretaker Pruitt and well," his arms stretch out as if to encompass the entirety of the world, "here we are."

"No, that's not all Charles. People fought back against the New Laws, and that's when the subversive's program first appeared."

Charles lowers his arms—his face turns severe as he nods agreement.

I want to know more, keep pressing them for information, but a crunch on the porch pulls our collective focus.

Victor has returned with two cans of potted meat in one hand and a can of peaches in the other.

"Breakfast anyone?" he says, rattling the cans.

"Oh, peaches! I love peaches, good job Victor," says Gette rushing from her chair to take the pastel labeled can—*Martha's Finest*—from him.

Gette's enthusiasm shines a little joy onto all of us, and we can't help but smile. Mirroring her relish, we dig into the cans with gusto. Our laughter and the sweetness of the peaches make the memories of last night almost fade away.

Almost.

After breakfast, Cornelia and I walk the hedgerow-lined drive. Distant cicadas and the low rumble of far-off rain wax and wane from our ears with each crunching step in the gravel. Reaching the end, we peer out from the safety of the hedgerow and look both ways down the road.

Nothing.

Letting out a sigh of relief, we bustle over to the mailbox—nervous energy propels us to make the mark and retreat to the safety of the house as fast as humanly possible.

Taking the same paint-pen she used to make the headstone from her pocket, Cornelia deftly traces the shape of a geometric lightning bolt with a broad downward stroke, a narrow jab to the right, then a final slash down ending in a sinister point as the pen lifts off the rusted metal box.

"Now we wait?" I ask.

"Now we wait."

Cornelia pockets the paint-pen then returns to the path. I linger at the mailbox. The sun is warm against my skin and the wind a cool kiss. Puffy white clouds share the sky with thin gray streaks lingering from the storm. I beg for an epiphany. I close my eyes desperate for a flash to show me the way out of our predicament. I want to use what I know for good, to put an end to the Caretaker's crimes. I want to stop Fowler from spreading violence across the country like a plague. I want to know who Hannah was, who Mother was, and why Father let her die.

Nothing. Only storm clouds and shadows.

I open my eyes, take a deep carbonized breath, then hurry to catch up with Cornelia.

She was meandering so I catch up in a few long strides. She

turns to me with a smile and offers me her hand. The cauldron in my heart threatens to burst. I take her hand in mine putting the lid back down. We stroll for a minute—our pace slow and meandering the way you do when you can't stand still but you desperately don't want to arrive where you're going. As comforting as her presence is, I can't help but feel some shame that I never connected with Mother this way. As much as I try, and no matter how urgently I want it, Cornelia can never be my mother.

I drop her hand.

"You know, Evelyn, I'm here for you. If you ever need to talk about anything, I'm here."

I give her a smile then turn my focus to my feet as they pass above the rock and gravel.

"Would you ever lie to Gette?" I ask.

Cornelia turns to me—her face serious.

"To keep her safe. Yes, I would do anything."

"Even if it would hurt her if she found out?"

The question hangs in the air.

"Sometimes mothers have to make hard choices to keep their children safe. Even if it means lying to them. Even if it will hurt them."

"But is that the right thing to do? How can the truth hurt more than a lie?"

Cornelia stops—the gravel crunches in protest.

"Lies hurt, but the truth cuts deep. There are some wounds you can never mend. Some truths make lies a kindness."

Exhausted and hungry, we sit in the parlor watching the day drag itself across the floor. The rectangular projection of the sun's path through the window fades until its final sliver vanishes. The winds grow strong and cold, and the house and trees shiver in response. As the silver-white glow of the moon swells in the window, the twin yellow eyes of headlamps fill the driveway.

Springing to life for the first time in hours, we creep low against the windows and peek out. An ancient truck—its body rolling like the surf from long exhausted shocks—crawls up to the porch and parks in a cloud of dust. As it settles, a silhouette appears.

Mrs. Sheffield returned as she promised she would. Danger past, we stand up and move to the foyer to greet her. Colleen wastes no time. Bursting through the door, she launches in at us.

"That was a damn fool thing you did. Every cruiser in the county is out looking for you."

Anxiety tugs at my frayed nerves.

"Did they make it? I mean, did any of them die?" I ask—the unknown fate of the Peace Officer stinging my throat like acid.

Mrs. Sheffield loosens the phlegm in her throat. "I wouldn't be here if they did. OSS scanner doesn't know what to make of it," she laughs, "they asked dispatch for Inspectors to investigate, but Einsam is refusing to send its resources away from the capital."

"Wait, what?" asks Charles for all of us.

"The OSS is scrambling all over itself. It thinks everyone is a subversive—even its own Officers. It seems those foreign rat bastards caught them with their pants down. Folks along the underground are saying they might take Einsam any day now."

Cornelia clears her throat. "If the subversives take Einsam, what does that mean for us out here?"

Mrs. Sheffield shakes her head. "Nothing good." She hawks-up a green-black wad of mucous out the front door onto the porch.

"Well, in any case," I say, "we can't stay here."

"She's right," Victor says, "maybe it's not the best option, but I think we need to ask Reinhardt for help."

"Can you take us there, Mrs. Sheffield?" says Cornelia.

Colleen rocks back and forth chewing her lip. Her fingers drumming on her side to the tune of her enigmatic agenda.

"I'm heading into town in the morning. You can hide under the bales of hay in the back of the truck. Be upfront and ready at first light. And you should put some ice on that," she says pointing to the kaleidoscope bruise on Charles' face.

Then without pausing for a reply, she walks back through the door, climbs into the truck and disappears into the night. Tension pushes the air out of the room. Gette fights back whimpers while the rest of us empathize in silence.

"We should try and get some sleep. I have a feeling that we aren't going to get any for a while," I say.

"I'll pack up what we can bring, but it won't be much."

Cornelia takes Gette up the stairs and Charles follows. Victor and I remain in the foyer. We meet eyes and stare for a minute. Words dance around my tongue and nebulous thoughts race in my head, but nothing comes out. I cross behind him, brushing his shoulder on accident then curl myself up on one half of the lumpy couch. I pull a dusty blanket over me and close my eyes. Dread pulls on me until I fall into a restless sleep.

We sit on the porch and await the rising sun. We dig into the remaining cans that Charles and Victor salvaged last night. Meat stews, chicken broth, mushy fruit. Unfortunately for all of us, there were no more cans of peaches. An uncomfortable silent breakfast in the bitter, pre-dawn cold.

Rays of golden sun silhouette the hedgerows on the horizon. Punctual, the sound of a car builds in the distance. The *rum rum* rumble of a truck comes down the dirt roadway toward the house. A trail of dust streams behind it—the rain already soaked away, evaporated and gone. Colleen's old beat-up truck pulls to a stop in front of the oak tree. The rumble of the engine cuts out replaced by the sound of bugs and birds starting their day.

"I've made a compartment for you underneath the hay. It's going to be really tight and hot. Sorry about that, but that's the only way I can do it. There're three checkpoints between here and town, so stay down, stay quiet, and I'll get you to the plantation in one piece."

"What happens if they stop you? If they check?" Charles says. His voice betrays his words. He knows exactly what will happen, but he wants to ask anyway hoping it will be something else.

Colleen looks at him and rolls the toothpick in her mouth around and around.

"Keep your masks off, it'll help you breathe."

She pulls her own mask on, walks around the back of the truck, and drops the tailgate. There doesn't appear to be any compartment just a stack of hay towering up over the cab. She punches her hands into the hay at the bottom, roots around for a moment, and then pulls on something. The bottom half comes away revealing the compartment. A wooden door covered with hay conceals it.

"Clever," Victor says.

"You don't get to be my age kid without learning a thing or two. Besides, this isn't the first time I've had to sneak past the Peace Officers," she winks and grins wide revealing scattered black teeth.

She points to a small lightning tattoo just below her left thumb. The same symbol she had us put on the mailbox. What does it stand for? Some secret society of farmers? Another day, another set of mysteries.

I move around back and climb up into the truck first. The compartment is short, just taller than my back lying down. I don't know how Charles and Victor are going to squeeze in here. The air outside the compartment is cool, but inside it's stifling. Holding onto my mask, I drag myself into the far corner and try to get comfortable. The compartment isn't wide enough for me to stretch out, so I tuck my legs up into my stomach. I rest my head on my mask—its rubber offering some support, but no comfort. The others follow in behind me. Charles has a particularly tough time of it. He's not a fat man, but he is very large. I'm cramped in here so I can't imagine what he's feeling.

All packed in like sardines, Colleen closes the compartment. It's nearly pitch black—there are only small needle pricks of light coming through the hay. With all of us in here, the heat has risen even higher. Sweat oozes up on my skin.

"Just hold on everybody, this should be over soon," I say. Probably more to console myself than everyone else.

The cabin door opens then slams shut. The truck struggles to start then roars to life. With every stroke of the engine, the bed rocks shaking dust and straw from the tower above us loose. Somehow it all manages to fall into our eyes. We cough and shuffle awkwardly trying to clear the crud from our faces.

The truck lurches forward and picks up speed. Every rock and bump in the road is magnified a hundredfold. The road dashes us about relentlessly. The metal floor is unforgiving, and the stacks of hay pressing down on us don't yield when I arch my back against them. I've never felt claustrophobic before, never felt like I was totally and completely trapped. But now it's taking every ounce of resolve I have not to succumb to panic. My mind is on fire; I'd chew my own arms off if it would get me out of here.

And it doesn't end. The road into town is way longer than I thought it would be. Time seems to stretch on without end making it impossible to determine how long we've actually been driving. Ten thousand miles or ten, either way all I can think of is having it end.

Mercifully, brakes squeal and the truck slows. The moment of respite vanishes as fast as it arrived. The reduced speed may have brought with it a reduction in the bumps and the battering—something incredibly welcome at this point—but with it came a new sense of dread—Peace Officers. We've arrived at the first checkpoint. Awareness takes the reins from panic stifling the air in my throat.

The truck rumbles to a stop. My knees, ankles, and shoulders ache—my heart pounds. I can hear everyone else's breathing—it sounds like shouting in a silent room. *They can find us. They will find us, and I don't want to know what they're going to do to us.* The rumble of the idling truck muffles our panting breaths.

My arm is desperate to stretch out to relieve the tension in my shoulder. It gnaws at me. I hear a voice deep in the primordial part of my brain screaming at me to *get out! Escape!* The demands fade into unshakable pleading, begging me to move. I hear the distinctive sound of Peace Officers speaking through their rebreathers. Their footsteps crunch along the ground around the truck. Their batons tap along its hull.

Their tapping moves toward the back—toward the tailgate. Animal fear tries to take control. *Get out, get out, we have to get out.* The rational part of my brain fights back. *Where do we go? We have no way out. Quiet, be still.* "Don't move," I plead with myself. My arm stretches out in defiance—my mind rages against itself. Gloved hands grasp the handle on the tailgate. The mechanism clicks open with a deafening *clang.* The tailgate drops with a deep thud—the noise reverberates down my spine. More indistinct chatter, more crunching feet. I'm drowning—it's all too much.

The tailgate slams shut. A few more muffled words and Colleen climbs back into the cab. Shifting into drive, she puts the truck in motion and back on the road.

A sobbing sigh rushes out in chorus.

From the first checkpoint, it takes about an hour to get into town. The other two checkpoints were far less eventful. Colleen must be recognized or be more familiar with these Peace Officers because they didn't even have her get out of the car.

We would slow to a stop, they'd exchange some indistinct chatter—far more familiar and friendly than the first stop— and we'd be back on our way.

The ride never gets comfortable, but I've grown numb to all but its hardest knocks. The contorted shapes of our bodies and the constant bombardment of the road, meld together into one long, agonizing exercise in patience.

A few miles outside of town, the roads drastically improve. Sounds of traffic, pedestrians, and everyday life begin to seep through the mountain of hay. The rumble of the truck mixes with the sounds of city life bringing unexpected comfort; things have gotten bad, the world is turned upside down, but not everything is gone, there is still some normal somewhere.

Off the straightaways now, I feel every twist and turn in the road. Each left turn sends my shoulder into the wall, and every right turn digs my elbow into Standish's side. Every time he winces and every time I whisper "sorry." "It's not your fault" or some variation his echoed response.

Just as we are finding positions of détente, the truck slows to a stop.

A final screeching of brakes and the lurching of the heavy load on the shocks signals the end. For a few moments, my body still vibrates and rumbles to the same pattern as the engine.

Colleen gets out of the cab. Hasty footsteps bring her to the tailgate. She wastes no time opening it and removing the cover. I had expected a burst of light, piercing rays to assault my massively dilated eyes, but the world outside is dark.

"Quick as you can—we don't have much time," Colleen commands as forcefully as whispers will allow.

The truck bounces as everyone clambers out. Victor and Cornelia grab Charles by the arms and yank him free. Gritting his teeth and breathing heavy, he does everything in his power to keep from screaming out in pain. My turn to escape.

Every joint aches but every inch forward fills me with relief. Dropping free from the tailgate is euphoric. I reach my arms up as high as they'll go. It feels good to stretch my back—to feel tall again. I quickly survey my surroundings. We are in an alleyway not too dissimilar to the service entrance at the apartment complex. Concrete walls, lines of blackened waste receptacles, discarded industrial things, and the ever-present yellow glow of streetlamps. The air has a strange smell. A mix of garbage, gasoline, soot, and something else—something unfamiliar. It's earthy, almost sweet, but, overwhelmingly, it smells of decay.

"This is where I leave you. Put your masks on and line up at this door here," Colleen points to a small utility door illuminated by a yellow light guarded in a steel shroud. "I have to get this hay to market on time or they'll suspect something is up. Don't trust Reinhardt, but he should be able to help. I wish you all good fortune."

"Thank you, Mrs. Sheffield, we wish the same to you," Cornelia says.

Colleen replaces the concealed wooden door on the compartment and slams the tailgate shut. The latch catches firmly, but it doesn't give me the sense of finality I wanted. It feels more like a journey that has just begun rather than ended. I turn away from Colleen and face the door. I look down at the mask in my hand and get ready to put it back on.

As I'm bringing my mask up to my face, a firm hand grasps my shoulder. I jump and spin myself around. Colleen is inches from me—her hot breath washes over my face reeking of tobacco. Her eyes burrow into me.

She digs into my other shoulder and pulls herself even closer—our noses are nearly touching. "Don't ever be in a room alone with Reinhardt. Ever." Her eyes shift over to Gette, "And you need to be her big sister now. There's a lot of foul things in this world, and it's up to you to stop them."

Colleen's words are disorienting. I know the world we live in, and the many dangers it holds specifically for women. I've been so wrapped up in the chaos, the subversives, and the Caretakers, that I'd almost pushed that out of my mind—almost. But I know she's right. War brings out the worst in everyone and makes cruel and unthinkable things commonplace. The weight of keeping myself and Gette safe and intact through this turns my guts to stone.

I can't think of any words, I'm not sure words are even good here, so I look into Colleen's eyes and nod. She squeezes my shoulder tight, pats it once, then turns and enters the cab. I turn back toward the group. Cornelia is helping Gette get her mask on, Victor and Charles have already fitted theirs and are now stretching against the wall trying to limber up. I look down into the mask. I know it's not armor, but sometimes being invisible is just as good. I plunge my face into the mask and tighten the straps down. *Here we go.*

CHAPTER NINE

THE ROOM IS NOT WHAT I EXPECTED. Small, concrete with two soiled wooden benches stretched in front of a scratched and dirty mirrored wall. About a meter above the floor, there is a silver metal hatch and a copper opening covered in wire mesh. It's claustrophobic, and the hum from the neon lights above is deafening. We file in behind the benches. I grab Gette's hand and give her a reassuring squeeze. A metallic voice crackles to life from the wire mesh.

"State your business."

I step forward, "We are here to see Reinhardt."

The speaker crackles with feedback, then the garbled words come through, "Are you expected?"

"Yes, well… maybe."

There is a lengthy pause. Staring at my reflection in the mirror, I see everyone else fidgeting looking at the door behind us. I make eye contact with Charles in the mirror. I try to convey with the smallest of nods that everything is alright, we just need to wait this out. He responds in kind.

Feedback breaks the silence. "Wait."

The electric hum of the speaker dies out, and we are left with only the buzzing neon lights. Hesitantly, I step over the bench and take a seat. Gette follows. She squeezes my hand, turns, and looks at me.

"I think I've decided I don't like hide and seek anymore."

I laugh, I just had the same thought. It seems so innocent when you play with your friends, hiding in closets, or behind the couch. But when you play it for real, and the stakes for losing are so high, it's not all that fun.

"I agree, Gette—hide and seek sucks," I say with a concealed smirk.

"You got that right kiddo," says Charles massaging his shoulders for emphasis.

Our smiles fade as fast as they cracked, and the conversation dies back into the hum. My leg bounces, what's our exit plan? If we must, we can run out the door—that is if it isn't locked behind us—and try to make it out to the town. But from there I have no idea where to go. In more ways than one, everything from here on out is uncharted territory. I want to talk to Charles about Reinhardt, to try to figure out who this guy is before we go in there, but they're most likely listening to us. We've run out of time to figure it out. I guess now the only thing to do is sit and wait. Angst, pain, and hunger wrestle for my attention.

Sitting still and staring at yourself in the mirror is not a very good way to stay awake. It takes a tremendous amount of willpower not to close my eyes and fall asleep. But holding Gette's hand serves as a reminder that I have to stay vigilant. Much to my relief, the hum from behind the wire mesh comes back to life with a small burst of feedback.

"Stand up and line-up against the wall. Place your feet apart and extend your hands up. Do not look around. Do not ask any questions. Comply, or leave."

I exhale sharply, I really don't want to do that, but I'm not sure we have much choice. Looking over at Charles and Cornelia they seem just as reluctantly inclined as I do. I take the lead. I rise then move against the right wall. I stand with my legs shoulder-width-apart and extend my arms up as high as they can go and still hold on to Gette's hand. I stare at the wall—the uniformity of the gray concrete has vanished. A swirl of grays and air-bubble craters shatter its flawless veneer.

Charles, Cornelia, and Victor shuffle into position—their shoes squeak on the polished concrete floors. They assume similar positions along the back and left wall. My skin tingles as though I pulled on a coat of briers.

There is a loud buzz and a deep metal *thunk*. A cool breeze floods in with the *clomp-klack* of heavy boots. Unknown hands begin to pat me down. They're forceful, and a few of their blows to my ribs twist my face up in agony. I can already feel my ribs turning purple. The hands stop their assault, and the guards step back—their jackboots click together as one. A baritone voice, amplified through a rebreather, answers the question hanging in the air.

"No weapons. They're clean."

"Take them to Reinhardt," commands the metallic voice.

A strong hand grabs my arm and yanks me in the direction of the breeze. I fight to keep my hold on Gette. A door, invisible when closed, stands open to the right of the wire mesh. Beyond it is a dim corridor lit by a stripe of lights running along the floorboards. It twists off to the left then the right. The men pulling us down the corridor are in uniform, but they're not the brown uniforms of Peace Officers. They're bright green and on the right shoulder is a patch with the symbol of a clenched fist holding a bushel of wheat. Under it are stitched the words *Reinhardt Agriculture.*

The journey is nerve-racking. A wave of fear ripples over me. Maybe they're handing us over to Peace Officers? But the thought quickly fades, I have a feeling Reinhardt doesn't much like Peace Officers himself. From what I gather, Reinhardt must think himself a beneficent feudal lord. The age of knights and dragons is long gone—if it ever existed—yet still, people build lives around those fantasies. Although I guess it's not that much fantasy if peasants like us have to come groveling to him for help. Where do we draw the line between fantasy and reality?

No labyrinth lasts forever, and his twisted maze ends. We

line up behind a door and the goon holding me presses a silver button the size of a two-Mark coin on the left-hand side. A computer voice answers, "Stand clear."

Inside the walls, gears turn and belts whine. Steam hisses loudly and some of it seeps through the edges of the door. A small blast hits my exposed hand. I recoil from the sting.

The door opens onto a room very different from the ones we've been in so far. The floors are covered in thick red carpet embroidered with gilded vines and silver trees. Plush red armchairs encircle the room—their intricately carved clawed feet disappear into the lush carpet. The walls are bedecked in ornately framed murals of joyful farmers thrashing fields of wheat with hand tools. There's a small table in the middle of the room with neat stacks of reading material. They even have the newest *Drumbeat*. Next to that is a silver tray with ornate carafes filled with steaming liquid—my bet's coffee—stacks of neatly decorated cookies lie next to clean, cream-colored teacups. The room is both impressive and laughably lavish. It looks like it was designed by someone who never had wealth then suddenly found themselves with riches; everything is nice, but nothing matches and most of it clashes.

The guards release us then line up opposite us. I can see now that the guard who was holding me has silver vines on his shoulders—he must be the captain.

"You are now permitted to remove your masks. Please help yourself to refreshment while you wait for Master Reinhardt."

The Guard Captain's baritone resonates in his mask to a sinister rumble.

Without pause, the guards turn to the left, snap their heels together, and march out of the room single file.

"Jerk really knows how to make an impression, doesn't he?" Charles says as he scoops up a handful of cookies from the silver tray.

I pull my mask off to reply—I'm hit with a pleasant aroma of coffee, cookies, and a not so pleasant smell of old potpourri.

"As long as he helps us, I really don't care what kind of hoops we have to jump through."

Cornelia pulls her mask off and looks at me sternly, "Don't be so brash, we'll do what we can, and none of us will compromise the group, or ourselves, to get out of here. Understood?"

"I didn't mean it like that," I say feeling the full brunt of Cornelia's undercurrent.

"I know sweetheart, we just need to be careful and stick together."

Charles interjects and breaks the mood, "These cookies are damn good." He takes a loud sip from a coffee cup, "and the coffee." He takes another mouthful, "Damn."

Gette laughs, "I want a damn good cookie." She says gleefully.

"Look what you did, Charles."

"Oh, I'm sorry. Watch your mouth there kiddo. But here, have a cookie, they really are that good." Cornelia stops and rolls her eyes. Gette bites into hers and beams. *Mmmm,* she exclaims. Charles looks at Cornelia, pouts then extends a cookie toward her.

"Fine, let me try the cookie too," Cornelia takes a bite. Her eyes widen. "Damn," she exclaims breathlessly.

We all break out laughing. I walk over and take a cookie from the platter. The exterior snaps under tooth with a delightful crunch giving way to a buttery smooth interior. Sweet, with notes of savory flavors I don't recognize, iced, and covered in crystalline sugar sprinkles. These cookies really are the best thing I've eaten in as long as I can remember. I grab five more and quickly devour them. Hardly has one cookie been swallowed before the next one makes its way into my anxiously awaiting teeth.

With the cookies all gobbled up, I pour myself a cup of coffee. I stir in a little cream and drop in one small cube of sugar. I use the delicate golden spoons to mix it all together. The clanking sound it makes reminds me of Margaret.

The coffee is good too and washes down the cookies well. I think we all needed that. Victor is just now getting to the table. As quickly as the rest of us, he scoops up a bundle of cookies. His eyes clamp shut, and he chews the first one with a slow beaming grin. I pour him a cup of coffee and make it up just like mine. Victor looks at me and tries to say thank you, but cookie crumbs start to fall out of his mouth. Gette giggles and I struggle not to spill the coffee I'm laughing so hard.

Having cleared the table of cookies and coffee, we sit in the padded armchairs and relax for the first time in days.

"Do we really have to go to Lufthaffen? I'm content to stay right here," Charles says. His eyes are closed, and he's sunk himself as far as he can into the chair. A big ear-to-ear grin splits his face.

"I'm sure they have chairs in Lufthaffen," says Victor. He too is slouched into the chair—eyes closed, his head up against the puffy wing.

I can't really think of a joke, but I want to tell one. I open my mouth to start when I'm cut off. An ornate set of double doors at the far end of the room opens. A tall, lanky man with slicked-back, black hair wearing a pressed and starched white suit opens the door and then bids us in. We stand and investigate the room beyond. It's decorated in the same style as this one, the red carpet flows seamlessly from one to the other. Ornate pictures hang in this room too, but instead of the pastoral fantasies, they're all different portraits of the same man. He has a thick crooked nose, a thin, wispy mustache. His brow is thick, his eyebrows bushy. His small eyes are dark, like the charcoal at the center of the flag.

"Welcome, please come in and take a seat." Reinhardt stands up from behind his desk. The portraits capture his face very well, especially the minute details like his wrinkles and liver spots. But in the portraits, he is fit—an Adonis riding horses and wrestling bears. His actual stature is much different. He stands not much taller than his chair, but almost half again as wide. He's wearing a black velvet suit—its buttons screaming as they cling to the bursting fabric. He gestures toward a set of chairs in front of his baroque oak desk with stubby sausage fingers covered in gold rings.

We enter, walking past the man in white to sit down and speak with the man in black. Once we are inside, the Man-in-White closes the doors behind us and stands sentinel on the other side—his heels casting a shadow on the razor-thin edge of light at the bottom of the door. Behind Reinhardt is a tall grandfather clock. It clicks methodically, building tension with each swing of its long, weighted arm.

"I assure you—I don't bite. Sit." He smiles. Normally the gesture you use when you want to make people comfortable. However, in his case, thin lips peel back to reveal gnarled, overlapping and chipped teeth.

There are three chairs. Charles, Cornelia, and I take one. Gette drops my hand and sits in Cornelia's lap. Victor moves behind me putting his hands on the chair.

"I got a message this morning, very early I might remind you, that you are all in some sort of a pickle?" He laughs until phlegm catches his throat and he has to cough to break it free. He pulls a stained handkerchief from his breast pocket and hacks into it.

"I do apologize—agricultural humor always gets me."

I feel so uncomfortable I might vibrate this chair to splinters and shoot out through the roof.

"We need transit papers to Lufthaffen for all of us," I say.

He leans back in his chair, interlacing his sausage fingers behind his head.

"Is that all you need?"

"That's it."

Meaty fingers stroke his clammy chin. "Five folks on the run. The capital on the verge of collapse. War coming any day now, and not thirty minutes before you arrived, I received a call from the Regional OSS Commandant. Be on the lookout for a band of subversives. Five of them, armed and dangerous."

My heart races, fists clench. The sound of grinding teeth fills my skull.

"Transit papers?" he says dropping his hand from his chin, "Done."

He sits back—his chair moans. I look over at Charles and Cornelia. I see my face reflected in theirs: utter confusion.

"Transit papers are simple things. I know the right people—I can have those whipped up by Martyr's Day."

A weight lifts from my chest—we can get the papers—but I'm dreading the answer to the next question.

"So, what is that going to cost us?"

He leans back in his chair again and stares off into the portrait of himself riding a horse into the sunset.

"Martyr's Day is only a month away. If you want those transit papers, you can work on my plantation for the month and we'll call it even."

"That simple?"

"That simple," he says leaning forward. His lips pull back revealing two rows of little white knives.

"And what about the Commandant?"

"Good advice to be sure. But I believe in giving people the benefit of the doubt, and you five don't seem all that scary to me. Now, I'm much too busy to handle the details right now, I'll have my man get them from you, you just hurry along with him to the dorms and start working. Before you know it, you'll be boating on the Great Inland Sea."

He stands, and without words, the Man-in-White presses open the doors and enters.

"Follow me," the Man-in-White says in monotone.

Bewildered, I think I would have more luck making sense of the Oracle Device's inner workings than the interaction we just had.

Left little choice, we follow him. I retake Gette's hand, as we walk back into the waiting room. I turn to make sure everyone's behind us and I see Reinhardt standing there behind his desk. His hands on his hips, a giant grin splitting his face like a knife wound. The double doors close on their own and he disappears behind them.

A stinging thought roils in my gut: we're never going to get those papers.

CHAPTER TEN

THE MAN-IN-WHITE MOVES FAST. Each stride of his long legs is almost double mine. Beyond the waiting room, the decor returns to the industrial gray of concrete and steel. Narrow corridors are bustling with workers in white jumpsuits veiled in elaborate rebreather helmets. Every door we pass is marked with a string of letters and numbers painted in black.

If you'd missed the sign on the ceiling telling you that you'd passed from corridor A into B you would have never known. Streams of workers emerge from one door, rush down the hallway, and then disappear behind another. Countless feet stomp. Doors hiss open modulating the hum and rattle of the machine rooms concealed behind them. My eyes are watering from the din.

The Man-in-White never questions his path. His hands stay interlaced in the small of his back while his head pilots his body through the maze like a prow. We struggle to keep up with him. Gette's grip on my hand tightens as she forces her short legs to move faster and stride farther than they've ever needed to before.

Left, right, then left again it's not long before I've completely lost track of how many turns we've made. For all I know we've doubled back several times. He could be leading us in circles but what could we do?

We cross through a final bulkhead of dull gray steel into a small room. The walls are the same uniform gray as the corridor with a similar band of recessed lights striping around the room at ankle height. The clean white light doesn't have the power to reveal details on the walls which soak it up without reflection. In the middle of the far wall is a narrow door flanked by two security guards. Their green uniforms send conflicting messages whizzing around my mind.

"One at a time please," says the Man-in-White motioning to the door with an outstretched hand.

Our eyes dart between each other. This could be a trap, a way of separating us. But we have little choice. We go through the door or we try to escape this labyrinth. Even if we did, the world outside may not resemble a literal maze, but the choices are just as limited.

"Can't we go through together?" I say smiling, holding up Gette's hand to the Man-in-White.

His face is utterly placid, "I'm afraid not. The intake device can only process one person at a time. Don't worry, it's quick."

Cornelia steps forward and takes Gette's hand from mine.

"It'll be alright darling. Evelyn is going to go first and show us how it's done."

Gette looks at me unconvinced. "I won't be gone but a minute," I say.

"Promise?"

"I promise."

The Man-in-White snaps his heels together. The chastisement echoes once then gets swallowed by the maze.

I stride past him avoiding his eyes. The door slides open with a hiss of steam. I step through the mist and disappear inside—the door closes on my heel.

"Welcome new employee to REINHARDT AGRICULTURE," the melodic female computer voice stumbles over the company's name. It pauses before continuing as if clearing its mechanical throat, "Please remain still while the Computerized Employee Registration and Processing Unit gathers your individual identification traits and assigns you an employee number. Your employee number is incredibly useful so be sure to remember it! If you forget your employee number, please contact the Human Resources department at REINHARDT AGRICULTURE."

It chokes on its final words then crackles quiet. The chamber is claustrophobic. Made of slick black glass, its contours gleam in the dim light radiating from the floor which twists and pools on every surface like water. Steam hisses then the wall in front of me slides open revealing an octopus of mechanical probes and instruments.

"Please remain completely still for processing. Dellios

Employment Services is not liable for property or bodily damage during intake."

The bundle of mechanical arms unfurls and swirls around me in a semi-circle. Bulbs flash, pincers take my hands and run frigid metal rollers down the length of my fingers. A rubber-coated instrument pushes under my lips and molds itself to my teeth. Distracted by the device measuring my mouth, a manacle clasps down hard around my left bicep. Blood throbs behind the blockage. I look down as best I am able with the teeth measuring device still fiddling with my molars just in time to see a gleaming metal syringe stab into the crook of my elbow. I turn away, sweat beads on my forehead. Finished with my molars the device relinquishes my mouth. I stretch my jaw—the taste of silicone clings to my tongue. An arm rubs a small cloth against my forehead then drops it into a transparent plastic bag held by another. A vacuum evacuates the air in the bag and it crumples up around the cloth. There's an ivory stain on the rag. *Are they collecting my sweat?* Before I can process what's happening, the arm tucks it away into the bowels of the machine. The manacle releases me, and the rest of the arms follow close behind retracting in a clattering of steel and squelching pistons. The panel clangs shut.

Hidden mechanisms click, skitter, and whir behind the walls. Steam hisses and with a click a metal door opens revealing a silver wand. It drops from the ceiling and unfolds into a long L shape. It emits a blinding blue light that sweeps over me. It rotates slowly until it's come full circle then retracts back into the ceiling.

"One moment please," says the machine's soothing lyrical voice. Hidden cogitators hum. Panic floods my brain. The computer will crunch the data, connect the dots, and figure out who I am. What will Reinhardt do then? This was a terrible idea—we should never have come here. So what if we didn't have a choice? This is the end of the road.

"Identity confirmed: Evelyn Brennan. Citizenship status: under review," I gulp hard, "Please wait." The hidden brain masticates this new finding. I make a hurried sweep of the pod for a handle or door release. Nothing. Body tingling, my throat starts to close.

"Work ban override: approved. Welcome worker 318117 to REINHARDT AGRICULTURE." Steam hisses, pistons activate, and the wall to my left slides away. "Please watch your step as you exit the Dellios CERPu 8000x." I spill out into the antechamber and clamber over to a hex-wedge bench across the room. The world is swirling. I'm electric and for the first time in a long time it's not because I'm terrified. *We might actually be safe here.*

I catch my breath and let my nerves settle. This isn't the end—we have a long way to go—but we can finally take a breath and get a real plan figured out.

Reclining into the wedge, I let my guard down. My body goes limp and I melt into the cloth cushion. This room is just as monochromatic and sterile as all the ones that came before it. I trace the lightbox around the room then up the slivers of light peeking through the door I assume leads to the dormitories. Satisfied, I turn my attention to the processing unit and listen intently trying to figure out what part of the uncomfortable and humiliating process they are going through.

When the door slides open, Gette stumbles out of the steam. I rush up and guide her over to the bench. She sinks into one of the six wedges. Tears bunch in the corner of her eyes threatening to rupture into waterfalls.

"I think I'm starting to understand why Mr. Herrington hated computers," I say with a smile.

"I'm with papa Herrington—computers are stupid."

I pull her close and rest her head on my shoulder. "It's going to be a tight squeeze for your dad."

Gette laughs wiping the tears from her eyes, "Ha-ha, yeah. Papa hates small spaces. It's because he's big-boned. That's what momma says."

We sit together, craning our ears to hear the CERPu claim another victim. Cornelia emerges next then joins us on the bench sandwiching Gette between us. Then Victor stumbles out. He's rubbing his left eye and he looks genuinely sour.

"Stupid thing almost scooped out my eyeball when it came at me with the wipe! What do they need a sample of our sweat for? This whole thing is ridiculous."

Cornelia's mouth moves as if to answer then her eyes land

on Gette and she stops. She thinks for a moment too long for it to be the truth then answers, "Maybe that's how they make sure you aren't sneaking in garlic bulbs or something."

Victor crashes onto the wedge behind me, "They can keep their stinking garlic."

"Yeah, garlic stinks," Gette adds pinching her nose.

"You two don't like garlic? Sure, it makes your breath stink, but roasted with butter on bread—" I let my words trail off as I smack my lips.

Gette scrunches up her face.

"I'm with you Evelyn—roasted garlic is divine," says Cornelia.

"Don't worry Gette, I won't let them make you eat any," says Victor with a wink.

The door slides open and the hissing steam cuts off the conversation. Charles wrests himself free of the pod. Chest seething, eyes ablaze, he stumbles forward on legs wriggling like rubber.

"I'd like to find the man who invented that thing and give him a piece of my mind." Charles pantomimes wringing someone's neck.

"And give him the garlic while you're at it!" Gette says.

"The what—"

Cornelia, Victor, and I burst out laughing.

"Do I want to know?"

Cornelia shrugs and beckons him over to the bench. He takes one long stride toward us when the humor gets sucked out of the room. The door to the antechamber slides open and the Man-in-White steps inside.

"I'm glad to see you are all," he spots Victor's purpling eye, "more-or-less no worse for wear. If you'd kindly follow me, I have many other tasks to attend to. I'll set you up in dormitory C-42."

Silent and obedient we rise and follow him back into the labyrinth of tunnels.

When we reach corridor C, it all begins to make sense. A large group of workers emerges from an even-numbered door leaving it open long enough to get a good look inside. Stacked five high, and farther back than I can see, are plain metal bunks. Each bunk has a stack of numbered lockers at its foot. Televisions dazzle for attention around the room. There is a small common area—hex-wedge benches circled around an even larger television—but the room is otherwise austere. Sterile.

The workers scatter throughout the hall, each finding their way to an odd-numbered airlock door. The revolving airlocks cycle quickly, but I catch a glimpse of something I wasn't expecting. Thick green trees. Wide, dense bushes. Bright red fruits. Behind just one of these doors there are more varieties of plants than I knew existed stretching off in endless rows. A line of overhead sprinklers showers them with clean, clear water—an ethereal rainbow dances in the droplets. The workers, faces visible in the large glass viewport on their rebreathers, tend to the plants and the many mechanical contraptions keeping them alive.

This is nothing like the pictures in the waiting room. Men and women don't toil under the sun, wiping sweat from their brow, a tall glass of cool lemonade waiting for them in the shade. It's nothing like that at all. It's industrial, regimented, and on a scale I'm struggling to comprehend.

The Man-in-White stops in front of C-42.

"There are five of you which will work out nicely. Proceed down the row on the left, and you will find your bunk second from the end: C-42-8." He pulls a data slate from his belt and punches in rapid commands. Moments later, the slate prints out a strip of paper. He tears it off and hands it to me. "This is the combination to your locker. Don't lose it or share it with anyone outside your bunk. Inside you'll find suits and rebreathers for the five of you," he sneers down at Gette. "I might have to go down to storage and find one for the girl." He chews back whatever condescending comment is swelling in his narrow head then snaps back to his task. "Once you put your suits on, operators will inform you where to go and what to do. They will convey your tasks through the helmet. Do everything we ask of you, and Reinhardt will do what he promised."

The Man-in-White doesn't wait for a response. I want to object, but he's already disappeared.

"I got a bad feeling about all this," says Charles.

"You and me both," I say.

"Come on, we shouldn't talk about it here—let's get inside." Cornelia leads the way into the dormitory. I follow her with Gette in tow. Cornelia reaches our bunk and stands impatiently at the footlocker. She extends her hand toward me and I give her the combination. She kneels and begins on the lock. *Twist. Twist. Click.* Hydraulics whine as they raise the lid. Inside are five neatly folded stacks: five folded coveralls, five pairs of knee-high, thick-soled boots, five sets of heavy white rubber gloves, and five rebreathers with oxygen packs.

"I'll stay here with Gette and wait to get one for her," Cornelia says. "But I imagine the rest of you should suit up and start working as soon as possible. I don't trust this, and I don't think he takes kindly to *deadweight.*"

"I don't like that they're going to separate us," Victor says. "How do we keep track of each other?" Something in his voice tugs on my ears.

"We'll be together here at least, and hopefully at mealtimes," I say.

"There better be cookies at every meal," Charles says.

"Somehow, I doubt it," I say.

We share a moment of stillness as the reality of where we are completes is descent through our guts. We can linger in this paralysis, or we can suck it up and get it over with. I exhale hard, stride forward, and pick up my suit.

"Let's get this over with."

CHAPTER ELEVEN

NOTHING COULD HAVE PREPARED ME FOR THIS. As soon as the rebreather's automesh makes its seal around my neck, a computer voice—dark and metallic like an angry machine demon speaking through a long pipe—begins barking odd, rapid commands at me.

"C-37. Row 84. Valve 92. Three quarters turn."

I start down the hall looking for C-37 when it barks again.

"C-37. Row 84. Valve 92. Three quarters turn."

Jolted, I pick up the pace, but I can't seem to find the door.

"C-37. Row 84. Valve 92. Three quarters turn."

Each bark louder and sharper than the last, the frantic beehive in the hallways crystalizes; we're all desperate to appease the angry computer in our heads.

The computer doesn't relent. *C-37. Row 84. Valve 92. Clockwise, three quarters turn. C-37. Row 84. Valve 92.*

Clockwise, three quarters turn. C-37. Row 84. Valve 92. Clockwise, three quarters turn.

Buzzing, stinging fire propels me ever faster. C-37! I race through the revolving airlock and break into a sprint as soon as I'm through. I need to make it stop. The rows are blowing by, one, two, three, but it's not fast enough. The commands are thunderous now, lapping over each other in a round.

Blurring by me is the verdant paradise I've always dreamed of escaping to—the better world I yearned for to get me through the night. Now here I am dreading the beauty around me.

79, 80, 81, 82, 83, 84. Frantic, swing around into 87 eyes hunting for the valve. A few meters into the row there's a panel covered in knobs of varying sizes. Joy swells with each step toward it. It'll stop, the shouting will stop. I square up to the panel and reach instinctively where 92 should be but the order doesn't make sense—the numbers are chaotically scattered across the board. Joy implodes into re-invigorated panic.

C-37. Row 84. Valve 92. Three quarters turn. C-37. Row 84. Valve 92. Three quarters turn. C-37. Row 84. Valve 92. Three quarters turn.

I fall to my knees and run my clumsy, gloved fingers over the tiny engraved number plates. They're impossible to see—they've been nearly rubbed away from countless searching fingers. My eyes aches from darting around the board.

There!

The ninety-two looks like two sticks falling over. I twist the nob into position and the commands stop.

Quiet crashes into my ears. The sound of millions of falling droplets filters through the helmet. I inhale—only now realizing I've been holding my breath.

"C-37 Row 1. Valve 42. Clockwise, one-quarter turn," the voice commands again.

It's strange to hear it so slow, so quiet. But I know it won't stay that way for long. I rush down the row as fast as I can to make it stop.

How long did that last? It's impossible to tell, each knob, row, and enclosure almost the same as the one before. All the soot and dirt in my jumpsuit has worked out of my clothes to cling onto my sweat-soaked skin—I should've taken it off. My ears are ringing, stars dance around the world. My desiccated tongue runs over numb lips in a fruitless quest for water.

I know I'm dehydrated, and I must be starving, but I'm nauseous.

The computer doesn't care, and I have to make it stop.

I reach enclosure C-35 row 19 and perform the demanded task. I grimace at the quiet knowing the next command is about to come. But it doesn't.

"Proceed to dining hall C-2," chirps the peppy synthesized female voice. Her words are like a cool breeze against the desert sun. A flood of emotions pours out—salty tears of joy hall onto my smiling lips.

I'd like nothing more than to take a leisurely stroll through the trees, getting to the dining hall in my own time, but there's no telling how long I have before the computer will start barking at me again.

I enter the hallway unsure where to go. Everyone else is running toward the far end of the hall so I follow.

The hallway chokes with people. There is a single door into the cafeteria and a single door out. I look around for Victor, Cornelia, or Gette. For a moment, I think I see Charles, then he turns to face me. Behind the glass a sunken face with dark circles for eyes stares back at me. His frantic pupils don't see me, they're too busy looking for the phantoms buzzing in his ears. The tide shifts and he fades back into the crowd.

Alone again, I let myself be pulled into the current. The hall is enormous. Thin silver tables run its length. They are tall, too tall to sit, and even if you could there aren't any chairs. The people in front of me are cycling through the tables. Pausing just long enough to rest their arms and hook up the meal bag onto their mask's liquid port. A lot of people don't stand around to eat choosing instead to rush straight back out into the hallway fumbling with the liquid port as they run.

My turn. A gaunt man with marble skin hands me a warm

silver bag. Blue mesh covers his stubble and thin graying hair. He doesn't even look at me. I take the advice I've gathered, and head straight back out into the hallway.

These gloves make getting the straw lined up in the liquid port impossible and I fumble with the straw all the way to the door. The straw clicks into place with a satisfying click and I take my first sip. This slop bag is far from food. Warm, and full of dry chunks, this is, unequivocally, the worst thing I've ever eaten. It tastes how I imagined the soup Charles found would taste but worse. I don't know what this is but calling it *food* feels like a crime.

It lumps in my stomach churning for a few seconds then a fire burst to life and warmth flood my veins. The nausea has gone away—I'm alert. The lights seem brighter than normal forcing me to squint. Every ache has vanished underneath a shellac of jittery numbness.

I'm not two doors down the hallway before the mechanical demon returns to life.

"C-33, row 19, valve 12. Full turn."

Vibrating out of my skin, I rush to obey.

CHAPTER TWELVE

"RETURN TO BUNK." I obey the day's final command with muted fervor—the glop's effects have worn off and my body is no longer ignorant of its pain. The electric buzzing that I thought was coming from the speakers, I now realize was the glop dancing around in my head.

I stumble down the hallway with the others, wait my turn, and file into C-42. I shuffle down to our bunk lightheaded and exhausted. I drag myself to our bunk then collapse onto the first level. I pull off the rebreather. I ignore the yellow sweat pouring out and take a deep gulp of non-recycled air.

I'd relax but this mattress is a lie, it's nothing more than cardboard covered in cloth flopped over bare metal. I want to sob. I want to cry away all of this. How can Reinhardt sit there, stuff himself with cookies, and get fat off our work? How do people do this their whole lives?

I sit up on the edge of the bunk and survey the room. The others are shuffling in removing their helmets to reveal drained, dripping faces. There are a few people who look to be my age, but most are older nearer Charles and Cornelia's age. But still, many more are as old as Mr. Herrington. There is a dejected acceptance in their eyes. At least that's what they want everyone else to see.

A small girl runs toward me. This must be Gette. I jump up to meet her. Picking her up in my arms, I squeeze her like a stuffed animal. I set her down and help her pull her helmet off. Her face is red, and her eyes are swollen from crying.

"I don't think I want to play Domnhall Says ever again either."

I smile at her, "You know, you're right—games aren't fun when they're work."

She smiles back. "I know, huh? That's why they're called games."

"Me and you should make our own game," I say giving her a gentle tap on the shoulder.

"Yes! That sounds fun. We should play the runaway game."

My heart pangs. "We will, we're going to. I promise. But before we can play that game, we got to play some more Domnhall Says."

"How much more?"

"Just until Martyr's Day."

"Okay," she says rocking her mental abacus back and forth.

"I can make it to Martyr's Day."

"I know you can," I say believing it.

"Not a day more?"

"Not a day more."

Gette extends her pinky out toward me. "Pinky promise?" There's iron in her voice.

I wrap my pinky around hers and give it a firm shake while looking her in the eye. "Pinky promise."

***

It isn't long before the others return to the dormitory. Everyone begins the tedious process of pulling off their rebreathers and taking off their boots. Stripped of their indistinguishable outer layer, they all look just as ragged as I do. Charles sits next to Gette and I on the bottom bunk shaking his head furiously.

"This is ridiculous. And where is that man in the white suit? I'm beginning to think this whole thing is a mistake." Cornelia plops down next to him resting her hand on his knee—the tiny bunk now full to bursting.

"We can make it through this Charles," she says.

She stares at him intently then jerks her head toward the others in the room. Most of them are glued to the news playing on the televisions bolted to the walls. But their ears are deft and alert—they shift, tilt and dip searching for gossip, looking for secrets. Understanding washes over Charles's face—his lips tense up. His eyes keep sweeping the room—studying.

Victor finds his way over to us.

"Well, that was a hell of a day," he says as he pulls off his rebreather. "I don't think I've ever been this exhausted."

"At least we're safe," I say, "but this is going to be the longest month of our lives."

"You've got that right," he says.

I try to throw him a reassuring expression, but from his expression, it doesn't seem to work. He slides in next to Cornelia—all of us now smashed together—and joins in our surveillance of the room.

"I'm going to do my best to keep an eye on Gette. I promise."

Cornelia turns to look at me. "The way they run us around, I'm not sure there is much you can do," she sighs, "I'm not sure there is much *I* can do either. We should all look out for each other, as best we can. We'll get through this." She gives us a hollow smile.

The bunks fill up back-to-front. When the last people arrive, it's clear they are the ones in charge. They strut in like roosters. They march straight to the back and enter the small restroom. The other bunks fall in line, front to back. There is a hierarchy here, and we're at the end of it.

"I guess I'll save our spot at the end of the line," I say.

"I'll come wait with you," Victor says perhaps a little too enthused.

"Sure," I say.

Victor jumps up and heads to the end of the line which is already wrapped around the room. Standing forces my aches back to the front of my mind. My knees feel like swollen water sacks ready to burst. I shuffle into line next to him.

"You know, I always wondered where our food came from," he says—his tone jovial. "I always thought it would be something magical. Endless stretches of trees tended by, I don't know, elves or something."

I look at him blankly.

"I never imagined I would be one of those elves," he says.

I smirk at him. He smirks back hoping to escalate the joke into laughter.

The idea is funny enough I guess. Mythical little elves fluttering through the forest tapping trees to sprout new *instant meals for one*. I'm just not in the mood for jokes. Something to break the overwhelming tension would be nice, but standing here with Victor… He keeps looking at me in that way, like I'm the most important thing in the world. Or like a ceiling tile on the roof—a gateway to another world, something you stare through not at. I'm too tired to be sure which. My biggest fear is that he does it because he likes me, because—if I'm being honest with myself—I have no idea what to do with that. It's like he's tossing me a hot iron to lug around when I'm already yoked to a boulder. I just can't.

The line shuffles forward and we line up with the television hung on the wall between bunks three and five. News scrolls across the screen in a tickertape fashion. Minor incidental things, nothing of importance. It seems they are going to cover this all up. The Caretakers don't want us to worry about what's really happening, so they give us petty celebrity news instead. I look away but the familiar trumpets of the *Nightly News* grab back my attention. The parade of triviality fades into the show's opening sequence. But from the first frame, it's clear this broadcast will be anything but familiar.

The scenes of towering cities are cut short and close-ups of the citizens of a bustling Great Society are missing. Instead, it lingers on the deep azure of the flag. When it cuts to the studio, an unfamiliar woman is sitting behind the desk. She's middle-aged with silver-gray hair cut and primped expertly into a bob—her nails are painted midnight blue. She wears the same collarless suit that Rourke did and speaks in the same deliberate monotone.

"Good evening citizens. My name is Annette Beall. I am the new host of the *Nightly News*. It is a great honor to sit in this chair. However, I wish it were under better circumstances. Over the weekend, subversive groups attacked the capital in Einsam. Some of you may have seen the transmission where the honorable broadcaster Desmond Rourke was mercilessly gunned down. We regret that the live stream lasted as long as it did. Such horrors should never be seen by you—the good and honest folk of our great country. The subversives wanted us to think that the Great Society is being torn apart—that we are on the verge of civil war. Those lies are the heart of their propaganda. These Subversives, these foreign devils, want to drive a stake into the heart of the Great Society, driving a wedge between Citizens and our Caretakers," she shuffles her notes, sets them aside then fixes her eyes straight into the camera lens—the intensity of her gaze makes the hair on my neck stand on edge. "I turn now to High Caretaker Domnhall who wishes to address you himself."

The studio cuts out to a wide establishing shot of the People's Acropolis. The massive stone and steel building where the Caretakers pull the strings on their byzantine labyrinth of bureaucrats and trained muscle. The camera sweeps up the meticulously clean marble steps—doubtless the work of a fleet of restless robots and a legion of starving workers. The frame comes to rest on the People's Podium. Beautiful at first glance, it depicts a man holding a great slate upon his nape and upper back. Yet the longer you look at the metal sculpture—its patina covering up the once mirror-like polish—the more it cries out for you to wake up to the reality staring you in the face. Enshrouding the pedestal is a thick glass shield encompassing much of the landing. Domnhall stands behind the pedestal. Wearing a simple, crisp white suit. He strikes a fatherly, peaceful demeanor. His face somber, but not sad—his eyes look up as though they are seeing beyond the present moment and into the future.

"Citizens of the Great Society. Subversives infest our cities spreading despair, panic, and death. But we are not afraid! We shoulder the heavy burden of civilization proudly. We will stand united against subversion, root it out, and cleanse our communities." He pauses for applause too crisp to be real. "The OSS safeguards our institutions. Peace Officers will protect your businesses, your schools, your homes. Our Guardians have been called back from the front to hunt the subversives down and rid us of these malignant, foreign usurpers once and for all."

Domnhall steps back from the podium. He raises his hands. On cue, thunderous applause—real or imaginary—bursts from the speakers with such intensity that they hiss with feedback.

The bathroom line shuffles forward pulling us away from the speaker—people around me raise their hands to their ears in protest. Just as sudden as its onset, the applause cuts out—the silence ringing like a bell. "Stand vigilant brothers and sisters. This is a time of darkness. Only by standing together can we emerge from it and return to the light. Every one of you fights subversion when you go to work, shop, or simply go out to eat and enjoy the company of friends. These subversives wish to destroy our civilization. To extinguish the light we shine across the world. Go about your daily business. Continue your hard work and dedication to the Great Society. We will prove to these subversives—we will prove to the envious world—that the Great Society may be wounded, but that which is righteous can never die!" His final words crescendo to a thunderclap.

Thrusting his fist into the air, invisible crowds roar their approval of the High Caretaker. Thunderous trumpets belt out the opening stanza of the anthem. Safe in his glass enclosure, Domnhall basks in the applause, shifting his furrowed brow and clenched fist back and forth. The image then abruptly shrinks into a small picture-in-picture floating in the upper right-hand corner of the screen. The drab studio of the *Nightly News* comes back into frame.

Beall holds her right hand to her heart. "Patriotic and uplifting words from our great High Caretaker Domnhall. It is our duty to march forward and continue carrying the torch of civilization into this dark night. I mourn the loss of my esteemed colleague Desmond Rourke who served our Great Society faithfully for nearly two decades. But I *honor* him by sitting here tonight continuing to broadcast the triumphs and glories of our intrepid nation." She pauses for a moment to collect herself—her own words threatening to rupture her veneer of plastic calm. "Stay vigilant citizens."

A radio broadcasting voice cuts in. The screen fades from the studio and cuts to a shot of the flag fluttering in the soot-filled air surrounding the Halls of Justice.

"This has been a special broadcast of the Nightly News. We return you now to your regularly scheduled broadcasts."

The screen fades to black, flickers, then returns to life. The tickertape is back, filling the screen with its endless stream of useless news and petty things.

"Can you believe that? That was… odd to say the least," Victor says.

I nod in agreement. "They never say things that candidly. I wonder if it's because Damian kept the broadcast going? Or maybe it's because of the way the Peace Officers reacted? Pulling off their masks like that—everyone saw that."

"I know," Victor says, "it's strange, everyone knows what happens—people aren't dumb. But when you see it like that for the first time," his words trail off, his eyes growing dark in remembrance.

His words land on a tinderbox of self-loathing like a lit match. "We're not dumb? I didn't know. I'm pretty sure no one at my school knew. Not all of us live in the same reality, Victor." I know he wasn't calling me out, but it still stings. He's forced me to remember how much I don't know and the price I've paid because of it.

We keep shuffling forward together, but our conversation has died—I killed it. I shouldn't have snapped at him, he didn't mean anything by it, or did he? Does he still think I'm a spoiled outsider? From the look on his face—lips pursed, eyes darting from me every time my gaze so much as brushes him—something is lingering here, festering, and it's no good for any of us.

"What do you think this means for us?" I say.

"I don't really know. But nothing good. If they're willing to come out and talk about it on TV, then things are really messed up. When things are swirling around, it's impossible to predict what people will do."

"Let's just hope we can get out of here and get to Lufthaffen before things get really bad," I say.

"Agreed." Victor seems nervous. His eyes dart away from mine at even the slightest crossing. He strokes his arm over and over again. I can't focus on him anymore if I want to stay sane, so I divert my attention to my surroundings.

Waiting in is agonizing. I don't know how many showers and bathroom stalls there are, or if that first group is just taking their sweet ass time, but my patience is wafer thin.

When they do finally emerge, they're coifed and gleaming in simple, clean white jumpsuits—their rebreathers nestled under their arms. They joke amongst themselves in booming voices as if the rest of us aren't even here. Patting each other on the back, and laughing in exaggerated bravado, they strut the length of the barracks. The waiting line scurries away from them—they act as though they are unaware that everyone has to move out of their way, but I see the smirks.

People divert their eyes and move aside with zero protest. Looking at their feet as the gaggle blunders past, these people have accepted their place on this arbitrary social ladder. I track the leader of the pack as he swaggers at the head of the gang. He's an older man, most likely in his fifties. He's balding, and his cheeks have begun to sag into jowls. A bristling handlebar mustache frames his gray-toothed mouth. He walks with his shoulders back in long strides like he owns the place—like he's not just another worker in a company suit. King of the dormitory, he surveys the line—his eyes dripping with contempt. My eyes lock with his.

"What have we got here? Newbies?" he says stepping forward invading my personal space. Our toes nearly touching, his hot, unpleasant breath steams over my face.

"Who, us?" I say, "We're just passing through."

He tilts his head to the right like a dog caught off guard by an unfamiliar sound.

"Just passing through? We'll see about that. Didn't anyone ever teach you respect where you came from?"

My eyes roll somersaults in their sockets. "Where I come from you have to earn respect. Strutting like a rooster doesn't mean you rule the roost."

I up his ante, stepping forward until our toes touch. I can't pinpoint where exactly it's coming from, but I really want to fight with this jerk. All these petty bullies want to be feudal lords. They all think they are god's gift to the world, better than the rest of us. Speer, Fowler, Reinhardt, and now this asshole. They claim their power through thugs, posture, and intimidation. They're all just sacks of rude, hot air.

"You better watch yourself, *girl.*"

Fists clench at my waist. His sycophants flock to his side.

"You've got yourself a pretty sweet assignment right now. But I say the word," he snaps his fingers together, "and things for you and your friends could get a whole lot rougher." A shit-eating grin peels his mustache back.

I want to scream. I want to smash my fist into his smug face. Tell him he's a fucking idiot. All the anger that has been welling up inside me demands to be set free to ravage and destroy him. I fight it down—my anger is my weapon, my fuel. I won't waste it on this worthless goon. Still sour—hitting him would do a lot to unwind the bundle of stress inside me—I resign myself to inaction. He's under stress and that's twisted him into this. He's just doing it to survive. Just like everybody else, he's trying to make it through one day at a time. I can relate to it, but I can't stand the way he does it.

I extend my open hand to him. He lurches back, startled and off-balance from my sudden change of tactics. "My name's Evelyn. It's a pleasure to meet you, *boss*." Confusion warps into imagined victory—his mustache dances with delight.

"The pleasure is all mine."

Squeezing my hand like it's a lemon, his grip nearly breaks my fingers. A tear wells up in the corner of my eye—bones smash into each other sending waves of electric fire down compressed tendons—but I refuse to let it fall. I stare directly into his eyes and squeeze back.

Confidence melts from his face. My refusal to back down undermines his whole charade, and I can see it begin to crumble in the twisting, twitching corners of his sagging face.

He drops my hand—dull ache replaces the shooting pain. His face immediately regains some of his oafish poise—surely he thinks that *he* defeated *me* by releasing his grip. He turns back and resumes his strut. His cronies jeer at me but do so hastily so as not to fall too far behind their master.

Victor leans in close. His lips whisper in my ear—accidentally brushing my helix. A shudder runs down my spine. "A little too soon to be making enemies don't you think?"

I turn to look him square in the face—a poorly concealed snicker on his lip. "I wasn't going to bow down to him. And neither were you," I say pushing my finger into his chest. "We're doing the same job as everyone else. He's just like us, and I won't let him get into his head that he isn't."

"I know but—" I cut him off.

"But what? The whole world got into this mess because people never stand up to bullies. They let them push them around, and I'm sick of it. I won't stand by anymore. I won't back down anymore."

"You think you're the only one who's sick of that? I am too! All you're doing is making it harder for us in here," he says his snicker melted into a frown.

He tries to turn away, but I mirror his movements. He's not entirely wrong, but he isn't right either. That's who I am, I charge in. Good or bad, nothing would be the way it is if I hadn't been myself. Should I just stop? Give up now? Would things really be better if I wasn't the way I am? *Maybe Mother would still be alive.*

Victor puts his hand on my shoulder. "I didn't mean it like that."

Chest seething, I realize I've redirected the rage I have at myself onto him.

"No, you're right, Victor. I keep fighting my own battles, and I forget about everyone else. I'm sorry. I'm trying harder than you know."

The conversation dies a second death. This time it stays dead.

It takes ages to get into the bathroom. When we finally get there, we invite Cornelia, Charles, and Gette over. Going inside, it is just as I should have expected it. Five showers, five stalls, five sinks. Inside each stall there is a fresh white jumpsuit, a towel, and an oblong toiletry bag. Pulling the zipper on the canvas bag, I take account of its contents: one small rectangle of *Smellright* soap, one single-use toothbrush, a sewing kit consisting of a needle and a tiny spool of white thread, one packet of powdered deodorant *mountain-rain*, and a single sanitary napkin. We all disappear into different stalls and fall into our own routines.

The shower floor is frigid. Strands of hair clog up the small silver drain in the middle of the concrete pad discolored white in swirling soap stains. I crank the single nob hoping that hot water will wash away the bitter cold crawling up from the floor. Instead, a torrent of ice assaults me. I double over involuntarily from the sudden onslaught. I should have known all the hot water was long gone by now. I take hold of the soap and attempt to lather up my arms. The cold has all my hair follicles standing on edge, and the soap seems to have little interest in lathering. Instead, it grates against my skin like sandpaper. Trying to scrub myself clean, I'm quickly raw. Shivering from the cold and the stinging swarm of angry wounds filling with soap, I go adrift in a sea of dread.

I endure the glacial rain only as long as it takes me to scour myself—head-to-toe—with the abrasive soap. When the water stops, the downdraft from the industrial ceiling fans sends new tremors up my spine. I rub my arms together vigorously trying to warm myself. It doesn't help a whole lot and only seems to add to the discomfort. The towel is starched and stiff—its fibers long since absorbent, after ten thousand bleach-filled washes. I attempt to dry my hair, but the burnt chlorine smell of the fabric repulses me and I give up.

Dry enough, I slip into the provided jumpsuit. Its canvas fabric is inflexible and not very comfortable, but it does offer a welcome reprieve from the bombardment of the wind. I wad up my old jumpsuit and go to discard it in one of five identical silver trash chutes arrayed at the door of each stall. I stand over the lid and press the lever with my foot. The top pops open with a clang. I hold my bundled jumpsuit outstretched over the waiting abyss of the can. Just as I'm about to release my grip and watch it disappear forever, I remember.

I pull my foot off the can. It clanks back down, angry it didn't receive its meal. I quickly unzip and reach into the hidden pocket and fish out the article and the storage sphere. Relieved that I remembered and frustrated that I forgot, I jumble the jumpsuit up again. This time I take special care to feel every pocket and check every seam. Convinced of its emptiness, I toss the jumpsuit into the mouth of the eagerly awaiting trash chute. *Clang.*

I ensure no one has seen—the sound of running showers and closed stall doors are all good signs—then dash into an empty stall and throw the lock.

I search for a place in the jumpsuit I can hide these safely. There aren't any zippers on the pockets of this jumpsuit like my last one so I can't trust them not to fall out. So, I improvise. The sleeve is done-up around the wrist in thick, clumsy stitching. Tugging at it with my teeth, a few threads work their way past my gnashing teeth and slip between them to my gums. The course thread rips them open filling my mouth with warm copper. I wince and fight back the string of profanities desperate to jump out of my mouth.

I press my index finger against my gums from the front and press my tongue against the top row of teeth in the back. I take a small reprieve, then keep going, biting at the threads until a small tear forms in the sleeve end. I hold the tiny folded article in my hand. Such a small, little thing, fragile and nearly weightless. It's more precious than a boxcar of gold. I crease the fold then slide it into the breach in the sleeve. I take the storage sphere next. Staring into its infinite facets, I see Damian, the execution in the square, the silver trucks. Blinking, I roll the sphere around in my hand. It catches the fluorescent light above and throws it around in unpredictable fractals. The images were never there, just superimposed by my brain. *Right?*

It holds so much potential. So many possibilities to flip the script on the Caretakers. But does it even matter anymore? And even if I could find a way of sharing it with the world, what makes me think they'll listen to a teenage girl?

Unable to look at it any longer, I push it inside next to the article.

I dig out the sewing kit and thread the needle. I start looping the needle and thread through the sleeve. I tuck my arm up against my body to make it easier, but it's harder than I thought it would be and it's slow going. I thought I'd do a better job than the clumsy stitches that were there before, but mine aren't any better. The sound of the showers stops. Times running out.

I whip faster—around and around the needle flies. The needle slips.

It stabs into my wrist. It didn't go deep, and there isn't any blood, but it stings like fire. I shake my head and refocus, glad no one was there to watch me do that. *Knock, knock, knock.*

"You okay in there Evelyn?" Cornelia asks, her head must be pressed right up to the door.

"Yes, everything is fine. Just finishing up now." She backs away from the door. With only a few precious seconds left, I whip the needle around in a few more frantic circles. Unconvinced it will hold, but out of time, I loop the end of the thread into a haphazard knot and close up the stitching. I use my incisors to slice the bit of leftover thread. I slide the needle back into the kit, and the kit back into the toiletry bag. I stand and take a moment to inspect my hidden compartment. It's crude, but no one should know what it is at a glance.

I take a deep breath, then step out. Cornelia is standing at the sink rummaging through her toiletry bag. She looks just as uncomfortable in her jumpsuit as I am.

"Oh, good, I was getting worried," she says turning her head around to see me.

"No need to worry about me." She turns back around, closes the toiletry bag, then stares down into the sink.

"This will be really tough Evelyn. It's okay to be upset. It's okay to be frustrated."

The sound of rummaging from the other stalls helps me deflect answering her.

"Right now…" I pause, trying to convince myself of my own words "… right now I think I'm okay."

"To be honest," she says, her feet and hands shuffling—eyes still transfixed on the sink drain. "I'm not."

I take the two steps to the counter. My wet feet stick to the cold concrete floor. I stare over her shoulder at her hands. Fingers spread and pressed flat against the concrete counter they look pale—like gossamer cloth pulled taut over bone. The red stumps of her fingernails—bitten to the quick—scream at me.

"I never wanted Gette to live in a world like this."

"We'll get her out of here," I rest my hand on her shoulder. She grabs my hand then turns her face from the abyss. I look into her eyes like I would a mirror, "We're all going to get through this."

Clang. Startled, we both turn to look. Charles is the first to emerge. His hulking frame is squeezed into his jumpsuit. A moment later Gette and Victor join us. The five of us, clad in identical white, practically glow against the water-stained concrete.

"That was a hell of a day," Charles says as he bends down and scoops Gette up effortlessly into his arms.

"I'm not sure if I can do this," says Victor. He's rubbing his arm nervously—his eyes bloodshot from recent tears.

Cornelia crosses over to him and presses his head down into the crook of her neck. Her fingers run through his ragged brown hair.

"We just need to keep strong until the rest day. It'll be a long week, but we can make it that far. Look how far we've come. We can't let a few valves slow us down now," Cornelia says. Her words stir a small glimmer of hope in my chest—it could be a lot worse.

"That's not what I mean," Victor says, "I seriously doubt Reinhardt is going to help us. I think once people find their way into this place they never get out."

"You're probably right," Charles says. Gette's eyes dart between her father, mother, and me.

"Like hell," I say, "don't worry Gette. Your mom is right—as soon as we can figure out what to do next, we'll get out of here."

"Absolutely," says Charles. Setting Gette down, he moves to the door. "At the very least, these cots aren't too bad. Sure as heck beats slinking around under hay bales."

Charles steps out into the barracks and cuts off our meeting. Cornelia shakes her head, picks up Gette's waiting hand, then follows him out. Victor stands frozen. The speed of his hand nervously rubbing his arm keeps accelerating and it sounds like he's trying to saw through a log.

"He doesn't get it. I've got a bad feeling about all of this. You feel it don't you?" he says—his eyes pierce into me desperately seeking my affirmation.

I know exactly what he means. From the moment we stepped through those doors, I've been uneasy. Everything is shrouded in unknowns and the nagging, itching knowledge that your every action is being monitored. I think we'd be fools to think we're safe here in the lavatory. For every mechanical eye you see, how many more are hidden behind a light bulb or peering through a grate? But more than feeling like sliced meat under a microscope, there is no telling if he'll help us or turn us over to Peace Officers.

I'm sure he has the power to destroy us if we don't comply, and I'm pretty sure he has the authority to do whatever he pleases with us. *Whatever it takes.* The Caretakers have always given businessmen like Reinhardt too much freedom—and it shows. He's built a shrine to his grandiose vision—rendered masterfully in oil on canvas. His cast of supplicants in his feudal colors. And perhaps most dangerous: The Man-in-White. A true believer in his feudal lord. The real power—the Daedalus. And even if he helps us and gets us papers, what then? It won't be long before the tides of war wash over this town then the next. How long before Lufthaffen burns? Will there be any place left to run?

"He knows. We all know," I say, "but he's trying to be strong for us, for Gette."

"I don't want strength—I want some honesty. We need to get out of here right now—tonight!" The grating rubbing stops. His hands, no longer nervous, are bundled into fists. The veins on the back of his hands bulge in throbbing pulses.

"And go where? We just barely got here. It isn't safe, but at least we have a place to sleep and something to eat. We'll get out of here. But we have to be smart about it."

"Smart? If we were being smart, would we have come here?"

After the die have been cast, he's so ready to offer up his opinion and tell me what we should have done. Boiling rage percolates out of me in the twitching corners of my eyes.

"Well if you're so smart, what would you have done? Huh? Where would you have gone?"

His hands relax, and his gaze shifts away from me and down to the floor.

"We need to figure out how to get to Lufthaffen," I say. "Fingers crossed your sister will be able to help us. I don't want to be here either but running out in the middle of the night with no plan, no supplies, and no allies is a recipe for disaster."

"I know that. I know why we're here. But I'm not happy about it."

"No one expects you to be happy. We just need to stick together. Can you do that, can you stick with us," I step into him and rest my hand on his shoulder, "with me?"

He looks up at me. His eyes are big and the whites spider-webbed red. A smile cracks his pensive face.

"Consider me glue," he says. I pull my hand from his shoulder and give him a gentle slug on the arm.

"Come on, I'm exhausted."

On my way to the door, I scoop up my toiletry bag then place my hand on the handle. I begin to push the door open when a freight-car load of anxiety slams down on my chest. *Breathe Evelyn, just breathe.*

I inhale deeply then let it out slow. Enough of the weight passes to allow me to move again and I step through the swinging door.

I feel their eyes burning into me. The agonizing exile of the newcomer tugs at my nerves. Boss hovers over a woman propped up on one arm in her bunk. Hunched low, his lips dance an inch from her ear. Her eyes sit like lumps of coal in a gaunt face. His lips stop their weaving, and he turns—glacially—toward me. Our eyes meet. He stands as rapidly as he turned—the same kind of cosmic speed the gods use to dish out their vengeance: eons. I break his vampiric gaze only to see it repeated on all the bunks from two dozen different eyes. More unnerving than their vacant eyes is the crushing silence in a room full of people. Victor was right, I made a great first impression.

"Goodnight Evelyn," Boss says, his words dripping with confident bravado. He flicks his head around and struts back to his bunk—first bunk. For a moment, the *slip slap* of his feet against the concrete floor is the only sound. The judgment of his thralls lingers in the air for a heartbeat then they too roll back and shut their eyes—just as their master commanded. *Just great Evelyn, you're so great at making new friends.*

I toss my toiletry bag into the footlocker and start the climb to my bunk. Making the swing around to my bed, I catch a glimpse of the woman Boss was just whispering to. Her eyes—like pits of coal—are still staring at me. A cold shiver shoots down my spine.

I pull the wafer-thin blanket over myself, and turn away, but I can still feel her eyes burning into me. My skin crawls with the eerie sense that she's the kind of person you don't want to cross. My heart thumps in my ears. The lights grow dim—undoubtedly automated like everything else in this nightmare.

Should I be scared? Should I try to sleep with one eye open? All pressing questions, but exhausted I close my eyes tight. I run my fingers along the hastily sewn seam. I feel the edges of the folded square and dance my fingers along the contours of the sphere. Moments later sleep comes for me like a vortex. But sleep does not mean rest.

Every dream is a nightmare. Peace Officers chase me down dark and twisting corridors. Mother screams at me. *Run!* Over and over the scene plays out like a macabre play acted out by the dead. I want to stop it, to rush up onto the stage and pull the curtain back. "Ah ha!" I would say to my spectral tormentors, "end this torture." But even in my dreams I'm powerless to stop what I set in motion.

I scream and fight and bang on the walls—my dream struggle feels uncanny, like my waking fight. Even here—my own imagination—I cannot make the visions stop no matter how loud I scream, or far I run. I try to close my mind's eyes—I don't want to see this—but it doesn't stop. Nothing can keep the nightmares out.

CHAPTER THIRTEEN

THERE ARE NO WINDOWS in this place, so it's nearly impossible to tell time. But the body can sense more than taste and smell, and it definitely *feels* early. My brow is covered in sweat and the thin white blanket—so thin as to be less useful than a sheet—is bundled up by my feet. I don't feel like sleeping anymore, and I'm not sure I could if I wanted to.

I slip down—my toes curl from the rush of cold pouring into them from the floor. Charles is asleep on the bottom bunk. His blanket appears doubly small draped over his hulking frame like a gingham blanket on a mountaintop. Victor is still asleep. His violent thrashing evident in the sheets pulled up from the corners. I look up at my bunk—number three—and see it in much the same condition. Following the bunk up, my eyes pass over Cornelia who's dreaming behind clenched eyes and stop at Gette at the top. We're all worried about Gette.

There isn't any space to express it with her always nearby and so many unfamiliar eyes watching. But this world of uncertainty and war is no place for little girls. Behind every one of these new people, Boss, the Man-in-White, Reinhardt, there lurks a predator. I can't shake Colleen's words from my mind. If bullets, bombs, poison gas, and legions on every side willing to use them weren't enough, there is no escaping the demons lurking within men. Normally only brave in shadows, wars offer the excuses men need to unleash their vile natures. *Was Mother that crazy? Maybe she just wanted to protect me?* I'm not sure what we're fighting for anymore. Is it enough to just want to survive? But it's not just me—perhaps for the first time—I know I'm fighting for someone else. Gette deserves a childhood. A life free from the unending dangers of war. I'll do whatever it takes to get her out of this forest of nightmares.

All the other bunks are still except for the occasional toss and turn and grumbling snorting snore. I slip on my boots then creep toward the hallway. I push the door open—its greased hinges making no noise.

The corridor is quiet, empty. The overhead lights are switched off. The only light is a dull, buzzing yellow shining out from the lights inset along the baseboards. The dim light gives the hallways an ominous sense of infinity. My hair is standing on end. I move each foot with care, but it doesn't help. Each step echoes down the hall until it fades away into the darkness.

I head toward the cafeteria. My ears straining over the buzz of the baseboard lights listening for movement. It's a short trip—dead end. The two doors to the cafeteria stand sentinel against the right wall. I try the handles, but they don't budge. Even locked, the door mechanism attempts to open. Hidden gears grind out a deep hollow resonance. I wince and wait to move until the sound fades away and no new ones stir. Silence is safety?

Curiosity unquenched, I make toward the other end of the hall.

A dozen paces in, I turn around. The end of the hall is invisible in a shroud of shadow. My heart lurches. If I run into anyone out here, I won't see them until it's too late. My heart drums. The rush of the unknown, of danger, skitters across my skin. I slink along the wall in a crouch.

I pass the many doors I frantically buzzed in and out of today. I peek through the small windows hoping to see something. Just rows of plants and miles of steam-belching tubes and those god-awful valves.

I pick up speed, but the *stealthy* crouch I'm in prevents me from going too fast. Speed and duck-walking are rarely mentioned in the same breath and tonight's excursion proves why. In an instant, the endless darkness fades into a close, and very real, end.

Opposite the cafeteria, the hallway comes to a stop—the exit. The exit door rises to the ceiling. Its hinges and seams are nearly invisible—the scant light revealing them in lines like ink on a page. In the middle of the door, there is a small wire mesh panel like the one in the first room we entered. Excitement rushes over me and I scamper up to the door.

Victor would be mad at me if he knew I was out sneaking about when I just told him to settle in. But I'm not trying to escape. I just want to know that I can if the need arises. That's not hypocritical, is it?

A spotlight cracks on. My hand shoots back from the door, and I find myself looking up at the exit from a constricted crouch. The spotlight illuminates me from above bathing me in a pool of light. My eyes tear at the sudden onslaught. I feel naked and exposed like a lone performer lit up on stage. A mechanical voice crackles to life from behind the mesh.

"Hallways are unpermitted during non-work hours," the voice says with slow monotone delivery.

I feel like I have to say something. Something believable. Every moment seems like too long to wait before I give an answer, so I blurt out the first thing that comes to mind.

"I just need to pop outside real quick. Forgot something in town." Even as the words are leaving my mouth, I feel like an idiot.

"Exit from the dormitories is only allowed on scheduled rest days. Return to your bunk immediately."

I stand to my full height and stare down my mechanical sentinel. White-hot anger flashes to the surface. How can they just lock us in here like this? We're people, we have rights. Don't we?

The mechanical voice barks again, "This is your final warning. Return to your dormitory immediately."

Pissed off, but afraid of the consequences—more for the others than myself—I turn around and head back.

I linger in front of C-42 trying to shake off the uncomfortable feeling that some mechanical eye just followed me down the hall.

Everyone is still asleep. I slip off my boots and return them as neatly as I can. Climbing into bed, I pull the wisp of a blanket up over my head. Eyes open, I fight back sleep as long as I can.

***

The next few days are a blur. The frantic pace, the terrible food, and the endless orders crash and merge into each other like a kaleidoscope of beige-colored boring. Even at the end of the long workdays, returning to the dormitories offers little rest. Boss—someone told me his actual name, Albert Konrad, but I like mine better—sees to that. When we all have nothing, you have to find something else besides money and muscle to exert power over others. With the little free time we have, we could be reading or watching television—all party approved content of course—but instead, we huddle together in tight cliques, afraid to talk to each other. Not from fear, but because Boss is playing us all against each other. Want the channel changed? Boss has the remote. Want to read the new edition of *Drumbeat* before everyone else dog-ears the pages? You'll have to get it from Boss. He shoves himself into everyone's affairs, spreads rumors, and gossips—*ad nauseam*. 'Did you hear what bunk four said about…' he'll say, or something to that effect, then trail off deliberately. This leaves bunk four panicked trying to figure out if it was something they actually said, or if it was just something Boss made up. All the while the other bunks huddle amongst themselves in feverish whispers. Boss wins because all the other bunks do their work for him—just like Mother, the best jailor is yourself.

Our knowledge of outside events and our desire to be anywhere but here has kept our group together. We don't speak openly in the dormitory, only chance words in the lavatory each night. We watch the endless tickertape on the television screens and keep to ourselves. There is no point settling in or ruffling any more feathers than I already have. We're not going to get sucked into this place.

The Man-in-White hasn't returned. I've seen him a few times in fleeting passes in the hallway. But it's always been just as I'm coming in or out of a room. I've never had a moment away from the barking orders in my helmet to stop him and ask what's going on. Where's the paperwork? Is Reinhardt going to actually deliver on what he promised? With each passing day, my doubts grow. Charles and Victor haven't said anything outright, but I know they're just as frustrated. Desperate, we did what everyone else did, we turned to Reinhardt for help. But now that he has us here, Reinhardt has no reason to help any of us. Trapped in his dormitories, we help him whether we like it or not.

I try to console Gette every night. She isn't crying as much as she was the first day, but she still cries every night. I can't blame her, I cry too. We all do. It builds up in you—the stress of this place—being trapped and helpless. There isn't a day that goes by that I don't wish I could go back in time to the moment just before we stepped through that alleyway door. I want to pull us around and try our luck finding help in town. I've even started thinking that maybe we'd be better off hitching rides from strangers on the byways—the Peace Officer's baton always around the corner—than being trapped in this place. Seeping into my thoughts these last few days is the hopelessness that maybe this is the end of the line. That we're already trapped in here.

The televisions continue to roll news in a tickertape along the bottom of the screen. But as the week progresses, the useless trivialities we saw on the first night have given way to a list of the victories and small accomplishments made by *Guardians and Peace Officers across the nation. Guardians advanced in force retaking Central City from subversives who fled their posts before our troops arrived.* Another headline reads, *one hundred subversives caught today. Swift trial tomorrow. Executions Friday.* All the news seems triumphant, glorious like the Caretakers are beating back the subversives on every front. Every day is an endless stream of reports. More battles, more victories over the subversives. The fighting seems to have no end, but always another victory. Always the war's end is just over the horizon—a horizon we can never seem to cross.

CHAPTER FOURTEEN

EACH DAY OOZES SLOWER THAN THE LAST. Time has stopped flowing and has chosen instead to move in fits and starts. Listening to the endless stream of barking commands and rushing around to perform the same task for the thousandth-time swirls everything together and numbs you to the changes. It's like mixing paint into a bucket of water. For a moment, you can distinguish the individual colors. Blues, reds, yellows. Before long though, the multi-hued clouds collide with each other. The once bright, unique shades get swallowed up into murky brown. Was this the first time I turned this valve? Or the seventh? Who knows? Both answers are just as likely.

Being in this dormitory is the strangest experience I've ever had. We're constantly working toward a goal that fades with each agonizing day. The Man-in-White still hasn't returned, and it doesn't seem like he ever will. We need to come up with a plan in case this deal—or whatever you call this—with Reinhardt falls apart, but there is so little downtime or privacy we haven't managed to put together anything. We've been able to regroup a little each night in the restroom, but with Boss pressing his ear to the door and hidden cameras and microphones, we can't really speak. The only time to be still and think is at night in your bunk, but you're so exhausted there is little you can do but fall asleep. They built this place with a cold mechanical precision. Everything is designed to keep us atomized, keep us busy. No one knows what's going on. No one knows how they fit into the group. We work alone, we dine alone, we agonize alone. There's no time. No time for trouble or anything else. Easy to control and easy to predict.

Waking up on rest day, I don't expect anything to be different. I roll out of my bunk and start getting ready for another day of valves, order, and glop. Still wiping sleep from my eyes, I crack open the footlocker and pull out my rebreather. I brace myself for the coming onslaught of commands but exhausted all I can manage is a grimace.

Sealed up—I take a deep breath of carbonized air.

Silence.

A swell of joy surges through me. I'm free—the gates have been flung open! But it's a hollow victory.

I'm in a strange place surrounded by less than friendly people in a town I've never been to. I don't have any money or a change of clothes. Are we even free to leave? Would we want to? Should I just sit on my bunk and watch the tickertape run by?

The rest of the room is alive with excited chatter. Outside of my head, not everyone seems to share the same outlook on our situation. Little gaggles, almost entirely comprised of members of the same bunk, take off together. People are betting on who made the most Marks this week, and who can drink it away the fastest.

Our bunk is slow to assemble. Trying to figure out the rest day rituals, we observe in silence. Boss and his gang are among the last to leave, "I made 100 Marks this week easy," he says wrapping his arm around a woman nearly half his height, "drinks on me!" The woman takes up his arm and strolls with him through the door. The rest bumble along after them singing his praises. We're almost alone in the room, almost.

The woman with the coal pit eyes has been staring at Boss. Her eyes fixated on him unblinking. Her jaw clenched—hands wringing the straps of her rebreather. When the door closes behind Boss and his posse, she turns her attention to us. Her eyes linger on Charles and Cornelia who are helping Gette get her boots on. Her gaze is just as withering, but she quickly loses interest. I guess we're not the only ones who don't like Boss. She leaves—her boots squeak with each step making it impossible to ignore. Alone at last, we turn to each other.

"So what are we going to do on our rest day?" Gette says.

"I'm not really sure what there is to do," says Victor.

"I'm not sure there is a whole lot we can do," says Charles. "But even if we can just get out of this place for a few hours and stretch our legs I'll be more than happy."

"I want to see if we can find some real food. Something you can sink your teeth into and actually chew," says Cornelia.

"I like the idea of that," exclaims Gette, "maybe some pie?"

"Peach pie," says Charles.

"Yes!" exclaims Gette as she leaps from the bunk into Charles's outstretched arms.

"Well then, I guess it's settled," says Charles while effortlessly swooping Gette up to his shoulders, "let's go find us some peach pie."

Cornelia scruffs Gette's hair, "Hold your horses you two. I'd like some peach pie too, but shouldn't we worry about more pressing issues?"

"Like?" Charles says.

"Getting our transit papers?" I say.

"Exactly," says Cornelia, "we need to fill out that paperwork for the Man-in-White."

"Hey," Charles starts raising an open hand in defense, "for the record, you brought up the idea of food." Giddiness drops from his face. "Agreed. We should try and track him down, fill out the paperwork, and then get pie."

"You've been talking this pie up so much I have a feeling we aren't going to be able to find any," says Victor.

"You've got a point Victor, let's not get ahead of ourselves. Let's handle some business first. Then we can go look for pie."

Gette's face slumps. The reality that there may not be any pie and that taking care of business here could take all day erodes her jubilance. Torn between the overwhelming desire to get out of the plantation as fast as possible and the need to get our affairs in order, I draft a solution.

"Why don't you two take Gette into town. Victor and I can meet with Reinhardt's aid and get the paperwork squared away while you go out and get us some pie."

"I don't know Evelyn, I don't like the idea of us splitting up," says Cornelia.

"If something happens, or they need our signatures, we'd have to come back anyway. Maybe it's best to go in a group?" says Charles.

Silence grows between us. The hum of the wall-mounted televisions and the overhead lights slur together.

"Together then," I say. "I'll lead the way."

I turn to leave without looking back. Heading down the hall, we easily pass the door that kept me locked in the first night. It stands ajar—its mechanical voice silent. Beyond it is yet another hallway stretching out like a spoke from a central hub. The hub has rounded concrete walls rising into a massive vault. Long cables extend down from the invisible ceiling—the piercing light from the suspended orbs fails to reach all the way back up giving the impression that they hang like stars in the sky. Benches curve around a central obelisk. It stands twice my height—its silver surface shimmering and alive. On each of the four sides of the obelisk are projected light screens and protruding black-mesh microphones. Three people stand around the obelisk speaking to the machine. Unsure what it does, I approach the open side of the obelisk.

"Step forward," says the machine's snappy voice. On the ground in front of the light screen are two painted yellow feet. I step onto them then look straight into the prismatic projection *Reinhardt Agriculture Worker Terminal 3*.

"Processing." Blue laser light projects out from the four corners of the light screen sweeping my body. It then turns its full attention to my helmet forcing me to squint.

"Identity Confirmed. Worker 318117. Weekly credits earned: six."

A small metal door opens, spits out six one-credit paper bills, then slams shut with a harsh metal *kur-thump*.

I flick through them, fold them in half then shove them into the front pocket on my jumpsuit.

"Step away," chides the mechanical voice.

"Actually, I had a question. We need to speak with master Reinhardt's aid. The man in the white suit."

"Processing request, standby."

I lean back giving everyone a cheeky smile and a thumbs up. The speakers crackle so I turn my focus back on the screen.

"Denied. Worker 318117's request has been submitted to human resources."

Flustered, I throw my hands up. "We just need to talk with him, it'll just take a minute."

"Step away," barks the mechanical voice. Emerging from the dark shadow cast by one the vaulted room's five buttresses, a green-uniformed guard takes a single step forward into the light.

I look down and obey, slinking off to the bench that wraps around the room.

"What the hell was that?" asks Charles as forcefully as he can without the guard overhearing.

"Not here. We should just get our Marks and go. We can talk about it outside. But I think it's safe to say we won't be seeing the Man-in-White anytime soon."

Charles bites his tongue. Shaking his head, he steps up to the terminal. "Unbelievable," he mutters to himself. The guard disappears back into the shadow.

I sit and watch as everyone follows my lead. The machine scans them, spits out their Marks, then barks at them to go away.

Thirty Marks between us, I lead us along the painted yellow line—scuffed and faded but visible—along another long spoke to the 'employee egress room' identified by the painted block letters on the bare concrete walls.

The single yellow line splits into seven. Short lines have already formed at each airlock. I follow the path to the far left. Reaching the line, I turn and watch Gette, Victor, Cornelia, and lastly Charles snake down their own line and join the queue. I try a smile, then turn back—eyes down, feet shuffling—to wait my turn.

The airlock doors fold open—the rubber seals on their edges squelch under the door's massive weight. Sunlight accosts us, and it's a moment before the world takes form from the featureless white brightness.

The central roundabout for the plantation has signs directing traffic to the various areas of the agro-factory. Shipping, receiving, personnel, office. The twisting octopus of hallways, dormitories, stockrooms, and countless greenhouses is imperceptible from the boxy white exterior. Just like the modern construction of Neptus Memorial, great effort has been put into making everything uniform. Streaking ash, like tee-shirt sweat stains, ooze from the off-white walls breaking up the regularity with a chaotically organic smear.

Stretching out toward the town in the valley below us is a line of workers uniform in their white jumpsuits and rebreathers. We slip into the procession, pausing momentarily at a small concrete portal. A metal wand sweeps the ID markers in our helmets. An amber light blinks then turns green. A Reinhardt security guard waves us through and we're out.

From our vantage on top of a gently rolling hill, the entirety of Bergholz is visible. Compared to Einsam, the town is minuscule. A dense core of two-story buildings covers a strip along a central two-lane road. Single-story buildings branch out snake-like from the core—their roads, curved and narrow at the middle, turn to a wide grid at the edge of town. Turning back to look at the plantation, it's easily the same size as the town. Bergholz sits in the shallow valley created by three hills. The sun is rising higher into the sky on my left and the two other hills lay a mile or so away. One is densely wooded while the other is little more than a grassy knoll.

Gette holds my hand, and she keeps up a good pace. By the time we reach the first house on the edge of town, my neck is sore from looking around. The air is as clean as I've ever seen it—I can see nearly a mile in every direction before the suspended particles blur everything into nothingness. The novelty of seeing the world beyond the next streetlamp and colors other than yellow and brown has yet to wear off. A familiar rumble grows louder with each step. My wondering neck fixes straight ahead, my eyes cast down to the white rubber boots in front of me.

A Peace Officer cruiser rumbles past us like a skulking panther on the prowl. I glance over and see myself reflected in the obsidian-black tint of the windows. I turn my head forward and keep my pace. My grip tightens on Gette, and I pull her closer.

Its lights burst to life swirling red and yellow. Its siren whoops—my whole body cringes. Black smoke belches from its smokestack. Its thick, diagonally grooved tires dig into the loose gravel road showering Gette and me in a spray of muck, ash, and stones. I huddle Gette's head into my body instinctively. The cruiser tears off. Like startled prey, the line jolts to a stop and lingers brittle as icicles until the cruiser's shrill whoops fade from our ears.

"Are you alright?" I say to Gette kneeling to check her over for injuries.

"Yup, I'm alright."

Cornelia takes two quick strides over to us and grabs up Gette's hand. "That was scary, huh?"

"They're not scary, just rude," Gette says a little too loud. A veiled head turns in the line ahead of us. Cornelia holds her index finger to her viewport making a cross with her lips. Gette nods in understanding then turns her attention down and away from prying eyes.

We let our subconscious' take over. Like water, we meld back into the stream unseen.

The houses on the outskirts are small single-story homes. Most have a front yard of dead yellow grass surrounded by glistening white-picket fences. We pass a dozen small children in masks holding large pails of white-wash lazily dabbing at their family's fences—their attention captivated by the weekly stream of workers. Every house has a flagpole jutting out from the front porch proudly waving the deep blue and silver flag.

Two blocks into town, houses give way to a park cordoned

off with rusting chain-link fencing. A large parking lot eats into the tawny grass. *Welcome to Patriot Park* reads the carved wooden sign stretching over the entrance.

Just beyond the park, two-story buildings begin to dominate the streets. The line of workers is breaking off and diverging now—small groups of people peel off disappearing into one neon-lit bar or another. This end of town, closest to the plantation, is lined with bars, greasy spoons, and a half-dozen red neon XXX signs blaring and obnoxious in the morning sun.

"Let's keep moving farther into town," says Cornelia. She steps into the lead, pulling Gette so close to her right leg they practically trip over each other.

I follow her lead, glancing back occasionally to make sure Victor and Charles are still with us. Soon the red neon disappears in favor of blues and greens and pastel sandwich boards. The streets are bustling now—our white suits make us sore thumbs amidst trench coat and fedora-wearing locals. The town square is lined with dead trees and a few full-leafed metal sculptures of trees trapped frozen in perpetual spring.

Stepping off the sidewalk, and out of the main flow of people, we cluster around a park bench to get our bearings. Gette wastes no time hopping up on the bench—her little legs bouncing inches above the mound of soot the sweepers missed underneath the bench.

"I think we should find a place we can have some breakfast and sit down for a while," says Cornelia.

"Agreed," says Charles, "these boots are digging into my ankles."

A commiserating look passes between us.

"That sounds good. Let's see what our options are." We each survey the ring of shops surrounding the square. Bit & Bobble Haberdashery, Walt's Hardware, Modeo furniture outlet, a Mountain Air showroom, Pritchett's department store—Mother loved shopping there—a barbershop and salon, a Guardian recruitment center, Citizen's Bistro—*now with glass-patio seating*—and Hall & Sons FHVAC. Across Main Street, on the other side of the square, is the squat city hall building which resembles the Ministry of Justice in miniature; a classical base of marble columns holds up a modern glass and steel building on top. On the corners are onyx statues of naked men and women posed as if they were shouldering the full weight of the building above them.

A gust of wind catches the cable on the town's central ten-meter flagpole with a clank. It draws my attention toward it but something else catches my eye. Erected in the yellow grass at the base of the hall's marble staircase are wooden gallows with space for five. Ghost-fire wraps itself around my neck and seizes the breath in my throat. I shudder and look away.

"I guess it's Citizen's Bistro then," says Victor, "unless you all want to join the army."

"Yes sir!" says Gette snapping a decent salute.

In the same instant, Charles and Cornelia shoot him a disapproving look.

He blushes bright red. "Just a joke," he says shrugging out his hands in surrender.

Cornelia sighs, "Victor—"

Gette interjects. "I know, mom. I was just joking too."

Cornelia sighs. "It's okay to joke, but let's do it inside, somewhere we aren't being watched."

"I hope this bistro has peach pie," Gette says absently kicking at the uneven cobblestones beneath our feet.

Cornelia leads the way across the square, and I fall in at the end of the line. While we were surveying the square, ash accumulated on us. Pure white and starched this morning, our jumpsuits are now nearly gray—oily shrouds weeping trails of black tears from our shoulders.

A large group of locals—indistinguishable from each other in brimmed hats, trench coats, and masks—reach the bistro just before we do. A line forms at the airlock, and we queue up without protest. My eyes stray as they always do when I'm shuffling forward waiting to transition from one world to another.

The town feels old. Yellows and reds poke out from beneath thick layers of gray and black. Airlocks and gasketed windows all seem to be bolted on—their glass and metal forms unmistakably alien on brick and wood bodies. Neon signs spit out their fluorescent glow with a crackling hiss that fills the air like a miasma you cannot escape. Narrow alleyways hint at more businesses tucked away from the main square. I drift toward the one closest to me on the right. Steam vents from boilers and pipes tucked away under the skin of the town. A haze of red tantalizes us to a business whose sign is just out of sight around the corner.

We shuffle forward—Cornelia is nearly at the airlock. I step out of line and stride toward the alley, hoping to catch a glimpse of the sign.

"Evelyn, where are you going?" Victor says.

I don't respond and keep moving closer. With a single step, my perspective on the alley shifts enough for the hidden form to take shape. *Martha's Café & Bakery.*

"Gette," I say turning back around, "I think I found pie."

"Pie!" Gette exclaims bursting from her mother's grasp and barreling toward me. Cornelia breaks out of the line and catches up to Gette with three long strides. I take up one of her small hands, and her mother takes the other.

"Slow down there little missy. I'm sure the pie will still be there thirty seconds from now."

I chuckle.

"Wait for us," says Victor. He and Charles take a few jogging steps to catch up.

Swinging between us, Gette leads the way down the short alley and around the corner. A small cobblestone path wide enough for a car—barely—stretches out a few dozen meters in both directions before twisting out of sight. The red glow of *Martha's Café & Bakery* is joined by the blue radiance of *Chestnut's: Treasures and Curiosities*. Covered food stalls and stacks of ash-covered books fill in the remaining gaps between apartments. I try and take in the sight of the street, but Gette is so insistent she practically pulls me into the tiny single-user airlock with her.

I drop her hand and step back as the glass cylinder swirls closed, hisses, vents and then grinds open. Cornelia and I start toward the opening.

"You go first, Evelyn."

"She's something," I say unable to keep from laughing.

"She's the best," Cornelia says with a confident smile.

Charles steps closer, "Hurry up and get after her before she eats the whole store!"

I step into the cylinder—my cheeks tight with joy. It whirls closed, but the mechanism is far from smooth. Metal grinds and moans as the air is pumped out through the exhaust fan and warm air is sucked in through the massive overhead filter.

A shrill whistle of escaping air accompanies the jerking motion of the door as it opens. Gette has already pulled off her rebreather and is plastered to the front of the long, glass counter. Three layers of baked goods fill the case. Pies, cookies, assorted loaves of bread, cakes, rolls, Danishes, and muffins. Each pastry arrayed in a rainbow of flavor combinations and decorations. I pull on my rebreather's retention levers by my chin popping the mask open. I tuck it under my arm and close my eyes. The aroma is intoxicating. The sweet-sour smell of yeast, caramelized fruit, cinnamon, and lavender. The warm, scented air fills my lungs and wraps warm memories around me—I dance with Mother in the mists of my mind.

"Welcome to Martha's. Let me know if you have any questions," says a young voice behind the counter.

I open my eyes, reluctantly giving up the fantasy behind them. Behind the counter stands a short woman probably only a few years older than myself. Her auburn hair is pinned up in a tight spiral with only a few stray wisps falling over her red-freckled cheeks. Her apron is a kaleidoscope of fruits and splattered flower, but the sleeves of her frock are as white as bleached bone.

"Well actually," I say stepping closer to the counter, "Gette here has her heart set on peach pie."

"Is that so?" the baker says with an amused smile.

"Yes ma'am," Gette exclaims, "it's my favorite."

"Well then today is your lucky day. We just got in a bunch of great peaches and it just so happens that my oven is full of peach pie right now."

"Really?" Gette's excitement is kinetic.

The hiss of the airlock draws my attention. Victor and Cornelia are already inside and seem to be equally transfixed by the aroma. Charles is still in the cylinder; the seal hissed open, but the door is stuck.

"A little help?" says Charles his words fighting back claustrophobia.

The baker notices and rushes out from behind the counter.

"I'm so sorry—here, let me help." With practiced motions, she grabs a worn wooden dowel that was leaning next to the air-lock, pokes it through the opening and wrenches the door open. Charles steps out and unlatches his rebreather in a single motion.

"I've had Hall in to look at it twice this week. He says it's not worth fixing yet, just a bit of binding from the building settling."

"I'll help you trap him in there—that ought to change his tune," says Charles.

The woman laughs then places the dowel back against the wall. "I might take you up on that." Awkward silence creeps into the room.

Ding.

A bell from the kitchen behind the counter summons the baker away.

"That'll be the peach pie," she says disappearing through the narrow opening.

Charles kneels next to Gette pointing to his favorites. Cornelia sets her mask into one of the cubbyholes underneath the front window then takes a seat at the largest of the three tables. I follow her lead and place my mask in the spot next to hers. Victor mirrors me like a shadow and sits down in the chair next to me.

"Even if we don't get any pie, the smell alone was worth the walk," Cornelia says. The tension in her face is beginning to uncoil and the hint of a smile is creeping into the corners of her mouth. "Let's hope there really is pie though."

We laugh in unison. The last thing we ate that even resembled food were the cookies in Reinhardt's waiting room. I can't help but think of the fairy tale of the children lured to their deaths with sweets. Though to be fair, those cookies were damn good.

Victor leans forward plopping his elbows onto the red-and-white checkered vinyl tablecloth. "I thought we were done for when that cruiser lit up this morning." His voice is barely a whisper, but I find myself looking over my shoulder nonetheless. We're alone in the bakery, and out of earshot of the baker, but my stomach knots up all the same.

"I did too," I say, "I still can't figure out why Reinhardt is helping us. What's he getting out of it?"

"We can be certain we aren't going to get anything from him for free. We should hold on to the wages we made this week, I've no doubt he'll hold it, and everything he's given us over our heads."

"Should we not spend money on the pie then?" says Victor.

Cornelia sighs, turning toward Gette. "Are you going to break it to her?"

Victor pulls his arms back across his chest. "I'd rather tickle a spider."

I don't know what I find more amusing: the thought of Victor tickling a spider, or Gette taking him out when he tries to take her pie away. My cheeks ache from laughing.

"Look mom. Look what we got!" Nestled in the baker's oven-mitt-protected hands, the peach pie is glistening golden and glazed.

She places it into the center of the table. "It could probably stand to cool for another ten minutes, but something tells me this little girl can't wait that long." Gette jumps into a chair grinning wolfishly.

Charles takes the last seat ruffling his daughter's hair.

"I'll bring plates, cutlery, and some fresh cream. Is there anything else I can get for you?"

"No Martha, this is perfect," I say.

The baker blushes, "Martha's my grandmother. My name's Mary-Anne."

Roses flash across my face.

"Oh, don't worry," she says placing a gentle padded hand

onto my shoulder. "If I had a nickel."

"You could get that door fixed," Charles says winking.

"Charles," Cornelia says shooting him daggers.

The moment stretches, but Mary-Anne's laughter pulls it back together.

"I think I should have left this one in the airlock. I'll be back with those plates."

Mary-Anne leaves briefly returning with a stack of plates, a silver bowl of cream, and a fist full of forks bundled in white napkins.

Gette digs into the pie as soon as a plate lands in front of her.

"That's really good," she says—her mouth full.

I slide a slice onto my plate and take a bite. The outside world drops away, and for those glorious minutes I retreat into the fantasy of Mother and me together and happy.

CHAPTER FIFTEEN

THE PIE WAS LONG EATEN by the time we left leave the bakery. Mary-Anne insisted we could stay as long as we liked, but the choke of customers itching for our table propelled us to leave. Reentering our rebreathers, the smell of the bakery lingered for a few short and glorious breaths until the carbon filters and ionizers stole it away.

The sun is high in the sky illuminating the town in harsh direct light. Filth—obscured in shadow and neon light this morning—clings to every surface. Under the sun's unflinching gaze, the façade falls away completely leaving only crumbling, sad stones tread upon by crumbling, sad people.

We head for the Mountain Air showroom. Its building is just as old as the others, but it has been so augmented and upgraded with glistening silver steel and grime-resistant glass that it's practically shouting, 'the Great Society is doing just fine!'

Gleaming modern signs advertise the new *Lux* line of masks. Its dream is alluring. We pull toward it without discussion and pass through its high-efficiency turnstile airlocks with ease.

Stepping inside, I pull my rebreather off and hand it to the attendant by the door. She is my age, slender and tall. Tight, short brown curls peek out from under her *Lux* mask bouncing just above the cuff of her neon-red, uniform shift dress.

"Welcome and breathe deep," she says—her voice slick as silk. "Let me know if you have any questions."

The *Lux* mask distorts her voice but not in the typical way. Normally it throws your voice down a well then makes it crawl its way out. The result is distant, echoing, and dark. It made someone like Victoriana—with a voice like spiced honey—sound like a haggard smoker. This is different. This is almost appealing. It takes your voice and elevates it, sculpting it from sound into music. If that weren't enough, the mask itself is a revolution. In place of rubber and steel, synthetics and fine-grain leather flow around the face organically. The filters are different too. Silver diamonds slot in seamlessly with the contours of the mask accentuating the design.

I float farther into the showroom. *Lux* masks in a dozen varieties and materials seem to float on pools of light—plinths of clear acrylic illuminated from below line the center of the room like classical columns. In place of walls, giant screens cover every flat surface. Videos of preternaturally beautiful people dancing—wearing little more than patent leather strips—loop all around. Music, driving and primal, blares from hidden speakers.

I love it. And I despise it. All of it. How could they do

this? They took everything great about stepping out of line and coopted it into perfect packages—prison cells curated just for me. This isn't the way Mountain Air works. This isn't the way the Great Society works. The changes are small, they don't adapt. And yet here it is. The life and organic freedom of the illegal club sitting on the shelf for $295.99.

"Aren't they just incredible?"

I blink back into reality. The manager is leaning on the plinth closest to me. He's wearing one of the new masks. It's a deep red upsettingly close to blood—the color matching a little too close to his red collarless suit.

"They are," I say with a sigh.

Either he didn't notice my frustration, or he doesn't care. He scoops up the mask on the plinth propping it up in one hand while running his fingers along the stitching with the other.

"We've never offered people masks of this quality before. This kind of needlework used to be reserved only for the High Caretaker and his closest advisors. Have you felt the different leathers? The sheepskin is my favorite, but we have a dozen different suedes, or synthetic's that wick away moisture and shuck off soot if that's more to your liking."

His eye ports are crystal clear revealing a lion's hunger. He thinks I'm easy prey and I'm going to buy one. Maybe he's not far off. If I were here with Mother, we would already be taking measurements and going through the material selections. She would have been so happy. I'd let her buy me a dozen masks if I could see her smile one more time.

"They are remarkable—beautiful," I say trying to shake the tear from my eye. "How do they change your voice like that?"

"Remarkable, isn't it?" He flips the mask over in his hand, "In the middle of the breathing chamber here," he points to a small black box. "This is the modulator that takes in your voice," he flips the mask back around again. "Hidden behind thin mesh slits on either side of the mouth are the speakers. It sounds great, doesn't it? Fully customizable, we can sit down and design your perfect mask right now if you like."

I place my hand on the mask and push it back toward the plinth. He fights me for a moment then relents. "They're very nice. But I'm just looking."

"I'll be here when you're ready." The hunt fizzles from his eyes for a moment then rekindles again. "Please excuse me and breathe deep."

Not waiting until his corporate-approved exit is spoken, he sets off across the store toward Charles who seems transfixed by a black and yellow mask across the room.

"How do I look?" says a baritone voice rumbling like thunder. I turn around, fear tingling down my back, then smile as I turn my gaze down.

Gette is wearing a mask from the *Authority* collection.

"Halt citizen!" says the miniature Peace Officer. Genuine laughter mixes with disquieting memories both distant and new.

I throw my arms up in mock surrender and breathe deep that fresh mountain air.

After apologizing our way out of the Mountain Air store, we duck into each of the stores in the square. With little money and no intention of buy anything, none of the stores are very inviting.

Modeo's doesn't allow us to sit on or try out any of the furniture. Signs saying 'You make a mess, you pay for it' hang everywhere on little chains. The sales staff watches us like hawks ducking behind displays as if we can't see them spying on us. It's only our first day in town but it's already quite clear that the locals don't like the people from Reinhardt's plantation.

We haven't been in Pritchett's ten seconds when it goes off the rails. As soon as we're through the airlock Gette spots a wide-brim yellow hat and rushes over to it. Before she even gets close enough to the mannequin to pick it up, the manager bolts across the room and snatches it from the display.

"Absolutely not," the manager says, wiping fiercely at imagined filth on the brim. "You'll have to pay for this."

Her accusations hit us like a grenade.

"I didn't even touch it," Gette pleads.

"Little liar, you've ruined it."

Charles and Cornelia finally process what's going on and

step forward hands up and pleading.

"Hold on, I'm sure she didn't mean to do anything. We can wash it off."

"But papa I didn't even touch it."

"Look here, it's ruined." The manager holds out the brim of the hat pointing to a phantom stain.

This lady's got some fucking nerve. "What stain?" I move between Gette and the manager. "We're sorry for bothering you, we'll be going now."

"Don't try and get out of it. I'll charge it to your work number."

Victor throws his hands up. "That's ridiculous, she didn't even touch it."

"I didn't."

The manager tosses the hat on the ground. "You've ruined it, and you're going to pay one way or another. Will that be Marks, charge, or shall I call the authorities and have them sort it out?"

Charles grabs my shoulder. Gette's fitting back tears.

"I don't know what I did, I'm sorry. Here," Gette reaches into her pocket and pulls out her week's earnings."

The manager swipes it out of her hand then riffles through the bills. "The hat's fifteen Marks."

"Unbelievable," Charles spits a little too loud.

"What was that?"

We pass Charles the little money we have left, he counts it out, then shoves a wad into the managers outstretched hand.

"Come on Gette." He scoops her up and turns to leave. Cornelia locks eyes with the manager and shakes her head in slow, deliberate condemnation.

Before stepping into the airlock, I glance back. She's picked up the hat and is already fussing with it on the mannequin—silver glinting in her eyes.

After that none of us felt much like going anywhere. It's well past lunchtime—nearly dinner—we're tired, humiliated and now almost broke. We duck into the alleyway hoping to split a piece of pie between us, but Martha's is closed.

Going back to the square isn't really an option either. The setting sun shines through the buildings like a magnifying glass illuminating the gallows across the street in bright yellow. To make matters worse, a convoy of Guardians stopped on Main Street across from city hall. They've spread out around their mammoth, six-wheeled transports erecting sandbag barricades on the buildings approach. The officer leans up against the gallows joking with two Peace Officers while smoking a long black cigarette through an adapter on his rebreather's intake valve.

Afraid of drawing unwanted attention to ourselves, we resign to walk back to the plantation. Rest day had started off well enough—any break from the regimented monotony of that place is appreciated—but it's clear we aren't welcome here. I never imagined how quickly the whole world could turn its shoulder on you. Without the right clothes, the right mask, and a fist full of Marks, you might as well be soot on the bottom of someone's boot.

CHAPTER SIXTEEN

WE TREK BACK TO THE PLANTATION sticking to the side streets and alleyways. Peace Officer patrols have steadily increased during the day and the main road is now bristling with them. Whether they are looking for us or not, it isn't worth getting close enough to find out.

The small pocket of dense two-story buildings passes quickly to single-story homes and business—their growing lawn sizes help us measure our progress. The sun is beginning its final plunge into twilight when we reach the seedy part of town.

With daylight fading, the red glow of neon reshapes the world. The white uniforms of the plantation workers glow red as they stumble out of buildings on their way back to their bunks.

Cornelia pulls Gette close and Victor starts walking a little faster—his footfalls nip at my heels. Charles on the other hand is totally oblivious and is entirely engrossed with what is going on through the window next to us.

"Come on Charles, best not to dawdle here."

"I know Cora, but—" Charles stands transfixed, mouth agape, at the kaleidoscope dancing behind the glass. "Look, it's the Brawl Ball championship. Einsam versus Lufthaffen."

"It's getting dark Charles—we should really be getting back," Cornelia's eyes dart around to the smoldering piles of cigarette butts, smashed liquor bottles, and soot-trampled flyers offering a good time.

"Let me just pop in real quick, check the score—I'll be right behind you."

Cornelia sighs, "Alright, but be quick—I don't want you to get locked out. No telling what happens if you do."

"Thanks Cora, I'll just be a minute."

Cornelia and Gette waste no time and resume their march with long strides. They're growing smaller like the trick people do to 'go downstairs' by squatting a little lower each time they step in place. But they aren't playing a trick, they're walking up the hill. It's then I realize my feet refuse to move.

"Evelyn, everything okay?" Victor says moving to my side.

I turn around to Charles still glued to the window. "You mind if I tag along?"

Charles blinks then turns to look at me. "You're a Crusader fan?" he says quizzical.

I shake my head no. "No, not a fan. Mother and I always called it Blood Ball. I don't understand the appeal of it. But I—"

I pause to even find the meaning for myself. "My dad watched it—every Sunday. I guess, I guess—" The words catch in my throat. I've been trying not to think about him.

Arrest her!

Why? Why would he do that? Why did he let Mother die?

My memories are all jumbled up now. If I replay my life, it should have a different ending. Father was always the supportive one, the one who kissed my cheek when he came home late smelling of coffee and cigarettes. It wasn't Mother. She was either pushing me away or clutching me so close I couldn't breathe. But I know that's all wrong now. I couldn't see it then—and I certainly can't see it all now. All I know is that she loved me, and he let her die.

Charles' heavy hand falls on my shoulder cementing the world back into place. "No need to explain. Come on, you and your shadow here," he jabs a finger in Victor's chest knocking him off balance for a moment, "are more than welcome to join me."

He smiles wide and toothy. It leaps across the air between us and curls up on me.

"Come on," he beckons, leading us into the airlock.

The hum of neon, crunch of soot, and rumble of traffic outside gives way to the clattering of pint glasses, booming laughter, and guttural cheers for the Brawlers locked in desperate melee on a dozen screens around the bar. Two rows of wooden booths with cracked red-leather seats are full to bursting and the long bar that wraps the length of the room. It's crammed with patrons desperately trying to balance their beers on slivers of free counter space. The smell of malt, hops, salt, and fried food sends my rumbling stomach into flips.

"Here," Charles shouts pointing to a small open space under a window. I gave him a thumbs-up unconvinced my voice will carry over the din. The space against the wall is narrow and we only just barely squeeze into it shoulder-to-shoulder. Charles doesn't seem to notice at all—transfixed on the screen, his surroundings appear to melt away from him and he is lost in the Ironclad's desperate surge toward the summit. Victor, however, seems far more enticed by the chaotic mix of plantation workers and farmhands, and when he thinks I won't notice, me.

It isn't a new look—he's been making it from the moment I smashed my elbow into his eye—but this close to him, the intensity is almost too much to endure. Electric tension is radiating from his arm—an arm trying its best to get as close to me as possible without actually touching me. I know he likes me. The looks, the way he follows me like a puppy. The way he waits for me to talk before he gives out his opinion to avoid contradicting me. He's genuine, brave, and, if I'm being honest, handsome. But he looks at me with lightning bolts in his eyes—a tempest barely contained under his skin yearning to tear free. I look at him and feel nothing.

I fix my eyes on the screen to avoid slipping him a glance that will only stoke the flames further. We're that age—I've had the talk—and it's not like I don't want something to happen. It's just…

I shake my head, breaking the train of thought, and re-focusing on the prismatic carnage on the closest screen. Two formations of Brawlers are arrayed on the field. The Einsam Ironclad—gleaming in silver and blue armor—are formed up into a wedge on the left of the central flat while the red and white Lufthaffen Vandals are arrayed like a diamond. I step up on my tiptoes and cup my hands around my mouth to better shout at Charles.

"Why are they formed up like that?"

Charles turns away from the screen with a smile so wide it's as if he's waited his entire life for somebody to ask.

"Well you see the time there in the bottom, right? That means the Ironclad only have ninety seconds left to tie up the game." Floating holograms show the score six to nine. "They need to score on this next tilt or they're done for. That's why they chose the flying wedge," Charles brings his hands together into a point and gestures a quick thrust. A passing waitress deftly avoids getting hit in the temple while holding a tray full of beers frothing over the rim. I watch her glide away—her body slinking and graceful like a panther. Charles continues oblivious to the calamity he almost caused.

"The flying wedge is like a spear. Coach Stueben knows his stuff. He'll lead them to victory." Then, without warning, Charles puffs up his chest and bellows like a war horn. "Urrah Einsam!"

My eyes flutter and I stumble back a step from the sudden assault. A moment later, the bar echoes Charles' cry.

"Urrah Einsam! Whoop whoop whoop." The crowd pumps their fists into the air with each guttural whoop. The chant still reverberating off their lips, the patrons chug their pint glasses and slam them down in almost perfect unison. Charles, not having a pint, slams his right foot against the ground.

Glasses clash. Feet stomp. Then silence descends like a hammer. My hackles stiffen, my fingers dig themselves into my palms. Teeth clenched—I'm transfixed on the screen. The bar drops away. There is only the arena and the spear ready to kill.

Breet. The whistle blow unleashes the final tilt. The Ironclad's spear charges up the sloped hill—the Vandal's shield surges forward to stop them. The flag-bearer raises the white flag high. The Ironclad chant out "Urrah Einsam!" and the crowded arena and the bar shout in response "whoop whoop whoop." Brawlers clash. Cleats tear into grass and shins and legs alike. Bones snap and the camera zooms to see their twisted angles. The white flag dips then resurfaces in a tangled sea of blood and pain. A small group breaks out from the writhing heap. They sprint up the steep slope toward the goal—the flag now tattered and splattered with red. A lone Vandal throws his arms out to stop them. The lead Crusader—a hulking brute of a man with muscle exploding from under his jersey—grabs the Vandal by the oxygen cables running along his helmet and wrenches him to the ground without losing his stride. The flag-bearer doesn't flinch. Crumbled on the grass before him, the flag-bearer plants his cleats on the Vandal's unprotected neck and kicks off. Blood fountains.

Unchecked, the Ironclad reach the summit and hoist the

flag up the goal post. The arena and the bar erupt with joy. Beer sloshes and voices shout themselves hoarse. I feel dirty—an unwitting accomplice to a crime. Everyone, so transfixed before, is looking anywhere but the screen—high-fiving and congratulating each other on a victory they had nothing to do with but take credit for all the same. No one is looking at the screen and the growing tendril of crimson dripping down the black field.

The game goes into overtime but it's over before the round of victory drinks hits the tables. The Ironclad won the overtime coin-toss, arrayed themselves in formation, and barreled up the pitch like thunder. The second spear tore through the Vandal's shield as easily as the first and half a minute later their white flag—a crisp, blindingly clean one—flaps over the goal post. The events happened so fast that most of the people in the stadium, and most people in the bar, were still lost in their revelry from the play before. When the bar realizes that their beloved Ironclad have won, the chant starts anew. This time, however, it ends in a fizzle rather than a roar.

The heat of the moment fades away. Every table scrambles to settle their tab and rush back home or to their bunk on the plantation.

Charles springs away from the wall grabbing Victor and I by the arm.

"Let's hurry up and get out of here before there's a rush on the airlocks."

Our feet agree, and we find ourselves back outside before the crush.

The sun is gone now—fading bands of purple and indigo struggle to project their light into the coming onslaught of deepest black. Charles leads with a brisk pace—his longer legs forcing me to the edge of running to keep up. Ahead, the plantation is illuminated like a city in miniature. Thousands of little lights silhouette the plantation's sprawling enormity against the night sky. A glance over my shoulder shows the extent of the town to be little more than we had seen today and a scattering of small homes and gas stations on the hills. One cluster of lights seems at odds with the tiny hamlet. On the grassy bluff where nothing stood taller than a shrub this morning, a ring of red lights tricks me for a moment that the sun has not dropped away after all.

There is a small line at the re-entry gate, so Charles slows his pace. My legs shout with joy—I hadn't realized how steep that incline really was. I form up behind Charles then turn around to watch the twinkle of the town. In the corner of my eye, I see myself reflected in Victor's visor—his eyes sparkling amber.

"That was a hell of a game huh?" Victor says absently rubbing his neck. My thoughts turn to the poor man and my hand can't help but paw at my own neck.

"I don't get the point of it. Games are fun—who doesn't like to play? But did he have to kill that man? Why not just step over him? They would have scored anyway."

Victor turns his gaze back to the town. "You're right. That was senseless." From his tone, I hear the unspoken *but*—he can't bring himself to disagree with me.

"Senseless," Charles says turning around, "but damn the Ironclad know how to finish a game. I thought we were lost for sure then—" Charles knives the clenched fingers of one hand through the other.

Victor whips back around. "Damian would have been so pissed—he was a Vandal through and through." His words started with joy but trailed out of his mouth bitter.

A figure steps out of the darkness behind Victor and clasps him on the back.

"What's this I hear about you being a Vandal fan?" The figure puts his fist up as though to attack. My hackles raise, blood thickens in my veins.

Victor steps back—his hands raised in defense.

"No, not me. My friend Damian. He always said the Vandals would win the championship one day."

The figure laughs. He steps closer bringing his face into the light. It's Boss.

"I'm just joking with you kid. You can like whatever team you want." He clasps a meaty hand on Victor's shoulder and pulls himself close.

Though his breath is safely contained within his rebreather, his rosy cheeks, sweaty brow, and fumbling demeanor are proof enough that he's had more than a few victory pints.

His eyes dart up, noticing me. "I didn't know you liked the

Brawl, Girl? Why didn't you say so?" he says making the suds clinging to his mustache dance.

Without warning, he stumbles from Victor's shoulders onto mine. He is a big man who would have been heavy enough, but his stupor has turned him into a semi-sentient potato sack—my heels dig into the soft ground. Before I can collapse, Charles swoops in pulling the heap off me and throwing the weight onto his own shoulder.

"Urrah Einsam!" Charles says instantly defusing Boss's confusion.

Belches of "whoop whoop whoop" erupt along the queue and echo down the valley.

We pass through the gate with little fanfare—the blue light sweeps us, the amber light flicks to green, and the gate raises letting us through. Methodical, mechanical, we march lockstep. We follow the same path that led us out in the morning and before long we're rounding the final corridor into C-42.

The bay is half full. They either never left—having decided a good book and some quiet was rest enough—or they returned early to avoid the mad dash for the restrooms. Charles hands Boss off to one of the sycophants from his bunk then rushes over to say hello to Cornelia and Gette.

It's late and the thought of returning to work in the morning makes my skin crawl. Cornelia and Gette have already showered and are curled up on Gette's bunk flipping through a magazine.

I take one look at the long line of drunk and stumbling people queued for the restroom and decide to tough it out.

I say goodnight, strip down to my jumpsuit, then slide into my bunk and close my eyes. Excited murmurs and talk of the game linger for hours as I fight to find sleep among visions of blood, gallows, and peach pie.

———

The mechanical dawn forces me awake. The line for the lavatory snakes down the bay. Ice radiates from the floor through my bare feet.

"Just until Martyr's Day," I whisper to myself as I pick up my toiletry bag and take my place in line.

CHAPTER SEVENTEEN

WHEN THE FINAL COMMAND BARKS at me to return to my bunk, I'm as brittle as glass. It's weeks' end and I've made little headway in understanding the rhyme or reason behind my actions. Every day I follow the commands static-blasted at me through the helmet and each day I get a little more compliant. Twelve days in, I'm completing each enigmatic twist, pull, or dial faster now so I'm rewarded with more of them.

Since the game, Boss has changed his attitude toward me. He still calls me girl, but his comments are now only in jest. This subtlety is often lost on his sycophants who cannot make up their minds to glare or smile at me—their faces are, as a result, often twisted up in grimaced smirks.

The glop has grown less palatable—something I wouldn't have believed a week ago—and even though I'm eating it, I can feel the gaps between my ribs widening. My eyes are sunken and heavy. The feeling is worse in the hour or so before each meal. The ache explodes—threshing across my skin to cover me in an itch I cannot scratch. Eating the glop numbs the ache and forces it back into the pit of my stomach but it never goes away.

The routine is unyielding. Tears come as often as panic attacks. *Just until Martyr's Day* I tell myself and count to four. It's enough to keep me going but only just.

Today, like all the days before it, ends with aching feet and a terrible biting lump in my stomach. I stumble into the barracks a little slower than everyone else and find the snaking queue already wrapped around the room. As usual, Victor is holding our bunk's place while Charles, Cornelia, and Gette share what precious little family time they can steal.

"I'm so ready for a break. Kick my feet up, get a slice of pie, and be anywhere but here," Victor says making space for me at the end of the line.

I crack a beleaguered smile. "I'm about ready to chop my feet off and buy some new ones. You think someplace in town sells new feet?"

Victor scratches his chin smiling. "I think I saw a bit and bobble shop, they should have a pair."

"Get to sawing then!" I say, already feeling lighter.

The line shuffles forward as the first bunk exits the lavatory and the second bunk enters.

The television nearest us is unobstructed now. Fire and smoke dance in the display while three tickertapes scroll beneath it with information relevant and not. Atop the footage are bold white letters: *So-called 'Citizen's Liberation Army' claims responsibility for fresh wave of attacks.*

Victor's eyes grow solemn. He jabs a finger at the screen, "Can you believe this? I thought subversives were the bad guys. Who are these people?"

I lose myself in the projected chaos—eyes desperately hoping to make sense of the competing text whizzing by. *Subversion in the heartland. How to tell if your children have been compromised. Reports of failed coup heroically stopped on the steps of the People's Acropolis. Foreign armies spilling across the northern border. Mountain Air stock up 19%.*

"Whoever they are," I say, "I don't think they're alone—how many groups were just waiting for the violence to start before they spilled out of the woodwork?"

Victor opens his mouth to respond but Boss's procession cuts him off.

"You two wouldn't be thinking about joining up with the CLA would you?" Boss says accusing us with a crooked finger. "We'll have to drag you down to town hall and string you up like rats." He pantomimes a noose around his neck. His fat gray tongue sticking out—his hands convulsing.

Victor's hands clench to fists—his eyes dart to me.

"You mean I'll get to hang out all day? Sign me up," I say and throw my fist up into the air.

Boss doubles over in laughter—a heartbeat later his entourage joins in.

"I like you girl," he says wiping a tear from his eye, "and your little boyfriend here." Boss throws an open hand at Victor catching him in the chest. He stumbles back, his face a firework display of embarrassment.

"*Hang* out," Boss says prompting himself into another fit of laughter. Still laughing, he moves to his bunk—his groupies scuttle along behind him anxiously trying to match their master's ebb and flow of laughter.

Alone again, Victor turns toward me hands raised. "He shouldn't joke like that."

"You mean that you're my boyfriend?" I jab at him.

Volcanos don't glow as bright and hot as Victor's face. "I don't know what on earth you two are talking about," his eyes search frantically for a distraction—he starts to itch at his arm.

I try to defuse the situation—everyone seems to be enjoying the joke but Victor and it's cruel to let him squirm.

"You're right—I have no idea what he's talking about," I say looking away to give him one less thing to make him nervous. I fixate on the screen and shuffle forward absently until it's our turn.

The shower is cold and saps the last bit of energy I have. Crawling into my bunk, I pass out before my head hits the pillow.

The artificial dawn provided by long humming fluorescent ceiling panels washes over me like rain. The walk into town is refreshing. The day is clear and bright—thin clouds cut the light into beams illuminating the contours of the valley. On the bluff where we saw the ring of lights last week there is a ringed palisade of cement barriers, concertina wire, and a small huddle of mobile buildings covered in thick cables snaking off to generators and satellite dishes. The presence of soldiers, though disquieting, quickly fades from my attention—their olive green and black paint scheme helping them disappear from sight and mind.

The slithering white stream of workers splinters as we pass the neon-drenched bars and brothels on the edge of town. Two Peace Officer cruisers stalk down the street toward us. Cornelia is in the lead, so we follow her as she splits off Main Street and guides us through the side streets. Heading deeper into the neighborhood, the homes are older and more well-kept. Fleets of children, laborer's, and domestic robots prune, paint, and sweep each home under the foliage of shockingly green and leafy trees.

Moving closer to the trunk of a towering oak, I run my hand along its rough bark. Shivers of electric excitement shoot up my arm from my fingertips dancing to the delight of the unnatural sensation. I look up its trunk to its full emerald canopy—golden light catches the leaves swaying in the gentle morning breeze. I close my eyes and run my fingers along the contours of the bark.

Cynicism snaps me back to reality—a tingle in my gut pulls my eyes downward. The ground around the tree is black from soot and ash—the dirt desiccated nearly to sand. *Trees can't grow in soil like this*. My eyes fan out from the base looking for clues and stop on a white metal stick hammered into the ground a foot from the roots. I look up and down the street and find hundreds more of them ringing each of the luscious trees.

I kneel next to the closest spike and wipe away the dirt revealing the logo. *Nurture-spike a Green Thumb product*.

Before leaving the neighborhood, I turn back to look at the stone and iron monument proclaiming *Welcome to Green Gardens* at the corner of Industry Avenue and Coal Drive.

***

Martha's is packed. Mary-Anne is handling the customers and their orders while two older women—who appear almost like clones of Mary-Anne twenty and forty years apart—bring trays of bread and stacks of pies in white boxes out from the back. We press ourselves against the far wall letting the smell of the bakery wash over us as we stalk the table we sat in last week waiting for an opening. A middle-aged man in work overalls is sitting with a woman ten years his junior in an orange and white dress. With them are two small boys and a girl nearly my age. Empty plates covered with pie crumbs ring the table. The man is still drinking his coffee, but the rest of the family is itching to leave. The woman takes one look at us hovering near the table and goes white.

"Herald," she says in a whisper meant to be overheard. "Those rats want our table. I bet they're foreigners Herald. Laura says the plantation is full of them."

Herald sets his coffee down. His wife and kids follow his gaze and land on me—their little freckled faces scrunch up. The littlest one—a boy of six nearly Gette's age—brings his hands to his puckered mouth pantomiming rat-like teeth and sucks his tongue against his three twisted front teeth. The mocking slurping sound hits me like a slap. His father shoots him a disapproving look but doesn't stop him.

"Come on kids. Let's go pick out your new masks." The family scoots back and jumps up in a chorus of screeching wood on wood.

"I want a *Lux* daddy," says the mocking little snot.

The mother sweeps her arms out corralling the kids toward the exit and putting herself between us. I catch the eye of the older girl as she's putting her mask on. She stops, mouths 'sorry,' then follows her family out through the malfunctioning airlock.

Charles scoffs in disbelief then takes the first chair. I sit next to him and help the others gather up the plates into a stack and wipe the crumbs into a pile.

Mary-Anne notices us over the line of customers at the counter. "Hi folks. I'll be with you in just a minute." She ducks back down to the register—the check spindle full to the point.

"Can you believe that crap?" Charles says jabbing a thumb toward the airlock.

"No," Victor says shaking his head, "I really can't. We're not that different—them and us. Can't they see that?"

"We need to remember that," says Cornelia. "It's easy to forget our shared humanity when we're scared."

"Why'd they call us rats, mommy?"

Charles and Cornelia share an uncomfortable look. Victor leans over and takes Gette's hands in his. "That's a thing people say when they don't know who you are. People are scared right now. But don't let it bother you, kiddo."

Gette smiles and seems reassured enough. I feel unsatisfied with the answer and I think Charles and Cornelia feel the same by the way they're both wringing their hands under the table. I try to shovel the disparate facts and emotions I have toward the phrase into a cohesive answer, but the words crumble in my mouth.

Mary-Anne emerges from the line to save us.

"Welcome back. Coffee and peach pie again?"

"Please and thank you," exclaims Gette. Mary-Anne chuckles revealing a pearly white smile.

"Let me just clean this all away and I'll be right back with your pie."

———

Our enjoyment of the peach pie lingers long after we leave

Martha's. Not wanting a repeat of the week before, we decide to steer clear of the shops in the main square and go to Patriot Park. Passing under the archway, dead yellow grass and barren soot-stained trees stretch out before us. Three gazebos form a triangle around a roughly circular pond—brackish coal-black water percolates from its central fountain.

Each gazebo has a zip-around urethane jacket. The closest two ones are full of picnickers. A small generator on the roof recycles and filters the air—its own black cloud of ash drifting peacefully above it like campfire smoke.

Walking past one of the gazebos, a feast of fried chicken, succotash, and mashed potatoes is laid out on a red-and-white checkered blanket. Each dish sits under glass domes nearly opaque from the condensed steam and heat inside. Mothers sit talking while fathers lord over brimming coolers of cola and beer. One group of kids is playing touch-brawl ball while two other little boys expertly pilot a kite in the gentle but steady winds blowing across the field.

I pick a spot on the gazebo's long bench near the middle. Watching the picnickers, my tongue searches for any remnants of the pie clinging to my teeth. The search yields nothing spurring my already growing hunger to writhe uncomfortably in my gut. I turn my attention away from the sputtering fountain—its babbling *glops* only making matters worse—to the kite gliding above us. A black diamond with blue and silver streamers, the kite is mesmerizing.

"Boy that pie was good," Charles says rubbing his stomach and staring intently at the hot lunch steaming a gazebo away.

"It's probably the best I've ever had. But I don't think we should talk about food, not unless we plan to get some," Cornelia says.

"You're right, momma. We should go back and get more pie."

"Little girls can't live on pie alone."

"Why not? I'm your little sweetie, aren't I? Papa says so. How am I supposed to stay so sweet if I don't eat enough pie?"

Cornelia's face twinkles with her smile. She shakes her head no, "What's something else to talk about? Anyone want to talk about their week?"

Thoughts of the week cluster up in my mind as a single monotone mass. I'd rather forget them than try to dissect and make sense of them. Gette shakes her head side-to-side, violently.

"Well," Victor starts, his mouth open ready to speak. I lean forward curious. "Nope. Not a thing."

Charles chuckles leaning back into the railing. "You had me going there for a minute. I thought you were going to say you liked it or something."

"God no," Victor snaps.

"Well," Cornelia imitates his pause, "what about the game?" She gestures toward the kids playing nearby. A girl in pigtails knocks over a little boy and scores a point. "You were so insistent to go last week, and you hardly said more than 'they won.'"

"It was a pretty great game actually. The Ironclad were down by three and then *wham!*" Charles reenacts the game with his hands by smashing a fist into a flat palm. "They drove the game into overtime and won."

"The crowd was really into it too," says Victor. "It was fun. It felt like old times sitting with Damian and dreaming of making it big."

"Yeah," Charles wraps an arm around Victor, "Damian was always our hope at breaking out of the Under City."

There isn't much for us to be happy about, but I can't sit here any longer listening to them reminisce about that game like everything was fine. It's not fine, and it should never be okay. Someone died, and we cheered and laughed.

"A player died, remember? How can you two talk about it like it's no big deal?"

Charles's face turns to steel. "Because it isn't a big deal. I'm sorry to disappoint you kid but if you haven't noticed how the world works by now, I don't know what to tell you."

"Charles!" snaps Cornelia. "I can't believe the way you're talking to Evelyn."

Charles snaps back. "I'm not the one always claiming to be high-and-mighty. This world is cruel. People die. And sometimes you have to kill those people."

"Papa," Gette's trembling hand rests on his arm to calm him.

"That's not what I'm saying Charles. Look let's just—"

"No, don't tell me to calm down. I won't apologize for the way things are. I didn't make them that way, and I've fought my whole life to change them. Don't lecture me on right and wrong. You don't know what it's really like to have nothing. To come from nothing."

Fire boils under my skin and I desperately want to let it out. But I hold my tongue because he isn't wrong. Crossing my arms, I sit and listen.

"You're right, killing is wrong. What the Caretakers do—the way they force us into an early grave with nothing in our brains or bellies—that's unforgivable. But judging the Brawlers for playing a game—a game that brought them out of the Under City, a game that gave them and their families' food and education—I can't just sit here and listen to that."

"He's right," Victor says. Siding with Charles against me is tying him in knots. He tugs at his mask with a sweaty hand. "There aren't many ways to get out of the Under City. Damian was always big and strong, and we all hoped he would be our ticket out. He got blacklisted from tryouts and he spiraled out of control. If Mr. Herrington hadn't of been there to straighten him out," he pauses—eyes glistening. "I don't even want to think of what would have happened."

"I had no idea," I say sickened by my ever-present ignorance.

"That's my point. You're so quick to judge everything."

"To be fair Charles, you and I haven't always made the best decisions. Evelyn may be naïve about some things but who isn't? She follows her heart and you can't berate her for that. Not while I'm here at least."

Charles sighs.

"I didn't mean to explode, Evelyn. It's just so damn frustrating being powerless. I couldn't save Bernard, the fate of my family is in the hands of a man I know nothing about, we can't afford to feed ourselves a proper meal. I just—"

I rest my hand on his knee. Raising the corners of my lips into a smile knocks a tear loose from my eye. Salt seeps through clenched lips.

He takes my hand in his. The fire of the argument has burned away but tension still hangs heavy in the air.

We each turn to our own distractions. The pond, the game, the billowing kite. I try to focus on the boundaries of the park and the mansions hidden in the trees.

A distant whine edges its way into consciousness. I scratch at my ear. The tone rises. Assuming it's a fly, I turn to engage the pest. The air shimmers with the falling flecks of soot but no flies are buzzing.

The sound grows even louder. Instinctively, I turn my eyes to the sky. A black plane, flying low and fast over the wooded hill, is screaming toward the town. Terror grips me.

"Look," I say pointing to the approaching aircraft as I stand. Everyone turns to look. Heads tilt up. The brawlers stop their game.

A heartbeat passes and the plane is looping above downtown. Without warning, red streaks fill the sky emanating from the Guardian battlements on the bluff. The plane dips its wings back and forth pirouetting through the hail of cannon fire. The *doof-doof-doof* of anti-air artillery rumbles over the valley. A Victory siren whirrs to life adding its high-pitched drone to the chorus.

The plane's right wing bursts into flame. A door on the side swings open. They're small but I can make out someone leaning out of the opening. A cloud of white papers plumes out the door. Another round crashes through the fuselage ripping the plane in half. The front half spirals toward the ground belching oily black smoke and red-orange flames. The tail section flits and bobs like a dropped piece of paper but it too is falling fast. Caught in the middle, the figure standing at the door is flung away. They plummet—a little black dot against a muddy blue sky—disappearing behind the trees and buildings on the edge of the field.

Following their descent, my heart jolts when my eyes track past the horizon.

The world rushes into silence—time oozes—then everything snaps back into place with a boom. The fuselage explodes on impact sending a mushroom cloud of smoke high into the air. The siren waxes and wanes its shrill alarm like the heartbeat of chaos. More tracers light up the air. A formation of black planes is swooping down from the north toward the battlements.

"Citizens! Follow me to the air-raid shelter." A tall, thin woman in a denim work frock is waving a red flag—a dark blue armband wrapped tightly around her bicep.

I look to Cornelia and Charles. The *doof-doof-doof* is deafening. The black diamond in the sky unleashes its own barrage at the bluff—dark green streaks tracing the carnage. Another plane bursts into flame then explodes violently. A torrent of searing hot metal fragments and flame rains over the town.

"Citizens!" the Blue Band cries again.

"Stay close!" Charles says as he scoops up Gette then leaps down the gazebo's three short steps. We spring to action and dart across the field. The other families have abandoned their picnics. The brawler's flag flutters on the ground—the kite soars away lost amidst the tracers and clouds of flak. Huddled together we move like a flock of frightened ducks wobbling back and forth—our destination uncertain.

The Blue Band leads us through the park's gates. Halfway across the parking lot she throws her hand up.

"Get down!" she commands. We obey, throwing ourselves down to the asphalt. It digs into the meat of my palm. The formation of planes whooshes overhead. Bullets snap and hiss above us and shrapnel turns up the earth on the embankment in front of us.

"Up! Follow me."

Standing, the pain in my hand is stinging and rivulets of blood bead down my wrist. Running in the rebreather is taxing. I'm already out of breath. Only the will to survive propels me forward. Victor takes my hand urging me on.

"We'll get through this," he says through heaving breaths.

The thin woman opens the gate of a house with a freshly white-washed fence.

"Quick, into the cellar."

She lifts the air-raid shelter's double doors open—small hydraulics keep the heavy steel from crashing down on our heads. I follow Charles down—still holding Gette like a stuffed animal under his arm. Victor and Cornelia are right on my heels.

The cellar is dark and cold, but it feels safe and already the thundering of the battle overhead is deadened. I grope my way through the dark to the back and slide to the floor. My heart pounds and everything is starting to swim. *Just breathe, Evelyn. Just breathe.*

"Deep breaths," I say to myself and anyone who's listening.

The other families finish stumbling in and the Blue Band pulls the doors shut. As they close, most of the sound fades away leaving behind only a faint whisper of what's going on outside. She fumbles around in the dark producing three small kerosene lanterns from a metal cabinet.

"We're safe here everyone. I'll pass out some water, but we need to remain quiet until we hear the 'all-clear' signal. Is that understood?"

"We comply," says one man but most of us just nod, too shaken for words.

We scoot in close to each other. I close my eyes. Explosions rumble through the earth and into my bones.

———

The raid only lasted for a few minutes after we found shelter in the cellar, but the all-clear took over an hour to sound. A single, long drone left to reverberate into a shrill vibrato that seemed to build and build forever until one moment it wasn't there.

The Blue Band opens the cellar standing at the top to help us out. The sky is thick with smoke. The wail of fire trucks and ambulances fills the air.

"We should get back to the plantation," says Charles. He tries to pick Gette up again but she stops him.

"It's okay Papa. I can walk."

"You're right," I say. "Lead the way."

Charles nods then bounds off toward the plantation. He's moving fast. I have to put my head down and really move to keep up. It's hard to keep pace and pull my eyes away from my feet, but I chance a few glances back at town. Streams of water cut vanishing slices in the columns of black smoke. The bluff is cratered and smoking, but the battlements seem to be intact. *I hope Mary-Anne is okay.*

Coming to the edge of town we slow to make our way through the crush of workers trying to get back up the hill to the plantation. Panicked, the group is being corralled by Blue Bands, Peace Officers, and Reinhardt Guards. A swell in the mob pushes me against the wall. I struggle to keep my feet on the soot-slick cobblestones.

I crash down hard, landing on my already injured hand. I wince and turn my hand over to inspect the damage. To my surprise, clung to the blood on my hand, is a pamphlet. Soot stained and now speckled with blood I pull it free and sneer at the renewed pain.

The Citizen's Liberation Army Fights for You! The Caretakers Lie. Foreigners burn our cities! Stand with your fellow patriots. Fight for the CLA! - First Patriot Ursula Fowler.

I clamber to my feet awkwardly—my full attention fixed on the small, blood and soot-covered paper. I read it again, then again. Is the CLA just a cover for the subversives program, or is this something new, something more? How can anyone fight in a civil war and not know what side they're fighting on? Transfixed on the page, I don't notice him approach.

A large man looms over me—my peripheral vision picks him up first. If they're a Blue Band or a Peace Officer, I'm screwed.

Boss grabs the flyer from my hand.

"What are you thinking girl? You can't be seen holding one of these." Crumbling the paper in his fist, he shoves it into the front pocket of his jumpsuit. Charles pushes through the crowd to me.

"Are you alright?"

"Yeah, I'm fine. Boss here was helping me up." Boss shoots me a stern look.

"You owe me, kid." He points an accusing finger then disappears back into the mob. Anxiety tugs at the back of my ears—a primordial warning that I'm being hunted. I look through the faces in the crowd. Everyone is turned toward the Reinhardt's Guard Captain who is blowing a whistle and demanding we line up single file. All but one. The coal-eyed-woman is burrowing her eyes into me. Unsure of what she saw, and powerless to do anything about it, I file into line behind Victor and march back up to the plantation.

⎯⎯⎯⎯⎯

Behind us, Peace Officers sort out everyone but the plantation workers. They demand papers on the spot, and arrest all those who can't produce them. The Blue Bands punch and kick. No one does anything. Even me.

The value of Reinhardt's protection is greater than the roof over our heads. His business is valuable enough that the law turns a blind eye even when war rages around us. The thought of staying at the plantation flashes for a moment. We'd have a place to sleep, eat, and we'd be shielded from some of the Caretakers' muscle. But even as I mull the thought it turns to ash. We still don't know if Reinhardt is actually going to help us and we've still haven't learned his price. We might be able to survive here but I want more than that. I want to live. I want answers.

Guards shuttle us back to our bunks with drilled efficiency. They run a brief headcount—the Man-in-White double-checking everything on his own datapad—then leave us. When the click-clack of their boot heels echoes away into the next barracks we finally dare to move. Whispers grow frm a murmur to a roar. Each bunk is checking itself over. Is everyone okay? What did they see? Do they know who was flying the planes? Would they have to evacuate? So many questions fly around the room that it's impossible to remember which ones we asked each other or simply overheard.

Speculation is abundant but answers are hard to find and the excitement fizzles away. Some people sob. Others lie in their bunks pressing their pillows down hard over their eyes to try to sleep in the fluorescent brilliance of the room.

We sit along the bottom bunk together, holding hands and watching the tickertape run across the television closest to us. We had started to feel comfortable—we were building a routine—then reality came to shut it all down.

The tickertape blinks to black. Static fills the screen. Anticipation rises like the tide.

"Citizens of the Great Society."

Ice runs down my spine. I know that voice. The voice that haunts my nightmares: Ursula Fowler.

"Our nation is sick. Infested with foreign subversives and crippled by corrupt bureaucrats. I offer you a solution. I offer you fire to burn out the infection before it consumes—" static reclaims the television.

"Ouch," says Victor pulling his hand from mine—its red and covered with my blood. I look down at my clenched, bloody fist. My chest seethes.

"I'm sorry," I say thinly—the lack of oxygen catching me off guard.

"It's alright. It's like seeing the boogeyman."

The pixels snap back into form. Trumpets and ukuleles ring out a chirpy jingle.

Mythic Mountain has the fun. Mythic Mountain has great rides.

Come on over.

Clean fresh air and sunny days, you'll smile all your woes away.

Come on over.

Food and games for Jim and Jane our spirits will emancipate your brain!

Come on over.

Take a trip, come and see, all the parking is free.

Come on over.

Images of Mountain Air Brand's *Mythic Mountain Park* saturate the room in a whirlwind of primary colors.

"Safety is our middle name. Step inside the world's largest geodesic dome with not only one, two, but three layers of Trust Corp. safety glass to seal in all that Fresh Mountain Air™. Come on over and take your mask off. We won't tell." The cartoon woman winks then disappears into a shower of silver stars that morph into the toll-free telephone number. *Book your hotel and tickets through us and save, save, save!*

More commercials play but I'm too stunned to see them. The tickertape is gone; all live feeds have been disconnected. The television is just a revolving carousel of shiny colors, vapid songs, and high-pressure sales pitches.

"I need to lie down," I say climbing up to my bunk without waiting for a response. I hit the mattress hard. I stare into the fluorescents above me until the pain is too intense and I have to turn away, tears streaming. Everything has changed but everything has stayed the same. I turn over on my side hoping to will myself to sleep. I notice the coal-eyed-woman. But for once she isn't staring at me, she's staring at Boss who's gesticulating what appears to be his heroic survival and rescue story.

Competing realities fight in my mind until exhaustion pushes them both aside and I drift into a short and restless sleep. *Just until Martyr's Day.*

CHAPTER EIGHTEEN

ANXIETY FROM THE AIR RAID has smoldered into a nervous miasma. Each workday exhausts our demand for answers. We'd probably still be worked into a fever pitch, but we're totally locked in. Between the looping commercials and the enigmatic Man-in-White, nothing resembling an answer has been able to satiate us. Left no other option, we've turned inwards to cope. It's exactly what they want us to do: Domnhall, Fowler, Reinhardt, they all want us to atomize ourselves. Starving and alone, we'll bite onto the first crust of bread offered to us.

I've tried to fight it. To keep the conversation alive among the group. But ever-watchful eyes and ears hold my tongue. I know I'm giving *them* power over me—even thinking of my oppressors in this way feeds the paranoia. Yet I can't figure a way not to.

I turn the gears when the voice commands. I eat the glop when the voice commands. And I return to my bunk when the voice commands. *Only until Martyr's Day* isn't breaking down the walls but it's keeping me in the fight.

Gette has lost some of her sparkle. The life that shone so freely in her eyes weeks ago, is now little more than a smoldering echo. Charles has grown wafer-thin; his temper on a hair-trigger. Cornelia is stretched between the two. Her eyes grow heavier with each passing day.

And Victor. I can't avoid Victor. He's been trying desperately to get my attention. To have me help him through this. But the closer he tries to get, the harder it is for me to even look at him. His every attempt to connect pushes me away like a magnet flipped the wrong way round. He wants something more and I know—no matter how persistent he remains—that nothing will grow. It seems harsh, but you can't blame a seed for not growing when it tries to take root in sand.

When florescent sunrise dawns on rest day a renewed vigor fuels my step. One way or another, next week will change things. Either Reinhardt will deliver on his promise and we can get out of here or the ruse will come to light. It makes no difference. We aren't going to spend another week in this ill-begotten place.

Gette wakes up as I'm returning to the bunk from the lavatory. The barracks is mostly empty now—most people wake before 'dawn' to get ready to bolt out the door as soon as the time-lock clicks open. Only our bunk and a few stragglers, content to read on their bunks all day, remain. It seems the fear of another air raid—or worse—is less powerful than the desire to eat some real food, stretch their legs, and drink it all away.

"Let's go to Martha's and stay until we pop!" Gette says,

eagerly pulling on her rubber boots.

"We'll see darling—hopefully Martha's wasn't damaged," says Charles.

"I do hope Mary-Anne is okay. She seems like such a nice girl," Cornelia says helping Gette finish dressing.

I ruffle Gette's hair then help her mother carefully slip the rebreather over her curly auburn locks.

"Only one way to find out."

The day is dreary. Gray clouds block the sun intermittently separating to reveal a wet soup of ash and mud. Biting wind slows our walk into town. Regular patrols of Peace Officer cruisers have been augmented with Guardian Sentinels—their massive weight and smoke-belching engines rumble across the earth and chatter in the loose stones. The vibration is impossible to ignore as it bounces in my teeth and rattles up and down my spine. Their metal tracks leave slithering trails along the roads to mark the passage of the dragons.

We keep our heads low and change directions away from any foot patrols. Either the protection of Reinhardt's uniforms or dumb luck guides us past the park into the square.

Looking down at my feet, I don't notice the mass of people stopped in front of me and I crash into a man. I snap into the present and expect him to scold me, but when he turns, I'm aghast. Death twists his face. He looks away from me as if nothing happened—his full attention having never truly left the scene in front of him.

"What is it?" Cornelia asks.

We turn to Charles who's a head taller than all of us. His face is pallid, pulled back and aghast.

"Quick, Cora, get Gette out of here."

"Charles what is it?"

"It's—" the words choke in his mouth.

"Papa, I can see it! You never let me know what's going on." As quick as her words, Gette tears herself free of Cornelia's grasp. Mother and father attempt to grab her, but she's quicker than us all. She darts into the street to get around the crowd and see what they're looking at.

"Gette!" I cry out already on the move to catch her. Four long strides—I've almost got her. Focused on the chase, I fail to see it in time. Gette bursts into the street then stops cold as if turned to stone. Barreling toward her, I shift my weight to slow down. My feet slip out on the slick cobblestones of the street and I crash hard into the mud. My knee stings and tears cloud my eyes. I stumble toward Gette wrapping my arms around her. I start to speak—to tell her not to run into the street. The words form *what were you thinking*—but the sight before me chills me to silence.

Five swollen figures swing from the gallows. A man in denim overalls, a woman wearing an orange dress with white trim, two young boys—no older or bigger than Gette—and a girl. A girl no different than me. Herald—his name only exists as a faint echo of his wife's voice—and his family sway in the cold driving winds. Staked with nails to each of their chests is a soiled gray parchment. 'Rat' is scrawled onto each one in sloppy black paint.

I slam the lids of my eyes closed. Sorrow and rage boil. Clasping my hand over Gette's visor, I pull us from the street. Charles is there. He takes Gette into his arms, cradling her face into his shoulder.

"Make her look!" a mask-garbled voice barks from anonymity.

"Kill 'em all," demands another.

We race out of the square, into the alley, and press our way into Martha's. Gette is bawling. Victor looks like he's seen a ghost and I can't make heads or tails of what I'm feeling. I want to scream and cry and break things and glue them back together. I want to burn the world away and blow the fire out.

Enraged, I collapse against the mask cubbies and throw off my mask.

Footsteps announce her approach. She rests a warm hand on my shoulder.

"Is everything alright?" I open my eyes and see Mary-Anne up close for the first time. Freckles outline the soft curves of her nose and cheeks. Green eyes twinkle under berry-blonde eyebrows.

She notices Gette and helps her down from Charles's arms. As she pulls the mask from her, the intensity of her sobs grow.

"That little boy. We saw him here last week. He wanted to get a new mask. He made rat faces at me." Her words unleash a torrent of tears. Mary-Anne pulls Gette into her flour-covered apron.

"It's okay sweet girl, it'll be okay."

"No, it won't be. It'll never be okay again."

I want to tell her, "No, you're wrong. Everything will be okay again. You'll see, it'll all be okay." But I know each word of that is a lie. Nothing was okay before. It wasn't burning, intense, and constantly in your face, but it was always there.

Cornelia turns to the window biting on her fist to keep her own grief contained. Charles rains swollen tears that bead up and splatter on his boots. Victor is splintering glass an inch from breaking. I reach out and interlace my fingers with his.

Peach pie heals wounds no medicine can cure. Though her first few bites were splashed with tears, by the end of her second piece, Gette almost looks herself again. Around me, my red nose and blushed cheeks are mirrored on four solemn, but friendly, faces.

We stay at our table most of the day. Partly because we've no will to leave but mostly because business is slow—only a handful of people trickle in throughout the day to pick up bread and pastry orders. We watch as each customer struggles with the airlock. It was bad before, but now it seems to bind every time. Despite few customers, Mary-Anne is busy in the kitchen. She's all alone today—her mother and grandmother curiously absent.

After helping a woman through the airlock by prying it shut with the stick she keeps by the door for the umpteenth time, Mary-Anne pulls up a chair to our table and sighs.

"Hall came by yesterday. To look at the airlock. I guess between the planes crashing and tanks rumbling up and down the street, the building has sunk down almost a foot. He's had to order a special jack to fix it." She pauses letting out a long sigh. "And with the way things are going around here, there is no telling how long that'll take."

"That's got to be frustrating," I say.

"Tell me about it. I'm about to just rip the danged thing out and just bake in my mask."

Charles chuckles, "You know that's not a half-bad idea. I'll help you do it."

Mary-Anne smiles wide. "Tempting. But I'm so slammed with orders for Martyr's Day Pies. I'll just barely get them done this week."

"Are they still going to hold Martyr's Day celebrations? With all the fighting, I thought maybe they'd cancel them," says Cornelia.

"That'd be the smart move, but Mayor Warren is determined to," Mary-Anne sits up to better perform her impression, "resist the vulgarities of subversives and rebels. Citizens of the Great Society will not yield!" She laughs. "They're out in the park building the bleachers and setting up the pavilions already."

"That sounds fun. Can we go watch?" asks Gette.

"I'd steer clear if I were you," Mary-Anne replies, "Blue Bands are rounding everyone up to help. They'll have you there past midnight!"

"Maybe next week darling," Cornelia says.

Gette nods her head in understanding then returns to playing with her fork that's long since been scoured clean.

The only other customer in the store rises from his chair with a squeak.

"Thanks for the pie," he says tipping his brow as he dons his mask.

"Come again soon," Mary-Anne says waving him off.

He enters the airlock but halfway through its cycle it binds up—steam escapes through the cracks with an angry hiss. Mary-Anne rushes over, uses the stick to pry the door shut, then backs away shaking her head.

"I'm telling you—just rip it out," says Charles.

Mary-Anne smiles at him gesturing 'almost' with her

forefinger pinched over her thumb. She starts back toward the kitchen, stops, then walks to the window and flicks off the neon 'open' sign and draws the blinds.

My pulse quickens as she returns to the table.

"You seem like good people," she looks over her shoulders anxiously. "If you want to get out of town, I can help you get to the rail hub in Mansfield." We pass a quizzical look between us.

The question sizzles in the air.

Charles moves as though he's going to talk but stops short. Cornelia fills in the silence.

"Your offer is very kind. And I know a month ago we would have welcomed it without hesitation."

Mary-Anne fills in the blank. "But—"

"But," Cornelia continues, "we already threw our lot in with Reinhardt."

"Meaning no disrespect—trusting Reinhardt was a bad move."

"We didn't have a choice," I say.

"Not a good one at least," adds Victor.

Mary-Anne leans back, defensive. "What did he promise you?"

"Clean transit papers," I say.

Mary-Anne nods. "And you're supposed to get them soon?"

"Martyr's Day," says Charles.

Mary-Anne sighs. "If his promises evaporate—which I'm pretty sure they will—my offer will still stand. I'll help you get out of here before that place swallows you up."

Every fiber of my being wants to jump up and say yes. We don't need Reinhardt and we still have so many unknowns with him. We don't really know her either but it feels safer than sliding toward the abyss like we're doing now.

"We may just take you up on that," Cornelia says putting her hand on mine. I snap my attention to her and nod my consent.

If I were alone, I'd have left already. But I can't make impulsive choices. I have to think of the group.

An unfamiliar tension mixes with the cinnamon and sugar in the air. Mary-Anne pushes her chair back and stands. Reflexively we follow—how can we keep sitting here after that?

"I'm going to close up early today so I can try and get ahead on all my orders. Here, I'll help you out."

We pull our rebreathers on and proceed through the troublesome airlock. I go last and as I step into the airlock Mary-Anne pulls me around.

"Stay safe out there. And whatever you do, don't trust Reinhardt."

I feel my words will betray my apprehension with the choice we just made so I nod my understanding. The airlock hisses and squeals as it pumps out the clean air and deposits me back into the gloom outside.

The weight of the world crashes back down on all of us. Just above the constant rumble of the tanks is the twisting squelch of the nooses in the square. The sound grates against my already queasy stomach.

"Let's find another way back to the plantation, I'm not sure there's anyplace else for us to be out here," I say.

Charles beckons us with a swooping arm to follow him. We snake through the alley away from the square and get lost in the maze of cookie-cutter homes.

———

Back at the plantation, we take our time in the showers. With only a handful of others in the barracks we have the hot water all to ourselves. For the first time in weeks, the shower is a place of relaxation and escape. The bar soap leaves my skin waxy and dry, but the relief of the endless torrent of steaming water melts away so many aches I hardly notice.

The squelch of the gallows, the thunderous roar of guns, and the desperate cries of Mother linger on the edge of my thoughts. I fight them away with the few good memories I have. I chant Hannah's name in my mind like an incantation hoping to reveal more hidden memories.

I linger until my fingers and toes shrivel to prunes. *Just until*

Martyr's Day. I repeat it to myself as I slip into a fresh jumpsuit, carefully remove the infosphere from the hidden compartment in the old sleeve and sew it and the article into the new.

I wring my hair out in the towel amazed at how long it's gotten. I let it drape down in front—fanned out it covers my chest. Long split ends break open as it dries. I braid it together loosely and toss it over my shoulder. Hoping to crawl into bed early and sleep everything away, I push my way out of the lavatory.

I climb into my bunk, pull the thin sheet over my eyes and drift to sleep. My mantras keep the darkness from creeping in until sleep sneaks up and takes me.

Breet!

A shrill whistle blast shoots me awake. I spring up in my bunk and spin to face the challenge. Reinhardt's Guard Captain is still holding his silver metropolitan whistle to the lip port on his rebreather. Four OSS Specters file in behind him and surround the first bunk.

"Albert Konrad?"

Boss, trembling, stands from his bunk. "I… I'm Albe—"

The Specter closest to him thrusts his nightstick into his solar plexus. Boss crumbles to his knees gasping for air—his face twists in agony, tears stream from his eyes.

"Search his bunk," commands one of the Specters. The Specters obey mechanically. Their mirror-like geometric rebreathers erasing their humanity.

Grabbing the bedposts, they topple the bunk over. Steel hammers against concrete like thunder in the cramped room. The person on the top crashes on their shoulder—the all too familiar crunch of bone stabs at my stomach. My heart is pounding, and I can't look away.

The Specters pull long knives from their hips and slice into the thin mattress. Wadding billows. Another one rifles through Boss's pockets while the one who struck him clasps Boss's hands in cuffs.

The Specter pulls out a soot and blood crumbled paper from Boss's pocket.

Boss looks at the evidence held above him.

"I can explain, I—" Another sinister blow to his gut drops him back to the floor. Sobbing, Boss struggles to breathe in a growing pool of snot and tears.

Approaching footsteps clack on the polished concrete floors. The Man-in-White struts into the room with his data slate. He pulls a stylus from its holder at the top. His eyes don't stray from the display as he methodically checks boxes.

"Sergeant," he says his voice flat, "I'll need you to sign for damages."

The Specter Sergeant takes the outstretched stylus and scrawls his signature at the bottom.

"Initials here please," the Man-in-White says dryly tapping at an empty box in the middle.

The Sergeant makes his mark then tosses the stylus back to the bureaucrat.

A sharp snap of his heels commands the other Specters to move and as suddenly as they emerged, they disappear into the hall dragging Albert by the arms. The Man-in-White surveys the room, checks over his data slate, then nods to the Guard Captain. Snapping his heals together, the captain follows the Man-in-White out of the barracks. The door slides shut with a hiss.

Stunned silence grips us. No one dares move. Boss's bunkmates are grief stricken. One lets out a sob and then the dam bursts and they collapse into tears. A man from bunk two walks over to them and helps lift the bunk back into place. He leans in and whispers something to them and their tears dry up.

Everyone gets the message and the room busies to ignore what just happened.

"I thought we were done for," I say just above a whisper.

"That was awful," Charles says, "that was just awful. He should have fought back. I wouldn't want to die without fighting back."

"What good what that have done him?" Victor says. "He was on his knees before he even knew what was happening."

"That may be true. But I promise you all, if they try and take you away, I'll die fighting."

"You can't die papa," Gette says. I'm still in shock, I can hardly imagine how she feels.

Cornelia reaches up to stroke her daughter's hair. "No, of course not, darling. Your father is just upset. Right Charles?" Cornelia's look is more troubled then scathing.

"Don't worry darling, I won't let anything bad happen to you. I promise."

Gette's eyes dart back and forth between her parents. Swollen to bursting, she blinks away her tears.

I look away to keep my own composure. Behind closed eyes a maelstrom of destruction consumes everything I've ever touched. I open my eyes to escape the thought. In the bunk in front of me I notice a void in the beehive of people preparing for bed. One bunk has been empty the whole time. The coal-eyed-woman is gone.

Terror races down my spine. Apart from myself, who else knew he had picked up that flyer? Why didn't she report me? Uncertainty gnaws at me. I lay down to keep the nausea at bay.

Head spinning, conscious crying, I stare into the florescent lights above until they blink out.

CHAPTER NINETEEN

AN OCEAN OF ANXIETY swirls beneath my skin. The endless repetitive tasks of working hours come as a relief from the moments of anxious stillness in the barracks. Paranoia and secrecy have solidified the cliques into polarized blocks. Even the smallest perceived slight or misjudgment in our daily protocols unleashes a tirade of shouting and finger-pointing.

With each bunk vying to prove their loyalty is greater than any others, subscriptions of *Drumbeat* and *Caretaker's Quarterly* have skyrocketed. The automated commissary that wheels through the barracks sold out of blue armbands the morning after Boss's arrest. Bunks one and two secured the supply and have hoarded the rest to dole out only to those bunks that prove their unwavering devotion.

Tensions from the air raid, executions, and arrests are unwinding themselves into fanatic displays of patriotism. Bunk seven, too low on the pecking order to buy up patriotic magazines or paraphernalia, has focused their time on staging a skit for Martyr's Day. Not to be outdone, bunks four, five, and six have begun practicing their own tributes to our fallen patriots.

Going a step further, bunks one, two, and three have formed an alliance putting their collective effort behind a three-act musical. The working title is *The Great Patriot*. Collectively, they've blown their savings and meager weekly earnings to buy instruments and cloth for costumes at inflated 'wartime' prices.

With five productions underway, we've been able to keep to ourselves hidden in the far corner of the room. It's both a relief and a curse. Charles and Cornelia have decided it best we don't talk about anything 'colorful' to avoid prying ears or upsetting Gette. She's young, and the things she's witnessed in the last few weeks have hit her hard, but she's more resilient than they give her credit for. They are using her innocence as an excuse to ignore the reality we're sitting in. No one dares talk about what will happen with Reinhardt or whether we should have just accepted Mary-Anne's offer without really knowing what it was. Victor would probably take my side if I broached the subject, but he's been walking on eggshells all week trying to make everyone like him. His sentences don't come out in fluid strings anymore. Instead he lugs each word out past trembling lips.

Seeing Boss beaten has brought memories of Victoriana in the parade grounds to the forefront of my mind. Her defeated wails and the soul-splitting yowl of Cinnamon echo when I close my eyes. I know I didn't set Boss up. I didn't make him take that flyer nor did I make him keep it. Some of what happened was on him. But I can't deny I played a role. He was trying to help me. He got too close and the maelstrom tore him away.

As painful as my guilt over his arrest is, it's a pebble next to the boulder I drag around for Victoriana.

Victoriana was my scapegoat. Every slight against, every act of oppression—real or imagined—I attributed to her. Her flawless façade the perfect vessel for my own weaknesses and fears. But since my dream of Hannah things have been different. Some of the silver strings lingered and pulling on them has scratched away some ink from my redacted memories. Flashing reveries flit and tease at the edges of my recollection. Images of Victoriana vulnerable and sad. Hopeful and kind. Phantoms lurk at the periphery of that horrible day on the parade grounds reminding me that not only did I set up an innocent person to be tortured, I think she used to be my friend.

CHAPTER TWENTY

MARTYR'S DAY DAWNS. The dew of apprehension clings the sheets to my skin. Abuzz, each bunk has been humming since before the florescent panels above us flickered to life. My legs drop to the ground like sandbags and I wobble as I stand.

"Are you alright?" Victor says throwing an arm around my waist to steady me. His fingers fall into the growing gaps between my ribs.

"Yeah I—" I hesitate unsure if by uttering my fears into the world I'll create a self-fulfilling prophecy. His amber eyes peer into me—his hands hold me warmly.

I cast the dice. "I've got a bad feeling about today. I really think we've made a huge mistake. We should have left with Mary-Anne last week."

Ice replaces warmth as his hands drop down to his sides.

"I think you're right. It's been eating at me all week. I, I haven't been able to voice it."

The Standish family returns from the lavatory fresh and ready for the day in crisp white jumpsuits. A smile wiggles its way onto my face.

"Whatever happens today," I say to Victor then turn to Gette. "There will at least be lots, and lots of—"

"Pie!" she says bouncing into the air.

Charles and Cornelia smile—their faces gaunt.

"Well then, what are we waiting for?" Charles rubbing his hands together and dramatically smacking his lips.

We turn to leave then immediately stop in our tracks—the Man-in-White blocks our way. The Guard Captain and two other green uniformed Reinhardt security guards stand behind him.

"Happy Martyr's Day," says the Man-in-White.

"Happy Martyr's Day to you too," I reply. Adrenaline surges. The barracks falls away. Backed into a corner, I'm loaded and ready to fight.

"Miss Brennan, if you would kindly follow me, Master Reinhardt would like to finalize his transaction with you and your," his face breaks its usually placid veneer as it scrambles to find a diplomatic word. "Friends."

Breathe Evelyn. Just Breathe.

"Excellent," I say trying to control my tone. "We'll gladly speak to Reinhardt."

"Oh no. Master Reinhardt has made it quite clear. You are to accompany me alone."

"Out of the question," snaps Cornelia. She pushes Gette behind her legs and Charles steps forward to wall her off.

"We deal with him together or not at all," says Charles.

The Man-in-White steps forward.

"You forget your place Mr. Standish. You are the master's guests. A guest has no right to make demands of their host."

The guards hold nightsticks at the ready—pistols hang in black leather holsters at their sides.

The world widens past the tunnel—the fire settles into glowing embers.

"It's okay Charles," I say. "Go to the park and have fun. I'll get this sorted out."

"Evelyn—"

I reach out a hand to his chest. "I'll meet you for pie." I wink. A deep, no confusing it for a blink, this is a signal pay attention, wink.

Charles nods.

"Lead the way," I say stepping toward the guards.

"Wait, there has to be another way," Cornelia says grabbing at my shoulder. Charles rests a gentle hand on her arm to stop her.

"It's alright. We'll meet her for *pie* later."

Unconvinced of my half-baked plan, but knowing it's the one we've got, she steps back and gives me her own, reluctant, nod of approval.

"I'll save a piece for you," says Victor. His hands are swollen red and twisted into fists. Water glimmers on the edge of his eyes.

"Right then," says the Man-in-White. "Follow me."

His long legs propel him at a break-neck pace. I surge behind him holding my shoulders back and head high to project what little confidence I have. Metal heeled boots *click-clack* behind me. The tapping of a headsman's drum. I fight the urge to turn back. *Breathe Evelyn.*

I follow the Man-in-White confident I'm headed into the dragon's den.

The twists and turns seem normal at first—this is a labyrinth after all. But soon the familiar concrete walls and twisting hallways pass away. Odd, I don't think we're headed to Reinhardt's office.

"Keep up," snaps the Man-in-White sensing I've lagged behind.

He widens his gait forcing me to focus on staying behind him and not letting the guards barrel me over. I force myself to keep pace—the coarse fabric of the jumpsuit chafing painfully with each step. Mercifully, he halts at a steel service door.

"Open," he commands, and the door obeys. Cogitators whirr and steam pipes rattle in their effort to obey his will. The metal door stretches a foot taller and wider than normal. It slides away seamlessly into the wall revealing a glass-sealed carport. A stretched, jet-black Duesenberg waits idling. Geysers of noxious exhaust pour from the twelve chrome pipes curving out of the long bonnet to protrude like spikes below the rear window. Three ventilation fans pull the smoke out of the glass box creating a vortex of smoke around the car. I stop—feet frozen to the concrete. The guards push me forward dragging me on my toes.

"You're fine. Just play along," whispers the Guard Captain—his hand separating my right bicep like a nutcracker.

I tug myself free. I can't keep a grimace from my face, but I straighten my jumpsuit. The Man-in-White pulls the lever on the rear passenger door. It swings up and back like a bird's wing. A plush red-leather seat reaches the width of the massive six-wheeled saloon.

"There's a present for you in the back seat."

My throat seizes. *Don't ever be alone with that man.* Colleen's words scream at me to flee.

The end of a baton rolls across my shoulder. I turn to face the Guard Captain.

"Don't make me put you in there." His voice resonates inhuman through his rebreather.

Run!

I shudder. *I can't. Not this time.*

I slide into the back seat. The Man-in-White closes the door then climbs into the front passenger seat. The masked valet puts the car in gear. Through the window, I watch the guards dash over to the control panel on the wall. Glass hanger doors peel open and the Duesenberg glides forward. The guards rush into another car and pull in behind us.

Across from me on the bar separating the front and back seats is a white box tied with a red ribbon. The slots of booze and tumblers are empty, and the ice bucket is nowhere to be seen. All the possible weapons neatly packed away somewhere else. I watch the Man-in-White in the rearview mirror. The instant he's distracted with the gate guard, I try the handle.

The lever pulls but the door doesn't give. I let it go slowly moving my arms only below the elbow. We're headed into town. I watch for another opportunity. Trembling, it takes a minute for me to realize only some of that is nerves. A Sentinel is rumbling down the street toward us with a Peace Officer escort. The Man-in-White shifts his attention to direct the valet to a side street. Seizing the instant, I scoot across the seat and try the opposite handle. The handle pulls up. Nothing. The bubble of hope bursts half-formed. My guts somersault. Seeing nothing else, curiosity and desperation take the better of me.

I pull on one end of the ribbon and the silk bow unfurls dropping to the polished wood floors. A red leather *Lux* mask is perched inside on a bed of black tissue paper. Having left my rebreather in the barracks in all the commotion, the gift is welcome only out of necessity.

"I trust it fits?" says the Man-in-White—his eyes scathing in the reflection.

I inhale until my chest fills to bursting then let it out slow and controlled. Tension sheds away. I flip the mask over. Its leather is supple, the details exquisite. Pressing it on, the smell of tawny rubber fills my nostrils then vanishes into a field of flowers. It forms to my face almost perfectly. Short tugs on the straps seat it in place. If I closed my eyes it wouldn't be hard to imagine I was standing in a mountain meadow. The sun on my face and the wind in my hair. But I can't close my eyes, and deluxe filters and scent modules do nothing to filter out the sinister intentions of this gift.

"I guess it does," I say. My modified voice—sultrier than I'm comfortable with—startles me.

"Excellent." I can't make out his placid face but his tone leaves little doubt he's mocking me.

We turn a corner near the park. Crowds are blocking the view, but the Martyr's Day celebrations appear to be in full swing. Peace Officers are screening people at the gate—Guardians crew a heavy machinegun from behind a sandbag pillbox in the parking lot. Bright, multi-colored tents fill the yellow grass fields. A short Ferris wheel twinkles and spins. We pull away before I can see much more—the trees of Green Gardens obscure the small windows.

Driving deeper into the neighborhood, the press of hyper-green trees blots out the sun on a cloudless day. I breathe in, hold it until my lungs burn and my fingers tremble, then let it out slow. Rinse and repeat, I steel myself for what's to come.

The valet makes exaggerated hand-over-hand motions on the oversized steering wheel pulling us into a long driveway. He flips the headlights on warping the tall trees into clawed fingers. The Man-in-White pulls on his all-white mask. He double-checks the seal and the straps just as the valet pulls under the arches of the massive portico. The Man-in-White steps out. In the heartbeat before he opens my door, I tuck away the red ribbon into my left pocket.

"This way," says the Man-in-White beckoning me inside.

I feign compliance and follow him through the revolving airlock doors.

The airlock rotates us inside so smoothly we don't lose our stride. The grand foyer echoes the decorations from his office. Gilded burgundy carpets. Ornate clawed chairs. Tapestries sway over travertine walls. Massive urns erupt with volcanos of flowers. Distant orchestral music plays at the edge of hearing. A domestic robot wheels up to me—its articulated body extending on gleaming pistons. Rotating brush arms sweep over me followed by a vacuum attachment. Another robot cleans my boots—its bristles tickling my calf just above the tops. The Guard Captain enters behind us, and now finished, the robots whisk off to their next chore.

The Man-in-White pulls off his mask extending it to yet another, different mechanical servant.

"Come miss Brennan, the Master is expecting you." He walks on not waiting for a response. I slip off my mask. A discord of scents crinkle my nose. Potpourri, ozone, oil, and sickness. I stifle a retch. Holding my mask like a club, I follow him. I glance back. The captain has taken sentry at the door alone. His two guards must be patrolling outside the house.

We pass through a long hallway of mahogany wood panels and ornate geometric sconces. Each room is decorated in its own style and no effort is made to bring cohesion to the overall design. The Man-in-White opens the double doors at the end then stands to one side indicating for me to step inside.

Reinhardt is sitting with his back to the door in an over-stuffed leather recliner. His thick fingers wrapped around a delicate crystal tumbler brimming with neon-green liquor. A beam of light splits the space in two separating him from the matching empty recliner next to him. The projected light fills the far wall with quivering white light. He notices us and turns in the chair to address us. The leather screams under his con-torting weight.

"I'm so glad you could join me. Please, take a seat." He motions with his drink hand to the empty chair—rivulets crash over the side and roll down his fingers. Fire engulfs the back of my neck. The mask's leather crunches in my hand.

"Do you like your present? I do hope that it fits. I can always get the *measure* of people." He pauses, mouth agape, hoping I'll take the bait and laugh at his pun. The Man-in-White lets out a controlled guffaw. Reinhardt giggles at his own joke—his neck undulates. I approach cautiously. Eyes searching for a way out or a weapon. The stark lighting frustrates the task. As soon as my feet pass the threshold, the Man-in-White slides the doors closed. They clatter then fall silent—the hum of the overhead projector and the twirl of the tumbler stifle the room. I try to let my eyes adjust, but the projector is too bright.

"Would you like anything to drink? I can make you a mocktail," he leans over on his meaty elbow, "or a cocktail. I won't tell anyone." He winks tapping his nose. His jagged teeth glisten like daggers in the dark.

Acid burns in my throat. "You wanted to see me?"

"Straight to business. I like that. Yes, yes, I did. I'm a man of my word and I—" He cuts himself off gesturing again to the seat next to me.

"Please, take a seat. I have something I want to show you."

Hovering over the chair, I weigh the options. I could bolt back through the door and maybe take the Man-in-White by surprise. Maybe I could sneak out of the mansion and find my way to the park and get lost in the crowd. Maybe.

Too many uncertainties. Every muscle and tendon protests staying. Every synapse urges me to find another way. I scan the room again. Gray outlines dot the wall. Paintings and plaques.

But not a single window or door. A drinks cart against the wall is bristling with thick crystal decanters. *If he tries anything I'll grab one and smash it over his head, okay?* My body grumbles but agrees. Resolved, I slip into the chair. The leather is silken and crinkles as I settle. His grin shines like a crescent moon against the gray blur background of the room.

"I'm sure you and your friends have been wondering why I decided to help you. Fugitives on the run from Einsam. Wanted for the murder of two Peace Officers and wanted for questioning in connection to the subversive assault on the broadcast tower."

My chest seizes. I scoot forward to the edge of the chair ready to run.

He laughs unleashing phlegm and quickly devolves into coughing. "So, I know who you are. What of it? Did I turn you in? Did I torture you?"

"No."

"No. Of course not. I believe in giving people the benefit of the doubt. People say all sorts of nasty things about me and well." He chuckles, "Only half of it is true." This brings on another coughing fit. He knocks back the remainder of his drink, clears his throat, then runs a mitt-like hand across his face to wipe away the sweat beading in the cavernous wrinkles in his forehead.

"I helped you because you can help me."

I bolt up.

"Evelyn, please. Please sit. You have my word," he crosses his gout-gorged arm over his heart. "I swear on my honor I intend no," his hand twirls in the projected light as he flips through the dictionary in his head searching for the word least likely to result in a decanter splitting open his forehead. "Perversion."

The word slithers across his lips. Mouth puckered in disgust, I slide onto the edge of the chair—eyes locked on the largest decanter.

"What is it you want to show me?"

He smiles pressing himself deeper into his seat. The recliner cries out a chorus of creaking metal and squealing leather.

"You don't strike me as all that important," he says. "You're a seventeen-year-old with no real affiliation to subversive groups or any particular knack for violence or frankly anything but getting yourself into trouble." His words sting true.

"But you have managed to make yourself the most wanted person by the Caretakers, the subversives, and the CLA."

"Wait what?" I say genuinely confused.

"Do you know who your father is? What he does?"

The bottom drops out of my stomach. I shoot a hand out to steady myself. I don't have a clue. I know he works for the government and that he manages something. But it was never to be discussed. The taboo was there from my earliest memories. He comes home late and you ask how his day was but nothing else. You don't ask. I lived that way so long only now does it seem strange. I never even thought to ask that question, it wasn't something that had words.

"No. I've never known what he does."

"That's rich. You know how much trouble you stirred up for your old pop? You know you got your mother killed, right? This whole shit show got sparked by your bumbling."

I'm trembling. Fires rage in my muscles. I should jump up, grab the crystal, and smash his teeth in. Yet as the fire stokes itself into an inferno, the cold winds of the void snuff it out.

He's right.

I don't know the details, but I knew the moment I stepped through the penthouse door that it might as well have been me with the gun to Mother's back. Tears tumble and splatter with each short, gasping breath.

He leans closer grinning ear-to-ear. "Your pop is the executive field marshal of OSS special operations."

"What?" my body drops away. "What does that mean?"

"What that means, miss Brennan, is your pop is the mastermind behind the subversives program."

He blurs through wet eyes. With each breath, I sink a little deeper into the chair.

"You stirred things up. You got Fowler thinking her own

plot to hijack the program had been discovered. The look on your father's face when they told him they found you in the Oracle Device," he chuckle-hacks more phlegm. "He went white as a sheet."

Confusion and guilt sweep me away in an undertow of pain.

"How, how do you know this?"

His ceaseless hyena's grin is eroding my self-control. "I'm on the council of industry. That was the most eventful meeting I've ever been to. You unwittingly got the whole system to turn on itself. Battle lines were drawn, loyalties questioned, and then your friend shot up the broadcast tower." He flips open a lighter igniting the end of a fat cigar. His face painted in the glowing embers.

"Why am I here?"

"Isn't it clear? You're my hostage. Offers have been pouring in for you for weeks. Money, favors, promises, secrets. Your head could get me so many useful things. Things a million Marks couldn't buy."

Knots twist in my gut.

He takes a long drag. "Computer, play the message from Allen Brennan."

Blood drains from my face. Cold fingers dig into the armrest. The white light shatters into a rainbow of light. Projected on the wall ten-feet tall, Father sits behind an oak desk. The seal of the Caretaker's office hangs on the wall behind him flanked by the white-and-red flag of the OSS and the deep-blue and silver of the Great Society.

"Evelyn, darling, if you're listening to this message, please do what Reinhardt tells you. He has sworn to keep you safe in return for certain promises I've made him. When the siege of Einsam lifts, I'll come for you." He closes his eyes—his throat struggling to keep his emotions down. "I never meant for you or your Mother to get hurt. You must believe me darling, everything I've done, I've done to protect our family. I love you Evelyn—"

"Computer, end playback."

Father vanishes from the wall. His words still slicing their way into my heart.

"Your father had the least to offer of the three—Fowler wants you quite badly—but I have a soft spot for little girls."

I explode to my feet. The earth sways and shudders. I can't tell if the earthquake is real or imagined.

"So it's all been decided then? I'm supposed to just smile and go to my room? What about Charles, Cornelia, Gette, Vic—"

Knock. Knock. Knock. Our attentions turn to the door.

"What is it?" barks Reinhardt—smoke frothing from his mouth.

The Man-in-White slides the door open. "Deepest apologies Master, but it seems we found a heartsick puppy trying to sneak in through the kitchen."

"Where is he?"

"Captain Miller has his men seeing to him." The Man-in-White smirks.

Reinhardt snuffs his cigar out in the ashtray fitted into the armrest then hoists himself to his feet—the chair sighs in relief.

"Come on miss Brennan. Let's go have a chat with your friend."

Quivering, my legs have taken root and I have to rip them out to follow. The Man-in-White is careful to keep his shoulders square with me then steps behind as I pass. Reinhardt waddles down the hallway to the foyer.

Forced down into a squatting stress position, the two guards have their nightsticks under Victor's armpits letting his own body weight do the damage. He tries to prop himself up. When he does they lash out, kicking his ankles with their steel-tipped boots. Victor moans through the gag in his mouth. Tears streak down his soot-covered cheeks.

"Let him go!" I shout racing toward Reinhardt fist raised and ready. The Man-in-White springs forward snatching my wrist in the air. He wrenches my arm down—something pops in my shoulder. Hot pain swells

"Be gentle with our guest," Reinhardt snaps at his henchman and he lets go of me. I cradle my arm rubbing my wrist. "Captain, get this rat out of my house."

"At once."

"No!" I scream dropping my mask.

It all happens so fast.

I lunge back, twist my hips, and fire my elbow up at the lanky man's chin. It connects with a *thud* snapping his head back. He crumbles to the gilded carpet like a sack of potatoes.

Reinhardt turns around. I yank the ribbon from my pocket and lunge at him springing off my right foot. With the ribbon stretched between both hands, I clothesline him. He stumbles back. His grubby hands claw at my face, but I fight through it and manage to wrap the ribbon around his neck. I pull hard and throw myself back—the mess of fermented emotions inside me explodes in a guttural scream.

We topple to the ground. He shoots an arm out to catch himself and his wrist snaps under his girth. His full weight bears down on me. Flashes of light chase dark splotches across my vision. Each breath is harder fought than the last with each bringing waves of cold fire to my compressed ribcage. Face-to-face, his clammy skin clings to mine. His spiced cologne fails to mask the odor of infection and decay. Hot air ekes from his swelling neck.

Shoving Victor to the floor, his captors turn their attention to me.

The guards drag their master off me, but I keep hold of the ribbon. I manage a single breath before their batons fall on me like hail.

Blood vessels rupture. Nerves shatter. Cartilage shears. I would scream had I any air.

I pull my hands up to shield my face releasing my stranglehold on Reinhardt.

Bang. To my left, a gunshot ruptures the room. Victor emerges from under the limp, dead body of Captain Miller. The guards freeze—their batons hang above me, their cruelty suspended. The guard on my left acts first.

She moves for her holster. Before she can undo the clasp, a bullet shatters the front of her rebreather—slivers of carbon fiber and bone explode amidst the scarlet bloom. The other guard drops to his knee drawing his gun at the same time. His pistol slides along the holster barking fire the instant it clears leather.

Bang! Bang! Two puffs of crimson mist out his back. He wobbles, trying to aim his pistol for another shot. Then, as if someone flipped a switch, his muscles turn to water. He flops back, pistol still clutched in his hand.

Fire shoots through my arms as I stand. Victor is clutching his left arm near the elbow. Blood gushes between his fingers to the beat of his galloping heart.

"Enough!" cries the Man-in-White. "Drop your pistol." Turned side face, an ornate silver pistol extends from his outstretched hands.

Bang.

The Man-in-White crumbles. Passing straight through

him—armpit to armpit—the bullet explodes lungs and heart.

Eyes quivering, I back away from the bodies as if the distance can erase this horror show. Victor still has the pistol raised—its slide clattering in his jittery hands. His left arm is limp at his side. Dark blood pools at his feet.

Reinhardt wiggles away clutching his wrist—his face ashen searches for air. Fire erupts in Victor's eyes. He trains the gun on the back of Reinhardt's plump head.

I slap the pistol from his hands.

"No. No more." The words fall from heartsick lips. Tears stream down my face.

"What have you done?" manages Reinhardt through gasping breaths.

"Evelyn?" Victors words slur. He collapses. I dive in and keep his head from hitting the ground. I grab up the ribbon from where Reinhardt tossed it aside and tie it tight around Victor's bicep pulling on both ends as hard as I can. The clatter of a rotary phone crashing to the floor snaps my attention back to Reinhardt.

Reinhardt has pulled the phone from the side table—his stubby fingers rotating the dial. I spring to my feet and kick the phone away from him. It tumbles away with a discordant wail—my big toe radiates with stinging needles.

"You're dead girl! Dead! I'll hunt you down to the ends of the earth."

"Come on Victor, we have to go."

Cradling my shoulder under his good arm, I pull him to his feet then help him to a chair. I search frantically, finding Victor's mask then my own among the carnage. I help him with his then snug mine into place. The smell of gun smoke and blood vanishes into lavender fields.

I cradle Victor again and make for the door. The fleet of domestic robots descends upon the nightmare in the foyer. Ever faithful, they begin to vacuum up the blood with their rotating bristle brushes.

I drop the world away. I push the foyer away, and the message on the screen. I drop everything that isn't running down this driveway. The drive stretches before us like a funhouse mirror warping into infinity. *Breathe Evelyn, run.*

Passing through the stone columns we hobble down the street in the trees' inky shadow. Springing some invisible snare, each step forward causes the world to tremble. Tremors rustle the leaves breaking up the canopy to let light fall like rain.

"What have I done?" Victor says.

"We can't think about it now. Keep moving, we have to find the others."

The scream of jet engines thunders down the valley announcing the arrival of warplanes.

The entrance draws near. Drained and exhausted my steps begin to stumble.

"I need to lie down," says Victor, his voice as thin as gossamer.

"We have to keep moving."

Just breathe, Evelyn. Just breathe.

The trees thin and the street widens into the main drag. Leaning against the mailbox to catch my breath, I see the outline of the park behind a row of houses. I take in a lung full of clean lavender air and watch as the world erupts into chaos.

CHAPTER TWENTY-ONE

THE FIRES OF EINSAM FOUND US. Ominous pillars of smoke, black as oblivion, blot out the sky. Galling winds carry embers from rooftop to rooftop and into the kindling twigs of dying trees. A melody of horrors shrieks all around us. The deep rumble of tanks, the crackle of fire, the *whizz snap* of bullets, and the piercing shrill of countless screams.

Beleaguered, I'm drowning in the chaos. Movement on my periphery explodes needles of panic in the base of my skull. I give over to instinct, pulling Victor next to me behind the stone pillar and out of sight. A Peace Officer cruiser screams past, lights swirling, siren blaring. *Stay down, not yet* rumbles a voice from my bones. Victor moans—his wounded arm quivering. I place my hand on his chest to hush him. He's frozen. He's going into shock and if I don't get him to safety soon, he's going to die.

I blink away the thought. *Just breathe, Evelyn.* Time drums in my chest—each heartbeat slides us closer toward the precipice. I peek around the pillar.

A column of black, armored cars races toward us. Trucks, delivery vans, and family sedans covered in bolted-on thick steel plates. The rag-tag arsenal is unified by a slapdash paint job of midnight black—a white eagle preens above CLA painted in white block letters.

I rush back behind the relative safety of the stone pillar pulling Victor's exposed legs closer. I close my eyes and listen as they pass. Engines roar, machineguns charge. The stampede rounds the corner to park just a stone's throw away.

Fighting erupts. A hail of automatic fire punctuated with grenades splits the air.

Now.

Ear's ringing, I pull Victor up. He's trembling uncontrollably. He's lost a lot of blood and he's starting to look like a corpse.

"Victor! Stay with me. We need to get across the street. Can you do that with me?"

Victor lets out a moan dropping his head ever so slightly to say yes. My stomach twists but I clamp down with all my resolve. *Enough.*

Taking most of his weight, I scan the street—a laser show of tracers and explosions cut across the smoke-filled sky. Up and across, we dash over the two lanes of asphalt. We keep our momentum and push straight through to the white-washed gate. I kick it open as we approach. A dull ache runs up from my heel and embeds itself in my hip. Victor is still moving but his eyes have rolled into the back of his head. I spot the air-raid shelter.

"I'll be right back," I say lowering Victor to the grass. Arm glistening with fresh blood, he melts to the ground.

Throwing the doors open, I rush back to him.

"One more big effort Victor. You have to help me get you down the ladder."

"Down the ladder," he murmurs eyes writhing under the lids.

I hoist him up—his body soft and limp.

We step on the first rung and nearly tumble. A muscle in my shoulder tears from the effort. Fresh tears and cries of pain flow unchecked. Victor's body surges with life just long enough to get us safely into the cellar.

Totally spent, I drag him over to the wall. Propping his feet up, blood rushes back to his head and some color returns. I hurry over to the cabinet where the Blue Band keeps the emergency supplies. I push aside the water bottles and lanterns—the shaft of light coming through the open doors is dim but enough to see. I spy an emergency kit and yank it free. I slam it down next to Victor and throw open the hinges. A large, brightly colored cartoon pamphlet sits on top. I unfold it—the big print making it readable despite my trembling. I flip through to the page on tourniquets.

Remove package 4 from the kit. Tear open the Stay Fresh™ package at the corner. Inside is one Med Corp. Insta-quet™. Simply wrap above the joint on the affected limb, secure the self-adhering sides together, hook the metal loops then hold down the red circle until it turns green.

I tear into the package and follow the directions. My jittering fingers bumble the clasps, but I get them fastened. I jam my thumb onto the red circle. Bound fibers release their suspended tension cinching the Insta-quet firmly in place. The flow of blood stops.

I turn back to the pamphlet flipping through looking for blood loss.

Remove package 7 from the kit. Tear open the Stay Fresh™ package at the corner. Inside is one Insta-IV™. Simply wrap below the elbow, secure the self-adhering sides together, hook the metal loops, then hold down the red circle until it turns green. Auto-Sense technologies will automatically guide the needle into the vein. After successful application, remove package 8 from the kit. Tear open the Stay Fresh™ package at the corner. Inside is one pouch of saline. Break off the protective cap then twist it into the nozzle on the In-sta-IV™. Don't worry, it can only go in one way so you can't screw it up! *(if using in conjunction with package 4 use opposite arm.)*

I follow the directions—saline drains from the pouch. Ex-haustion racks up and down my battered body. I crumble to the floor next to him. Adrenaline wearing off, every breath brings searing hot jabs of pain in my chest where batons splintered ribs. My switchboard of nerves and emotions is lit up on all channels. Lightheaded, it's a miracle I stay vertical. Sleep pulls at me. *You're not safe yet. You have to get out.*

I plaster over the blinking red lights in my mind and scramble to my feet. "Victor. Can you hear me?"

"Evelyn? Are you alright?"

I shake my head in disbelief. The mysterious cocktail of drugs I just injected him with are working better and acting faster than I could have imagined. Maybe there's hope we'll get through this.

"Do you think you can stand?" More tears soak into the plush padding of my new mask.

"Yeah, I think so," he says, his voice brittle.

I fish out some medical tape from the kit then wrap the saline pouch to his arm.

I help him to his feet. His body is still soft, but some strength has returned to his muscles and his temperature is returning to normal.

"Alright, one step at a time. Let's get up that ladder."

We turn to leave—a shadow cuts into the light. A figure stands over the doors silhouetted with sun and fire. The Blue Band is there—a gaggle of huddled people behind her.

Bullets hail and bombs blast raising the tense moment into madness.

"Give me your hand," says the woman.

Victor accepts, and she helps him out. I follow behind.

"Thank you," I say.

She doesn't acknowledge me, turning instead to the huddle of trembling people behind her.

"Quickly, get inside," she says—her confidence infectious.

The traumatized families rush into the cellar. She follows them underground eyes piercing me through her mask as she pulls the double doors shut.

Supporting him, we dash from house to house. Keeping the fences between us to conceal our passing. We slink behind the last house before the street widens and the two-story buildings of downtown pop up.

The park is a hellscape of fire and blood. The pavilions have crumbled into infernos—plastic sheeting and diesel from the generators mix together to fuel an unquenchable fire. Hundreds of bodies lay burned or bleeding on the yellow grass field. Peace Officers, Guardians, and soldiers dressed head-to-toe in black are scattered about. But most of the dead are families in suits and ties and bright summer dresses. A blue balloon dances in the wind still tied to the wrist of a small boy.

The lights on the Ferris wheel have gone out but the structure still spins sending each chair through the fire at its base like a rotisserie. A gun battle still rages at the far side of the park. A Sentinel comes to life rolling over its sandbag emplacement near town hall. Two squads of Guardians follow in its path. The tank opens fire—the *kurr-whoosh* of its main cannon slams into my chest. I follow the soldiers with my eyes taking deep lavender-scented breaths.

Screaming past, a flight of silver warplanes buzzes the rooftops. Earth-shattering concussions ripple through the ground moments after they pass. A cloud of fire billows up from the road snaking out of the valley toward Einsam.

"We need to get across the street," I shout to Victor.

"There?" he says pointing to a blind alley to our right.

"Let's go," I say moving low and fast.

Victor's call comes just in time. Scrambling over a fence we clear out of the yard and get across the street. Glancing back, a CLA technical has taken position near where we were hiding. A heavy machinegun slung from a slapped-together sling on the bed of a truck—that a week ago was probably delivering flowers—opens up on the squad of Guardians still in position around the square. Two Guardians drop, their comrades scramble for cover. But they recover fast.

An avalanche of death falls on the gunner. He falls over his weapon tangled in the sling. The driver tries to pull away but a salvo of rocket grenades blast through the armor plates. The cabin bursts into flame—red tongues lap out through cracked windows painting them black. The truck rolls forward coming to a stop when it collides with a traffic barricade.

The fire and smoke cover our next move. Darting from cover to cover, we inch closer to the square. The red neon of Martha's illuminates the far side of the alleyway calling to us like a lighthouse.

"We're almost there, Victor. Stay with me." The last sprint sapped him, and his eyes are starting to roll back into his head again.

"Just a few more feet. Come on, one last sprint."

Our footsteps echo on the cobblestones. Steam vents sting as we pass. I tumble through a pile of garbage hidden beneath a mound of ash. We crash down hard—slag poofs up around us.

"Come on Victor, we have to keep going."

"I can't," he says—his words scattered and faint.

He's ashen and limp sinking into the fluffy pile of soot.

One look and I know he's spent—teetering on the edge of death. I scoop him into my arms, his limp weight dangling over both ends.

My ears are ringing so loud now everything else fades away.

Reaching the airlock, I press Victor into the cylinder basked in the red glow of the neon sign above.

Steam hisses and the gears grind. The cylinder binds. Human shapes—warped through the soot-covered glass—rush to his aid. The door completes its seal. The door opens and they pull him to safety. Optimism springs in my heart.

I watch the cylinder cycle back. Each whir and hiss reassuring.

I step inside. Air vents and the glass rotates around. Mary-Anne is tending to Victor near the counter with Cornelia and Gette. Charles is waiting with the stick to let me inside. A nervous, tear-spattered smile blooms under my mask.

The roar of jets arrives just before their bombs. The building shutters.

Kurr-thump.

The cylinder binds again. But this time it's something more; the walls are coming down. Mortar wiggles free of brick—floorboards splinter. Hydraulic arms tremble inside the wall as they attempt to force the door open. The shifting wall snaps the plumbing like twigs. Steam shoots out catching Charles in the face. He stumbles away screaming, then surges back to set me free. Cracks in the glass around me branch and splinter. A deep, guttural groan issues from the girder above the door. The stick shatters in Charles's hands.

"Hold on!" He grabs the edge of the cylinder with his massive, calloused hands. Veins swell in his forehead and snake down his arms. I join in—joints paling from the effort.

"Almost there."

The door flies open. I tumble out as the roof collapses. Charles swoops over me, his body a shield. A steel beam pops out of the wall. Falling in on itself, the archway collapses—windows and airlock shatter. The floor buckles, dropping a foot before the vaulted ceiling of the cellar catches it.

"Charles!"

All the air is pounded out of my lungs. Legs pinned beneath stone radiate electric fire. Something hot, mushy, and wet flows over my hair and down my back. A thunderstorm of pain crescendos—tempest waves crash against me relentlessly.

Firm hands pull me free. Wailing rises above the ringing in my ears.

Mary-Anne drags me away from the rubble. Leaned against the wall, the horrific scene snaps into view. Shielding me from the collapse, Charles took the brunt of the impact. The steel girder that burst free from the wall sliced deep into his head.

Cornelia drags his body from the rubble. Her arms bright red with blood. I reach a trembling hand to my neck. It comes away sticky with blood and brain.

I rip my mask off and vomit on the floor. Blood, soot, and bile mix with cinnamon to assault my senses.

Cornelia wails.

Gette is frozen—her eyes dilated and colorless, lips quivering.

"Papa?"

I rush over to Cornelia. His face is pink and glistening from the steam. I retch, but already empty, nothing escapes.

"Charles!" She cradles his head in her arms. I try to find a pulse. Not giving up I press my ear against his chest and hear only the rumble of distant battle.

There are no words. Nothing I can possibly say or do to make any difference. Husband, father, friend. He snapped from those things in one moment to a corpse in the next.

Why can't the world stop? Just for an instant. A heartbeat. A whisper. One moment where you can step outside everything, bottle up all the hurt, and just scream. Scream until every drop is boiled away.

But you can't. And the world never stops.

Cornelia is obliterated. Pain starts in her gut then heaves itself up to rattle from her lips. Mary-Anne is trying to console her. Her words inaudible over the deafening roar ringing in my ears. Trapped where she stands, Gette is starting to dissolve—the quiver in her lips growing wider her eyes blinking faster. I crawl over to her on legs like wet sand and wrap my arms around her. No words come to mind. My mind is numb. A crinkling white noise of emotions I cannot process.

Warplanes scream overhead. Wind drives down the alley blowing soot and embers into the bakery. I huddle Gette into me to shield her unprotected face.

"We have to get out of here," I say rooting through the rubble for Gette's mask. "Help me find her mask—we need to go!"

"No. I can't leave him. I won't leave him."

Victor wobbles then slumps over hitting his head on the ground.

"Help Victor!" I shout. The world is a blur.

"Charles. Charles, get up!" Cornelia pounds on his barrel chest.

Mary-Anne stands, trembling.

"Where are their masks? We have to get out of here, it's not safe," I say.

"Their—masks?" she stumbles away from Charles.

"Mary-Anne! Listen to me. Where are their masks?"

Awareness blinks back into her eyes. "Here, over here." She rushes to a nook by the tables. She grabs up three Reinhardt Agriculture rebreathers, then drops one.

"Bring them here," I say.

A deep-toned oscillating rumble grabs my attention.

"Help her with her mask," I say instructing Mary-Anne. She finds her way over and starts pulling Gette's mask on—Gette stands a statue, eyes fixed on her father.

It's not safe you need to go. Compelled, I crawl over the crumbled entrance and look up at the sky. Only a sliver of blue is visible between the smoke and surrounding rooftops. A hulking silver plane—four massive jet engines under its wings—looms over town coming toward us. The air raid siren winds up. Doors unfold the length of its distended belly.

"Go get your mask on!" I scream at Mary-Anne—Mother's face flashing before my eyes. I snatch the second mask from

Mary-Anne and rush over to Cornelia. She's buried in Charles's chest and though winded and drained she continues to wail.

"Cornelia, we have to go. They're going to blow us up if we stay here."

"I won't leave him."

"You'll die!"

"What does that matter?" she says. The whites of her eyes completely taken over by red—her face long with grief.

"Gette needs you," I take her blood-covered hand, "I need you."

The first bomb lands sending a shower of dust from the floor above. I move my eyes to Gette. Cornelia's follow.

The second bomb hits and the world heaves. The tall oak cabinet in the corner crashes to the floor with the cacophony of broken china.

"Come on," I thrust the mask into her hands and pull her to her feet. Looking down at her husband and across to her daughter, she makes her choice. She dons her mask in one instant and scoops Gette up in the next. I help Victor to his feet.

"Come on, we need to get away from the buildings." I start for the door.

"No, wait." Mary-Anne says. "There's a better way. Through the kitchen follow me." We dash through the door into the kitchen. A cramped space filled to the brim with ovens, mixers, and crates of jams, and fresh fruit. Mary-Anne braces her feet against the oven then pushes against the center wood-topped island. It slides out of the way exposing a wooden hatch.

"Inside." She pulls up the hatch revealing a vacuous cavity below. Anticipation of the next bomb prickling down my spine like needles, I hop down onto the ladder. Victor shuffles in and I help keep him from falling. At the bottom, Victor scrambles out of the way. Cornelia lowers Gette down by her arms. I grab her by the waist and set her down.

The third bomb hits. The concussion is earsplitting. The ground below me writhes like gelatin. Cornelia jumps down holding her arms across her chest. She lands straight-legged and falls wincing. Mary-Anne throws herself through—the building collapsing above her. She flies into my chest knocking the wind out of me as we crash to the ground. A fiery wooden beam crashes through the hatch missing our legs by inches.

We scatter like bugs from the light. I help Victor to his feet then check on Cornelia. She waves me off and rushes to her daughter.

"My darling little girl."

"Papa?" Gette asks.

Cornelia cracks into a million pieces. Tears splash from the corners of her eyes as she shakes her head no.

"We're not safe here. Follow me." Mary-Anne gropes along the wall then flips a switch. Yellow industrial lights blink to life stretching off into the distance. The tunnel is far longer than I imagined, and now illuminated, only just taller than I am. Mary-Anne breaks off in a crouched run. Cornelia and Gette follow, then Victor. I go last to make sure he doesn't fall.

Bombs rain. Dust showers. Lights flicker. On we run in the darkness. On and on until the booms turn to thuds then to a far distant rumble.

CHAPTER TWENTY-TWO

THE TUNNEL CLOSES IN. The horizon recedes before us fixed forever just beyond our grasp. Standing under one light, you can look in both directions and see an infinite string of them in both directions. A trick of the darkness and claustrophobia no doubt, but the helplessness it spawns is very real. A gaseous malignance deepens the shadows into oblivion.

I shake my head to keep depression from turning my feet to stone. I tune out the lights and the length of the tunnel. The rumble of bombs, and the panicked pace of our collective anxiety venting from our masks. I focus on Victor's back. I help him when he stumbles, and I urge him forward when he slows.

I push all thoughts away until there is only moving forward. No tears or remorse. No second-guessing or fear. I gather up each thread: Mother, Father, Victoriana, Fowler, Hannah, Reinhardt, Charles. I wind them around each other until the end of one is indistinguishable from the other. I kick the tangled hydra's head into the hidden recesses of my consciousness. I give up the existential, the intangible, and grasp onto the mundane.

I'm hungry. Tired. My feet ache. And there is a faint crackling with each labored breath. Ice washes over me until I no longer feel the cold, until I feel nothing at all.

Emerging from the darkness, the small vignette of a ladder surrounded by concrete reinforced walls grows from a speck to the ground beneath my feet.

"I'll pop inside and let grandmother know it's us. Wouldn't want her to pull the shotgun on us."

Mary-Anne climbs the ladder disappearing through the hatch to the unlit room beyond. I slump against the wall. The others do the same. Victor is turning gray—the life drained out of him. His eyes are open little more than slivers.

"Stay awake Victor. You can rest soon, but you have to stay awake."

"It hurts," he murmurs slurring the words.

Cornelia holds Gette in her arms—their eyes hollow, bodies blood-stained and soiled.

"Stay with us Victor." I grab his good arm and shake him. His muscles are limp—he topples forward from the nudge with no reflex to catch himself.

Cornelia perks up. Her face twitches from the sudden impact of mind re-entering body.

"Get his mask off—he can't breathe."

"What about—"

"Do it!" she snaps.

"Ow!" Gette gasps pulling her arm from her mother's seizing talons.

I pull off his mask and tilt his head up. He wheezes in a long stream of air.

"I'm so sorry darling—I didn't mean to grab your arm like that. I'm sorry."

Gette stares at her mother, incredulous.

"Victor! Stay awake."

Cornelia springs to her feet—her eyes metamorphosing from sullen to steel.

"Help me get him up the ladder."

I nod my head—shaking away my hesitation.

She takes his good arm and I push up on his back. The life has run out of him. He offers no help only stammering words of pain.

One hand clinging to the rungs and the other gripped under his right armpit, Cornelia pulls him up like a leopard taking a kill to roost. Victor's legs wobble under his weight—his feet slide off the rungs. I keep him climbing, wrangling his spaghetti legs into position.

Light blooms through the cracks overhead. Mary-Anne

pulls the hatch open flooding the tunnel with light. She takes Cornelia's hand pulling her free. More hands—smooth, leathered, and wrinkled—envelope Victor and raise him up. They rush him away, disappearing beyond the lip.

"He's going to die isn't he," Gette says still sitting, staring at her feet.

I kneel taking her hands in mine. Her father's blood on my hands shoots a lightning bolt through my mind nearly ripping down the wall of ice keeping things in check.

"Maybe," I say unable to hold back the truth. "But we're going to do everything we can to save him."

"Did we do everything we could for papa?"

I want to say, "Yes. Yes, we did." But I don't even know if that's true. What could we have done? His brains were spilling on the floor. Fissures snake up the dam. I'm frayed. I need this to end, I need to wake up from this nightmare. *Just breathe, Evelyn.*

I take three, long, lung-bursting breaths.

"Your papa is a hero. He saved my life. We did everything we could."

Gette explodes. Tiny fists slam into my chest—her anguish echoes down the tunnel. She flails against me—her blows painful and stinging. I wrap my arms around her pulling her in for a hug. She struggles against me.

"Not enough!"

I absorb her accusations and pull her tighter into my arms.

"Why'd he have to die?"

I cannot fathom an answer.

Her fists flail until the fire burns out. Sobbing, she melds into my arms hugging me back. Her little fingers clawing at my back. Keeping one hand wrapped around her, I push off the concrete with the other. We climb the ladder and emerge into the blinding light of a storeroom.

Shielding my eyes, the world dissolves into focus. Shelves of canned goods, preserved meats and vegetables cram the floor-to-ceiling shelves. Directly across from us, the door to the kitchen stands open. Placemats and silverware litter the floor around the stout oak table. Women buzz around the table tending to Victor who's prostrate upon it. Cornelia spots us and rushes to her daughter. Gette pulls herself free and jumps into her arms. Cornelia looks at me, her eyes glistening. I stroke her shoulder as I pass to the table.

"That was quick thinking you did back there kid," says the oldest woman to me. She's hunched over the bullet wound cleaning and bandaging it with skillful hands.

"What can I do to help?" I say.

"Stay out of the way," she snaps. She pauses looking up from the wound. Her eyes linger on my blood-soaked hair. "Mary-Anne,"

"Yes, Oma?"

"Get this girl cleaned up and get some food in all of 'em. Your mother and I will save the boy."

Mary-Anne hands off the saline bag to her mother.

"Come on, the washroom's through here."

I nod curtly at Oma. She mirrors the gesture then turns back to helping Victor. Cornelia and Gette follow behind me through the short hallway to a large washroom at the end.

"I'll scrounge up some clean clothes for you. Take your time. There's plenty of hot water in the tank."

"Thank you," I say. Mary-Anne whisks away.

Cornelia sets Gette down on the counter and helps her peel her mask off. The sight of her sorrow racked face is too much to bear—I close my eyes reflexively and look away as if it will help.

"I'm going to help Evelyn wash her hair real quick sweetie. I'll be right here."

Lips pressed together so tight they look as though they'll burst, Gette nods.

Cornelia follows me into the washroom and closes the door behind us.

"Oh god," Cornelia says trying to find the end of my mask's straps in my blood knotted hair.

"Maybe I should just hop in the shower and let it run off for a while."

"No, let me help get your mask off. You won't be able to get it out with the strap covering most of it up."

She dives into the mess, digs out the strap ends, and loosens them. We pull the mask up and free—a dozen clumps of hair yank out of their roots. I grimace but keep it to myself. She throws the mask into the sink and runs the hot water—the mirror steams up like a halo around the basin. Turning the water off, she helps Gette down.

"Go ahead and get in the shower. We'll give you some privacy."

"Thank you," I say.

Cornelia's face is stoic, but her eyes are dilated and glistening.

Alone, I look at myself in the mirror. My hair is red with blood—rivulets run down my forehead and temples. My arms are bloody to the elbow. I unzip the jumpsuit with trembling fingers. My shoulder erupts in pain as I pull my arm free. I kick off my boots and finish undressing gingerly. My ribs are purple and black. Cuts and scrapes cover my legs. Every part of me is covered in ash. Soot clings to sweat lines and clumps in my body hair. I'm thinner than I remember—bones casting shadows where none ever have before. The sight of myself breaks the wall and the world plunges into the sea.

I force myself into the shower and turn the water on full blast. I don't have the energy to shiver while the water warms. I keep my eyes and mouth shut as blood and tears stream down my face—my sobs imploding in my bruised chest. The drain swirls red.

I manage to find shampoo and wash away the gore—my scalp stinging from the ferocity of the scrubbing. I clean myself with the washcloth until it's too soot-filled and grimy to help anymore.

Just breathe, Evelyn.

Brick by brick, I rebuild the barrier in my heart.

When the water finally runs clear, I turn the handle and step onto the cold warped-wood floors. The steam extracting the smell of mildew and age from the walls.

Knock. Knock.

"I've put some clothes by the door when you're ready," says Mary-Anne who, by the sound of her voice, is pressed against the door.

"Thank you—I'm nearly finished." I run a wide-toothed wooden comb through my hair breaking through the knots. Finished, the comb has as much hair as I do. I crack the door—cool air rushes in contracting my skin. I pull in a stack of soft cotton clothes. A pastel yellow blouse, wool pants, and simple cotton undergarments.

Pulling on clothes other than a jumpsuit feels good. I could almost feel normal again. I take up the soot and blood covered sleeve of my jumpsuit and tear open the stitching on the hidden compartment. It's almost a shame to split the seam—after a month of nearly daily practice my stitches look better than the machine's. The article is smudged from sweat and stained with blood. I press it into my pocket then pull out the sphere. The cool blue depths are invisible. Crimson black blood mars its pristine surface. I run it under a hot tap—the blood splatters away. The urge to smash the damned thing against the wall flashes bright. Fingers constrict to crush it. Hand quivering, the fire burns out. Clenched fist uncurls to reveal the beautiful, crystal object.

"I hope you're worth it."

It doesn't reply. I shove it into my pocket next to the blood-soaked article then quickly straighten up the mess I made. I pull my mask from the sink, and with towel in hand, exit the room drying it.

"The clothes fit," Mary-Anne says. She's leaned against the wall, one leg perched behind her like a chair. I can't help but study her shape—I can't decide if her position is comfortable or not.

"Yes, thank you. It's nice to be out of a jumpsuit."

"Come," she says standing, breaking my trance, "help me make dinner while they shower."

I nod and walk briskly to follow her. "How's Victor?"

"He's stable. Oma gave him something to help him sleep. He looks like he's dead, but I promise he isn't."

I smile but my eyes can't help but shoot over to Cornelia and Gette.

Mary-Anne slips past them into the kitchen. Turning sideways, I step past Cornelia and Gette. I give them the most optimistic smile I can muster. A faint glimmer of joy flashes in their eyes.

Black-and-white family portraits and landscapes hang on the walls next to old tools, muskets, and the occasional animal head. The wood walls bring everything together making it feel like it jumped off the set of a pioneer film.

Victor is motionless on the table—a morose tableau of bloody gauze, drained saline bags, and a half-empty bottle of moonshine. The women are sitting around the living room fireplace drinking the clear liquor from glazed earthen mugs.

"Pour yourself a cup," says the middle of the three.

"Be a dear and bring the bottle while you're at it," says Oma.

I move to the bottle—my every step, heartbeat, and breath slowing as I approach. Victor's eyes race under his eyelids. Thick droplets of sweat bead and fall from his brow. Tremors ripple down his body—the slight ever-present motion of life. But his left arm is completely placid below the elbow. It looks necrotic. I lean in and snatch the bottle—a tsunami crashes and falls inside it. I drag myself free of the gloomy veil. Mary-Anne meets me in the living room with two more clay mugs.

I sit in the only empty chair—an uncomfortable straight-backed oak chair draped with quilts that do little in the way of cushioning.

"I've seen worse," says Oma finishing the last of her drink in a single swig. "He'll live. Don't you worry about that."

Mary-Anne fills her grandmother's outstretched mug. She fills the two she grabbed and offers me one. Notes of peach tickle my interest. I bring the mug closer to sniff. Stinging vapor wrinkles my nose and burns my eyes.

I set the mug down on the table next to me.

"Thank you for saving him. And thank you for taking us in. I'm Evelyn, that's Victor," I say nodding toward the table without glancing back.

"It's nice to meet you Evelyn. Cornelia introduced us to Gette—what a precious little girl. My granddaughter tells me you lost a man?"

"Charles," I say, his name fire in my throat. "Gette's father."

Mary-Anne's mother turns to the fire's crackling embers. "I know how hard it is to lose a father so young." She turns back to face me—half of her face lit up in the orange glow of the fire. Laugh lines and crow's feet are the only subtle clues to her age. "My name's Mabel. You've met my daughter, Mary-Anne, and this here is the matriarch of the Mulholland's: Martha."

"It's a pleasure to meet you Evelyn," Martha says raising her mug to me before slamming it back. That's the second glass I know of. In the flickering firelight, I can just make out the outline of something on the crook of her hand by her thumb.

Mabel rises and moves to the window and pulls back the yellow floral curtains. A starless sky hangs above inferno drenched hills. Red and green tracers split the air like a nightmare meteor shower.

"You folks trying to get to Lufthaffen?"

"That's the plan—Victor's sister lives there and she might be able to help us."

"Not a bad plan," says Mabel closing the curtains. "We'll help you."

I shift in my seat unable to get comfortable. "What'll it cost us?"

The crackle of the fire takes over the room above the rush of the shower and the far distant rubble and snap of war.

"You folks got messed up with Reinhardt without knowing what he wanted. That was dumb, but I like that you're learning. We're going to help you because it's the right thing to do. But mostly because I can't stand Maurice and his whole pestilent brood." Martha hacks into the fire.

"But if you're thinking we can hold your hand all the way there, well, that's just not realistic."

"We can get you to the rail hub in Mansfield," says Mabel picking up where her mother left off. "Mary-Anne is sweet on the stationmaster there. We'll slip you into a coal train then send word ahead that you're coming."

"We write to each other is all," retorts Mary-Anne, blushed from the moonshine and her mother's words.

"How…" I pause trying to put the question together, "Why are there tunnels? Are you subversives?" The question falls from my mouth as I say it. I shake my head and wave no, "That's not what I meant to say."

Martha laughs, pouring herself another glass. "The Caretakers have more enemies than some foolish nonsense about foreign subversives. People have hankerings for things the government won't supply. We fill that need—been doing it since I was a little girl and I'll do it 'till the day I die."

The shape on her hand snaps into focus in my mind. "Do you know Colleen Sheffield? She was the one who—"

"Colleen Sheffield," her mouth curls like she just bit into a lemon. "Spineless harpy. I should have finished her when I had the chance."

"Come on mom, that's water under the bridge."

"Like hell it is. She sold her people down the river for a few bucks and some favors. Her kith and kin, Mabel. That's unacceptable."

"She's part of your organization though, right? She has the same lightning bolt tattoo on her hand."

"Having the bolt don't make you part of the Lightning Underground. She set up a meeting with that gouty bastard, didn't she?" Arthritic fingers curl into fists that still tremble with deadly potential.

Cornelia and Gette emerge from the shower clean and in fresh clothes. Cornelia's dress is a little too long on her but

Gette's fits her perfect.

"Never throw out perfectly good clothes I always say," Martha says clambering up to inspect the fit on Gette. "You're such a sweet, precious little thing." She pulls Gette into her with a fierce, protective hug.

Despite freshening up, Charles's death clings to them like mud.

"Are you hungry sweet thing?"

Gette shakes her head no—a river of pain threatening to burst from her hazel eyes.

"Thank you for your hospitality," Cornelia says. "I don't think we have the stomach for food right now."

"Rest then," Martha says. "Best thing for you. Mary-Anne why don't you show them to bed?"

Mabel steps over stopping her daughter with a gentle hand. "If you don't mind, I'd like to take everyone's picture tonight, so I can get to work making up their papers. It'll just take a moment."

"Of course," Cornelia says. Her eyes the only chink in her armor.

Mabel leaves the room—a log collapses spraying a column of hot embers up the river stone chimney. Footsteps above us and the groaning of ancient wood beams telegraph her search through the attic.

She returns with a large mahogany box with simple brass

hardware. She plunks it down on the writing desk in the corner. Flipping it open, she reveals an assortment of pens, papers, blank visas, stamps, and an antique box camera with a massive silver flash. A geometric black box—gold circuitry tracing around the edges—is the only thing in this box made in this century.

"I'll snap a few pictures and then you can be off to bed. Mary-Anne, can you pull the curtain?"

Mary-Anne obeys. Standing in the corner rolled up around a wooden dowel is a large cloth. She places it in a stand, unfurls it pinning it in place with clasps nailed to the wall. This isn't the first time they've done this.

"If you could stand on the X," Mabel points to the small X painted near the middle of the cloth.

Cornelia goes first, her hand dropping from Gette like pulled sugar.

The bulb explodes filling the cabin with light. I blink away the afterimage as Mabel ejects the spent bulb with a *thunk* and pops in another.

"Alright sweetie, your turn."

Gette drags herself to the X. *Snap*—the burnt-out bulb crackles like a cigarette.

"All done," Mabel smiles.

"It's just this way." Mary-Anne leads them away—each step fighting its way through a quagmire of suffering.

As soon as they disappear, Mabel splashes more moonshine into her cup and knocks it back. Her face sours suppressing a shudder. "I can't bear to see it Mabel," memories stirring droplets in her eyes. "This world chews up little girls." She blinks away her ghosts and turns to me. "Was Charles a good man?"

I inhale sharply—my own memories eating away at my defenses. I knew Charles about as well as I really know any-one—I'm always keeping people at a distance or pushing them away. He wasn't like that though. He went out of his way for his family and friends. He was passionate, and he defended his own like a golem. Far from perfect but genuine, loving, and kind.

"He was," my voice trembles—a large hot tear streams down my right cheek and explodes at my feet.

Mabel wipes away the tear with a firm swipe of her thumb. She smiles, her own tears pooling in her lashes.

"Come now, let me get a picture of you before you're too red to recognize."

I chuckle releasing a fresh stream of tears. I wipe them away with my sleeve and stand in front of the X.

The world explodes in white light. The spectral echo of the flash fades from pure white to red to nothing in a shrinking circle ever flitting from view.

"I'll have to get Victor's when he wakes up, but this'll give me a good start on the papers."

"I'm going to keep watch in the attic," says Martha.

"You think there'll be trouble?"

"No, but sure has a way of finding you when you aren't looking."

"I'll check on you in an hour." Martha nods then disappears. Her footsteps reverberate through the rafters then fade back into the crackle of the dying fire. Mary-Anne stalks back into the living room. The dim light casts graven shadows into the contours of her face.

"You two should get some sleep. I'll get the papers made and wake you before first light."

"Shouldn't I help take watch with Oma?"

"No, you're going to have a long day tomorrow—you need the rest."

"Are you sure—"

Mabel raises her hand and Mary-Anne's protests evaporate.

"And you should really drink that," Mabel says pointing to my untouched glass of moonshine. "Chases the nightmares away."

The mug is cold. Lifting it to my lips the peach and turpentine aroma water my eyes. Ember's light dances in the ripples of the glass. I steel myself and take a sip. Expecting fire, it's surprisingly sweet. I lean into the taste, savoring the same grove of peaches used in the pie. Then the mood shifts, and fire strikes the back of my throat with a vengeance. Involuntary reflux forces me to cough as my body desperately tries to expel the poison—white-hot pain dances through my ribs. The initial shock gives way to warmth, radiating and calm. I throw caution to the wind and down the rest of the mug. The fire comes straight away, rolling down my tongue to fill my stomach with flame. A shudder racks my body then the world slurs. The light from the fire follows me around the room in ribbons. My cheeks are tingling and hot.

"Come on," Mary-Anne says, "let me take you to bed." I grin like a fool—eyes blinking sloth-like. Thoughts and fears melt from my mind and the blank space lures me to sleep in the darkness.

She guides me with strong arms to a bed where I sleep before I've begun to fall.

I awake in the darkness. The crystalline void stretches off in an infinite gradient of purple never reaching black. Remembrance snaps the phantasm into shape. Feet collide with the platform and before me stand two doors.

Both doors are equal in height and float equidistant from me. Yet the door on the left all but fades from view—the door on the right glows with ethereal light. The strand around my wrist leads through the keyhole. Guiding myself upon its mooring line, I float to the door and pass through.

I'm back in my childhood bedroom sitting on the floor.

Dolls and plastic horses are scattered on the ground around me like the horrendous aftermath of a tornado. Across from me is a little girl. My age, she's blonde and perfect. Her resemblance to the dolls is uncanny and I drift away wondering which came first like the chicken and the egg. A glint flickers in her eyes and tugs at the corners of her mouth.

"Let's play hide-and-seek," she says with a voice like spun sugar. "I'll hide first. Close your eyes and count to ten. No peeking! Ready, set, go!"

She springs from the floor and the world disappears behind my hands.

"One," I count aloud. Her feet pitter-patter to the door.

"Two." Door handle twists, bolt clicks.

"Three." Footsteps echo in the cavernous living room.

"Four." Echoes fade.

"Five," I strain to hear her—my heartbeat thrums in my ears.

"Six," my breath quickens with anticipation.

"Seven, eight, nine, Ten! Ready or not here I come!"

I jump up, then decide to play it cool. I can't rush out of the room—she'll think I cheated. I'll start here, throw her off the scent. I step carefully over the scattered toys and pull open the closet. I rifle through the hangers making sure to do it loud enough that she hears me. Next, I pull off the bed's duvet.

"Nope, not here. Where could she be?" That'll trick her. I already know. She's behind the couch, she has to be.

I twist open the handle and burst from the room like a snake-in-a-can. In the corner of my eye, Father is sitting on the couch—Blood Ball highlights blaring. Mother is sitting at her desk through the open door to her room. Her face is cast in dancing blue and white light front the projected light display.

Mind still on the hunt, I leap behind the couch.

"Ah ha! Got you—" My accusing finger falls limp at my side.

"Daddy, did you see where Victoriana went?"

He mutes the blaring announcer on the television and turns to me.

"I don't know," he leans in closer to whisper, "but I think your sister might know."

Grasping the spine of the couch, I pull myself over and kiss him on the cheek. He's turned back—television blaring—before my feet land on the polished concrete floors. I turn to the wall of windows, then keep turning, until I spot the door to Hannah's room. I rush through the door with abandon.

Sitting with her back to the door hunched over a book, she nearly jumps out of her skin. "Hey, you need to knock!"

"Come out, I found you," I say oblivious to my sister's request—I'm on the hunt. Hannah sets the book down on her desk and walks over to me.

"She's not in here silly goose." She ruffles my hair.

"Nice try, but I know she's here," I dart to the closet and throw open the door.

Dark and empty.

"She has to be here," backing away from the closet, webs of searing hot anxiety constrict around my chest.

"Here!" I say, pulling the bedding—my breath comes in short gulping gasps. The edges of the world turn to black.

"Here!" I say looking under the bed.

Nothing.

Panic swells up and swallows me. I fall to the floor rocking on my knees.

"Where is she?" I say hyperventilating.

Hannah rushes over. Taking me in her arms, she strokes my back.

"*Shhh* Evelyn, just breathe. Just breathe, Evelyn. Everything is going to be okay. Come on, I'll help you find Victoriana. Something tells me I know where she is."

The tempest fades and I look up at my big sister. Her almond, honey eyes sparkle beneath a halo of jet-black hair.

"Come on, little goose."

She takes my hand in hers, but before I can take a step, the silver leash wrapped around my wrist yanks me back. Disembodied I watch myself walk off with her.

"No!" I cry in vain—my screams swallowed whole by the merciless void.

The apartment rockets away—the leash digging into my skin.

"Let me go back to her!" The silence ricochets my words into nothing.

———

I shoot up in the small bed panting and drenched. Feet falling to the cold wood floor, I hold my head in my hands desperate to find my way back to her.

The house creaks in the small hours of the night. Silver peeks through the tops of the windows while orange dances through the gaps at the bottom. Breath condesing in plumes of vapor, the cold shivers away the path back to sleep. I pull the duvet around me taking the bite out of the cold, but a deep chill is still crawling up through my toes. My head bobbles on my shoulders and my stomach hangs in my gut like a rock.

I try to walk it off—first the bed then the floors singing to the night like mice. Eyes adjusted to the dark, I wade through the blurred, blue-black world. My fingers tracing my path along the smooth pine walls.

Illuminated at a writing desk in the corner of the living room, Mabel is hunched over her work. Quill in hand, the magnifying glass warps and exaggerates the small black-and-white image of my face.

"Can't sleep?" she says acknowledging my presence. I shake my head gliding across the floor to her side.

"I'm just putting the finishing touches on your travel papers *Sarah*." I lean forward. Underneath my portrait is a name written in perfected bureaucratic hand: Sarah Goodman.

"The name's a little much, but I never claimed to be creative."

"No, I like it. It sounds ordinary—invisible."

She smiles, teeth beaming in the lamplight. "You don't mind if I take credit for that?"

I smile and shake my head.

"And there." She crosses the final T near the bottom of the page. The ink shimmers and moves in the light. She blows on it gently drying the ink which snaps itself, unmoving, onto the page. She passes it to me. It's perfect, like the one I used to have. Rotating it in the light, I inspect the watermark—the seal of the Great Society appearing and disappearing in a holographic rainbow—and rub my fingers along the embossed seal *Department of Citizen and Labor Affairs.*

"It's beautiful—your work that is."

"Thank you. I've had some practice."

"Wouldn't it be easier to print it out? Why go through all the trouble of doing it by hand?"

She smirks. "Kids, always wanting things right now."

My cheeks glow hot. "No, no, I didn't mean it like that. It's just you've had to stay up all night to do it."

"I'm only kidding with you. It's a fair question. When digital cameras and laser printers trickled out of the military and into people's homes, there was a whole cottage industry of fake papers. The bureaucrats couldn't keep up, so they started embedding watermarks and protections into the inks." Her face lights up, the nuances of forging documents finding a way to bring some joy to this joyless night. She catches herself in my expression and shakes her head laughing. "There I go, about to drag you down a rabbit hole. Anyhow, long story short, if you try and print it today, tiny IR sensitive flakes in the ink will light up like Martyr's Day."

"I had no idea."

"We learned that lesson the hard way."

"So it's the old way or no way?"

"They can slow us down, but they can't stop us." Mabel pulls out the last incomplete passport. The photo is missing but she goes about filling in the details she can.

"What should your *brother's* name be?"

We could name him after Charles or Damian—a small token of remembrance—but those wounds are too new for it to be a good idea. I try to compile a list in my mind of common names no one would ask twice about.

"Robert? Bob is about as invisible as it gets."

"Bob Goodman," she says aloud as her hands deftly scrawl the name with a fountain pen.

I turn to look at him. In the dull light, he's silhouetted blue against the dark—his chest rising and falling rhythmically under a patchwork quilt.

"How is he doing?" I ask.

"His fever broke not long after you went to bed. He's stable, but—" her words trail off into a thundering silence.

"But what?" I say.

"I don't think he's ever going to use that arm again. The bullet made a mess of his elbow—nearly everything connecting his lower arm is frayed or severed. If we could get him to a hospital they could stitch him back together, but," she scoffs, "taking him there would be a death sentence."

I let the weight of her words wash over me. What had Victor been thinking? That he was going to storm in and rescue me? Did he have a plan, was he even thinking? Probably not. He was probably driven by whatever fantasy of me lives behind his eyes.

I slide my passport into my pocket then walk the few short steps over to the table where he's sleeping. I pull over one of the carved pine dining chairs and sit down next to him. I squeeze his good hand tight laying my head down on the table next to his.

CHAPTER TWENTY-THREE

DAWN RISES before I've come anywhere near rest. Martha passes me on her way down from her lookout in the attic—scoped rifle tucked in her arms. Mabel greets her, and they whisper something too faint for me to hear. They disappear together.

Mary-Anne, looking rested and put together like only a person long accustomed to early mornings can, emerges from the hallway as a rooster crows. The chill of the house fights against the first warming rays of the sun sending fresh shivers up my spine.

"Help me in the kitchen?" she says tying on an apron.

I rise to join her, leaving my blanket folded in the seat of the chair.

I do as she tells me, but mostly I stand slack-jawed and yawning as she whips together a feast of potatoes, sausages, and eggs faster than I manage to make some burnt toast.

"I'll finish up here, can you go wake them up?"

I smile, relinquishing the apron I had no right to be wearing.

Golden light illuminates a path down the hallway. I peek through the open door to the spare bedroom to find Cornelia already awake perched on the edge of the bed lacing up brown leather boots.

Unsure of how to talk about anything that's just happened, I stick to the pressing concerns of the morning. "Breakfast is ready. They haven't told me the plan yet, but I think they want to get moving pretty soon."

Sunken eyes turn to see me. "Thank you, Evelyn. We'll be out shortly." I start to smile then decide against it. Gette is bundled into a twisted mess of sheets and pillows behind her.

I leave them electric and not at all at ease.

Despite hunger and delectable offerings, none of us seems able to swallow more than a few mouthfuls—our stomachs are already full of apprehension. Victor is awake but distant. Mabel tied his arm up in a sling which he has chosen to ignore completely. He hasn't so much as glanced down at it since he woke—his eyes unable to fixate on anything but me.

"These will be good enough to get you past Peace Officers and most checkpoints. If they get their hands on you these won't hold up long when they're run against the central database. So it goes without saying—don't get caught." She waits a moment for us all to inspect our identities. "Finish eating, then Victor come with me and I'll get your picture taken. Mary-Anne see if you can get through to Mansfield and let them know you're coming. Everyone else, Martha is in the shed getting The Mule ready."

She reads the confused expressions on our faces and the excited one on Gette's then clarifies. "It's a tunnel car, not a pachyderm."

Gette's momentary excitement fizzles away and she hunches back down poking at her food with a fork.

"Alright then," says Martha rising from the table, "let's get this going."

———

The tunnel in the shed is twice again as large as the tunnel we escaped in. Constructed in the same fashion—wooden ribs holding back smooth earthen walls with a central string of dull-yellow lights—except for a set of narrow steel tracks running off into the distance. Anchored on the concrete landing is The Mule. A squat hobbled-together cart with recognizable elements from a lawnmower and diesel generator. Painted with flourish on the side is a cartoon mule kicking lightning bolts from his back hooves.

Huddled together, the seven of us fit comfortably on the long bed.

"Hold on tight—I 'aint call it The Mule for nothing," Martha says cranking the engine to life.

She isn't kidding, and with a surging lurch, we speed down the tunnel. Wind thrashes my hair and billows in my clothes.

Shivering, I press myself as low as I can—hands clenched onto the railing only inches away from the wood ribs whizzing by—my mask keeping the wind out of my eyes. Once the sloshing in my stomach and the tingle of my spine simmered down, it's almost fun.

I didn't realize how comforting the rumble of the generator was until Martha killed it. Letting us coast on the rails, the shriek and rattle of the cart echoing down the tunnel becomes audible. Lapping back over on itself and warped in the cavernous resonance of the tunnel, the sound slithers into my ears like a worm.

The end draws near. Mabel and Mary-Anne pull on the hand brakes. Piercing steel cries stab at us once then bounce back and away to assault us again. As we glide to a stop, the stone in my stomach turns to a boulder.

"I'll stay with The Mule and keep her ready in case we need to get out of here in a hurry. If I don't see you again, I wish you good fortune." Martha's matter-of-fact tone cannot betray the fluttering of her eyes behind her mask.

"We're forever in your debt," says Cornelia lifting Gette over the railing.

"Nonsense. This is the least we can do."

I help Victor climb out then we follow Mary-Anne up the ladder.

The room beyond could be anything and each rung swells the possibilities. Mary-Anne helps me out and I turn and help Victor who's struggling with only one arm.

The warehouse we've climbed into stretches three stories above us. Soot covered windows block out nearly all light. What scant light there is splits the space in shafts coming through the windows either broken or propped open with wooden dowels—the vacuous coal piles eliminate refraction keeping the light trapped in rectangular pillars.

"I'm going to go find David and make sure the plan is still in place. We should be back shortly. I'll tap like this," Mary-Anne rasps her knuckles on a grime-encrusted support beam next to her. *Burap, burap, buarp.*

"If you don't hear that knock, get back in the tunnel and get to safety with Oma."

"We won't leave you behind," says Gette her fists and eyes dancing on the edge.

Mary-Anne takes her by the shoulders—their masks pressed filter-to-filter. "Oh, sweet thing, don't worry. I'll be back." Unconvinced, Gette huddles to Cornelia's side.

"Right," Mary-Anne says brushing the accumulating soot from her blouse.

"Be quick," Mabel says voice brittle and thin. Mary-Anne rushes off, sliding, and trudging through the mountains of coal.

The rail yard howls with activity. Engines rumble and air horns slice through the stillness—their commanding voices whooshing away even thoughts not firmly held down. I crouched on my haunches until they cramped and forced me to straighten them, now I'm sitting in a lumpy pile of coal. Our clothes, so pristine this morning, are now soiled beyond recognition. Our every cough and shuffle echoes through the warehouse. Gette is acting out some scene with two lumps of coal. The larger piece lies still in her hand while the little one prods it over and over again to move.

Cornelia and Mabel are hyper-alert—their eyes darting to investigate the slightest sounds. Victor has retreated into himself. Rocking back and forth his face is turned up in agony and he's grabbing at his arm above the bandages.

Each tumble of a coal-lump down a pile or the whistle of wind in the rafters sends needles on a rampage through my veins.

Burap, burap, buarp.

Threadbare, we snap out of our skins at the start. Bumbling footsteps crunch through the soot toward us.

Mary-Anne emerges over a heap. The crescendo snaps—our shoulders relax, and the roof settles an inch lower. A plump young man with a fine woolen trench coat trimmed in fur follows behind her. His cream calf-skin gloves are stained black from catching himself. A laden satchel hangs over his shoulder. The duo pauses to catch their breath.

"I have a coal train leaving for Lufthaffen in fifteen minutes. Bulls are checking it over now, and then Specters will sweep over it with dogs. When the red light turns amber, you'll need to run to the second to last car—Mary-Anne will show you the way. Get inside fast and stay quiet. I've arranged for someone to come get you on the other end. Best of luck."

"David, the bag," says Mary-Anne in an unfamiliar tone.

"Oh, right. I scrounged up some pain pills for him," he gestures to Victor—David's face grimaces at the wound. "I've also put some food, a little water, and some reading material in here for you. It isn't much, but it should help the ride be a little more bearable." Closest to them, I reach out and take the supple leather strap—it's heavy for its size.

"Now I have to get back to the radio room before anyone notices." David embraces Mary-Anne holding their foreheads together for the few moments they have left together.

"Thank you, David," says Mabel.

"You'd all do the same. Now I gotta go." He turns and bumbles back through the soot.

Mary-Anne leads the way across to the back corner of the warehouse. "Come on, let's get in position."

Rusted holes in the corrugated siding peek out onto the rail yard beyond. Bulls in blue work suits are scouring every crevice of the fully-loaded train two tracks away. The tapping of their batons fades replaced by the slathering, snarl snap of hounds.

Encased in grotesque armored rebreathers, the Specters' hounds are cyborg monsters. Their barks are bowel-loosening rumbles enhanced by their exoskeletons. They surge forward, sniffing, and snapping—their chain leashes tugging on the arms of their dread masters.

One of the monsters stops mid-stride and turns its red, augmented eyes to the warehouse. I leap out of my skin pulling myself away from the peephole. The world fades away and my ears shout at my heart to stop beating.

"What is it?" asks Gette who's desperately trying to find her own viewport. I hold my finger up to the red leather of my mask. Gette sits down understanding—Cornelia runs her hand down her back.

"Hounds?" Mary-Anne says with her lips and a tiny gasp of a whisper.

I nod frantically. Both petrified and deeply curious, I press the glass of my mask viewport back to the hole. The hound has lost interest and is dragging his Specter toward the engine.

The coil of nerves unwinds in my chest and I breathe deep reflexively. My battered ribs ripple with fire. Mary-Anne peers through a gap of her own.

"We should get ready. Cornelia, Gette, Victor, and Evelyn.

That's the order I want you to line up behind me. Keep your head low and run as fast as you can. Don't look around. Mabel will watch our backs and David is looking out from the tower. I'll help you inside the car and then you're on your own."

She pauses to let our jitters settle and the plan to sink in. I look to each of their faces. The boulder in my gut grows a little bigger.

"I think we're as ready as we'll ever be," I say.

"That's good enough. Alright, let's get lined up."

Mary-Anne hustles over to the door. She clears away the thick soot from the hinges and makes room for it to swing in. Mabel takes position looking through a small hole at the red light. Mary-Anne crouches like a coil ready to spring—one hand on the handle and the other steadying her on the wall. Cornelia mimics her and Gette and Victor follow suit. Mother holds her daughter's hand. Legs bounce, hearts race.

"Now."

Mabel's words crack like a starter's pistol. Mary-Anne throws open the door and leaps through at a sprint. Cornelia lunges after her pulling Gette along. Victor lags, I hook under his good arm and pull him into a run.

Suddenly emerging into the light turns the world white. The rail yard gravel crackles under our fast feet. The outlines in front of me grow in detail as my vision returns. I tune the rest out, shutting down flashes of hounds tearing out my throat.

The twenty meters evaporates. Mary-Anne holds open the small hatch on the second-to-last car. The locomotives roar into action—the dead metal hums with infused life. Victor disappears inside. I scurry after him, ribs exploding from the effort. I yank the satchel through. Mary-Anne lingers in the opening.

"Good luck," she says slamming the door shut.

The metal latch closes with a definitive *clank*.

The car is half empty with soot ash. It grates against my exposed skin and works its way under my clothes, but it conforms around me enough to relax. Eyes closed, I focus on keeping my breaths shallow to lessen the liquid fire that seeps from my ribs every time they expand.

The lurch of ten thousand horses starts us on our journey. Catching up to my breath, I open my eyes. The open-top car frames the sky like a cinema screen. Blue sky peeks out from behind thin gray clouds. I watch shapes twist, form, and melt away. Then the belching black smoke from the engines reaches its inky tendril back to us blocking the sky from view.

Numb hours pass with little to break the daze. Sapped, hungry, and on the edge of despair we've hardly moved from where we landed. Occasional breaks in the smoke offer fleeting glimpses of the brown-black sky. But the wind, so quick to shift, always returns the ominous black cloud overhead. The sun had long set by the time I noticed the single twinkling star shining through.

Stomach rumbling, I sit up as best I can. *How long do ribs take to heal?* Rooting through the bag I find a *Meal for One.* I twist the cap from its silver package and greedily slurp it through my mask's liquid port. Squeezing out the last few drops of *deluxe turkey dinner supreme,* my heart pangs. *Was this Mother's last meal?*

Light glints in the darkness. Gette sits up pushing her mother's sleeping arm off her.

"Can I have one?"

"Sure thing, kiddo."

I root around and find another. Gette struggles both with the cap and the liquid port but gets it all the same in the end. She doesn't say it, but she doesn't have to. Her scrunched-up face tells the truth.

"Yeah I don't get it either. It's not deluxe or supreme."

"Yeah, more like turkey de-yuck."

I laugh and regret it. My chest bursts like a kicked anthill. I crunch forward trying to stop the pain with my fingers.

"I'm sorry," Gette says looking away.

"No, it's not your fault. That was funny."

The traumas behind her eyes are dragging Gette away so I change the subject trying to pull her back.

"Did you get any sleep?"

"A little. But I had nightmares—don't make me go back to sleep."

"I won't make you." Wind howls, wheels clatter, metal groans.

"Why don't you climb over here and help me see what's in this bag?" I say beckoning her over with a wave.

Life flashes in her smile. She crawls out of her mother's arms and over Victor who's passed out on his side, his wounded arm to the sky. The soot shifts around us and we settle in.

"Let's see. More *Meals for One*, some water, a flashlight, and—" I pull a red, leather-bound book from the inside silk pocket. Flicking the light on, I read the title scrawled in gleaming gold letters. "Anwen the Dragon Slayer and other tales of heroic deeds."

"Will you read it to me?"

I can't help but smile.

"You hold the flashlight and I'll hold the book." We shift the soot to position ourselves and I begin.

"Anwen was the only daughter of Bronwyn and Berwyn. Her hair flowed in an untamable mane and glowed red like an amaranth flower. She was bold and brave. The townsfolk called her little dragon. Bullies and thieves knew to steer clear of the fiery lass lest they feel the bite of her wooden sword."

"I like her," Gette says pulling the light away in her excitement.

"You know, you remind me of her a little. No, more than a little. I might just start calling you that from now on." Gette grins. "Come on little dragon, what do you think happens next?" Beaming, Gette turns the light back to the page.

I read the whole story through twice before the gentle swaying of the train and exhaustion lull us to sleep.

Convulsing shivers rattle me awake. Rubbing my arms vigorously, I open my eyes wide to acclimate to the darkness. With each breath condensation mists over my lenses shifting the world in and out of a dreamlike haze.

At some point in the night Gette pulled away from me and cuddled up with her mother. Cradled in Cornelia's arms, she trembles from cold and what I can only imagine are frightful dreams.

I pick up the book from where it fell out of my hands and return it to the silk pocket. Pulling the bag to me, I try to use it as a pillow. I fight with the coal to find some comfort, but no manner of writhing makes it less miserable.

"Can't sleep either?" Victor's voice carries just above the rumbling clickety-clack of the train.

I turn and see him looking at me. I nod my head and sit up. I scoot my way over to him—my feet send avalanches of coal down the shallow slopes. Next to him, I catch the glimpse of a smile under his mask. But it fades as fast as it formed—caressing his shattered arm his gaze turns to the sky.

I follow his gaze up. Thick plumes of smoke blanket the sky—a gray canvas highlighted yellow and orange from city lights. Small breaks in the blanket reveal the darkness of the night above.

"My sister tried to get us out of Einsam once. She took us so far from everything that you could see the sky. We were just little kids—I was maybe five. She must have been thirteen or fourteen. That last night we were on the run, we lay there under that massive sky. Countless stars looked down on us. White, blue, yellow, red—god, there were so many. I didn't really appreciate it then. The sky or what she was doing. I just thought we were on an adventure." Victor's eyes move to Gette. "I hope we can find her—I think you and Olivia will like each other," he says with a smile crinkling the corner of his eyes.

"Oh yeah?" I say reflecting his smile.

"Oh yeah—you're peas in a pod you two," he chuckles.

"Is that so?" I move to play punch his arm then remember it's shattered, we're sitting in a boxcar, Charles is gone, and the world is on fire.

He notices my hesitation in the corner of his eye and pulls his body away from me hiding his left arm in shadow as if that'll make it all go away.

The click-clack counts the time as minutes of silence pass. Looking back to the sky, Victor picks up his thought.

"She always has a plan. Maybe she doesn't know where we're going, but she keeps moving forward. She doesn't let you stop and get stuck where you are." Victor's eyes flick to me then retreat as quick as I catch them—the light of a solitary star twinkles in them.

"Look!" he exclaims pointing to the break in the smog with his right hand.

A gap in the twisting rivers of smog open a portal on the blackness of space pierced only by a single blue pinprick of light. I look up, mouth agape, unable to blink until the smog closes in again and the star's light fades again from view.

"When our parents died, we were all alone—we had nothing. She kept me safe, always made sure there was food on the table."

The emotion in his voice threatens me to break. *I wish Hannah were here.*

I force myself to speak—to push down that tiny voice in my head. "It must have been hard when she left."

Victor nods his head. "It was. We'd moved in with Mr. Herrington by then. He convinced us there was a future. That we could fight back from inside."

"Is that why she left?"

"Yeah. She believed if enough good people got into the system you could soften it—make things better. She landed a job with the Lufthaffen port authority. We needed the money and it put her in a position to make a difference." Victor shakes his head. "I should have gone with her. I stayed to help Damian. To help Mr. Herrington. I—"

I scoot close and put my arm around him.

"You made the right choice. If you'd left Einsam, I don't know where I would be."

Tears glisten in his eyes and break away as he smiles. He leans into the hug.

Returning our attention to the sky, we watch for breaks in the smog until sleep takes us both.

Sweat pooling in my eye sockets startles me awake. The sun is high in the sky above us, but it's only just now broken through the smoke to boil me in my mask. Similar discomfort drags us all out of sleep.

I pass around the water sacks and then smash up a handful of pain pills and mix them with into one of the water pouches for Victor. I don't know if it's safe, or if it'll even work, but I can't just do nothing—he's turning pale again and his bandages are almost soaked through with blood.

I read Gette more stories of heroes and monsters, dragons and wizards.

The day slinks along shifting the hidden shadows in the soot pile.

When next we see the sun, it illuminates our destination in radiant columns of golden light. The train slows, and the honk and clamor of cars joins the shrill music of the rails. Buildings appear over the lip of the car and tangled nests of power lines crisscross the sky. The setting sun is replaced with the hum and glow of countless neon tubes—their collective kaleidoscopic brilliance revealing more than the daylight. Airships dangling massive neon billboards beneath them float silently through the growing forest of towering skyscrapers.

Lufthaffen is taller and brighter than Einsam—its hundreds of chrome and glass skyscrapers illuminate a bustling metropolis still untouched by the ravages of the war nipping at our heels.

The train pulls us into the heart of the city before convulsing to rest. Momentum swirls inside me stirring up idling tensions and resting fears.

Steam hisses, brakemen bark. I slide over to the hatch—air lumps in my throat.

"Ready?"

A silent nod passes between downturned faces.

Clunk.

The door grinds open and I pull myself free in an avalanche of soot. Jagged grains work their way into my boots and bite at the soles of my feet.

I crouch low and scan my surroundings. The rail yard is

sprawling. Work lights sweep through the darkness. Steam and smog billow from a dozen active trains. Pebbles dance to the same deep bass rumble that's clattering my teeth.

Whooot!

The air horn's blast hits me like a bucket of ice water. Rattled, I make one more sweep of the rail yard. We're as safe as we're going to be. I turn back to the hatch.

"Coast is clear, but we need to move—quick!"

Gette's hand emerges from the porthole sending a soothing wave of resolve over my flayed nerves. She slides out without trouble and Cornelia manages but tears roll down Victor's face as he stifles the pain of contorting through the opening. He stumbles forward and it's all Cornelia and I can do to keep him from falling.

"Are you alright, do you need help?" He nods no but he's being stubborn. He's clammy and losing color and he can't seem to keep his eyes open. "At least put your arm around my shoulder."

I guide his good arm around my shoulders before he can think to say no again. His arms are soft, and his legs are about to lose their fight with gravity.

"Right. I don't know where to go but let's at least get away from these trains and spotlights."

Everyone nods. I breathe in deep and press forward.

I haven't taken my second step when terror slams into my chest.

A figure takes shape in the wall of steam ahead of us. I pull everyone behind me, holding the satchel in front of me like a shield. Teeth clenched—my eyes dart frantically for a path out of this labyrinth. Panic, like frostbite, constricts my limbs.

Their shadow grows as they approach until it towers over us in the hissing steam.

CHAPTER TWENTY-FOUR

I WON'T LET IT END LIKE THIS. Muscles bound to snapping, I wrench the bag back ready to hurl it at the boogeyman looming in the haze.

The shadow grows well beyond human height stretching up into the rail yard's thick miasma as high as the megaplexes. But just as rapidly as it appeared, it shrinks down into a child-sized silhouette.

A boy no older than Gette emerges from the steam. He's swimming in a patched leather jacket hemmed to half its length but still entirely too long. His respirator is clogged with glistening black sludge. Molasses eyes ripple with spotlight beams behind cracked goggles strapped to a precariously perched leather ushanka that must have belonged to the same person as the jacket.

"Sarah Goodman?"

His words knock me off guard and I drop the tension in my arm.

"Uh…" I'm slack-jawed. Were we set up? Then why go through all the trouble with the trains? Is he on our side? Can we trust him? Do we have a choice?

I turn to Cornelia hoping to find an answer. Her eyes say run. Action burns in my chest. Victor's clammy hand clutches mine—Gette squeezes my leg until it tingles.

The fire snuffs itself out. We can't run, we can't fight. The only way out is through.

"Uh yes," I cough, clearing the fear gummed up in my throat. "That's me—I'm Sarah Goodman."

"Then you need to come with me right away! The shift change!"

A quizzical look passes between us. Cornelia nods, Victor and Gette squeeze tighter.

I start moving. "Lead the way."

He motions for us to stay low then darts down the row of trains, snaking left and right to navigate the maze of boxcars. I struggle to keep up and keep an eye on the others. Cornelia urges Victor along and I take Gette by the arm.

Emerging from the labyrinth of trains, he holds open a gap in the chain-link fence—concertina wire glints in the blood-like bath of Mountain Air advertising. Searchlights scanning the yard sweep overhead missing us by lucky meters.

We sprint a little farther stopping behind the shelter of a dumpster overflowing with rotting food. Rats scurry away to steam pipes carrying off a smorgasbord of rot.

"Ready?" We've only just stopped but the boy looks like he'd rather shake himself apart than sit still.

Victor's a little gray and Gette is shaking, but we're not too bad considering. "I think so."

"Good, good, good. Almost there." He shuffles forward along the alley wall to the corner and signals for me to follow.

I mirror his urgency doing everything I can not to think about the grime on the wall and the greasy rat trails I'm trudging through. We chance a peek together.

"That's the checkpoint. Show 'em your papers, keep cool—Shepard will take care of the rest."

Portable watchtowers anchor prefab metal walls bolted across the sidewalks. A slalom of concrete barricades funnels traffic past Peace Officers with inspection mirrors.

"Are you kidding me?"

"It's just a checkpoint—she's waiting."

"Our papers aren't going to hold up to scrutiny.

Cornelia and Victor move up behind us.

"What's going on?"

"He says we have to go through the checkpoint."

"No way. Victor can hardly stand and I'm not going to just hand my daughter over."

"Sheesh, I'm just trying to help." He throws his hands up. His ushanka starts to slide off the back of his head. He manages to catch it just in time. "You can make your own way if you want, but you won't get far." He whips his head around the corner again keeping one hand firmly pressed on the top of his hat.

"You gotta go now. If she's not there to help you…"

This is suicide. Cornelia shakes her head and pulls Gette behind her. Victor moans, his eyes are glassing over. We're out of options and we're running out of time.

I nod to Cornelia with grim resolve. She closes her eyes—ash falls in the pregnant pause. Her eyes open with a nod.

"Here's your opening! Good luck!"

A gap forms in the listless people shuffling down the side-walk. He waves us on. The time for hesitation is over. I pull Victor to his feet then stride confidently out of the alley.

Neon signs flash animating stars and arrows declaring all manner of sales. Food vendors and hawkers compete for the crammed walkway from their plastic shelters. Thin huddles of trench-coated citizens shuffle along ebbing and flowing into the hundreds of stores and apartments hidden in the megaplex engulfing the street. Street sweepers and their dinner-plate-sized sidewalk cousins roam like sharks.

The checkpoint looms before us. Floodlights and machine guns in the towers sweep over the backed-up traffic. Barbed wire funnels foot traffic into the small portals on either side of the street. Peace Officers check each person's papers with a handheld scanner that baths them in searing green light. A silent determination is made, and they are directed to one path or the other. So far everyone has gone to the right.

"Just breathe everyone." I say it aloud hoping in vain that it will dislodge the anchor on my chest.

I pull our papers from the satchel with bouncing fingers. Victor's hand is ice cold. Scratching fire skitters across my body. Each step forward adds another timpani to the orchestra whooshing in my head.

"Halt citizen. Papers." His mask infuses his dispassionate tone with a commanding bite.

He snatches my passport, folds it open, and presses it down on the glass. A bar of green light comes to life under the glass and creeps across it. I'm dizzy. Bile builds in my throat.

The green light flicks off. Words flash on the screen, but they slide over each other in a swirling blur. The Peace Officer stiffens and lifts his concealed eyes to meet mine.

"Left gate." There's nothing blasé in his voice now.

Blood streams out of my head like a dam burst. The ground is coming up at me, but firm hands keep me on my feet. His inhuman eyes trace themselves across the hands propping me up.

"You three, left gate," he barks jabbing his baton at Cornelia and Victor.

With fight and flight impossible we stand teary-eyed in a frozen stupor.

"Comply!"

Skittering flames reignite.

Chatter irrupts in the line behind us. Rough gloved hands corral us through the left gate.

Inspections resume behind us without missing a beat. "Halt citizen. Papers." The authority in the Peace Officer's voice is already waning.

Beyond the gate, Peace Officers wave through the cars slowly snaking through the maze of concrete barriers. Diesel generators feed searchlights through braided steel cables bolted to the megaplex's façade. People that made it through the right gate shuffle along the edge of the megaplex separated from us by a wire fence. They rubberneck as they pass soaking in as much information as they can for their watercooler story about the subversives at the checkpoint.

A petite Peace Officer guides us to windowless rectangle that would be more at home on the back of a truck than a sidewalk.

"Stand here." She motions to a corral made of three prefab fence units.

I squeeze Gette's hand. "We're going to be okay." My muffled words are carried off down the concrete canyon by the howling wind.

We shuffle into the three-sided cage and huddle together to shiver away the cold. Satisfied, the petite Peace Officer stomps over to the squat building, knocks, and waits to enter.

She disappears into the hut. My mask is fogging up. Raindrops flash into steam on the generators. There isn't anywhere to run. Every path out is barricaded or surveilled. One of the spotlights keeps sweeping over our heads and the message is clear: don't even think about moving.

I adjust my grip on Victor, he's growing heavier by the minute. The door to the hut swings open with a startling bang. The petite Peace Officer returns with the sergeant and hands over our passports.

"Let's see what's going on here." She flips mine open. Raindrops turn the ivory pages brown. "Just arrived from Mansfield huh?"

I start to answer but the question was rhetorical—her eyes never lifted off the page. I kick myself—*shut up*.

She flips through the rest of the pages then makes a perfunctory glance at the others. Victor moans, his eyes are listing side to side.

"Problem is Sarah—these work permits are expired. Not a serious crime, routine mistake. But I'll have to detain you until you can sort it out with Citizen and Labor—" Victor's legs give out and she swoops in to catch him.

I scramble to help. His skin is pimpled and quivering.

"Corporal, help me load him into the van."

The corporal pushes Cornelia and me aside and takes Victor under his injured arm. He moans—his legs wobble and fumble for footing.

The sergeant looks back, "You three, let's go."

Cornelia and I share a panicked look. That boy said we'd get help from them, but this is going south fast. Do we just go along? What options do we really have? If we grabbed Victor, where would we run? We're caged in and the only way out is through.

The corporal is practically dragging him—his feet dart and slide in the muck searching for grip. I rush forward and take Victor's other arm. She's leading us to a van. My stomach clenches. If we hop in there, that could be the last thing we ever do. If we're lucky, they might drive us to the pits and put us straight onto a chain gang. Or they could line us up against an alley wall and leave our bodies for the rats. I can reach the corporal's baton and try to knock her out before she draws her pistol but then what?

I help her load Victor into the first row of seats in the van then clamber into the back with Cornelia and Gette. The corporal slams the sliding door shut—it seals with a wheezing hiss then locks with a *clang*.

Rain hammers on the roof. I reach forward and keep Victor's head from flopping against the window.

"It's going to be okay. We're going to get you help."

Victor moans. Cornelia squeezes my thigh. Gette's leg bounces in rhythm with her shaking head.

The corporal climbs into the driver's seat. The sergeant stops her door from closing.

"Keys corporal. I'll take them in."

The hammering rises to a roar as the clouds tear open. The corporal hesitates. Her head swivels between her sergeant and us—her hand never giving up the grasp on the keys.

The sergeant steps back opening the door all the way. Rain pours in.

"Don't make me ask again."

With insubordinate reluctance, the corporal twists the keys out of the ignition and slams them in the sergeant's outstretched hand.

The corporal rushes to the street, stopping traffic with a raised fist and shrill blast of her whistle. The van rumbles awake, and the sergeant pulls us into the road. We snake through the maze—a dozen black eyes follow us—then as soon as we are free the sergeant pushes the van to its limits.

"Sorry about all that—you're safe now." She looks back at Victor, "We aren't far from the Lighthouse—Keep him awake."

Relief shimmers through me. The boy was right.

"We made it Victor. It's going to be okay. They're going to help you."

Victor moans. I'm losing him.

"Tell me about your sister. Tell me about Olivia."

I catch his eyes blinking open through the reflection in the glass.

"She's… she's a lot like you. I bet you—"

His eyes roll back, his muscles lose their tension. He melts into the seat.

"Victor!"

I pull out some slack on my seat belt and lean over the seat in front of me. His breaths are shallow and fast. I pull off his mask and he gasps. Life pulses then fades through him with each unfiltered breath. His forehead is on fire—his skin is beaded with sweat.

"Faster!"

Rain and the engine's roar drown us in a sea of noise. Each gap between his breathes brings me to the edge of the abyss. Then, his chest swells and it's like the sun is bursting over the horizon.

My seat belt slams me back into my seat sending the frozen city hanging in the windows—a specular neon blur—crashing back to life in a squeal of breaks. A swarm of dark figures rush the van. They push past me and pull Victor onto a stretcher then disappear through an open door—the warm light inside spills out illuminating our path.

"Follow them, I need to hide the van. Hurry." The sergeant's concern filtered through her voice modulator knocks me off balance.

My hands are hard to control, and I fumble with the seat belt. As soon as I'm free, I rush back and help Cornelia get Gette out. We pull her along and step through the door.

It's a small utility room littered with shovels and brooms. A small airlock at the end stands open—steam rising around it in lazy tendrils. Flashes of the bakery airlock—of Charles—melt my feet to the floor. Gette drops my hand. She's staring at the airlock—tears cloud her eyes.

I offer her my hand "Victor needs us, we have to be brave."

Together we step through. *Whir hiss whir.* I pull off my mask swapping the salty, leather lavender of the mask for the metallic, smoke and gunpowder of the room. A few dozen lights flicker with yellow life revealing wood walls charred black and pockmarked with bullet holes. *Die Rats!* is tagged all over the walls in sloppy red paint.

Flyers, crumbled and ruined, litter the floor. *The Lighthouse welcomes all.* I bend over and pull one from the floor. Layer of dirt and ash shuck off it revealing a line drawing of a light-house splitting the darkness.

A slick muddy trail leads across the sandstone floor and up a flight of stairs. I follow the trail and the sounds of Victor's rescuer's up the stairs with my eyes.

There is a woman on the landing looking at us. My heart plummets to the floor. Her hair is hacked short and oil black but there is no mistaking her.

Faint, I stumble—Gette takes my hand, steadying me.

My mouth trembles open. "Victoriana?"

CHAPTER TWENTY-FIVE

VICTORIANA SCARED ME LESS AS A GHOST. It was easy to hide from my sins when she was a relic of a former life. But there she stands, a living, scathing reminder of the poor choices I've made. Even standing across the room from me it's clear she isn't the same person who she was on the field that day. But neither am I.

Victoriana is alive and resolute. But she hasn't managed to crawl out of the hell I put her through unscathed. Her bouncing blonde locks have been hacked away and time has betrayed their false pallor and reveled the ink at its root. Gone too is her perpetual effervescence popping and sparkling like an agitated seltzer. In its place is a look of steel—her eyes no longer glisten, they burn.

Her mouth opens but before she can say anything her eyes lock on me and recognition turns her face to stone. I think I'm going to puke. Searing through me like a hot knife, only her eyes betray recognition.

"We're doing what we can for your friend." Her words nail me to the spot. All the sweetness is gone from her voice revealing the solid core and unshakable confidence within. Is this why people have always flocked to her, why they've always loved her? Was there always substance I couldn't see?

I dare not move. Air turns to concrete in my lungs. Oblivious, Gette and Cornelia walk straight past me toward the staircase.

Victoriana's stance waivers, her fists clench—she's ready to throw us back out on the street. Gette breaks from Cornelia's hand and bounds up the stairs.

"Where is he?" Gette asks, washing away the contempt swelling between us. I draw in a tingling, heavy breath.

"He's in good hands. They've taken him to the infirmary," her eyes break from mine and when they blink open, the embers in them have been extinguished. Vicky takes Gette's hand and gives her a you-have-nothing-to-fear-your-friend-is-safe smile. "I'll take you there." Victoriana turns her attention back to me—her eyes scream rot in hell.

Vicky doesn't wait to watch me squirm. She leads Gette down the hallway. Cornelia's halfway up the stairs before she notices I'm not behind her.

"Evelyn?"

"Go, I'm coming, I just need to catch my breath."

She doesn't believe me, but I wave her on and she doesn't

fight me. Getting to Victor is the only thing that should matter right now.

Her footsteps fade into the dull hum and rumble. Distant metal clanks. Sprites dance in my vision and I can't catch my breath. How can I face her? What if she tells them what I did to her? I've told them the short version—the version where I made an honest mistake—but not the truth. Gette will never look at me the same. How could Cornelia ever trust me around her daughter again? How will Victor stomach the sacrifices he made for me knowing the kind of thoughtless monster I was… Or perhaps the thoughtless monster that I still am?

I could make a run for it right now. If I turned back into the alleyway, I could be ten blocks away before anyone figured it out. I'd rather run straight back to the checkpoint and turn myself in than climb those stairs.

Victor screams.

I pull my feet from their nails and force myself up the stairs. I can't undo the things I've done, but I can take control of who I am now.

Earnest voices and muffled action swells as I make my way toward the light pouring from the open door at the end of the unlit hallway. Nerves build to a swarm of flies ready to tear their way out of me. A pungent wash of fetid copper hits me in the nose and clings to the back of my throat. *Just breathe, Evelyn.* I steal myself and cross the threshold.

The room still has the trappings of a classroom on the wall, biology posters, cartoon atoms and hydrocarbons holding hands. But the chairs have been cleared out and the tables turned into makeshift operating tables. Stained bedsheets cover the tables, trays of metal tools—probably last used to dissect a frog—sit next to *All Better* first aid kits.

A small group is huddled around Victor. A tall, muscular man in piecework medical garb is reworking the stitches on Victor's elbow. A middle-aged woman is holding up an IV bottle while a few other people are keeping Victor from slumping off the narrow chemistry table.

His screams have faded into a sobbing moan. Victoriana and Gette kneel beside him reassuring him softly. Cornelia catches sight of me in the doorway. She's ransacking the first aid kits.

"Help me find something for his pain."

The task propels me into action and fights back the medusa of dread, anxiety, and despair trying to turn me back into stone. I grab one of the few bags she hasn't unzipped already. Obnoxiously bright self-adhering bandages and perky pain pills aren't what we're after, and there probably isn't anything of the level Victor needs, but we have to look anyway.

"Just a few more," says the man stitching up Victor's arm. He's nearly as pale as Victor is and he doesn't seem confident in anything more than his stitches.

I unzip a new bag. Tossing aside the same useless bandages,

I come across a blue bottle of *Drift Away. Life got you down? Drift away!*

"What about this?"

I hand the bottle over to Cornelia. She snatches it and starts interrogating the label. "Two of these should take the edge off—no more than that." She lowers the bottle and brings her eyes to mine. "He might never wake up."

I swallow hard. One of the young women holding Victor steady steps forward and takes the pills from Cornelia.

"I'll get him some water," she says, leaving the room through a large hole torn through the lath and plaster on the back wall.

"There, all stitched back up." The surgeon plunks his bloody needle and thread onto one of the silver trays then makes for the sink.

Cornelia moves to Victor's side and strokes his forehead.

"How are you feeling?"

Victor opens his eyes releasing a new wave of tears.

"I just want to sleep. My arm is so cold."

"Hang in there, we've got a pill for you. It'll help you sleep." Cornelia takes the pills and water from the young woman and helps Victor sit up. He struggles with the water, most of it spills out the side of his mouth, but he manages to get the pills down.

"There, that wasn't too bad? It should help real soon."

The room grows solemn, all eyes are on Victor, and no one dares move. The medicine acts fast. His arms grow limp, but his breathing grows deeper and falls into a healthy rhythm.

The room swells with relief. Victoriana takes the IV from the middle-aged woman.

"Thank you, everyone. I think that's about all we can do for him right now. Let's help make our guests a little more comfortable. Books, can you show them where they can freshen up?"

The young woman who got the water starts to say yes but Cornelia cuts her off.

"That's very kind, but we'd like to stay right here with Victor if you don't mind."

"Absolutely," Victoriana says, "I understand. You can wait here as long as you like."

Books nods in agreement. Everyone but Victoriana and the surgeon filter out of the room. The surgeon comes back over to the table, his hands are shaking. Victoriana grabs his shoulder. "You did great."

"I did what I could. He's banged up pretty bad. I fixed the tourniquet and got those stitches straightened out, but he needs a real doctor. If we can't get him to a hospital, I don't think he's going to make it. Not unless we…" His eyes drift over to the small hacksaw on the tool tray.

Cornelia steps in front of the tray. "That has to be our last resort—if we can't control the bleeding, we'll kill him."

Books returns with the lanky guy with a stack of folded blue blankets.

"It's not much, but you'll be warm." They try to hand Cornelia one, but she's fixated on Victor, so I take it instead. The lanky guy unfurls one and wraps it around Gette.

The middle-aged woman returns with a big box of pumpkin cookies. She opens a wrapper and offers it to Gette.

"I saw these down in the kitchen and I thought they might be just what you needed."

Gette's eyes dart between the cookie, her mother, and Victor's limp, bloody arm. Sensing that she's about to breakdown, I step forward and take the cookie. The woman is taken aback, but smiles then takes out another cookie and unwraps it. I take a bite. It's tender and heavily spiced.

"It's good, you should try a bite," I offer Gette the cookie. She hesitates, wipes the tears from her cheek, then breaks off a corner.

"Can we save one for Victor?"

The woman pulls out a cookie and places it on the table across from Victor.

"There, he can have it when he wakes up. I'm sure he'll be really hungry."

"That's good 'cause he likes cookies, and he'd be sad if we ate them all without him."

Cornelia, Vicky, and Books wave off a cookie, but the lanky guy and the surgeon take one.

"So, he's going to pull through after all." The lanky guy says, his mouth full of cookie. Books jabs him hard in the ribs. Victoriana shoots him a disappointed glare then turns her attention back to Gette.

"We have to figure out how to get Victor some more help, but he's going to be just fine. You were very brave in getting him to us, and we won't let you down." Vicky rubs Gette's arm and the dam bursts.

"He's going to die isn't he!" she sobs, throwing the rest of her cookie across the room. A rush of arms and bodies swoop in to try to comfort her, but she fights through them all and dashes under a table. She coils up under her blanket begins to wail.

"He's going to die just like daddy. Then we're going to die too. You're all liars! We aren't going to be okay."

The surgeon pinches the bridge of his nose as tears wash down his face. Cornelia crawls under the table and puts her hand on Gette's covered back. I join her and put a hand on her back too—her lungs are heaving.

"We can't make his arm better, but we're going to find people who can. We'll get him to a hospital, someplace that can help him. You're right, things aren't okay, but we can make it through them if we stick together. Can you stick with us little dragon, can you stick with Victor?"

I poke my head under the edge of the blanket. Her glistening, bloodshot eyes threaten to break me into a million pieces. She sniffles and wipes at her nose.

"I won't let him down." I give her a big smile then reach out and scruff her kinky curls. I turn back to Victoriana, "Vic—" she cuts me off with a sharp jerk of her hand.

"No names if we can help it. You can call me Torchbearer, he's Stitches, she's Squirrel, and you know Books. And of course, her shadow, Spooks."

I look around the room, lingering on every new set of eyes. "Thank you for helping us. For taking the risk of sheltering us."

Victoriana's eyes burn through my head and send my hackles to full alert. "That's what people do for each other."

I gulp hard.

"You've already risked so much, I don't want to burden you with getting Victor more help, but we have to do something."

"We're in this together," Vicky says, "don't you worry about that."

Stitches speaks up. "Do you think we could sneak him into Geovanni General?"

"Too risky," says Spooks, "Dr. Chen was arrested last week, and now they're checking patients on the hour."

"What about Dr. Goupta?" Stitches crosses his arms over his chest.

"That's an option," Books says rocking her head back and forth. "But I don't know if she has the tools she needs."

"The Twins then. They can help us for sure—I think they might be our only option," Spooks says then finishes off his cookie.

"No," Vicky says, shaking her head at him. "I'm sure they could, but they have to be a last resort—the bargain is always in their favor."

Victor moans then tucks his legs up into his chest. Forced to take stock of ourselves and the situation. Where are the other options?

"Spooks," Victoriana says, moving toward the large room beyond the hole in the wall. "Can you start making calls—see if you can track down Dr. Goupta?"

Spooks smiles, "On it, boss." He bounds up then disappears into the cavernous room.

"We'll be right across the room if you need anything," Victoriana says making eye contact with Cornelia.

"Thank you."

Vicky smiles genuinely then ushers everyone out of the infirmary.

"Why don't you go keep an eye on what's going on?" Cornelia says just above a whisper. She looks down at the tangle of blanket that swallowed her daughter. "We'll be fine on our own for a minute."

I nod to Cornelia and rub Gette's back. I crawl back out from under the table and move over to Victor. He's sleeping now and the life is returning to his cheeks. His elbow is bound in gleaming white bandages with little dots of red. Transfixed, I watch the dots expand as the world around them falls away.

I'm standing over the Man-in-White's motionless body. His bright blood soaking unseen into red carpet. He was alive and then he wasn't. A flash of anger, panic, and fear—a single jerky squeeze of Victor's finger—and it all ended. In the moment, the world is a blur, thinking fades, and a primeval, sinister impulse takes the reins. The impulse needs control only for a moment, a single action often begun and ended in a heartbeat. But then it has you, forever. It has your life—your happiness. It keeps you safe, keeps you alive, but at what cost?

I want to judge him for killing the guards, for nearly killing Reinhardt. But how can I berate him when two Peace Officers rot in the earth—in long, shallow graves alongside countless other nameless martyrs—because of what I did in the space of a single breath?

A single action, a few neurons sparking one way instead of another, and the universe is permanently altered. Mr. Herrington lived his life fighting for a better future, Charles devoted himself to helping others—they did so without ever sending their opponents to the grave. And now that they're gone, we, the bloody-handed youth, attempt to fill their shoes.

I'm slouching low—the weight of everything crushing me. It comes and goes in waves—each eating away at the shore just a little more. I stare at my shoes to wait it out. I draw into myself and retreat onto a perch on the mountaintop in my mind to watch the turbulent tides recede.

Wiping tears off my cheeks, I force myself across the threshold into the cavernous room beyond. Once a lecture hall, the room has been transformed into a command center. It immediately draws to mind the communications center the captain set up in the parliament building. Where the lectern once stood there is a hydra of projected light monitors, and a dizzying array of input devices all snaked together with thick metallic cables dangling down through a rough-cut hole in the ceiling above. Spooks is in the heart of it—his fingers dancing in projected light, his face shrouded in a helmet display. Filling the rest of the room—where students once sat discussing the virtues of business—are boxes and supplies. Books is taking inventory on a datapad, her face dower. A few dozen other people mill about the room keen on their tasks.

Victoriana stands in the center of it all like a captain on her ship—her eyes scan over all the details, and she seems pleased with the work being done. She's stooped over a desk set up next to the communications array. Behind it, on the chalkboard, is a cryptic map. In place of traditional symbols, or recognizable landmarks, the map is drawn from strange geometric shapes, and lines that seem to twist and weave about randomly.

I start toward her then freeze when blue lights in the communications array flip to red.

Cogitators whir desperate to keep up with the incoming data. Behind me, the door to the auditorium bursts open. Jumping out of my skin, I pivot on one leg dropping low anticipating an attack. A wiry teenager still dressed in armored riding leathers races to the coms pulling her helmet and mask off as she strides down the steps two at a time.

"What is this, Jack?" says Spooks, whirling around in his chair to meet the young woman bounding toward him. Victoriana rushes over to the nest of monitors. Work stops. Everyone huddles close.

Jack sets her mask and helmet down on the table, taking a moment to shake the ash from her dense halo of curly hair. "I just barely made it back. I was on my way down to the lower Lighthouses when they closed all the checkpoints. They tailed me with a Vulture for a minute, but I lost them in the alleys. I don't know what's up, but whatever it is it can't be good." Victoriana soaks in her words, cradling her jaw in her hand to think.

"What did you think she was going to say, Spooks?"

He uncouples his display helmet revealing sunken eyes and a wispy mustache.

"Well for starters, I've lost all contact with the other Lighthouses. On top of that, my tap on the encrypted lines just blew up—there's so much chatter between the ministry and their field offices we're essentially running dark. I can't decipher any of it, but I think a lot of PO's are on the move."

Hazy knowledge gleaned from Victor stirs a question. I push my way to the front, "Aren't those communications quantum locked? How are you intercepting them?"

Spooks leans forward in his chair. "That's right—they should be impossible to intercept." He grins. "Jack and I rigged up a series of thermal cameras to monitor the cables. We can't see what they're saying, but we can tell when big orders roll out."

Victoriana scowls at me and throws her hand up, "We're getting away from it. Jack, why'd you rush back? What's going on?"

Jack leans against the desk pushing away keyboards and other input devices—her ebony skin paling white.

"Sweepers."

Panic ripples through the room—my neck hair bristles. The OSS is a massive organization with hundreds of thousands of people carrying out the will of the Caretakers. Peace Officers are the largest, softest branch of the stick. Sweepers are the fire-hardened tip.

"Keep calm everyone. We're going to get to the bottom of this." Victoriana turns her attention from the group to Jack. "Do you think we're safe here—do we need to get out?"

"No, it looked like they were headed into the Under City."

"Okay," Victoriana chews her next words knowing they could determine if we live or die. "Books, take as many people as you need to get us ready to go. If things go south, I want to be able to leave without hesitation."

"On it."

"Spooks see if you can get me anything specific, any details."

"Understood."

"Jack? Are you up to another run?"

Jack's face is somber. She stands straightening her overcoat. "Where do you need me to go?"

"Come into the office and we'll plan it out. Let's get busy people." She clasps her hands and the room buzzes to life. Books rounds up nearly everyone, including Cornelia and Gette. I'm left standing alone. I start to drift toward Books when Victoriana's voice stops me in my tracks.

"You're coming with us."

CHAPTER TWENTY-SIX

I SLINK INTO THE SMALL OFFICE where Victoriana and Jack are pouring over a map on the wall and slide into a chair. Their fingers trace a few different paths each accompanied by its own string of expletives. With no time to bemoan, they pick the least terrible option in front of them. Jack will take one of their two quadcycles to the farthest Lighthouse in Waukegan and alert them if she can. Victoriana and I will head to Earl's to warn them and hopefully bring Dr. Goupta back.

They hug—their eyes sullen. Jack nods at me as she passes to the door, her round, high cheeks and almond eyes exuding teenage confidence. She closes the door softly behind her then silence descends.

Victoriana scowls at me across the desk. Her fingertips rap the oak in a never-ending cascade. Her gaze is piercing, and I can't help but squirm.

"You really had to pick the worst possible moment to show up, didn't you?" she says, shifting her eyes away from me to the map of the city pinned to the wall. All the blue lines leading to blue circles have been crossed out in red. Dashed green lines, longer and winding, connect the few remaining blue circles without thick crimson slashes through them.

She sighs theatrically, her fingers tracing a circuit around three isolated blue circles. "But there are much bigger fish to fry."

I shift uncomfortably in the chair. The thighs of my woolen trousers slowly saturating with the deluge of sweat secreting from my palms. Mouth agape, I fail to find words. Her exasperation is palpable. They may be colored shapes on a map, but I know they are more than that. Other Lighthouses full of people like me, like us. In the frozen knowledge of the map they are both living and dead. Yet even this offers no comfort because their state of being cannot be so easily bifurcated. They could be bleeding or shot, beaten and scared, or worse—gagging and writhing, moments from death, in the soot deep below the earth.

My impulse is to race there as fast as possible and save them. But it could be a trap. They could be long dead—cold and rotting in heaps—under the watchful eye of waiting Peace Officers or OSS Sweepers laying in ambush. Running in like heroes only to get cut to ribbons or arrested and tortured is not an option— how can we help Victor, or anyone in the other Lighthouses, if we end up dead ourselves? Maybe I could go alone—Gette and Cornelia will get along without me—but Victoriana can't risk it. The Lighthouses need her—we need her. But she might not even want my help at all. Her hesitation at the thought of working with me is understandable. From her perspective, how can I be anything other than a threat?

I wish I could wave a magic wand that would explain everything and apologize. But I think in the current state of affairs—the thick, choking tension pressing all the air out of this room—that I'll have to convince her through my actions. I only hope I'm up to the task.

"Spooks can't get through to these three Lighthouses," Victoriana says still studying the map. "New roadblocks prevent the usual routes into the Under City—they've closed up all of the major entrances. We've even heard reports of plain cloths OSS using the Ratways and getting people trying to escape."

"Ratways?" I say, wanting to clarify and convey—hopefully—that I'm paying attention.

Her eyes roll into the back of her head so fast I'd be surprised if she didn't give herself whiplash. Her lips begin to curl up in frustration, but they stop mid-snarl. She inhales deeply, holding it in for a few beats then slowly exhales.

"Topsiders call people in the UC Rats. It's not a compliment. Ratways let people get around without constant checkpoint and body searches," she says, her voice tight-roping on the edge of anger.

"I always thought there was just a massive rodent infestation in the city. I never put that together…"

"That's because you never… you were never part of that world. You dipped your toe into it, but you've never been a part of it."

My face goes flush. I want to snap back at her, *I'm not an idiot—I've seen things you couldn't imagine!* But I hold on to the reins long enough to let reason shine through the tempest of self-righteousness clouding my mind. I looked at people like ants. I distanced myself from everything. I wanted to know the truth, but I never wanted to live with it.

"That makes a lot of things Speer used to say make so much more sense," I say.

"I bet he's loving the civil war—it'll finally give him an excuse to strap his jackboots on again."

"He was a Peace Officer?"

"Oh wow, you really weren't paying attention at all were you? He was in the OSS. He went on and on about it in ninth year."

"Yeah, I really don't remember," I say.

"Wow, what a shocker," she says, turning her chair around to face the map.

Not wanting tensions to build up again, I jump back into the conversation we were having before I derailed it.

"So, the Ratways aren't our way into the Under City, and the roads are out, what's left?"

"We'll have to use one of the old bootlegger entrances." Her finger moves down on the map to a jagged black lightning bolt.

"The Lightning Underground," I say, relieved to finally contribute something.

"That's right." She rubs her eyelids with forefinger and thumb. "You know, I'm surprised you've made it this far."

I flush again. My eyes drop to my feet, and my spirits drop with them. She isn't cutting me any slack, and each knock stings sharper than the last.

"Me either," I offer.

Her chair squeaks. Turning to me, I see concern wash away her frustration.

"I'm sorry Evelyn. I didn't mean it like that. I know you've been through a lot to get here," she pauses and looks away. Her face scrunches up tight mulling over what emotions should take precedent. In a flash, the bundle unwinds into an angry flash. "But I'm still freaking pissed off at you," she says finger jabbing out at me like a knife. Her tone softens but keeps its cutting edge, "But this isn't the time. You're trying to help, and I'm taking pot-shots at you." Her accusatorial finger unfolds into an extended hand. "Truce?"

"Truce," I say—the roughness of her hands clashes with the symmetrical perfection of her face.

As abruptly as she extended the olive branch, her demeanor changes. Her ears, arched in alert, drop into a casual slump. Shooting out of her chair, she begins rooting through a credenza on the wall behind her. The room fills with the sound of papers rustling over each other like dried leaves. Cutting through the shuffling, a delicate metallic jingle—the unmistakable sound of keys clanging against each other. She returns to her chair gliding into it with grace—the chair squeaks anyway.

"I think we can take the quadcycle through the alleys along Neptus Boulevard," her fingers run along one of the widest paths through the city. I count with my fingers every time her path crosses a checkpoint and stop when I run out of digits.

"It's littered with checkpoints though. Will we be able to get around them?"

She smiles, her perfect teeth glistening. Her left hand opens revealing a shimmering set of keys.

"I'd like to see them catch us," she smiles, stands, and moves for the door. I follow her back into the lecture hall. Cornelia and Gette are silhouetted at the far end of the room by the light of the infirmary behind them.

"I'll catch up—I just need to let them know them where we're going."

She stops, and her eyes soften. "I'll meet you in the alley— don't take long."

Victoriana makes a quick pass through the room giving instructions and encouragement then disappears. I shake away the anxiety of the room and focus on Cornelia and Gette. I meet them halfway—Gette leaps into my arms and nearly topples me.

"What's going on?"

I shift her weight to my hips then brush a curl out of her

eyes. "Peace Officers are out looking for their friends, but we're going to get there first and warn them." I choke on Victoriana's name and decide against it, "Torchbearer and I are going to bring back a doctor for Victor."

"We'll come with you!"

"I don't think so kiddo, I need you to stay here with your mom and watch over Victor."

I smile and her face sours. She writhes herself free and crosses her arms over her chest.

"You better come back." Gette's face quivers with sadness and rage.

I kneel, pry her arms out of their cross, and embrace her. "I promise."

***

The sun is nearly set now. The omni-glow of the sun reflecting off the suspended soot has been replaced by the sickly yellow gloom of streetlamps. The occasional punch of bright red neon flickers on airship advertisements floating in and out of view above. I take a deep breath of carbonated, lavender air and step through the airlock and into the alley.

Victoriana is waiting by a large storage container tucked away behind the corner and partially concealed by steam rising from subterranean vents. She reaches into her shirt and pulls out a key dangling there on a thin silver chain. She uses it to open the padlock on the storage door. It opens with a *thunk*. She unhooks the latch then swings the double doors open. It looks like a portal to the void. She disappears into its all-consuming darkness. I hesitate, unsure if I should follow.

Without warning, a blinding yellow light cleaves the darkness. A resonant metallic rumble shakes through the container's walls and blasts out at me. I cover my ears too late to stop the ringing. Bursting from the darkness, Victoriana sits confidently perched atop a sleek, black quadcycle. Her oiled leather boots dig out the kickstand. She sits up to finish buttoning her armored riding coat.

"There's another riding coat on a hook just inside to the right—a helmet too," she says.

With adrenaline adding a bounce in my step, I hurry inside the storage container and pick up the coat. Flexible gray pads cover the leather in flowing curves. I test one unsure of its ability to save me from a fall—moved slow it flows like water but struck it's harder than steel. I secure the first flap to the left, then zip up the right. Victoriana revs the engine impatiently. I grab up the helmet and head over to the quadcycle. I throw a leg over—bruised core muscles groan. The helmet is snug, but I tighten the strap down under my chin anyway. I lean in close and wrap my arms around her waist.

Victoriana wrenches the throttle back. The quadcycle bellows—its tires squeal on the slick soot-covered cobblestones. We lurch forward. My stomach slams into my spine. My head sloshes for a moment then re-settles. Adrenaline surges.

We are lightning leaving thunder in our wake. Hissing steam vents, honking traffic, countless shuffling feet, all the sounds of the city have disappeared beneath the engine's roar. My skin is electric. I'm starting to anticipate the turns by feeling the muscles in Victoriana's stomach tense and twist just before the tail on the quadcycle shoots out behind us. I feel alive, excited, and for the first time since I can remember a genuine smile covers my face.

The ride is a whirl of rumbling excitement. Caught up in the fun of it, I barely noticed where we went or how long it took us to get there. By the time Victoriana slows the bike to a stop, the sun has fully set. The engine grumbles then, with a twist of the key, it dies with a throaty huff. I wobble off the quadcycle still exhilarated from the ride. Victoriana climbs down taking off her helmet in a smooth and effortless motion. Confident and cool, she heads straight for the door partially concealed behind a veil of rising steam and falling ash. Gaining my legs as fast as I can, I follow her into the tunnel.

CHAPTER TWENTY-SEVEN

VICTORIANA NAVIGATES THE PASSAGEWAY with dancer-like grace. I do my best to keep up, but my body is having none of this. Ribs bruised, ankles swollen, and profoundly exhausted, each inch forward comes with a riotous wave of protest.

The path is straightforward—there are no side tunnels or dead ends to navigate through—but its path is anything but linear. Parts are chiseled out from the concrete foundations of the skyscrapers above while others use the gaps and pockets in between underground infrastructure. Welded tabs on water pipes serve as ladders while bundled cables carry us over open sewers.

Plunging deeper, the honk and bustle of the city fades away into the bass groan of the earth writhing against the foundations of the metropolis above. Steam hisses through hot pipes blistering to the touch. Water, both potable and gray, whooshes up and down in a jumbled tangle of clay, iron, and plastic pipes.

It soon feels as if we'll go all the way to the center of the earth. Sweaty, heart racing, chest heaving the descent finally relents and light—visible but dim—promises an end. Yet as our feet draw near, horrific warped sounds slither their way to us. Pressing into the galling underground wind, Victoriana slips down into the hidden room. She helps me down through the hatch, and the chaotic sounds take form. Sweepers got here first.

"Shit—we're too late," Victoriana says. "Keep your voice down and stay low."

I nod—all the wind tied up in my throat. Victoriana scuttles forward pushing her back into the counter. I follow. Glancing up, we're behind the bar of a speakeasy. A mercury mirror runs the length of the wall fitted with shelves stocked with bitters and spirits. The mirror lets us peer out on the rest of the bar and the front windows and the street beyond unseen. We can't see much, but what we can see terrifies me.

Bodies cover the floor. Scattered around upturned tables and fallen chairs, they are mortified at grotesque angles. Their fingers flay and bend like gnarled wood, their legs tucked up or splayed out. Surveying the scene, I lock eyes with a corpse. A young man frozen in terror—his face gaunt and screaming. I slam my eyes shut. Writhing biting ants crawl down from my neck and up from my ankles and wrists. I swat away at the phantom pests—my shallow breaths fogging up the inside of my mask. *Kur-doof!* My skin leaps out of itself—a shotgun blasts nearby.

"Stay low," Victoriana says. Crawling on all fours, she moves out from behind the bar scurrying to the wall beneath the window. *Just breathe, Evelyn.* I bite down on my fear and scamper after her. I drop the rest of the world away and focus only on her silhouette. I scoot in beside her. *Thump, thump, thump.*

The sickening crash of metal splintering wood echoes through the ten-meter-wide streets of the canyon-like stretch of concrete row houses holding up the city above. The snapping splintering intensifies until the battering ram delivers its final ear-splitting blow. The shattered door explodes open slamming into the concrete wall behind it. Screams bellow. *Kur-doof.*

Tears pool around my nose. I dare a glance through the window—my feet slide on a piece of broken glass in the soot.

Two doors down, a Sweeper team is entering an apartment hive. The armored brute holding the battering ram—white composite armor splattered black and red—stands idle by the door while a half-dozen shotgun-toting Sweepers pour in. A Specter in the middle of the road is orchestrating three more teams working their way across the other side of the street—his hound slathering and snapping at the bodies in the street.

Muted shotgun blasts silence the screams.

Each second howls in our ears. Fingers and toes twitch in the soot. Electric fire dances on our skin.

"We need to keep moving," Victoriana says. Her voice sounding like a trumpet to my nerve rattled ears.

I shake my head no so fast tears fling from my lashes. "We need to get out of here. We can't help anyone," I say.

"No, we have to find a way."

The hound's bay ripples down the street. A diesel truck engine rumbles to life behind the buildings *swept clean*. Looking through the window, the warped reflection of a silver truck—riding low on a belly full of poison—rolls forward. Walking alongside are four people in silver suits. They have oxygen tanks on their backs, and every seam on their suits is taped securely. Wielding silver wands tethered to the truck on long, braided steel cables, they spray frothing torrents of clear liquid. The geysers of liquid poison reach up three stories to the ceiling and run all the way down through the clogged drains in the streets below. It clings to every surface running down like snot before evaporating into a milky cloud. Air currents carry the mist through cracks in the seals around windows and doors and settles like a morning fog. The fresh wave of engineered death spills over the windows and oozes through the door.

The phantom swarm of stinging ants erupts in a new, intensified assault. Liquid fire writhes across my exposed skin clawing at my mask's seal around my neck. Blind panic consumes me. I thrash about trying to stomp out the invisible ants burrowing into me. I'd scream, but I have no air—even with my mask on, I'm too scared to breathe. Shotguns blast, screams echo, dogs bark.

The world swirls with black and red and pain. The electric cry of nerves sizzles in my brain. The mist's deathly fingers envelop me. I fall in a gnarled ball to the soot-smeared floor.

"Evelyn? Wake up, wake up Evelyn."

Swollen eyelids open on the perpetual gloom of the Under City. Victoriana kneels over me. She's shaking me awake with red, blistered hands. I look down at my own—the movement ignites a blaze of pain around my neck. They are lobster red and glistening with distended pus-filled blisters. I dry heave at the sight and immediately implode on myself from another wave of pain from my ribs and flash fires up and down my spine.

"We have to check on the Lighthouses. The Sweepers have moved on, we have to act now."

Forcing myself to my knees, Victoriana helps me to my feet—her hands steady me, but her touch is searing.

"Lead the way," I say.

Victoriana stops at the door, looks both ways then dashes across the street. I mimic her steps—my every movement stoking fires or bursting blisters in a confusing eruption of agony and relief. One look at her and I know she's suffering too. Her usually graceful movements are minimal and reserved. Her hands are flayed out to keep her fingers from accidentally rubbing against each other and inadvertently starting another fire.

She leads us down the street past a dozen scenes of carnage and cruelty. Families dragged from their homes shot, bitten, and blistered. Some are in their pajamas, others just coming home from a long day in the coal pits. A woman lies dead slumped across the three short steps leading into her humble home. Blisters have disfigured her beyond recognition and swelled the inside of her mouth and throat shut. Her mask lies just beyond the reach of her outstretched fingers. Next to the mask is a clump of the woman's hair torn out when the Sweepers ripped it from her face.

I turn away—her silent anguish pours into my heart like hot ash. How is this justified? The Under City is the backbone of the Great Society. The workforce that drives the engines of industry, fills the ranks of the army, and patrols the glistening—by comparison—streets above. Are film crews about to show up and spin this as a subversive or CLA attack? Calculated and cold or rash and fiery, what end could possible justify such means? I've been clinging to the hope that if I could expose the kind of atrocity that just happened here, I could get the nation to open its eyes—to show it a better way. But that hope has burned away. You can't put a ribbon on a corpse and will it back to life—survival is the only real hope we have left.

Victoriana motions for me to get low. The Lighthouse is just around the corner.

"There should be four families hiding in the attic of the repair shop. With any luck they're still alive and Dr. Goupta is with them."

Victoriana points to *Earl's Neon Repair & Sign Emporium* a building curiously missing an obnoxious neon sign. The door is knocked in and the windows shattered. An outline of drips frames the wall like salt stains. Victoriana scans the street and I double-check. Only blowing soot and tattered blinds flapping through broken windows.

We fly across the street and through the open door. We huddle behind a stack of *out of order* signs. Heart rate and vision calmed down to normal with controlled breaths, I scan the room. The shop is piled high with signs, boxes of bulbs, and miles of spooled wire. Faint sounds of struggle and violence tug on my ears but I can't tell if the rampage is ongoing or replaying in my mind.

Victoriana creeps to the back. Her every step is careful to miss the shattered glass covering the floor—Sweepers tossed over whole rows of shelves turning organized boxes into a chaotic mess. Already soot has blown in through the open windows causing everything bathed in the yellow light from the streetlamps to sprout a fuzzy coat of industrial moss. Crossing into the back of the shop, Victoriana freezes in her tracks.

Earl is slumped in the corner—a gory smear paints his final moments on the wall. His name—embroidered red on a white patch—gleams in the dim monotone gloom.

"Fucking monsters," Victoriana says, crossing the room to close his blistered, condemning eyes.

"There is a false wall here," Victoriana points to a rack of tools on the wall, "help me move it." She gestures to where I should grab. Wrapping my hands around the handle consumes them in fresh pain. I bite my lip and heave on the door. It cracks open with a whoosh of air. Sliding it the rest of the way open, Victoriana takes a flashlight from the workbench and illuminates the ladder to the hidden attic. I climb after her careful to keep my eyes from lingering too long on Earl.

Each rung creaks. At the top we find a small room only a few meters square. Victoriana illuminates its every crevasse and finds nothing and no one. I move to a table on the far side of the room. The light catches the crests and currents in the disturbed dust. A bowl of chili sits half-eaten. I follow the splatter of chili finding the spoon resting on the floor. Something under the chili catches my eye. I brush the bowl aside and pull up a lithograph. A jagged-edged cartoon rat points a skeletal finger to the neodeco city above. *The Rats will have their day*. A vision of endless war—blood pouring from the streets above to drown everyone in the city below—sends a tremor up my arm. The copy falls free, drifting back to the table.

"What is it?" Victoriana says, taking up the flyer.

She scans it intently—her eyes tracing the accusing arch of the rat's finger.

"Earl was just telling me about this. Militias are forming in the Under Cities. Not just here, but in Einsam, Engelstadt, Whitehaven… this is so much more than subversives." She sets the paper back onto the table, holding it there with her eyes closed until her lungs stop gushing like a bellows. Her composure snaps back into place—like clipping on a mask—and she restarts her search. "Look around for anything that could tell us where they went."

I rummage through the table only half aware of what I'm doing. Split a hundred ways—ears listening for approaching footsteps, body screaming for rest, and mind transfixed by her ability to put a brave face on even though she wants to scream—I hunt around the room, shuffling papers aside, lifting coats, and pushing aside curtains hung over cinderblock walls.

"I think I found something," she says, snapping me from my trance.

Plucking a small note from a dust pile by the ladder she reads aloud, "Cannot stay here any longer. Trying to get out of the city. Run."

"What do you think we should do?" I ask.

Victoriana reads the note a thousand times. Her hands clench the paper so tight the edges crinkle and curl around her fingers. She lets it go—it falls back onto the swirling dust on the floor.

"We have to get out of the city before it's too late. We have to get on a boat and sail as far away from this horrible place as possible."

"How?"

Victoriana retreats into herself, wracking her brain for a solution. While she hunts, we linger in stillness. Crushing silence fills the gaps between our ragged breaths. The poison itches, crawling like ants across my skin.

Victoriana snaps out of her trance, moves to a metal cabinet next to the landing, and pulls out something small. I catch a flash of silver and reach out instinctively to catch it. It's a metal tin with a simple white paper label. *Salamander ERS. For external use only.*

"You ever used that before?"

I twist off the lid and stare into the familiar clear, viscous gel. I look up to find that she's returned to rummaging through the cabinet. After a frenzied search, she returns to the middle of the room with a pump-handled spray bottle marked *Neutralizer.*

She pumps the sprayer then locks her somber, electric-blue eyes with mine.

"We need to meet with the Twins."

CHAPTER TWENTY-EIGHT

VICTORIANA MAKES QUICK, PRACTICED WORK of the decontamination process explaining each step as she goes. The neutralizer should make the nerve agent inert, and the salamander gel will radically improve the natural healing processes on our damaged skin. If we wanted to be absolutely sure, we'd need to shave our hair, burn our clothes, shoes, and masks—all of it—but she doesn't think we need to. As she talks, she touches the short, jagged strands of her once luscious hair. *I wish she trusted me enough to tell me what happened.*

We pause to cover Earl with a canvas tarp to give him a fraction of the dignity he deserves. Numb, we steel ourselves for the return journey to the surface. We dash from *Earl's Neon Repair & Sign Emporium* the moment the coast is clear.

Victoriana leads us back through the streets. The sight of bodies—now becoming familiar—racks me with fresh waves of horror and guilt. Overstimulated nerves and a threadbare mind save me from spiraling deeper—an icy malaise frosts over my thoughts deadening my body to the ravages of exhaustion.

Snaking back through the tunnel, I can't help but think that we're climbing back from a journey into hell.

Emerging in the alley, the world hums along oblivious to the horror unfolding beneath its feet. Palpable normalcy accentuates every flake of falling soot and beehive rattle of neon. Victoriana climbs onto the quadcycle pulling a silver cylinder from the fold-away compartment. Her blistered thumb depresses the small red button with a sharp *click*.

"And now we ride for the rendezvous point," she says, pulling on her helmet.

"That simple?"

"That simple."

———

We ride along the edge of the Great Inland Sea. The final rays of twilight turn the sky upside down in the lake—rippling and featureless like the void of space, punctuated by the lights of boats and steamers like stars. She guides the quadcycle behind a block of storage containers and kills the engine. I pull my helmet off and some of the sounds around me trickle back in. Distant foghorns, and the rhythmic slapping and gurgling of a gentle tide crashing back and forth against the wooden pier beneath us. Our footsteps creak the wooden boards, and a faint, filtered smell of salt brine trickles in with each breath.

Victoriana steps up to the small shack. *Knock, knock... knock.*

The rap of her knuckles fades into the night. Nearby, a metal buoy bobs in the water, glimmering red from the stray streaks of neon. Somewhere in the distance an ambulance wails.

The door creaks open. "Quick, get inside," says a woman's voice with a coastal brogue.

We waste no time—I close the door behind me as I step off the pier into the shack.

"It's safe to take your masks off, Hansruda just checked."

A small red light illuminates a thin rectangular table covered in papers and maps. Against the far wall is a compact field communications terminal. The woman who opened the door stands closest to us. She is tall with a stout build—her light hair is coiled into a bun on her head. Behind her is a man. He's shorter than her, closer to my height, with broad shoulders. His face is gnarled, leaving much of it hidden in shadow. Neither of them is wearing a mask.

"Evelyn, I'd like you to meet Gwendolyn and Hansruda." Victoriana pulls off her mask and takes a seat at the table. Gwendolyn grabs my hand with an iron grip, then releases me to go and sit—the blisters on my hand throb. Hansruda remains still. Removing my mask, the full aroma of sea air—salt, fish, garbage, and motor oil—makes me cross-eyed. Before I can sit, Hansruda barks at us.

"What is so important you couldn't use the regular channels?"

Victoriana fiddles with the collar of her jacket.

"I need to get my people out. Tonight."

Hansruda and Gwendolyn laugh in concert.

"Out of the question. We can't make any more trips, it's too dangerous."

"You just took three families over two nights ago. Did you lose your boat or something? We need one more run, that's it."

Gwendolyn slips into a chair. "You know things have changed—that's why you're here. We have a mission here beyond ferrying people around for you. When times were good you could give a little to get a lot, but as you've made clear yourself," her weathered face cracks a grin. "Times have changed."

Victoriana's fingers dig into her knees under the table while her facade—visible to the Twins in the red lamplight—remains calm.

"What do you need us to do?"

"We need you to deliver a package," he says—his voice a mix of heavy brogue and smoker's lungs. "We are not trying to be greedy, it's just *quid quo pro*."

"What kind of package?"

"Does it matter?" Gwendolyn says.

"Yes, yes it does matter," Victoriana says.

Hansruda hunches forward from the window, "I think what we meant to say was, do you have a choice?" His smile glows red.

The sloshing of the sea beneath us echoes the tumult in my stomach.

"No, I guess we really don't."

"No, you don't," says Gwendolyn picking up the conversation where Hansruda left it. "We need one of your people to take the package to the *Café Savoy* in Liberty Plaza. We have an operative in deep cover. Her investigation is stalled unless we get her that package," she says, tapping her finger against the wooden table.

"But you can do us one better," says Hansruda—the conversation flowing from their two mouths like one. "Our operative has been unable to record sensitive meetings concerning the foreign trade minister at the café. We need pictures, video—something concrete that links the trade minister to the Regional Caretaker. The package will ensure she completes her objective and the kit we'll give you will ensure yours. If you can deliver the package and return to us with intelligence our bosses find useful."

Gwendolyn jumps back in, "Then we'll pull our boat up to the dock and we can sail away. Simple as that." She claps her hands together for added drama.

The pier creaks in the pause. Distant foghorns drone.

"I think that's where Evelyn can help. She's new to the city. No one will recognize her, and," Victoriana leans back in her chair, crossing her arms—the words sticking in her throat. "I trust her completely."

Gwendolyn turns to me as if noticing the furniture had

someone sitting in it. "This isn't a trivial task. What skills do you have?" Gwendolyn jabs at me.

"I," I stumble over what to say, "I'm observant."

"No, I mean *real* skills. Surveillance? Infiltration?"

"I'm observant, and a quick learner."

Hansruda scoffs and moves to the window—his colossal form silhouetted against the glowing sea.

"What did you expect? I just have some spec-ops person lying around to do your dirty work? Evelyn has a singular focus, and a knack for not getting caught." Victoriana turns to me. Her expression, exaggerated in the red light and black shadow, torments me. Visions of the computer lab, inspector Aldridge, the parade grounds flicker before my eyes. Tension builds in my throat and coils itself into a knot. I swallow hard and try to refocus on the present.

"Fair enough," Gwendolyn says. She takes a long pause, looking to Hansruda who remains silent standing sentinel in the window.

Nothing has changed, the air still smells of the sea, my hands are still blistered and sore, waves still lap gently against the pier just below where we sit. Yet, everything has changed. Foreign operatives, government conspiracies, and now I'm a pawn in someone else's game. But this isn't just about me anymore, and in doing this I could get Cornelia, Gette, and Victor to safety. I guess I'll have to suffer the consequences.

"I'm in," I say. "What exactly do I need to do?"

Hansruda moves to the corner of the room—his hulking frame glides silent as a wraith. He kneels and rips open a duffel bag. *Zwiish.* He roots around for a moment then stands holding a headset.

"This is expensive, so try not to break it." He tosses the headset at me. Panicked, I throw my hands up to catch it. My mask and helmet clatter to the floor. Hansruda laughs.

"That joke again, really?" Gwendolyn says as she reaches down to scoop up my mask and helmet from the floor.

Hans doesn't seem fazed. A small smirk fills the corner of Victoriana's mouth in shadow.

"That's the safest, most secure way to secure intelligence there is," Hansruda says.

I look down to the headset in my hands. It's heavy, made of plastic and steel. Two hexagons anchor a strap that crisscrosses to secure itself snugly to the top of my head. All the elements look simple—clean lines and smooth materials betraying the complex engineering inside. The apparatus that rests over the right eye, however, is vastly more complicated. Small brass, gold, and silver gears trace intricate lines around three glass lenses as thick as a finger. The red light reveals hidden depths of complexity within each lens shimmering like stacked oceans. Twisting it reveals swirling shapes that dance and change with every subtle movement of my hands. On top of the already complex mechanics, a detailed labyrinth of gold and copper circuits slither along the straps terminating in unseen tangles inside the plane, smooth hexagons.

"It works with your eyes and brain, to capture everything you see and hear," says Gwendolyn.

"How do I store the footage I gather? How do I get that to you?"

Hansruda smiles, revealing a mouthful of chipped and cracked teeth. "We'll cross that bridge when we come to it," he takes his index finger and taps firmly against his temple. "It'll store it right in here. If the Caretakers wanted to get this information, well," he scoffs, "they'd be SOL. It's massively encrypted, and apart from the synced extraction module, the only way to read the information would be to cut it out of you."

"Hans, you really need to learn how to stop sometimes," Gwendolyn leans forward putting herself between Hansruda and me. "Don't listen to him—the information will be safe in your head Once you've delivered the package and gathered the foot-age, we'll get you to our safe house in Norland to download it."

"So, it really is that easy?" Victoriana says interjecting herself back into the conversation.

"It's that easy." Gwendolyn's smile is warm and genuine, but the red light and void-like darkness contouring her face project something rather more sinister. "You help us, get us something we can use, and a boat will be waiting to take you and a handful of others to Norland." Gwendolyn places a small storage sphere onto the table and pushes it toward Victoriana. She snatches it up and quickly conceals it in a pocket on her arm. "Once you're back to the Lighthouse, that'll give you all the details we have on the trade minister. It's patchy, but it's a good place to start." Hansruda takes a sleek brown leather briefcase from against the wall and places it on the table.

Victoriana grabs the briefcase—her eyes searching it, uneasy.

"Well then, we'll see you soon."

Victoriana turns to leave. Hesitant, but unsure of what else to do, I follow her lead. She pauses at the door to put her mask back on. I start to do the same, then realize I need to put the headset on. I move it back and forth a few times to figure out the best way, then I just take a stab at it. To my surprise, it fits snugly—I can almost feel it shape itself, warm and alive, to my face and head. Once on, it feels as though I'm not even wearing anything. Closing my left eye, the world intensifies with amplified details and the added ghostly tendrils of multi-spectrum light. Putting my mask on is a little trickier than normal—the straps catch on the hexagons behind my ears—but with a few quick adjustments I get it sealed up. Halfway out the door, Gwendolyn's voice calls out to me.

"Good luck, kid." I lock eyes from across the threshold, nod, then hurry to catch up with Victoriana.

She's already made it across the pier and is making the quadcycle ready for the return journey. I pull my helmet on as I walk, my head growing abnormally heavy. I feel like one of the buoys bobbing in the sea next to me.

"Well that wasn't what I expected, but at least it wasn't worse," she says, stepping onto the quadcycle. "Let's just hope you don't screw it up."

I start to protest, but before words can escape, she throttles up the quadcycle and the roar of the engine drowns me out. Lights stream past us as we tear through the city. Frustrations with Victoriana bounces around inside me, but the exhilaration of the ride quickly pushes it down. For the rest of the ride back all I can think about is that now I'm an international spy for a foreign government. It's exhilarating.

Yet I can't let myself enjoy it. The briefcase in my arms seems innocuous at a glance, but through the headset it's a vacuous black rectangle—a portal to the abyss cradled in my arms.

CHAPTER TWENTY-NINE

WE RETURN TO THE LIGHTHOUSE through the concealed alley passage. Dark and silent, we traverse the smooth wooden stairs like ghosts. I feel light as a feather, still electric from the ride and our meeting. The salamander gel is doing its job—the blistering has reduced leaving my skin pink and warm to the touch. Even so, each step still rings an alarm bell of discomfort somewhere in my body.

The hallways are still. Sparse dim bulbs keep us from running into the walls but just barely. It's as if no one is here and that's probably exactly how it's meant to be. Victoriana doesn't seem to notice the dark or the quiet. She heads straight up the staircase and makes for the main hall.

Without the bustle of activity, the main hall is far less inviting than it was earlier. Stepping inside feels like descending into a cave. The only light comes from the various blinking blue and red lights on the computer array. The projected light displays kick into life as we approach—our every sound echoing to thunder in the rafters. I throw a hand up to shield my eyes but it's too late; blue streaks dance in my clenched eyes. I blink to clear them. Victoriana has pushed on and taken a seat at the terminal.

"Take a seat," she says gesturing to the other empty seat at the terminal. The metal bucket chair is even more uncomfortable than it looked. She rolls the small teardrop storage device in her palm—its pearlescent blue stands in stark contrast to the red blisters on her skin. She pulls a hexagonal module to the end of its tether and presses the storage device to its surface. The solid surface of the hexagon gives way—little mechanical fingers pull the teardrop inside. She hammers out some commands on the input module. A line blinks in blue on the screen *Execute?* She turns her attention to the two imprint viewers on the desk behind the display—a tangle of braided metal cables linking them to the terminal.

"Put one on. Let's find out what the Twins want us to do." Victoriana picks up the viewer closest to her and slides it on. It looks like a metallic snake has latched onto her head. Shaking off my trepidation, I set the briefcase down carefully next to the terminal. Next, I pull off my mask, helmet, and the headset and drop them to the floor next to me. The viewer is heavy—a solid mix of steel, silicone, and copper wire. I slide it on. It's not comfortable in the least and all I can see is a small slice of light under my cheeks. I try and adjust it but nothing I do takes the weight off the bridge of my nose.

"Ready?" Victoriana asks.

"Hit it," I say trying to sound more confident than I am.

She taps the input module. Electricity jolts through the headset. Muscles seize. The hall falls away as the sphere plunges us into its depths—I grit my teeth for the ride. An overwhelming wall of information flashes in the eyepiece while maps, pictures, audio clips, and videos flood my thoughts. I greet them like memories—like something I've always known. The longer I watch the images, the more familiar they feel. My brain throbs—warm and alive—from the sudden burst of activity. The viewer isn't merely showing me the information, it's storing it directly into my memory. Far less invasive and consuming than the Oracle Device, but the effect is the same. Memories and thoughts that aren't my own, suddenly *are*. One hundred years of global trade mundanity and every trivial regulation ever passed suddenly feels as ordinary as door handles. The machine transfers the secrets from the teardrop into the hidden folds of my mind, and with each passing moment a picture, global and twisted, takes shape.

The Great Society sits in both a privileged and rejected space among nations. The Caretakers have, since Neptus, believed themselves apart from and exemplary among nations. International agreements, accords on human dignity, war crimes, and the establishment of international law, were beneath them and attacked as a loss of sovereignty. A true pariah state, it is illegal for the hundreds of foreign nations to deal with, what most call, *The Failed Totalitarian State*. Not all use that name, some still call us *The Republic*, the government Neptus fought so hard to overthrow, or they simply call us the *Former Republic*. Nowhere outside the geographic boundaries of our state are we in any way perceived of as *great* and by many we're not even a real society.

But politics is fluid. Climate change and failing crops forced desperate Caretakers to seek relief from the international community. A limited trade deal was enacted that allowed the Great Society to give up its chemical weapons stockpile in return for food and high-value consumer products from around the globe. *Weapons for Wheat.* Per the deal, the Great Society relinquishes its chemical stockpile to the Confederated Free States, who then turn around and pay for the *Imperium's* wheat which is shipped back to the Great Society. *The Vechnar Imperium,* a vast poly-ethnic empire stretching across the whole of the great continent, prospered immensely from the deal. Two centuries of climate change have turned their once uninhabitable permafrost into endless steppes of fertile earth that is now the breadbasket for the entire planet.

Many have long suspected corruption, and black-market dealings happening under the guise of the *Weapons for Wheat* agreement. Yet despite suspicions, even the Confederated Free States, those traditionally most hostile toward the Great Society, have seen their coffers overflow with a new, massive market for their consumer goods. The tensions within the High Caretaker's office have pitted the Great Society against itself; some grow fat, living lavishly off the trade deal's newfound wealth—scandalous photos of High Caretaker Domnhall flash in my mind—while the diehard nationalists abhor any foreign interference and plot to rid the Great Society of *subversive* foreign influence. Fowler's actions are beginning to make a twisted kind of sense.

This is where the target comes in—Peter Ivanovic. A stocky, middle-aged man with bushy eyebrows and short fingers. From the rural countryside of the Vechnar Imperium, Peter emerged from University with a mind for numbers and a truly unique gift for bureaucracy. Born into poverty, and making a meager bureaucrat's salary, Ivanovic's mansion and vast landholdings on the central steppe have raised many eyebrows. For the last ten years, he's been the trade ambassador for the Great Society's Heartland Delta—a vast region that stretches from the Great Inland Sea in the North down to the fertile lands fed by the Great River and all the way down into the Burning Gulf in the South. This is truly the wealth of the Great Society—nearly every product that sits on a shelf, every morsel of food crammed into a packaged good, comes from the Heartland Delta. I'm to go to the *Café Savoy*, gather intelligence on Ivanovic, and pass along the briefcase. My contact will approach me. Simple, straightforward, perfect.

The surging electricity fizzles to a stop. The flurry of images fades along with the tension in my muscles. I melt down into the chair under the pressing weight of the viewer. It all rests in my mind now as memory. But it doesn't sit easy. It feels packaged and clean—like a scalpel carved a neat chunk out of my brain and inserted plastic replacements. The connections are too perfect, the motivations too clear. It all makes too much sense. Despite the sterile order of the info-dump, other things pull into finer focus.

Things must've been tumultuous if the Caretakers were

willing to threaten their hold on power by opening themselves up to the rest of the world. I guess when their workers were starving and dying in the fields, they realized they had no power without them. The protests in the article—still folded up in my pocket—are starting to make sense. *Weapons for Wheat* cracked the Caretaker's veneer of infallibility, and people seized the moment to demand change. I still don't know all the facts, but it seems like people genuinely wanted to open up—to become part of the rest of the world. And it seems like it almost worked. Domnhall's response to his eroding power—manufacturing an existential threat to the nation's existence with the subversives program—mirrors the foundational lies that built the Great Society. Neptus and Daedalus did everything they could to undermine democratic institutions and align the interests of state with those of industrial plutocrats. The crackdowns, disappearances, and the use of chemical weapons are all pretty strong evidence that the Caretakers are truly afraid of losing everything—and are willing to do whatever it takes to hold on to what they have. That's what's so unsettling. Desperation doesn't inspire people to orderly, rational thinking.

There's something disturbing missing from these memories. There seems to be clear purpose—identify the Vechnar Imperium as the ones facilitating the Great Society's contempt of international law. But any reason for doing so is left out. These artificial memories tell the detailed history of trade agreements and alliances, without ever revealing the histories these nations share—the interdependencies between the Confederated Free States and the Vechnar Imperium are evident in the absences. It feels as if I'm being described a dance over the radio, and in a foreign language—I'm being *told* how majestic and smooth the motions are while straining at the headphone to listen beyond the static.

None of this sits well. I know the memories I saw in the Oracle Device are true. I smelled the smoke, tasted the brandy. I pulled the trigger. But this is different like I'm being tricked into believing one thing and not another. It pushes me—harder than necessary—to hate the Great Society and to blame the Vechnar Imperium for everything wrong—Peter is simply the figurehead, the focal point of my frustration. A perfect balding middle-age scapegoat.

The truth will come out one way or the other—once an action ripples its way through the universe, no amount of obfuscation can remove it—but I fear I'm going to have to pay for this lie before it does. This perfect plastic truth is going to cost me, and what troubles me most is not knowing how I'll pay.

The earlier excitement of being an international spy is all but evaporated. Despite my high-tech toy, I'm nothing but a pawn in some larger game. Yet, if I manage not to screw this up, I can get Victor the help he desperately needs.

I reach up and pull the viewer off my head and set it back on the terminal. I rub at the ache radiating from the bridge of my nose back into my eyes. Movement in the darkness sends me into high alert. A slender figure emerges from the shadows heading straight at me. Ice flashes down my skin. I jump up and square off, ready for a fight.

"Relax, just me. *Spooks*," he relishes in adding needless breathiness to his nickname.

I relax my guard to match his impish demeanor. My nerves still very much on edge.

"Aptly named," I say.

"I have a knack for that," Victoriana says.

Victoriana plops her viewer on the terminal and comes over to us. Her eyes a million miles off, still chewing on the fresh imprint.

"What were you two looking at?" Spooks says, shifting his attention to her.

Victoriana's face sours. "Too much. I'll fill everyone in," she pauses to rub her bloodshot eyes, "in the morning."

"That bad huh?" He shuffles awkwardly, clearly not the response he was hoping for. "Well, if you have a minute, I'd like to talk to you about something."

"Of course," she says stooping down to collect her mask from the floor. She snaps the concern off her face, "What's up?"

He pauses, brings his hand to his mouth, then rubs his lower jaw. His eyes dart from me to Victoriana and back again. "I was hoping we could speak in private," he says.

"By all means—I'll head to bed. I've had my fill of secret meetings. Plus, Spooks gives me the creeps."

Victoriana raises an arm to stop me. Her hand comes to rest on my sternum. A silver needle of sensation zips through me like a shiver. "Let's keep this to ourselves until the morning, okay?"

"Sure," I say. I turn to leave, pause, and pivot to face Spooks. "Are they still with Victor?"

"That little girl wouldn't let him out of her sight, so Books got them all set up with a cot in the infirmary," he says.

"That's our little dragon."

"Clean up a little before bed—end of the hall, can't miss it." Victoriana's smile gleams in the scant light.

"Thanks, I will."

We nod goodnight then I collect my headgear and pick up the briefcase and step past them—body and mind threadbare and pulsing.

Following her directions, I find it as simple as she said. I dip into the bathroom and do my best to scrub the soot from my hands and face. I'm too tired to shower, maybe in the morning. Fighting to keep my eyes open, I start down the hall-way toward the infirmary. Neon advertisements pour through the hall's atrium windows. I fumble through the red darkness careful not to make a sound.

I find my way back to the infirmary, and an intangible fa-miliarity and comfort washes over me. Three cots have been set up around Victor though only one of them is being used.

Gette's curled up with Cornelia. Both are fast asleep. Victor is still sleeping, but he's not at rest.

I don't know what he's dreaming about, but I'm positive it has something to do with what happened at Reinhardt's mansion. Taking a life stays with you forever. Even when you sleep, it keeps you from having dreams—hopes for the future replaced by nightmares. I see him, and I see myself.

I zip off my new overcoat, fold it, then place it with my mask, headset, and helmet on an empty table. I kick my boots off and slide the briefcase under the bunk. Cautious not to bump his arm, I curl up next to Victor and pull a thin wool blanket over us.

I close my eyes and try to fall asleep. I'm exhausted but the thought of tossing and turning all night—of reliving nightmares like Victor is—tugs at me and keeps me from falling over the edge into unconsciousness. But you can't fight the inevitable forever. Drifting away into nightmare, the *click-clack* of bureaucrats on their typewriters slithers its way into my regular fare of guilt, death, and shame.

I awake before dawn. Covered in a cold sweat and feeling as though a small elephant sat on my chest all night, I sit up next to Victor and try to rub the sleep out of my eyes. Cornelia is still wrapped up around Gette—her arms and legs are tangling her in a protective embrace.

Charles didn't have to die, such a stupid waste. He was a

good person, and he didn't deserve to die like he did. Growing up everyone lies to you about death. They claim if you are great and noble then you'll die with honor and dignity. Charles was great and noble, and he died under a pile of rock and rubble. Why didn't the rest of us die? We were all clumped together, it could've been any one of us. A few inches to my left, and maybe I'd be the one bundled up under the stone at Martha's Place. The mix of nausea and hunger sends me reeling. I push my way out of the infirmary and go on the hunt for food.

Following the sounds of clanking utensils and muffled conversation, I make my way to the dining hall on the first floor. Pushing my way inside, I find Victoriana, Spooks, and Books sat around the end of a long tables eating what looks like gruel from small cafeteria bowls. My entrance is impossible to miss—the sound of the door echoes in the cavernous space and my footfalls ring out like a steeple bell. Books waves me down to the end of the table. Squirrel pokes her head out from behind the double doors that must lead into the kitchen. Her apron is brimming with wet potatoes turning the white fabric translucent.

"Sit down, Honey, I'll bring you some breakfast," she says adjusting the precarious load of food.

I pull a seat out from the table and wince as it screeches across the floor. Squirrel returns from the kitchen saving me from looking at the tense staring faces at the table. She sets down a cup of water and a bowl of steaming mush.

"Here you go, Honey." She steps back from the table, wrings

her hands in her apron, then steps forward again. "I'm sorry about that mess with the cookies yesterday—I wasn't thinking, I should have waited until you had all settled in. I mean your friend was still right there bleeding, you know?"

I scoot over a little to create a sliver of personal space. "Your heart was in the right place. The timing might not have been perfect, but it wasn't thoughtless."

"That's kind of you to say…" she pauses, searching for the name she hasn't been given.

Victoriana interjects, "I haven't decided on names for them yet."

The cook grins then grows dour. "That's just as well—rumor has it none of us will be sticking around here much longer." She forces a smile, "I'll catch your real name when we're sailing away."

Conversations stop. Desperate eyes dance over us then converge on Victoriana.

"Well the cat's out of the bag now," Victoriana says rubbing her temples. "*Drifter* and I returned from the Under City late last night. As you can plainly see," she gestures to the blistered, pink-wet skin on her arms and neck, "Jack was right—they 'swept' the Under City last night."

Squirrel's perky posture slumps. "My god…"

Spoons drop into bowls.

"Holy shit—are you two okay?" Books says, the news nearly

knocking her from her chair. "Did you find Dr. Gupta? What about the other Lighthouses—Earl?"

Victoriana shakes her head slowly. "It was hell—pure carnage. I've never seen anything like it. They pulled people from their homes. Ripped the masks from their faces…"

Tears well in Books' eyes. She wipes them away and turns to Spooks. "What about Jack, have you heard from her?"

Spooks shoves his coffee away and hangs his head. "No. Nothing yet."

"Spooks stayed up all night keeping the coms open," Victoriana says offering her a hand to Books and Squirrel. "Shepard and Zip are out checking Jack's hideouts."

Spooks cuts in, taking Books' other hand. "We're guessing she's staying off coms in case they're bugged."

The gravity of events pulls on us all. Mocking stillness rings in our ears.

Victoriana clears her throat and shakes away the moisture in her lashes. "We spoke with the Twins late last night. They've agreed to run another ferry and take us to Norland. If everything goes to plan, we can get everyone out tonight."

Books yanks her hand from Victoriana's. Sorrow turns to fire in her eyes. "Wait, what? You're just going to abandon the other Lighthouses?" Tears rain on her shaking fists. "You're just going to abandon Jack?"

"We're not going to stop looking for her, but I'm responsible for the lives of everyone in this Lighthouse. We saw what's coming for us if we wait, and the Twins are the only ride out of town."

Books shakes her head then tosses her hands up. She lingers like that for a minute, fiery retorts dancing behind her sealed lips, then slumps down in her chair—her arms limp beside her. "Their price?" She says, her umber cheeks glistening with tears.

"We've agreed to do something out of the ordinary. We're going to snoop on the foreign trade minister at a café downtown then deliver a package. It's straightforward and if we get it done today, we can sail out tonight."

"Just snooping? Really?" Books says, shaking her head. "No, I don't like this. It's too risky. They want you to waltz into the Ministry district with a 'package?' Haven't you looked around? What could they possibly want delivered other than a bomb?" Fists clenched, her trembling shakes free fresh tears. "We aren't subversives, we aren't murderers. That's not what any of us signed up for."

"Yeah," says Spooks scooting himself closer to Books.

"What choice did we have? What real choices do any of us have?" Victoriana says, doing her best to appear calm. "We all knew there was a price for their assistance. Do you think the Lighthouses could have existed without them? We'd still have hundreds of mouths to feed if they hadn't of gotten them safely across the sea."

The tension at the table is troubling. I don't know anything about the logistics or politics of the Lighthouses—I don't think Victoriana wants me to know—but it's clear they're dangling from a thread.

"Oh, so blowing people up is okay now because you say so?"

"We're just as upset as you are Spooks, but dial it back," Squirrel interjects.

"I'm sorry," Spooks says, throwing his hands up in frustration. "But we're still royally screwed. If we get caught snooping around embassies, or the Halls of Justice, we're dead. Shepard's worked too hard to get the Peace Officers to leave us alone. Those agreements go out the window if we start to look more like subversives."

Another piece of the puzzle falls onto the board—that's how they can operate right in the middle of the city. But it doesn't fit neatly anywhere—another middle piece and there are no edges in sight.

Victoriana takes a deep breath and holds it for a whole measure—the tone of the room simmers. "That's why Drifter will do it," Victoriana says, staring intently at me. "She's not officially part of the Lighthouse, and she's already on the run. If she screws up, it won't be that hard for us to distance ourselves from her. I didn't put her in the log so we can claim innocence if they catch her."

I sit frozen. Hans and Gwen are using me for their ends, and Victoriana for hers. If she were anyone else, I'd be furious. What makes them think they can play me like this—use me? But this is starting to feel like atonement, and I've done enough wrong to deserve it. I speak up before anyone can steal my moment.

"My only objective is to get my friends to safety. I understand the risks, and I'll do everything in my power to keep you out of this. You need the Twins, I need you, and now you need me. Torchbearer's right, who said anything about choices." I finally pick up the spoon and take a bite—it's watery but satisfying.

Books leans across the table, placing her hand on my shoulder, "Alright then. What's the plan?"

"I need to get to the Café Savoy as early as possible. How we make that happen…" I shrug gesturing around the table for the answer.

Victoriana hangs her head into the cruck of her elbow. "I'll drop you off near the embassy. We'll have to hurry if you hope to catch whatever it is, they want you to see," Victoriana says her voice muffled into her arm.

"I'll keep my eyes and ears open for anything that can help us," says Spooks. "Books why don't you—"

Books cuts him off, "I'll get everyone ready to go."

"Right," Victoriana stands and clasps her hands together. "Before we rush off, let's take a minute to finish our breakfast. Thank you, Squirrel—it was a beautiful meal."

The cook smiles but her joy has vanished. I manage a few more bites before tension fills my stomach with twisting snakes and I can't eat anything more.

CHAPTER THIRTY

WE CLEAR OUT OF THE DINING HALL as the sun throws its first rays through the narrow neodeco windows that slash down the walls like gills. Victoriana is in a rush to get moving—the sun has nearly risen, and we have many miles of twisting alleys to pass through.

I creep back to the infirmary, trying to preserve the pre-dawn stillness. I run my fingers along the walls counting the times my fingers plunk down the rough gouges left behind by bullets. The scars of violence grate against my fingertips while humming stillness radiates in my ears. I wish there were a way to go back in time and fix things with Victoriana. We could sit at the end of one of these desolate corridors and she could tell me her story, the story of these walls, and confide her hopes in me.

Light slashes through the darkness and the constant rumble of the city swells enough to rattle in my teeth. A swirl of antiseptic, blood, and urine greets me as I cross the threshold into the infirmary lifting the last echoes of daydream from my mind.

I tiptoe over to the bunks. Gette and Cornelia are still sleeping peacefully, but Victor is quivering in the grip of a nightmare. His face muscles twitch as silent words fall from his lips. Pain slithers up from my gut and wraps itself around my heart. I cradle his head in my hands. I scrunch my eyes as hard as I can to keep tears from falling. The tremors in his muscles ease and his breathing softens. Something like rest washes over him, and happy tears roll down my cheek as I smile.

"You're going to be okay, Victor—I'm going to get you help."

I breathe deep to collect myself, then turn to collect my things. I slide the briefcase out from under the cot and the thought of it exploding—shattering me, Victor, Gette, and Cornelia into a million pieces—flashes before my eyes. My hand trembles on the handle. It's too late to equivocate—if I don't do this, Victor dies. I turn to leave—he task ahead of me a roiling thunderhead in my mind.

"Evelyn? Where are you going—it's so early?"

Gette's voice freezes me in my tracks—I can't stop myself from wincing. I didn't want to explain that I might not come back. I won't have the strength if I have to say goodbye.

"What's that?" she asks, pointing to the headset the Twins gave me last night.

"Oh, this? It's just a super-secret spy helmet," I say trying to be both excited and silent at the same time—a fool's task.

"Really!" Gette nearly shouts in her excitement, "Can I wear it?"

"*Shhh*, your mother is still sleeping."

"Oh, right," she says, shushing herself while holding a finger to her mouth. "Can I wear it?" she whispers.

I smile wide fighting back laughter—I love this kid. "I'll let you wear it when I get back, now go back to sleep! I have a feeling it's going be a long day."

"You'll be safe?" she says, noticing the blisters on my arm.

"Of course, I will."

"Promise?"

"Pinky promise."

I smile and extend my right pinky to her. Her eyes light up. She wraps my pinky in hers and shakes. Satisfied, she snuggles back up with her mother and falls asleep in an instant. I cross the infirmary's threshold and sigh. The pressure is palpable now—so many people are counting on me.

I pull my mask on over the headset then strap the helmet down tight. The added layers help bolster my confidence. Tingling with the uncertainty of what's to come, I make my way down to meet up with Victoriana in the alley.

The corridors of the Lighthouse are stirring with activity. Exhausted, sleepy people rub their eyes and shuffle down the hallway toward the cafeteria. We nod at each other in passing. Each footstep brings me closer to the alley, and each adds another brick to the growing mountain of anxiety in my gut.

The glow of the sun is warming up the windows—swampy heat swirls in my mask. I close my eyes and listen to the rhythmic sounds of my breaths. I listen until they are slow and even. *Just breathe, Evelyn.* I pass into the utility airlock and transition to the unforgiving world outside.

Victoriana's leaned up against her quadcycle. Dressed in a slate, ankle-length twill trench coat, patent leather riding boots, slick composite mask, and scraped-up helmet, she strikes an imposing image. It takes me a second to realize Books is standing next to her. Their discussion dies when they see me. Shifting my gaze to Books, I'm amazed by the power a mask and the trench coat have to conceal. Her sinuous features and pear-shaped physique are invisible—she could be anyone, a nameless, faceless, *ant*. I'm sure if I had a mirror, I would be the same. A bustling worker ant. Does that make Victoriana our queen?

"Books made something for you," Victoriana says, adjusting her body language from familial to authoritative.

"I had a chance to look at the papers you came in with. They were good enough to get you into the city, but they don't permit you to be walking around. If you are doing this strictly by the book, you would have needed to go to the Halls of Justice and register your stay with the city. They would have processed you and given you proper papers." She steps forward handing me a pocket-sized blue passport. "But in the process, they would have done a facial scan, and you'd be on your way to the pits."

I run my fingers over the embossed cover of the booklet—workers reaching for a lump of coal, silver lines radiating out around them. I flip it open. Its pages are thick and laminated. Staring at me on the first page is a picture of myself in my school uniform. The dark wooden stage of the gymnasium behind me. My face is somber, and my eyes are hollow like Victor's.

"Where did you get this?" I say, truly confused and unnerved at how easily—and quickly—Books was able to find out every detail of my life and forge my identity.

Her cheeks rise in her mask giving her eyes a feline angularity. "You'd be surprised what's floating around. Just have to know where to look, *Sarah*."

I look back at the document. Under my twelfth-year class photo is the alias Mabel gave me: Sarah Goodman.

Victoriana reaches over and plucks the passport from my hand.

"Not your best picture, but Sarah Goodman? Really? Name's a little on-the-nose, don't you think?" She says, her full attention turned toward Books.

"One, it's early. And two, I had like half-an-hour to whip this up. If you want art," her hands twirl up in jest, "you can't rush it. When you rush it, you get good enough."

"That's all I need," I say taking back the booklet from Victoriana's gloved hands.

"Now if that's all, I have a half dozen more rush jobs to get to," Books says.

Victoriana steps mask-to-mask with Books, grasping her hand firmly. The intensity in Victoriana's eyes sends a shiver down my spine and she's not even looking at me.

"Thanks, Books," she says. The words fall from her lips like silk. They share a moment, then Books steps over to me.

"Good luck," says Books.

"Thanks," I say as she walks away, disappearing behind the utility door.

"Ready?" Victoriana says hopping onto the quadcycle.

I slide onto the back, the sensation no less foreign and exciting than last night.

"Ready," I say with uncommon confidence.

The quadcycle roars to life and we streak down the alley. We ride into the heart of the city until the roar of the engine is lost in the morning din.

***

Using the alleyways, we make great time through the city. Lines of traffic, held up by checkpoints every few blocks, turn to streaks as we zoom past down hidden pathways. Idling cars belch smoke making the atmosphere nauseous and dense. The rising tide of fumes forces Victoriana to slow down—even with the quadcycle's headlamp, we can hardly see the path before us. The slick soot-covered ground tugs at the traction, occasionally pulling the bike to one side. Twice we nearly touch the ground. Every time it happens, I squeeze Victoriana around the middle and brace for what I know is our impending crash. But each time she deftly maneuvers the bike, pulling us out of the fall. It's as if she can see a path that I can't, like every patch with traction is illuminated to her skilled eyes. I never knew she rode a quadcycle, or that she was skilled at it. I want to ask her so many things. But the wail of the engine eliminates any possibility of conversation.

In the heart of the city, Victoriana pulls the quadcycle to a stop. We hop off and push it behind a steam vent concealing it in the hot billowing vapor. Like she's lived in this city her whole life, she navigates us through the alley to the street. The traffic here is at a complete standstill. The amount of engine exhaust pouring from the stranded vehicles makes it feel more like the mouth of a volcano than a plaza. The sidewalks are double-wide, and every inch of them is crammed with people. Orderly, they move in currents. And although they're all wearing trench coats, the quality of the cuts and the sparseness of the clinging ash give away their status. Nearly all of them are carrying fine leather briefcases and wearing *Lux* line premium masks. The sound of their thousands of handcrafted leather shoes thundering on the pavement mixes with a deafening syncopated *rum rum rum* of the entrenched traffic.

The sight of them all sickens me. These are the bureaucrats and technicians—the desk jockeying clerks that hold the whole thing together. Without their forms, committee meetings, and rubberstamps, the Great Society could not function. They're hustlers performing a never-ending shell game. They keep everything moving around—they stir the filthy pot—and keep everyone waiting, focused on their own myopic goals. They all just say they're *doing their jobs* and when push comes to shove no one blames them. They look at the Peace Officers who enforce the law with baton and rifle. They blame the Guardians who crush out resistance with tanks and bombs. But behind it all, sanctioning and processing their orders in triplicate, are the legions of bureaucrats wearing designer watches, fine leather goods, and hiding behind the newest luxury mask. And all along Father sat atop the heap.

Around the corner from the throngs, Victoriana holds her hand against me. "Wait," she says keeping her eyes peeked around the corner. Trusting her, I comply—eyes wandering around the dancing particles held aloft by the rising torrents of steam. Over the din, a deep rumbling begins to resonate. It shakes the cobblestones of the alley and works its way up the bones in my leg.

"Look now," she says, pulling me around the corner.

A Guardian Vulture swoops low over the traffic. Two massive propellers, shrouded in rings of steel, force great drafts of air down at the tips of the vehicle's curved wings. Clouds of exhaust and soot swirl like tornadoes trying to escape the black-winged monster. The vehicle's hooked body angles down like a hammer ready to strike a blow.

"The Caretaker's motorcade will be coming through any

second now," she says, her words barely audible.

The Vulture swoops low. The throngs of cars push themselves apart honking and screeching as chrome strikes chrome. Those walking struggle to stay standing in the massive gale of wind. They race indoors. Many even dart into our alley, holding their briefcases like shields to ward against the flying debris. The scene on the street is all chaos—an opaque swirl of fumes. But above the vulture, the air has cleared enough for the People's Acropolis to come into view. Not as magnificent as the one in Einsam, Lufthaffen's Acropolis is still an astounding structure. Thick marble columns hold up the first level and form the foundation for the heavy arches supporting the intricate carved façade. But as the building stretches into the air, its form changes from classical to modern metal, concrete, and steel. Four great iron atlases, one on each corner, stand erect holding up the towering concrete structure above. Massive lamps illuminate their strained and beleaguered expressions—their endless burden highlighted as architectural beauty.

A path appears in the traffic and a column of jet-black vehicles roll across the roundabout to the base of the steep marble steps leading into the belly of the beast. Yellow triangular flags flying from the hood shutter and snap under wind's relentless assault. Their edges fray as they fight to stay attached to their bending metal anchors. Through the crowd, it's hard to tell, but I see the doors open and huddled, dark shapes emerge. The headset analyzes the figures seamlessly feeding details into my thoughts. Caretaker Ashford leads the entourage up the stairs two steps at a time—each of her retainers fights to keep pace while holding black umbrellas over her head. Through the flashes of people visible between swirling smoke and umbrellas, I catch the profile of Peter racing up the marble steps at her side. Armored Guardians, encased head-to-toe in nanocomposites and steel, flank them on the stair like sinister shadows.

Just as suddenly as they appeared, the motorcade tears off. The Vulture shrieks after them. Smog billows in its wash. Impatient traffic refills the void with urgency. The scene returns to what it was when we arrived. It's as if nothing has happened. This highly militarized and opulent spectacle of power must happen every day. The people huddled for safety in the alleys filter back into the streets. All of them checking their watches then doubling their speed.

Back to some kind of normal, Victoriana pulls a small silver cylinder and a small square credit-chit out of her pocket. "When you've made the delivery, and gathered as much intel as you can, press down on this." With her thumb, Victoriana mimics pressing the rubber button on one end of the cylinder. "And when you're hungry or whatever, you'll need this. It only has twenty-five Marks so make sure it lasts you all day." She shoves them into my hand.

"I have to go, make sure everyone is ready to leave." She turns to leave.

"Wait," without thought, my arm shoots out—both items falling free. Hand firmly grasped on her arm, I force her to stop.

She turns back to me, her eyes bloodshot—she's been crying.

"Can we talk about us? If things don't go as planned, I won't have a chance to tell you—"

"Tell me what?" she steps into me ferociously. There it is, bottled and festering for years—her cauldron of anger toward me is finally bubbling over. "Huh? That you set me up? That you wanted me dead for being your friend? You pushed *me* away remember? I was always there for you, and then one day," she snaps her fingers, "you stop talking to me, stop looking at me. What is that about? Other people exist in this world besides you, Evelyn."

I want to speak but only sobs some out. Tears cloud my eyes, snot streams from my nose.

"What could you possibly say to me?"

I muster the courage and let the words loose.

"I'm sorry. I'm so, so sorry."

She backs away, shaking her head, tears clinging to her long lashes.

"No, I can't accept that. You have to earn that."

"How? Please tell me."

"Figure it out."

"I'm begging you," I reach out and take her arm—my fingers digging into her forearms.

She yanks her arm free and squares up to me. "Don't screw this up." She turns around sharply—her shoulder catches me in the chest forcing me against the blackened brick wall. She disappears through the steam vent.

Bursting from the haze, she streaks off through the alley¬— her tires throwing up plumes of wet soot.

Closing my eyes all I can do is heave. I know I screwed up. I admit it. I was selfish, arrogant. I didn't think anything would happen to anyone else because I never even thought about them. I got people killed. I killed. I've sunken as low as I can go, what more does she want from me? She won't let me apologize—she won't help me. Will she be happy only when I'm swinging from a noose? I'm so angry I'm shaking. I feel like I could burst into flames. Perhaps I will, and I'll take this damned city with me.

She's right, this is exactly what I did to her. I threw her into a world she didn't want to enter. Aldridge beat her within an inch of her life—I can't forget the way she looked bruised and battered on that stage. Publicly humiliated and forced to watch the sadistic murder of Cinnamon all because I didn't want to get caught. No, I need to be honest. If I can't be honest with myself, who can I be honest with? I did it to get her in trouble. I wanted to see her pretty face turn sour.

I slump down into the piling ash. The cylinder and credit-chit are both nearly buried. I scoop them up—flicking off the ash. Slipping them into my pocket, I turn the corner. The Acropolis is hidden—veiled in fumes. I slip into the sidewalk's flow and fight my way upstream.

Not wanting to get swept up, it's nearly impossible to look and see where I'm going. Navigating the throng is a skill of feeling and sound, your eyes will always fool you. They are so easily tricked by the repetitive shapes of cloaked people and ash encrusted windows. You must rely on your ears to hear the gaps, your skin to feel the push and pull of the herd. I meld with the crowd, learning its patterns and flows. Like the sea, the tide must recede.

Within minutes, the overwhelming majority have found their port of call. Filing into the many sprawling lobbies. Waiting in endless lines for airlocks. With the streets thinned out, I can once again use my eyes to survey the city. The Acropolis looms on the north-east corner of the roundabout—the Great Inland Sea glowing behind it. Surrounding it are skyscrapers built in a similar style—classical carved stone foundations with sleek metal and glass pillars shooting into the sky. Advertisements burn and crackle illuminating the windows red. Shops, restaurants, and professional services line the bottom level, with industry, hotels, and apartments reserved for the upper floors. Concrete barricades line the perimeter of the Acropolis. Metal sentry turrets sweep back and forth across the roundabout—their optical modules glow like spider's eyes. Surveillance modules hang along the walls of the buildings. Their mounting plates have thick bolts, many splitting the façade behind them. Wires haphazardly dangle from the oscillating modules before snaking into hastily drilled holes.

Behind those mechanical eyes are a fleet of Inspectors diligently staring into flickering projection screens looking for subversives—looking for me. Scanning the buildings nearby, I see a second-floor solarium. Two doors down is the *Café Savoy*. Its first floor is set up with tables in the typical fashion, but above it, on the second floor, the glass solarium is scattered with smaller tables making it a perfect vantage on the Acropolis.

I walk at a normal pace. Keeping my head low, I follow the same rhythms I observed before. Casually, I step into the building's airlock. Steam hisses and a large jet of cool air blasts me from above knocking most of the soot from my coat. It *dings* open.

"Welcome to Clermont Tower," says an unexpectedly enthusiastic computerized voice. Activity bustles in the lobby. A coat-sweep bot rolls up to me deftly vacuuming away the soot as I walk. Professionals hurry out of elevators—never fast enough for the impatient mass waiting for their ride. To my left and right stretches a long marble corridor lined with shops. Dozens of nimble squeegee drones dart out from the walls in the narrow gaps between busy feet. They leave a sparkling trail in their wake that is, moments later, tarnished by the ashy footprints of the next guest. Another drone darts out to rectify the transgression and on and on it goes. I force myself to look away—the futility of it stirring existential dread within me.

I return my attention to the task at hand. The café is just a few feet to my right. The maître d'—smartly dressed in an asymmetrical cross-buttoned cerulean suit—waits just outside the truly awesome entrance arch. Reminding me of the great oak tree at Glen Fois, smooth curvilinear lines twist elegantly into root, stem, and leaves. It's a carved tree—frozen in stone—yet my eyes wait impatiently for it to sway in the breeze.

"Welcome to *Café Savoy*. Table for one?"

His words, his suit, the opulence behind him, all stir up uncomfortable memories. These kinds of places were the only ones Mother liked to dine in. She would dress me up and drag me around to them. She sipped her coffee so agonizingly slow. Once I fit in here, but now I feel like a stain. Wearing soiled hand-me-down clothes and a filthy overcoat, I feel like one of the people Mother would steer me away from in the streets. I miss her.

"I would like a table in the solarium."

"Right away ma'am. May I take your coat and mask?" My fists cinch around the leather strap of the briefcase.

I hesitate. His outstretched hand demanding an answer. The mask is the only thing keeping the headset strapped to my face invisible. If I stand out now, I'll glow like a signal flare if I'm sitting in the solarium with a foreign bit of spy tech strapped to my face.

I click the clasp on the helmet and pass it off into his outstretched hands.

"I prefer to keep my mask on. One can't be too careful at a time like this."

He maintains his composure, but I can see it cracking. "And your coat ma'am?"

If I were here for coffee, I'd ditch it in a heartbeat, but I don't know what the day holds. I hesitate long enough for him to get the signal.

"Not a problem ma'am, the *Savoy* is happy to accommodate." Bowing his head, he whisks my helmet away to a skinny boy standing by the coat closet. His winces a little when the maître d' makes the handoff.

"Follow me please," he says as he glides toward the stairs.

I reassure myself that no one can hear my heartbeat or listen to my thoughts—if I play it cool on the outside, they'll never give me a second glance.

We pass by tables filled with bureaucrats, officials, and Guardian officers. Some sit astute, sipping their coffee and taking notes. Others gorge themselves, slurping oysters into their mouths one after the other like an assembly line. But all of them have one thing in common: power. From the silver stars on their epaulets to the glistening-gold fountain pens, these people drip with un-challenged confidence. *I need to get out of here.*

I take a deep breath and push back on that impulse. No, this is exactly where I need to be. I just need to make the handoff, so I can get Gette, Cornelia, and Victor out of this place. If I've learned anything, it's that what I plan and what actually happens rarely match up. The best thing I can do is to make the most of the situation and capitalize on my invisibility.

I follow the maître d' up the steps to the solarium. The

treads are made of a polished pale wood—the risers a swirling black-and-white marble. Warmer than below, the solarium is—thankfully—less crowded. With fewer conversations spilling over each other, it should be easier for me to catch their words. Metal arches—hammered into the fluid shapes of abstract trees—hold up great, thick panels of glass. Three propeller-type fans list above us in lazy circles. To the left of the stair is an ornate wooden bar. The woman behind it operates the many levers and knobs of steam belching espresso machines—her face collected and at ease, eyes unmoving yet seeing everything. Is that my contact?

Five roundtables with four chairs apiece fill the middle of the room. Three of the tables are occupied. At the table closest to the stairs sit three people in fine suits—their briefcases tucked in close to their feet. A man frantically takes notes as the woman to his left confidently gesticulates the growth potential of agricultural yields next year. The third person sips coffee—their head and shoulders are squared up to the woman, but their eyes continuously drift up to the fans listing above. *Not this table.* I shift my body language away from that side of the room, drifting to the left toward the bar and the other two occupied tables. Though he has his back to me, the maître d' keenly observes me in the reflections cast on the window and fluidly changes his course. At the next table is a man and a woman. Not dressed up for work, but for a night out on the town. *An odd thing at 8:45 in the morning.* They're holding hands across the table. Two small plates with delectable looking berry Danishes pushed aside to make room for their arms. She's making plans for the day. Art museum, lunch at the *Imperial Hotel*, a night at the Opera. While she speaks, he caresses her hands. She has long slender fingers—her nails exquisitely lacquered in white. His right thumb makes small circles on her left ring finger. It's then I notice, she's not wearing a ring, but he is. I struggle to contain a sigh. *Not this table either.*

Feeling like I've made a mistake coming upstairs, I contemplate heading back downstairs. It will be noisy and hard to hear, but I should at least be able to eavesdrop on more important conversations.

"Foreigners. Lying snakes, the lot of them," says an OSS officer to the woman beside him at the table.

Bingo.

The maître d' leads me to the overhang of the solarium. There are three sets of stuffed leather chairs separated by slender side tables. He extends his arm out to the set of chairs. I choose the chair against the left wall—angled in toward the rest of the room, I can see the table behind me in the reflection.

"This is great, thank you," I say.

He nods politely and disappears downstairs to retake his post at the entrance. Situating myself in the chair, I set the briefcase down between my feet. I wriggle around until I can clearly see the OSS officer's face in the reflection. Oblong with a thin black mustache, his parsed lips dance under the effort of keeping his words from flowing freely. The woman he is with has her back to me, but from her posture and the fine detailing around her collar, she has to be someone important.

"I won't be attending. I don't condone it," he says it, in a methodical, measured tone.

"It's just a party, Frank," she says with serpentine dominance.

"You know how much pressure we're under. I can't afford the time or my staff. I agree with you that is a problem, but he's a problem we can see. I'm far more concerned with the ones we can't. This whole damned city is infested with rats," he says, sipping his coffee at the end to add finality to his words.

"He doesn't bite Frank, and you're going to that party. That's not a request—that's an order."

He shuffles uncomfortably in his seat. His gaze shifts to the windows—our eyes meet in the reflection. I can feel him homing in on me when a dark form breaks the vision.

"Welcome to the *Savoy*, my name is Charlotte. What may I offer you?"

The OSS freak me out. Inspector Aldridge was always so cunning and ruthless. When she turned her eyes on you it was if she was going to spill your guts and divine your secrets from the entrails. This officer has the same eyes, the same look that nothing comes between him and his objective. Charlotte doesn't know it, but she may have just rescued me.

"Coffee. Cream and sugar, and one of those berry Danishes."

"Of course, but," Charlotte hesitates trying not to offend me. Her mouth opens to form words, but she thinks better of it and instead motions at her face with her finger.

"Oh, right," I say my face turning warm. "Just the coffee then."

"Of course," she says. Her eyes dart down at the briefcase before she wheels around back to the bar.

Come on focus, it's not worth blowing your cover over a berry Danish. Or is it?

"Not all combatants slither in sewers or wave flags on the battlefield," she says leaning toward the officer her elbows sliding along the marble top of the table. "I need you, Frank. Ashford trusts the man too much. I need you to go and keep an eye on them. She lets her guard down around him, and I need to know if she's been compromised."

The officer leans in, he looks around with rapid, twitching glances. I anticipate him looking back at me in the mirror, so I look away, out the window, and try to appear intrigued with the forms of swirling soot.

"Why didn't you just say so?" he says—bringing my gaze back to the reflection, I watch the emotion on his face lighten.

"Because frankly, I shouldn't have to. You're pretty damn dense for a Specter, Frank."

His posture immediately stiffens up—his face hardens.

"Careful Rachel, there's a big difference between what I do

and what you're asking me to do."

"There's no difference. You are loyal to the Great Society. You swore an oath to root out subversion. That's all I'm asking you to do, look into it."

"It's not so clear-cut. When I'm down in the Under City driving out Rats that's one thing, but when you asked me to spy on a Care…" Charlotte approaches the table—Frank cuts himself off. He shoots her a withering stare over pursed lips.

"May I offer you any more coffee? Perhaps something to eat?" Charlotte says standing hands crossed, polite, completely ignoring Frank. The promise of coffee changes his attitude and he drops the jagged sneer from his lips.

"Yes actually, I would love another cup…" Rachel stands— forcing Frank to shoot up out of deeply entrenched habit.

"I think we're done actually. Aren't you finished, Frank?" A silver cream jug still sits on the table between them. In its warped reflection, I'm still unable to make out her face, but I can still see Frank's clearly. He's dropped a few shades in color. He tugs at the edge of his jacket straightening it. "Yes, Madam Secretary, quite finished."

Rachel steps off toward the stairs in long strides. Frank dutifully follows in behind her. After they disappear, I can't help but focus on the *whoosh-whoosh* of the fan filling the awkward silence. Charlotte lets out a laugh under her breath. Wiping down the table with a rag, she shakes her head. She replaces the chairs to their regular spots then returns to her post behind the bar. I sink back into the chair. It's comfortable and it threatens to put me to sleep. The droning *whoosh* of the fans above and the sight of honking traffic and billowing fumes act as a strange sort of lullaby.

"Your coffee, cream, and sugar." Charlotte places a silver tray with a carafe of coffee, a small silver milk jug—clear droplets condensing on the surface—and a small dish of sugar cubes onto the table next to me.

I perk up—the leather chair crunches with my excited movement.

"Thanks," I say, looking into her warm brown eyes, "I really need it after that."

She smirks—I can see she's holding in laughter and much more.

"The things people say in public!" I laugh, trying to get Charlotte to drop her guard.

She scoffs—*yes*. Kneeling next to my chair, she glances over her shoulder quickly then turns back to me, "That's not even the half of it. That's the third girl that guy has brought in here this week."

I feel my eyes bulge and my skin turn red. Charlotte laughs, "I know, right? Tell me about it." She rises back up, winks at me, then takes her leave.

I lean forward and pick up the coffee carafe. Steaming murky coffee pours into the cream-colored cup. Poured cream swirls in ethereal clouds. I plunk one, then two sugar cubes into the coffee causing a tidal wave of ripples to bounce around.

I unhinge the liquid port straw and dip it into the coffee. I close my eyes and drink it all in. I think I've found the contact.

CHAPTER THIRTY-ONE

I TAKE THE TIME TO FINISH MY COFFEE. Smooth, sweet, and bitter, it washes over the mass of frustration and anxiety swirling in my gut. Sipping from the fine porcelain cup, I nearly forget where I am—looking out of the solarium I could be back in the penthouse overlooking Einsam.

Enthralled by the momentary reprieve, I don't realize as my mask's straw ventures to the bottom. A mouthful of coffee grounds shatters the illusion and its acrid, indigestible reality hits me with full force. I can't run, I can't hide, and I can't pretend. I could be sitting in a café halfway around the world, sipping on coffee and eating Danishes but no amount of aloof feasting can undo the world—it's always there waiting for you just outside the door or at the bottom of your cup.

Setting the cup aside, I pick up the briefcase and make my way to the bar. I know the instructions said that the contact would come to me, but that's what the wink was for right? The Savoy is thinning out, and the once oppressive din wafting from downstairs has simmered to a tolerable rumble. I slide myself onto one of the bar's smooth copper stools and admire the artistry. A thick elegantly carved bar, its patina is dark from constant use, appears to float above bulging steam containers. Atop the bar, are a dizzying array of hissing gadgets, valves, stems, and dials. Pressure gauge needles dance the fine line between white and red. Charlotte holds a copper carafe full of milk up to a steam nozzle. Actuated by hidden foot pedal, steam erupts from the nozzle into the milk shrill and frothing.

Willing to gamble, I cast the dice. I loosen the straps and pull off my mask and headset. The world wobbles while my eyes readjust to seeing without the headset's optics. Nerves in the base of my skull dance like crinkled aluminum foil. I blink it away. Play it cool.

"I believe this is yours," I say, sliding the briefcase onto the counter.

Charlotte looks up from making her drinks. Her chipper demeanor vanishes.

"You were instructed to wait—I was to come to you."

"I did. I thought," each word trips out after the other, "but you winked. Right?"

Charlotte scrunches her face and yanks on the steam handle—its hiss masks her groan.

"Why do they keep sending me amateurs? You've done it now so here we are. Order a pastry then go back to your seat—I need you observing there by the window."

Embarrassment shoots like flames across my face. Sweat beads on my brow.

"Right, shit, sorry," nervous, I glance back at the table of OSS soldiers. "I'd like one pastry please," I say trying to sound normal.

"Absolutely, I'll bring it to your table," her server's tone clashes with the daggers in her eyes.

My stomach flips. What am I doing? I grab the straps of my mask and start to stand.

Screech. At the far table, an OSS soldier rises from his chair, straightens his coattails, then strides toward us. His mirror-polished boots *click-clack* on the glistening marble floor. Before I can move, he's behind me. The uniformed spook wraps his fingers around my right arm.

"Lovely day out isn't it ladies?" he says, his breath a hot mess of cigarettes, coffee, and mints. Every muscle clenches. His face is smooth—not even a trace of stubble darkens his jaw. He's young, a fanatic. His boots are reflective enough to illuminate a dark alley, dining at the *Savoy*—he's looking to get noticed. I glance out the window to the miserable orange malaise.

"Yes," I say, hoping my terrible acting skills are enough to get out of this, "I was just saying that." I try and pull away—his grip tightens. Charlotte catches my panic and draws his attention.

"Need a coffee for the road sergeant?" Charlotte asks while checking her wristwatch.

His grip relaxes.

"Before I came over here you two were chatting up a storm." He looks back and forth between us, wagging his finger searching for one of us to say something. Exasperated by his moments-long wait, he jumps back in. "Well deal me in. I want to know what has the power captivate two fine ladies like yourselves."

"Nothing really," I say, "just shooting the breeze." I smile a leave-me-alone-asshole smile.

His grip tightens again. He leans close enough for me to get a full blast of his pungent cologne—it's cheap.

"Then shoot the breeze with me."

Charlotte's eyes linger on the briefcase. He starts to follow her eyes. I panic.

"We were just talking about our masks. I mean, is it even safe to take your mask off inside with," I look over my shoulder then back into his gray eyes doing my best to sell the charade, "*them* lurking about."

"Is this true?" he asks.

Keep Your Opinions to Yourself. The slogan on the posters is more than just cheery banter. Ordinance Nineteen prohibits publicly discussing affairs of state. Is this his angle? Write us up for a citation to get promoted?

"Answer me!" he snaps. A twinkle in his eye suggests a joke—it's anything but funny.

"Yes," Charlotte avoids his gaze and checks her watch instead. "I heard people gossiping that they were about to attack the city."

"Is that so?" his face curves into a smile. He drops my arm and pulls himself onto the stool next to mine. I look at Charlotte. At first glance she appears as cool and calm as when I walked in. But her eyes have started to flutter, and the skin behind her ears is growing a deeper and deeper shade of red. I have to look away from the gut-turning tension—his elbows hooked on the table, his eyes drilling holes in Charlotte's head. The table of OSS agents he left behind has already forgotten him, far more interested in their jokes and coffee than his personal quest.

"Nonsense," he says, "utter nonsense. *They* are none of your concern." His tone takes on a sickening tambour. He turns his torso toward me, keeping it square. His intentions solidify—I'd prefer he wrote me a citation. Throbbing pulses of blood radiate up my neck swelling my head like a balloon.

"Don't worry," he says, puffing his chest out, "I won't let *them* get you." My fingers wring tighter around the layered straps of my mask and the headpiece.

I want to run. Bolt down the steps, push my way past the maître d', and disappear into the streets. But that's the last thing I should do; I'd run straight into the jaws of the beast. No. Sometimes the safest place in the storm is right at the heart of it. If I can keep myself composed—a big if given my knack for spycraft—maybe I can wiggle Charlotte and I free of this python.

"Well, if you promise," I say, emulating the breathy voices

all the young ladies have in the daytime filters.

His lips twist up into a smile—his eyes glint. He adjusts his elbows on the counter in such a way that it forces his arms to flex—the bulging of his sleeves more a result of exact tailoring than herculean physique. He turns his attention back to Charlotte who is now frantically checking her watch.

"I know they seem scary. Filthy rats scurrying under the city waiting to get you," he bursts forward slamming his hands together like jaws. "Snap!"

Charlotte startles. He straightens back up laughing.

"Sure, I can't get you anything for the road?" Charlotte says, rubbing her thumb over her watch face.

"All business this one," he stabs a finger at her and tries to enlist a sympathetic nod from me. His gall fills me with rage. He interjects himself as if everything is his business. He feels entitled to do as he pleases; his uniform and jawline inflate his ego in equal measures. I can't commit to acting his fool. What was I thinking? Victoriana does it. She plays people, shows them what they want to get her way. But I'm not Victoriana. How does she do it?

Holding myself back from punching him in his aquiline nose, I sit frozen. My face drops all the pretense of enjoying his company.

Charlotte interjects before he can respond. "Because if not, I really need to get back to work."

He straightens back up. His face turns up, quizzical.

"Are you two really that worried about rats?" His eyes and pointer finger dart between us.

Laughter erupts from his chest doubling him over. His fist pounds the carved wooden bar—empty teacups dance to his beat.

"Afraid of rats? Broads," he says, throwing a mocking hand up like he's speaking to an audience of subordinates. I'm sure he's imagining them shaking their heads up and down like automatons. Charlotte's eyes pierce through him like bolts of plasma. Unable to contain the boiling discomfort, I stand.

"No, no, no. I didn't mean anything by it. Come on sit," he shoots a hand out and snatches my wrist. I pull back. He digs in. His icy fingers ratchet down like a beast on prey. He yanks me back down into the seat. My shoulder throbs—my right hand curls into a fist.

"You've got nothing to fear with me around. I've been stomping rats all week," he scoffs in false modesty. "Hell, pretty soon real estate will be booming down in the Under City—there is so much free space down there now. Maybe I could get a place for us?"

The cauldron bursts. Images of the Under City. Mounds of men, women, and children shot, burned, and discarded. The muddy pools of blood and ash. Toys left burning, dropped from panicked hands. And here he is, fresh from carnage flirting like the world is all sunshine and rainbows. He's no man—he's a monster. Should we not slay monsters?

Rage commands me for a split second.

Slap.

I draw my hand back, stunned. He clutches at his cheek. Charlotte tenses like a whip about to crack.

"Are you a rat lover?" he says twisting my wrist at an unnatural angle. His bony face sours to vinegar.

"And you?" He directs his rage across the counter to Charlotte, "Conversing with rat lovers? I ought to take you both in now. Assaulting an officer of the OSS? Conspiracy to commit subversion? I could see you both hang."

"No, please, no. I don't know her at all. She came up to me. Caretaker's mercy, please. I had nothing to do with this." Charlotte's hands fold up in supplication—eyes wet from well-practiced theatrics.

In a flash, the vinegar disappears from his face—his lips crack open and his tongue slithers across his upper teeth.

"Well. If you promise me you had nothing to do with it, I'm sure there are ways we could make this," a slack-jawed grin spreads across his face, "disappear."

Crack boom!

An invisible hammer slams into my chest followed by a cacophony of clangs from the racks of teacups and saucers sliding off the wall and shattering on the floor. His grip loosens, and I burst free from him. Jumping to my feet, I back away from him pressing my back to the wall at the end of the counter.

"What the hell was…"

His words are cut-off by another explosion. Far deeper in resonance, the *whump* slams into the building like a god's angry roar. The solarium shudders—the glass visibly rippling under the strain of the colossal pressure wave. It rattles through my knees and nearly topples me—my grasp on the bar keeps me from collapsing into the shattered glass littering the floor.

The OSS sergeant springs from the stool, having lost all interest in Charlotte and me, and sprints back to his subordinate's table. They've all stood up—half of their chairs lay motionless on the floor.

"Downstairs now! Get your kit on and form up by the front airlock."

They jump at his bark and break off down the stairs. Feeling like this is my chance, I start to move away from the wall toward the stair hoping to slip out. Catching my movement in his periphery, the sergeant whirls around, his outstretched hand leveled at me like a knife.

"Don't you move a muscle. I'll be back for you, rat!"

My feet transform into lead weights. Locked with mine, his eyes quake. If I stay here and wait for him to return. . . The thought spirals into pits I dare not fall into. But what choice do I have? I have to go down the steps and out the airlock. All of which puts me at risk of running into him again. I need to get out of here, but apart from jumping out the second-floor window, how do I get out? Knowing I've blundered into a sticky situation, again, I slink back to the wall. Its solidity is reassuring. I watch him turn and disappear with his cohort down the stair.

Talons take up my arm. Brown eyes ablaze with conviction peer into me.

"You nearly got us both killed," Charlotte's head trembles back and forth in disapproval, "I'll take the briefcase now. Come on," she scoops up the briefcase and pulls me behind the bar. "We can take the service tunnels out of here."

Nestled amidst shelves, now empty, is a slick oak door. She types a number into the keypad on the wall and it slides open. The room beyond has none of the glamour and elegance on display in the front of the house. Typical sterile gray walls lined with wires and conduits in thick braided bundles trace themselves haphazardly around the room. A single yellow bulb shrouded in a gray-metal cage lights the space just enough for you to trip on shadows.

She takes off at a sprint. I do my best to keep up with her avoiding bundles of burlap sacks full of coffee and giant barrels of flour and sugar. She pauses at the back airlock. Along the wall are hooks with name placards above them. Charlotte runs her fingers along the swirling lines of her scrolled name.

"You know, I actually liked this job," she says just above a whisper.

She lets out a sigh then pulls on her bright yellow overcoat. Slinging her purse around her shoulder, she picks up her mask and slips it on. It's a *Lux* with delicate couture angles and supple black leather giving her a feline silhouette.

"You can follow if you want, but I'd get as far away from the square as you can kid," she says, pulling on long leather gloves.

Her demeanor has flipped like a light switch. The bomb blast knocking away any last pretense she had to play barista. A zealot's determination burns in her eyes. Coupled with her words, my stomach flips in knots.

"Give me the briefcase back," I reach out for the handle.

Sharp and swift, her whole body comes together to deliver a blow to my sternum. Gasping for air, I writhe sprawled out on the floor—my battered ribs igniting with pains new and old.

Checking her seal, she steps up to the airlock—her fingers twitching around the briefcase.

"Get that headgear on kid, you're gonna want to record this," she yanks the lever—the airlock swirls to life with a hiss of escaping steam. The door swivels closed, and she vanishes into a cloud of mist and gusting air.

CHAPTER THIRTY-TWO

PAIN HAMMERS IN MY SKULL like a steam mallet. I twist to stand but nausea collapses me back to the floor. *Get up Evelyn, you have to stop her.* Sobbing, I force myself to my feet. I'm a curse—the deafening silence before the storm. Everything I touch crumbles away. I never should have agreed to hand off that package. We all knew what it was. Maybe I should have waited, asked Cornelia and Victor. But what choice did I have? I can't lose any more of them—I won't let them die crumbled in the sewer. My conviction for peace—so interwoven with who I am I don't know what I'd be without it—is tattered with each choice I make. I've become the evil I wanted to conquer. I handed the subversives a bomb.

I crumble to my knees—blistered hands rubbing away tears from my bloodshot eyes.

Enough. There will be time for tears later. Get up Evelyn, you have to stop her.

I fill my lungs and hold it against the protest of my ribs. I hold it until the storm dies down and I control my own mind again.

Up, mask on, out the airlock. The alley is bathed in neon red from the massive Mountain Air advertisement bolted to an airship overhead. Racing toward the square, a few dozen meters down the alley, Charlotte stops to open the briefcase.

Pushing everything else to the background, I rush at her at a sprint. There is no plan, I have no idea what I'll do when I reach her, I only know that I must. Engrossed in prepping the bomb, Charlotte does not see me approach—the wind-up of air raid sirens and a cacophony of emergency vehicles masks my crunching steps in the soot.

Muscles quivering with electricity, there is only her—a yellow ghost in a field of black. I throw myself in the air at her like a spear. She catches me in the corner of her eye and with drilled speed reaches into her purse pulling out a pistol. She brings it around a heartbeat too slow. My knee connects with the side of her face. Her jaw pops and we both tumble into the ash—her pistol clatters away on the cobblestones. Charged up, I bounce back to my feet—body numb and weightless. She recovers quick and unleashes a hail of blows to my face and chest. I stumble back—each hit a dull shockwave. The pain isn't registering, but my body has had enough. Millions of neurons band together to shift me from fight to flight.

Adrenaline waning, my pinprick of vision explodes into a panorama of vivid colors. The scream of fighter jets overhead, the rattling of machineguns, and the wail of emergency vehicles rages through my bones. I try to run, but she hasn't given up her assault.

Her foot arcs through the air colliding with my jaw. *Snap!* Molars chip showering my tongue with shrapnel. A nauseous pulsing consumes me. I fall back—tailbone taking the brunt of the impact on the filthy cobblestones. Gasping for air, the alley wobbles—waxing and waning before me like a funhouse mirror.

Charlotte picks up the briefcase, collects her pistol, and turns to the square. The first bomb collapsed the entrance of the Acropolis sending the atlases crashing down onto the quagmire of traffic below. Vultures sweep the air blowing soot into the jutting flames. Fire trucks battle back the inferno with a dozen hoses. Laden ambulances struggle to escape the choked confines of the square. She's racing toward them, bomb in hand, to deliver the second, lethal blow. Just like in Einsam, the first bomb wasn't meant to kill. It was there to draw a crowd.

Defeated. Spent physically, and presiding over a body politic in open revolt, I pull myself through the ash. *Just breathe, Evelyn.*

Soldier's shadows stretch across the alleyway. Startled, she freezes in her tracks. Charlotte raises her pistol.

"Rat!" The OSS sergeant bellows as he rounds the corner from the square. He takes aim. Charlotte fires first. Her bullet turns the sergeant's white uniform red.

His squad comes around the corner shooting. A hail of bullets shreds her—tracers zip overhead, stony shrapnel pings off my back. Their bodies—soldier and spy—fall to the earth in unison. The briefcase sends up a puff of ash. The squad moves in to make sure she's dead—a Specter cradles the sergeant in his arms. My hand finds the metal cylinder in my pocket.

A star bursts into life. In a blinding flash, the end of the alley disappears. The world falls into neon. A coming rush builds from nothing and swells to infinity in the space of an instant.

Cold, I drift into the static white and ringing void.

———

The crystalline void emerges from the static. Inky purples consume white noise. Familiar now, I lower myself onto the platform and approach the single remaining door. Icy tendrils slither up my arms as I twist the nob and press inside.

A pungent mix of sour mold and lacquered oak tickle my nose while biting cold radiates up through my feet.

"I don't like this place, daddy—I want to go home."

"We will darling, very soon."

His hand pulls my reluctant body forward. Shelves tower over me stretching into devils' fingers in the flickering light. The echoes of our footsteps grow louder the deeper we go. Panic threshes on my skin, sweat beads on my tiny brow. He's taking me to the underworld. He's taking me to Hannah. I jerk my hand free and fall to the floor in a puddle.

"I don't want to die, daddy. Why is Hannah in a place like this?"

He scoops me in his arms—they wrap around me like iron bands. "Hannah is in a better place full of sunshine, fresh air— she's happy."

"How can she be happy, she's dead? I don't want to die, don't make me die too."

Hot tears splash in my hair. "I won't ever let that happen. Everything is going to be okay. I'm going to make it all okay."

I press my eyes into his chest blocking out the world. He carries me through the rain.

Deep inside the earth, a dragon belches fire and snorts steam. Its muscles writhe against its steely scales. Its claws gouge deep ruts into the stone. Trembling, he runs a hand down my back.

"Everything is okay, darling. Look."

Watery eyes peer past his arms to the strange device. Steam hisses, lights blink. Pistons fire and things whir and turn. Its rumble rattles my teeth.

"I'm scared, daddy."

"Just breathe, Evelyn. It's all going to be okay."

He climbs the steps up to the machine. He presses me into a tangling nest of squirming metal fingers. I scream.

"It's okay, darling. I promise—everything will be okay. I'll make all the nightmares go away. Just breathe, Evelyn, just breathe. I'll make the nightmares go away."

The fingers pull me into their embrace—a million microscopic needles plunge into my skin. I scream, but the device won't let it escape. Steam rises, and the door drops away. Father's fingers glisten with falling tears as they dance on the controls.

Then there is darkness.

"Evelyn? Wake up, please wake up."

The world flickers back. I hear her words through ringing static, my eyes clamped shut—the afterimage of the blast still dancing there. I open them a crack. Knelt over me, Victoriana is shaking me by the shoulders.

"Vicky?" A sigh of relief bursts into a smile. She falls onto me, pulling me into her embrace. The sensation of her arms filters into my brain like sludge.

"We have to get out Evelyn. Books and Spooks are getting everyone to the docks as we speak. I just need you to hold on to me."

I push myself up. A burning mountain of rubble has replaced the end of the alley. The skyscrapers on either side have leaned into each other—glass and steel bubble from the pressure and threaten to burst. Victoriana pulls me to my feet—I wobble on legs of shifting sand. Her arms steady me. The quadcycle is only a few steps away. She helps me over then hops on.

Victoriana flips a strap around me and clips it onto the bike with a metal catch. "Hold on tight, this is going to be rough." The quadcycle roars to life. The sudden lurch forward nearly tosses me off, but the strap does its job and keeps me steady. She flips the tail around—away from the carnage—and guns the throttle.

The engine bellows down the urban canyon. With what little strength I have left, I cinch myself like a python to her torso and press my face sideways against her back. Fighter jets streak across the sky through a maze of tracers and sweeping searchlights. Burning airships crash in slow motion against skyscrapers shining red in the reflected firelight. The sun is high in the sky, but the dense haze of soot and coal-black smoke from a thousand fires smothers it in a blanket of ash.

Victoriana propels us through the city with reckless speed. We slide through narrow gaps and around obstacles so closely my pant legs flutter against them as we pass.

Just breathe, Evelyn. Just breathe. I draw away from the city, from our flight, and into the darkness Father carved out in my mind. I dig for the earliest memory I have but I can't go deeper than the penthouse windows. I was seven, and I remember opening the door—1745 glistening in silver. I rushed inside to the windows. Compelled, I pressed my nose against the glass and there she was. The Mountain Air cartoon, elegant and cavalier. *Remember, a filter a day keeps death at bay!* Mother was there to comfort my tears, but this wasn't the first time I'd looked through that window. We hadn't just moved in. The spare room was already boxed up, the house purged of all the things that reminded me of her. All except the small black-and-white clipping of a bright and better world. A single silver strand keeping Hannah from fading away forever.

CHAPTER THIRTY-THREE

THE WORLD IS A HELLSCAPE OF VIOLENCE. Planes spiral after each other in concentrically tighter circles until one plane or the other blunders a step in the dance. Those planes and airships that misstep—or purely at random—burst into puffs of red and orange and black showering the city below with fiery shrapnel. Heavy guns *doof-doof-doof* from their fortified positions adding their own sinister flak to the already sunless sky. Ambulances and air raid sirens compete to produce the greater shrill.

Embattled by memories, I hardly notice the shift from riding to standing. Every step forward expands the world two steps beyond my grasp. Both worlds offer no reprieve. I yearn for a third path, a liminal place between them where neither can touch me. I pull the infosphere and article from my pocket and clench them one in each hand.

Just breathe, Evelyn. Everything will be okay.

Hansruda and Gwendolyn have held up their end of the bargain. The small gray tugboat Astrea bobs gently tugging on its moorings. Victor shakes his way out of Cornelia's support and rushes down the pier towards us.

"Oh my god, are you okay? When I woke up, they told me you'd gone—I was so worried about you. They want us to get on the boat, did you know about this? What about my sister—we have to get Olivia!" Cornelia and Books come up behind him—Gette wrapped around their ankles.

"There's no time Victor, I'm so sorry, but we have to go. Now." Books grabs him by the shoulder.

Victor jerks his injured arm away. "No, I can't leave without her."

"Victor, please," Cornelia pleads, "there isn't time."

"No, we have to go back for her."

Victoriana swoops in and grabs him. He struggles, but she persists, and resting her hands on his chest his anger turns to tears.

"I promise you we'll come back for her," Victoriana says, cradling his head on her shoulder. But right now, we need to get on that boat so we can get you the help you need."

"Come on!" bellows Hansruda from the deck.

"You can cry on the boat, come on." Gwendolyn wraps a firm hand around Victor's good arm and drags him to the boat. Victoriana retakes my arm, Gette looks up at me with turbulent eyes.

"See Little Dragon, I promised I'd come back."

She takes my hand and all together we rush down the pier.

Hansruda and Gwendolyn settle us into the cargo hold and set sail. The waterline bobs halfway up the round portholes. The oscillating *whump-whump-whump* of the engine lulls me toward sleep. Gette is curled between her mother and me. Victor slouches next to Books across from us while Victoriana makes the rounds to everyone to see if they're okay.

Hand trembling, I unclench my fist revealing the infosphere. Scarlets and ambers flash in its wine-dark depths. I curl my fingers around it and hold it tight until all its ice leaches away into my blistered and bruised fingers.

Drifting to sleep, I watch the city shrink on the horizon. As I slip into exhaustion, I catch my last glimpse of the city raging, violent, and burned.

CONTINUED IN THE GREAT SOCIETY TRILOGY BOOK THREE:

BROKEN

ABOUT THE AUTHOR

G.K. Lamb writes speculative fiction, science fiction, and fantasy. His debut young-adult dystopian series is the *Great Society Trilogy*: *Filtered, Burned, and Broken*.

Trained as a historian and documentary filmmaker, he explores themes of memory, history, and truth through a cinematic lens.

He holds a BA and MA in history from Northern Arizona University. He lives in the Sonoran Desert with his wife, two cats, and dog.

Thank you for reading! Please add a short review on Goodreads, Amazon, or wherever you like to discuss books.

We'd love to know what you thought!

If you would like to learn more about G.K. Lamb's other publications, please visit: www.geraldklamb.com